Carol Marinelli recently filled in a form asking for her job title. Thrilled to be able to put down her answer, she put 'writer'. Then it asked what Carol did for relaxation, and she put down the truth—'writing'. The third question asked for her hobbies. Well, not wanting to look obsessed, she crossed her fingers and answered 'swimming'—but, given that the chlorine in the pool does terrible things to her highlights, I'm sure you can guess the real answer!

Louise Fuller was once a tomboy who hated pink and always wanted to be the Prince—not the Princess! Now she enjoys creating heroines who aren't pretty push-overs but strong, believable women. Before writing for Mills & Boon she studied literature and philosophy at university, and then worked as a reporter on her local newspaper. She lives in Tunbridge Wells with her impossibly handsome husband Patrick and their six children.

ITALY'S MOST SCANDALOUS VIRGIN

CAROL MARINELLI

THE TERMS OF THE SICILIAN'S MARRIAGE

LOUISE FULLER

MIX
Paper from
responsible sources
FSC
FSC C007454

book is produced from independently certified FSC™ paper
to ensure responsible forest management.
more information visit www.harpercollins.co.uk/green.

MILLS & BOON

First Published in Great Britain 2020
by Mills & Boon, an imprint of HarperCollins*Publishers*
1 London Bridge Street, London, SE1 9GF

Italy's Most Scandalous Virgin © 2020 Carol Marinelli

The Terms of the Sicilian's Marriage © 2020 Louise Fuller

ISBN: 978-0-263-27827-9

ITALY'S MOST SCANDALOUS VIRGIN

CAROL MARINELLI

CHAPTER ONE

'LET'S NOT GO THERE.'

'No, no,' Dante Romano responded to his brother with a black smile. 'Let's.'

The board had convened for a meeting at the head-quarters of Romano Holdings in EUR District, Rome, and though it was a frosty January day the subject matter was hot. Yet again the latest salacious articles regarding their majority shareholder's rather wild private life took precedence.

Dante Romano, the subject of said articles, sat at the head of the table, both unapologetic *and* confrontational as his brother, Stefano, did his best to steer the meeting away from an unpalatable topic. Except Dante was more than willing to face it and turned to his uncle. 'Perhaps you would care to clarify that, Luigi?' Dante's rich, deep voice could cut ice, as could his dark eyes. He looked across to his uncle, a substantial shareholder, and dared him to go on.

'I am saying that we are a long-standing *family* business.'

'We all know that.' Dante shrugged.

'And as a family business, we have a certain reputation to uphold.'

Dante drummed his fingers on the highly polished table, refusing to make this easy on his uncle. 'And?'

'Headlines like the ones over the weekend don't help to portray us as a reputable, wholesome family—'

'Enough!' Dante's patience had run out. 'We're hardly in some shed, bottling wine and oil to sell at the market. We're a billion-dollar company. Who the hell cares who I'm sleeping with?'

He looked around the table that consisted mainly of extended family, all wealthy and powerful thanks to the Romano name. Few would meet his eyes, though his younger brother, Stefano, did. Ariana, who was Stefano's twin, was forgiven for looking down at her nails, clearly uncomfortable with the subject matter.

But Luigi pushed on. 'With your father so ill, with so many changes still to come, we need to show stability, we need to get back to the values your grandfather built this company on...'

Famiglia, famiglia, famiglia. Dante had heard it a thousand times before and was more than sick of hearing it.

Dante loved his family, yes.

But to him love was a burden.

After this meeting, Dante told himself, he would go down to Giardino delle Cascate, kick a stone and scream—because the fact was, the Romanos were not the perfect family.

Dante had always loathed that his mother portrayed them as such when he had, after all, witnessed many rows. There were so many secrets at this table: Luigi himself had nearly destroyed the company with his penchant for casinos, which Dante had uncovered some years ago. That was the first time he had saved the company. In fact, Dante's eternally suspicious nature came from the belief that he felt lied to.

Always.

'Hold on, Luigi.' Dante would not back down. 'My grandfather *was* running a tiny family business from a shed, but then my father came along and set the Romano world on fire with his vision—'

'And also his family values!' Luigi was pretty formidable too, but he was no match for Dante.

'Until he had an affair with his PA,' Dante said.

'Really,' Stefano interjected again. 'Let's not go there.'

But there was to be no holding back Dante. 'Why not? My father was all about family values until he left his wife of thirty-three years and married someone younger than his own daughter.' He pointed to Ariana, who sat there with her lips pursed as Dante blew the lid off the uncomfortable truth. 'So don't you dare lecture me about family values. Not one of you.' He looked around the table but, still, very few dared meet his eyes. 'I don't have to discuss this with you. I give enough of myself to the company without having to explain my personal life. I am single and, despite the board's desire to have me settle down, I shall remain single and sleep with whomever I choose.'

And all too often he did.

Women adored him.

Adored him!

It wasn't just his undeniably handsome looks, with thick raven hair and black, bedroom eyes. Neither was it all about his stunning body, which he happily shared in his endless appetite for sex. Possibly his obscene wealth played its enviable part, along with his stamina in the bedroom.

There was more to it, though.

His arrogance, his insolence, his completely untamable ways would be offputting for some, just not when combined with Dante's charisma and his sudden smile.

For—and this was the kicker—he could be so charming.

Even when he was being a bastard.

'Come on, *bella*,' he would say as he ended the affair—they were all called *bella*, or *beautiful*—it was easier than remembering names. 'Would a diamond bracelet help dry those tears?'

Or a car, perhaps?

Earrings, maybe?

And, yes, they did sort of help, because the women had been told from the start it would never go anywhere, and had very willingly entered the glamorous—temporary—highs of Dante Romano's life.

They just weren't so willing to get out from between the silk sheets and the caress that smile gave.

Dante wasn't smiling now, though, as he told the board how it would be. 'I shall party on and I shall continue to enjoy the fruits of my work. I work damned hard, and you all know it. Were it not for me, we *would* be back in the shed. I didn't save this company once,' he reminded all present, 'I saved it twice.' When his father's divorce had hit, Dante had taken the helm and completely restructured the company, hence the reason Luigi was no longer a major shareholder. But, as Dante had pointed out, thanks to *his* business acumen, Luigi was still doing *very* nicely.

Yes, there were tensions indeed.

Dante leant back in his seat, not quite finished tearing Luigi to shreds, but, glancing down, he saw on his silenced phone that the doctor at the hospital was calling.

It was no surprise as he was expecting to be contacted today.

Dante had visited his father in a renowned Florence hospital last night to discuss his transfer to a private hospice here in Rome.

It made sense because Dante himself was mainly based in Rome, Stefano hopped between Rome and New York, and, though Ariana spent a lot of time at their Paris office, she was often in Rome too.

Last night, though, Rafael had said he had changed his mind. Dante had listened to his father express his desire to return to the sprawling family home in Luctano, nestled in the Tuscan hills and surrounded by his beloved vines.

'We can do that,' Dante had said. 'Of course we can.'

They were close, though they had not always got on so well.

Growing up, his relationship with his father had been distant at best, given the impossible hours Rafael had worked.

The same impossible hours that Dante now took on.

When he was seven Stefano and Ariana had been born and the family dynamics had changed. The fighting between his parents had stopped, perhaps because of the rapid growth of the family business meaning that there were fewer money concerns. Or perhaps, Dante had privately thought, because he had been shipped off to boarding school in Rome, and the family had bought an apartment there where his mother had spent a lot of time. Yet holidays had been wonderful, and his father would take time off in the summer and teach him, carefully, the intricacies of the lush land and its produce that had always been the foundation of their business.

But it had been in his midtwenties that Dante had stepped in and put his business mind to the grindstone when the company had been close to crashing. His father had put all his energy into the product, and had left the business side to Luigi, who was impulsive, made poor decisions, and spent too much time and profit in casinos. Dante had taken over the administration of the company, which had brought with it an unexpected bonus: the relationship with his father had changed, first to one of mutual respect, then that of confidants, and finally to friends.

Until Mia Hamilton had come along.

Dante could not bring himself to be nice towards her.

She had been plucked from the relative obscurity of trainee executive assistant in the London office and promoted to the esteemed role of Rafael Romano's Personal Assistant, although Dante thought of her as his father's Personal Assassin.

. Still, following his father's diagnosis, Dante had pushed animosity aside—at least towards his father—and had done—and continued to do—anything he could to make the time his father had left easier on him. Although Rafael being at home in Luctano would make things far from easy for Dante.

The logistics did not concern him for he had his own helicopter and used it with ease. And certainly they could afford a virtually hospital-calibre set-up in his father's residence.

What concerned him was that *she* would be there.

At least at the hospital Mia had the decency to step out when his family came to visit. Dante rarely acknowledged her, referring to her as 'Stepmother' any time he did.

He loathed his father's wife with a passion, and having to deal with her in the family home in his father's final months did not appeal.

Still, it was not about Dante, so he would call the hospital back to make the necessary arrangements for his father to be cared for at home. For now, he would get on with the meeting.

Except his screen lit up and he saw that the doctor was calling him again.

Someone of importance was calling Sarah, his PA, Dante guessed, for now she glanced down at her own phone and then looked straight up to him in that particular way she did when there was a call Dante needed to take, and the hackles on the back of his neck rose.

'Why don't we take a short recess?' Dante said smoothly. 'And when we return, perhaps we can discuss something other than my sex life.'

He strode out, leaving Luigi looking like thunder, and headed straight for his office.

There had, in fact, been four missed calls from his father's doctor and as the screen lit up again he took the call.

'Dante Romano speaking.'

And just like that it was over.

He was told that his father's condition had deteriorated suddenly, and even before a call could be made to alert the family that the end was near, Rafael Romano had passed.

Dante had known this day was coming for months and yet the news of the death of his father brought the ice of the winter outside right into his soul.

He looked over towards the Basilica dei Santi Pietro e Paolo, the church set on the highest point of the district, and fixed his gaze on its enormous dome. He could not fathom that his father was gone. 'Did he suffer?' Dante asked.

'Not at all,' the doctor assured him. 'It was very quick. His lawyer was there for a meeting. Signora Romano was walking in the hospital grounds, but your father was gone before we could get her back to his side...'

Dante did not need to know *her* moves. Mia Romano was irrelevant and would soon be carved out of their lives like the cancer she was. He thought of his father dying with the family lawyer beside him. Ironic, really, when it should have been family. He moved on to ask about the person who mattered, the person who had been a loyal wife to his father for more than three decades before that grifter, Mia, had come along. 'Has my mother been told?'

'No,' the doctor said. 'Just you. Signora Romano thought it better that this call come from me.'

Well, at least Mia had got that much right, for there was no way Dante would have wanted her breaking this news to him.

Dante had hated her on sight.

Only, that wasn't strictly true.

Dante had hated her on *second* sight.

The first time they had met she had quite literally stopped him in his angry tracks, for he had been furious with his father about a rumoured affair, though he had not known at that time that his mistress was Mia.

She had worn velvet stilettos and a lavender linen shift dress and had been delightfully pale for an Italian summer. She had worn her blonde hair up and back from her face, allowing full access to sapphire-blue eyes framed with pale lashes.

'Who are you?' he had asked when he'd strode into his father's office.

'Mia Hamilton,' she had said, and had told him in less than perfect Italian that she was his father's new PA and had been brought over from the London branch. Her poor Italian should have been a red flag—his own PA was fluidly multilingual, as was Dante himself, but he had been too enthralled in that moment for logical thinking.

And as he had looked at her and continued to look, Mia had stared back at him. For how many seconds their eyes had held Dante chose not to count. He recalled with perfect precision, though, the slight flush that had spread up her long slender neck and to her cheeks and the thick yet exquisite tension in the air as they'd assessed each other with desire in their eyes, but then his father had come in.

Or rather, *thank God*, then his father had come in!

It was easier on his soul to omit that memory.

To simply erase that first kick of lust.

His father had asked Mia to leave the office, and in an angry confrontation Dante had found out why her less than impressive linguistic skills had been overlooked. And he had later found out how focused, determined, resilient and tough the very prim Mia Hamilton could be.

As well as ruthless.

No, she refused to remain his father's mistress, and would settle for nothing less than to be Rafael Romano's wife.

The newspapers had been full of the drama of the irretrievable breakdown of the long marriage of the golden Romano couple and had been lavish in their vilification of Mia. She had been branded as a gold-digger seeking a sugar daddy, and it had been a sustained and savage attack.

The Ice Queen, many had later called her—the press, his family, the board—for she never betrayed even a hint of emotion. Even when the soon-to-be ex-wife, Angela Romano, openly wept in a televised interview about the end of her marriage, Mia Hamilton merely went about her day and was photographed shopping in the tree-lined Via Cola di Rienzo.

Yet Dante had not joined the pack in its condemnation of her, for his animosity towards Mia was *deeply* personal.

His blistering, disdainful treatment of her was really about self-preservation.

Dante had shored up the business himself—anything to get her gold-digging hands away from it. And while he told himself he wanted her on her knees, begging, the deeper truth was that he just wanted her on her knees.

A fast-track divorce had ensued and it had all gone through uncontested, so just over six months after the day he'd first laid eyes on her Mia Hamilton had become Mia Romano.

Naturally, Dante had not attended the wedding.

He had responded to the invitation with a handwritten note, stating that he had always considered marriage to be a pointless institution, and never more so than now.

Neither had his siblings, nor indeed any of Dante's family, attended.

His mother now lived permanently in Rome, and dear Mia, his stepmother, had her stilettoed heels firmly through the doors of the Tuscan residence.

The family home.

Thank God *he* had taken care of the business.

The only small positive to come from his father's illness

had been that Rafael's high-profile social life in Rome had been curtailed and as a result Mia had been rather tucked away, no doubt screaming to the hills that the glamour of being Signora Romano had been denied to her.

Yet he could not think of Mia now.

For his father was gone.

'Thank you for all you did for him,' Dante said to the doctor, and pressed a tense palm to his forehead when he thought of the unpalatable task ahead. 'I shall let the family know now.'

Rafael's *real* family.

When the call had ended, Dante stood for a silent moment, gathering his thoughts.

The wheels would soon be set in motion. His father had planned his own funeral with the same care that had seen that first vineyard and property on a Tuscan hillside grow into the vast empire it now was.

And, God knew, despite their differences at times, Dante would miss him very much.

'Sarah…' he pressed the intercom '…would you ask Stefano and Ariana to come into my office, please?'

'Of course.'

'And Luigi,' he added.

The twins were twenty-five to Dante's thirty-two.

Stefano was inward with his emotions and stood silent and grey as Dante imparted the sad news. Ariana, the absolute apple of her father's eye, had no such reserve, and sobbed noisily.

Luigi sat with his head in his hands, stunned at the loss of his older brother.

'We need to go and tell Mamma,' Dante said to his siblings, as he offered Luigi use of his helicopter to take him home to Luctano to tell his wife.

It was wretched, Dante thought as he headed back into the boardroom, that the board would know what had happened before Mamma, but Ariana's cries might have reached them, and the three of them leaving together would speak on its own.

He looked down at the solemn faces. Some were already crying because, though Rafael Romano had been an arduous boss, he had also been devoted and passionate and respected and loved.

'The news is not to leave this room,' Dante said, his voice a touch gravelly, but apart from that there was little to betray his emotions. 'A formal announcement shall be made in due course, but there are people close to him who need to be told properly.'

They all knew who that meant as Dante walked out.

'We need to go now and tell her,' Dante said, and put an arm around his sister. 'Come.'

'Poor Mamma,' Ariana gulped. 'This will finish her.'

'She is strong,' Dante said, and they took the elevator down. 'She's a Romano.'

Still.

Despite the divorce, his mother had not reverted to her own familial name, but had been given permission by the judge to keep the Romano name. In the vast scheme of things, it had been a minor point, and Dante had not given it much consideration, and neither did he now.

In the car, Ariana sat quietly sobbing as the car threaded its way through chaotic streets; Stefano called Eloa, his fiancée, and told her the sad news.

'Mamma should have been with him,' Ariana said as they neared the luxurious Villa Borghese where Angela Romano had a penthouse apartment. 'It is all *her* fault.'

'No,' Dante said, knowing his sister referred to Mia. 'There is much we could blame her for, but not Pa's death. When we get there we need to be...' His voice trailed off as a couple approaching the apartment building caught his eye. They were holding hands and the woman was suddenly coquettish—his *mother* was suddenly coquettish—running a little forward as the man pulled her, laughing, back to his side. And the man was somewhat familiar, though Dante could not place him... 'Drive around again,' Dante ordered the driver, and Stefano looked over at his older brother.

'Why?' Stefano asked.

'I need a moment to gather myself before we tell her.'

Stefano frowned as he ended his call to Eloa and Dante saw the question in his eyes, for usually Dante baulked at nothing. 'She needs to be told,' Stefano said. 'It will soon get out.'

'Of course she needs to be told,' Dante agreed, and took out his own phone. 'But we should alert her first, not just turn up unannounced. That would be too much of a shock...'

He was grasping excuses from thin air as he called his mother and it went straight to messages. He called her again and thankfully this time she picked up.

'Dante?' she said. *'Pronto?'*

'Stefano, Ariana and I are on our way to see you.'

'Why?'

'Mamma,' Dante said, 'we shall be there in a moment.' He took a breath. 'We have difficult news to share with you.'

As he ended the call Ariana looked at him accusingly. 'You are too blunt, Dante. Why would you tell her over the phone?'

'Because they were married for more than thirty years,' Dante snapped, his mind whirring from all he had just seen. 'She might need a private moment to gather herself.'

And to get rid of her lover!

Who was he? Dante could not place the face, but really that was the least of his concerns—he was simply stunned to see his mother with another man. And while, of course, his mother was right to move on with her life and deserved happiness…

He just didn't want to have found out on this day of all days.

Dante wondered if his mother would have the same consideration as they took the ancient elevator up to the penthouse floor.

Thankfully she had, for there was no sign of her lover when she wrenched the door open.

'Dante, what on earth are you—?' Then she saw the tear-streaked face of her daughter standing behind him, and the pale features of Stefano.

Angela Romano stood frozen and stunned as realisation hit.

'Come on,' Dante said, and led her through the entrance and to the lounge where she took a seat.

'No, no, no,' she said.

'Mamma, it was quick and it was peaceful. He had his dignity right to the end. He was having a meeting with Roberto. I saw him just last night and we were talking and even laughed…'

'I should have been there to say goodbye to him,' Angela said, and started to cry.

Yes, Dante thought as he sat with his mother while she wept, she should have been.

'What happens for the funeral?' Angela gulped. 'I haven't been back to Luctano since…'

Since the affair had been uncovered.

The scandal had been enormous, and his mother, who felt the family home had been tainted, had moved into their most lavish apartment in Rome.

'Luigi and Rosa have said you are welcome to stay with them,' Dante said. 'Or there is the hotel.'

God.

It had come to this.

His mother, who had lived in that town all her life, reduced to being a guest in a hotel—even if the Romanos owned it.

Dante was black with anger as he poured his mother a brandy and one for himself, though he did his best not to reveal it. But as the conversation turned to funeral arrangements, Dante felt a deep and urgent need to see his father for himself. 'I'm going to call Sarah and tell her that, after the pilot has dropped Luigi home, I want him to collect me and take me to Florence so I can see him,' Dante said. 'Do any of you want to come?' Stefano shook his head and Ariana started to cry again and said *no*.

'I'll be back tonight,' Dante said. 'And then we shall all return to Luctano together on the eve of the funeral.'

'It's my fault,' Angela sobbed, 'I should have been a better wife. I should have held on...'

Dante frowned, because she had said the same thing when they had found out his father was dying. 'Held on?'

But she was crying too hard to answer him and so Dante held his mother's heaving shoulders. 'None of this is your fault.'

He knew *exactly* where the blame lay.

Dante called the hospital and said he was on his way, and to please not move his father yet, and then he called Sarah to arrange the pilot and also—

'It's fine,' Sarah said. 'I'll feed Alfonzo.'

Damned dog.

He was the bane of Dante's life, and the reason he preferred to take women to hotels rather than home, to avoid having seven pounds of blind, ancient Bichon baring his teeth.

'Thank you.'

The helicopter took him to the Florence hospital and Dante made his lonely way through long corridors and to the private room where his father lay.

Mia had gone by the time he arrived, though he hadn't exactly expected her to be sitting at the bedside, quietly weeping. He was just grateful that there was no awkward meeting or standing back to let her pass.

Rafael Dante Romano looked peaceful, as though he was asleep, and there was the sweet vanilla scent of orchids from an array of blooms in a vase by his bed.

'You knew, didn't you?' Dante said as he sat beside him. 'That was what you meant last night when you told me you wanted to return to Luctano…'

And then he took his father's cold hand and his strong voice finally cracked as Dante asked a question he hadn't dared to when his father had been alive. 'What did you have to go and marry her for, Pa?'

Dante wasn't referring to the pain his father's second marriage had caused.

It was the agony of wanting his father's wife.

CHAPTER TWO

MIA WATCHED FROM the comfort of the sumptuous Suite al Limone as Dante's helicopter approached in the rainy, grey, cloud-laden sky on the eve of Rafael Romano's funeral.

Very deliberately she did not look over to the lake.

This morning, when she had been riding Massimo, Mia had come across the freshly dug grave and it had spooked her so much that she had swiftly turned the old horse around and kicked him into a gallop.

The Romano family residence was nestled in a valley on the outskirts of the Province of Luctano, in the fertile Tuscan hills. The endless vines that neatly laced the hillsides were, apart from a select few, now owned by the company. Who owned those vines, along with the residence, would be revealed tomorrow after the funeral. One thing was certain, it wouldn't be Mia. Both she and Rafael had long ago agreed that she would stake no claim to it.

And, though she didn't want it, Mia would miss it very much.

She would miss the horses in the stables and the beautiful rides that she took most days. Miss, too, standing here at her window, watching the dogs head out in search of truffles, and times spent sitting by the vast, still lake, or walking around it in an attempt to make sense of her jumbled thoughts. And she would miss the quiet comfort of this suite that had been both her refuge and her retreat.

The Suite al Limone was just that—a gorgeous suite with silk lemon walls and exquisite furnishings. The lounge room was both elegant and cosy and she loved nothing more than to curl up and read by the fire on winter nights. The bedroom with its high four-poster bed was both pretty and feminine and, Mia found, soothing to the soul.

Suite al Limone had been her private space for the last two years and had allowed for gentle healing, and although she truly didn't want the property, Mia wasn't quite sure that she was ready to leave it behind.

But there was no choice, and it had little to do with the contents of Rafael Romano's last will and testament. He was to be buried on the grounds tomorrow and so Mia would be leaving that very night.

Although she was dreading the Romanos' arrival, Mia was relieved to see Dante's chopper, for the blend of low clouds, rain and high winds were not the best conditions in which to fly. Her stomach lurched at the mere sight of the difficult landing, and she held her breath as the helicopter tilted a little to the side and then righted itself before finally touching down. As well as the helicopter's arrival she could see the headlights on the cars snaking their way around the hill towards the residence.

Mia had not seen any of the Romano family since Rafael's death, but on the eve of the funeral there were certain traditions to be upheld. Certain wishes, Rafael had specified, that needed to be carried out.

The family *would* eat together in his home tonight.

Angela would not be joining them as, despite keeping the Romano name, she was no longer his family, but Rafael's children, brother and his wife, and some cousins, too, would together toast Rafael on the night before he was laid to rest.

Mia watched as the youngest, Ariana Romano, got out.

She was gorgeous, long limbed and with a mane of raven hair, and she was as spoilt as she was beautiful. Next out was her twin brother Stefano, and Mia saw that he had brought Eloa, his stunning Brazilian fiancée, with him. Stefano was just as good looking as Ariana and just as arrogant.

All the Romanos were arrogant, but it was the eldest brother who excelled at it—and here Dante was, emerging from the helicopter. Mia braced herself for the appearance of whomever he was currently dating, while telling herself it mattered not. Instead of a leggy supermodel, though, her breath sucked in when Angela Romano emerged. She was dressed from head to toe in black and relying on her son's arm to get down the stairs.

Ah, so that was how it was going to be played, with Angela taking the part of the *real* grieving widow.

If only they knew!

Mia's lips pressed together and she watched as Angela was gently bundled into a silver car and driven out of the vast estate.

Stefano, Eloa and Ariana stood under black umbrellas and watched the car leave. They would then get into another that would drive them to the main residence. Dante, though, had chosen to walk. For a brief moment he glanced up towards the residence, and Mia stepped back quickly from the window, even though he was surely too far away to see her.

Of all the Romanos it was Dante who made her the most nervous, for his loathing of her was palpable. He insisted that they all speak English when Mia was around. But it was not to be polite; instead it was a snub at her Italian and also, she was certain, to ensure that she got the full gist of every one of the constant low barbs that were aimed at her.

Mia was dreading facing him.

Whenever they met, his black eyes seemed to look straight to the centre of her and silently tell her that he knew she did not love his father. That he knew she had only married Rafael for his money and that the marriage was a complete and utter sham.

The worst part for Mia?

He was absolutely right.

Dante just didn't know the full truth.

And neither could he *ever*! Mia had been well paid to ensure that.

Yet it wasn't just the sham of her marriage that caused Mia to be nervous when Dante was around. He evoked in her unfamiliar feelings that the very inexperienced Mia did not dare explore and did all she could to avoid.

But in a few short moments there would be no avoiding him.

There was a knock at the door and it was the housekeeper, Sylvia, to tell her the family would arrive in five minutes or so. 'The children are making their way towards the house,' she said, and Mia found her lips pressed into a wry smile.

They were *hardly* children.

'And the guest cars are approaching the grounds,' Sylvia said.

'Thank you,' Mia said, but as the housekeeper turned to go Mia called her back. 'How are you doing, Sylvia?'

'I'm all right.' She gave a tired shrug. 'Just so sad.'

'I know you are.'

'And I'm worried too,' Sylvia admitted. 'My husband and I…' Her voice trailed off, but though she didn't come out and say it directly, Mia knew the lovely couple had worked and lived on the grounds for many years and must be deeply concerned as to what the future held for them. 'We will miss Rafael so very much.' Sylvia's eyes drifted to the cases Mia had packed in preparation for her leaving. 'And we will miss you too.'

'Thank you,' Mia said, and, rarely for her, she gave the housekeeper a hug, for though Mia was not touchy-feely at all, she adored Sylvia. After a brief embrace Mia pulled back. 'I'd better head down. I'll greet them and have a drink to be polite, but then I'll be taking my meal up here.'

'Of course,' Sylvia said, for, like all good staff, she knew better than most the true situation.

When Sylvia had gone, Mia briefly checked her appearance in the full-length antique mirror. She wore a very simple black dress, stockings and low-heeled shoes and her blonde hair was tied back in a low bun. She took out a strand of cream pearls that had belonged to her mother and put them on, but then wondered if that was too much jewellery for a grieving widow to wear.

She truly did not know how she was supposed to act, let alone how she actually felt.

Numb was perhaps the best word, for even if it had been a marriage of convenience, Rafael had become a very dear friend and she would miss him dreadfully. She had decided she would deal with her feelings later, once she was well away from the Romanos.

Mia made her way down the grand staircase. Thankfully they hadn't quite arrived so she headed straight into the lounge where *apericena*—pre-dinner drinks and nibbles—was to be served before they moved through to the dining room.

She stood by the fire, hugging her arms around herself and taking a couple of calming breaths as the main doors opened and the Romano family started to arrive.

How to play this?

She had no idea, Mia thought as she gazed into the fire. They all loathed and detested her and believed her to be the cause for the break-up of their Raphael and Angela's marriage. Would they even want her to go out now and greet them?

Mia very much doubted it.

Over the last couple of years, whenever one of them had visited the Romano residence, Rafael had, of course, been here.

It felt very different to have them all here without Rafael.

Mia could hear the low murmur of voices as more cousins arrived and then, more loudly, Sylvia tried to steer them through to the lounge. *'Apericena?'* she offered, inviting them for a pre-dinner aperitif, but no one came through.

It would seem Mia's absence had been noted for it was then that she heard Dante's deep voice put to its poisonous best.

'So where *is* our stepmother?'

Mia's skin crawled when he called her that, and he insisted on doing so at every available opportunity.

The difference was that tonight it angered her.

The sound of his confident footsteps on the marble told of his approach to the lounge.

'Ah, there you are,' he said from the doorway.

There was no attempt at politeness for appearances' sake.

They had never so much as touched.

No air kisses, no shaking of hands. There was nothing other than the cold touch of his contempt that reached her.

It had always been difficult here at home but the tensions between them had escalated in recent weeks. When he had come to the hospital to visit and had arrived at Rafael's room she would stand and Dante would step back as she walked out as if he could not bear for even as much as the hem of his coat to brush her. From the moment Rafael had told Dante that Mia was his mistress it was as if there had been prison-cell doors that had slammed closed between them.

And those prison doors had never, in these two years, parted as much as an inch.

They spoke as if from behind bars, and only when they

had to, but Mia was grateful for those doors now and the boundaries they had long ago established. Dante was tall and forbidding at the best of times. At the worst of times— and this was exactly that—he was like the devil himself.

She did not want to know that devil unleashed.

He wore a black suit and his white shirt was a little rumpled, which was not up to his usual standards of perfection. His hair had been superbly cut, though he had not shaved, and his black eyes were a little red, but apart from that you would not know he was mourning. And, yes, he was absolutely beautiful, but she utterly refused to admit that now, even to herself.

'I'm sorry for your loss,' Mia said, and knew how stilted and wooden she sounded.

'But not sorry for your gain,' Dante retorted.

Rather than bite back, instead she was all steely politeness. 'Your suites have been prepared.'

'There was no need for that. My brother and sister are staying at my uncle's and I am staying at the hotel.'

'Well, should anyone change their mind—'

'I very much doubt it.'

Dante having cut her off, she stood, her arms still around herself as he walked through the lounge, ignoring the tray where drinks had been set up. Instead he went to a large buffet and opened a crystal decanter and poured himself a glass of amber fluid.

'Aren't they coming through?' Mia asked.

'You really expect us to have a drink and mingle?' Dante checked, and gave a black mirthless laugh. 'I don't think so. I sent them straight to the dining room. We all just want this dinner over with, Mia. Let's just get it done and then we will be out of your hair.'

'Fine,' she said, and went to head out. 'I'll leave you to it.'

'Oh, no, you don't,' Dante said to her departing back, and watched her stiffen. 'You *shall* join us for dinner.'

'It's a family dinner,' Mia said, her cheeks a touch pink as she turned around. 'You've all made it exceptionally clear that I'm not welcome in the fold.'

'It was my father's wish that we all dine together and it is also the only chance to go over tomorrow's arrangements as I am heading to the vigil soon. I won't have time to waste explaining things twice.'

'What is there to explain? Everything's been organised.'

'The cars, the seating, the eulogy, the timing of the wake, the reading of the will…' He ran a list by her, tapping the fingers of his hand as he did so. 'Or do you just want to waft around tomorrow, dabbing at your crocodile tears, having had absolutely zero input as to the final arrangements for your own husband's funeral?'

The very last thing she wanted was dinner with the Romanos but, it would seem, she had no choice.

He did not await her response. Dante turned and headed off to take his place at the table.

'*Is* she joining us?' Ariana asked, because, despite Rafael's instructions, none of them thought she would have the gall to.

'I believe so,' Dante said.

'She's got a nerve—'

'Cut it out, Ariana,' Dante warned.

He did not like the group attack mentality; heaven knows, he had dealt with it enough himself at work and in his family. Dante himself would face anyone one on one and let them know his mind, but he would not have them sit there and gang up on Mia.

He was also aware he had gone too far with his animosity back in the lounge, but the sight of her had been like a kick in the guts. The house, when he had stepped in, had been so silent. In an Italian home, there would be crying and keening, such as would be taking place at his aunt's now.

Yet Mia had stood there so still and silent and dignified. Finally she walked into the dining room.

Still silent, still dignified and still completely capable of turning him on.

CHAPTER THREE

THE SEAT AT the head of the table was left empty out of respect for the recently departed and there were a lot of side looks as Mia took her seat at the opposite end of the gleaming table.

Mia was, after all, the lady of the house.

And they *detested* her for it.

Wine from the private Romano vineyard, the one still owned by his father, was served and toasts were made.

Dante kicked off. *'Dei morti parla bene.'*

Mia knew that one: *Speak well of the dead.* And she took a sip of the dark liquid and forced it down, for to her it tasted like medicine.

Then Stefano offered a toast, and though Mia couldn't quite make out what he said, she politely raised her glass.

But then Luigi offered his toast and he stared right at Mia as he did so. *'Dove c'è un testamento, c'è un parente.'*

Where there's a will, there's a relative.

It was a familiar saying following a death, but the implication that Mia was here for the money was made exceptionally clear.

Dante looked over at Mia, who didn't as much as blink as the less than veiled slur was hurled, but neither did she raise her glass, and despite himself he rather admired her resilience. And, despite his loathing for Mia, Dante found himself leaping to her defence. 'That is true, Luigi. I have no doubt you will be in the study tomorrow for the reading of his will.' He looked around the table. 'All of you will be.'

Mia had not expected even a sliver of support from Dante, and though grateful she dared not show it.

It felt odd to be in the same room as him, odd to be sharing a meal.

She felt odd whenever Dante was near in a way that was less than becoming, for he made her aware of herself, just by being himself.

As the *primo piatto* was served, Dante got straight down to business. 'It was Rafael's request that he return to his home one last time. The hearse will be here at eleven and the funeral procession will leave shortly after that.' Mia swallowed when he looked at her. 'Naturally, you will be in the car behind the hearse,' Dante informed her.

'With?' Mia asked, because her heart was hammering at the prospect of sitting alone.

'That is up to you—whoever you've invited to support you on the loss of your husband.' He did not wait for her to respond. 'I shall be in the vehicle behind with Stefano, Eloa and Ariana. Luigi...' he turned to his uncle '...your family shall be in the car behind that...'

'Surely Mamma should be in the procession,' Ariana said.

'Ariana.' Dante's voice was a touch impatient. 'She is so overwrought that she can barely stand. At least this way she can be seated in the church when the procession arrives.'

'But it's not fair that she won't be in the procession when she was his—'

'Enough!' Dante warned.

Ariana was the first to leave the sinking ship. With a loud clatter, she threw down her cutlery and stormed out, and it was just a matter of moments before a car was summoned to take her back to be with her mother.

There was silence after she left.

Dante gave up on the pasta and declined more wine, asking for brandy instead, before continuing. 'The procession will move slowly through the grounds,' he explained. 'First to the stables, and then on to the private vines and residences and then it will do a loop around the poppy fields. This will give the staff a chance to come out and pay their respects before they make their way to the church.'

It was going to be a long procession, Mia thought. Even though most of the land that surrounded them now belonged to the business, Rafael's private property encompassed the staff residences, lake and poppy fields and was still huge. Mia took in a shaky breath at the thought of sitting alone in the vehicle behind the hearse and she tried, *how* she tried, not to recall her parents' funeral.

They ate in silence for a while, and for Mia it was excruciating, but as the plates were being cleared, she felt Sylvia's hand come down on her shoulder, giving a little squeeze of support, and Mia briefly glanced up and gave the housekeeper a small grateful smile.

Dante noticed the supportive gesture, for he always noticed what was happening around Mia.

The staff adored Mia—that much was made evident whenever he visited here—and that confused him. They were always discreet, but little things, like that touch of support, made it clear to Dante that Mia was both respected and liked in the household.

She looked stunning in candlelight. Her lips were a little swollen, but apart from that there were no signs of tears. Dante doubted she had shed even a single one for his father.

Perhaps drawn by his scrutiny, she looked over and Dante realised she had caught him staring at her, and when he perhaps should flick disapproving eyes away he did not, for, despite his best intentions, his eyes were not disapproving...

Mia felt trapped by his gaze.

She could hear Eloa talking yet had little idea what was being said, and she was peripherally aware of her wine-glass being topped up, yet it felt as if it were just her and Dante at the table.

For two years Mia had forced herself to ignore him and be her aloof best, she found that she too could not look away. For two years she had trained herself to deny the slight prickly sensations his presence evoked, and to ignore the stir of unfamiliar arousal he triggered, but she was unable to stop it now. Mia felt the creep of warmth spread up her throat to her cheeks, and down to her breasts. Dante made her, without words, want to shift in her seat; he made her want to touch her own mouth to check on it for it felt too big for her face.

And even as she willed him to look away, Mia found that she could not.

The prison doors felt as if they were parting as, for the first time since the day they'd met, she allowed herself to meet his gaze and be held there.

Oh, prim Mia, Dante thought as it was *he* who finally removed his gaze, *you are so not.*

The second course—suckling pig—was served as the atmosphere at the table grew increasingly tense. Now it was Mia who wanted to fling down her cutlery and head upstairs, but instead she asked for a very small portion, though it was almost impossible to eat even that much.

'Where is Angela to be seated in the church?' Luigi's wife asked Dante.

'Wherever she chooses.'

'But what pew?' Luigi persisted on his wife's behalf. 'Surely the children of the deceased should be at the front and their mother with them.'

'Mia shall be seated at the front,' Dante said. 'Etiquette dictates that the ex-wife should be discreet and stay back...'

Though Dante knew, of course, that there wasn't a hope in hell of that happening tomorrow. His mother would be sitting behind Mia like a cat put out in the rain, Dante thought, and he felt a rare prickle of sympathy in Mia's direction for the circus his mother created. Very deliberately he pushed that thought aside and got on with explaining the order of events tomorrow. 'He shall be buried back here by the lake, in a very short ceremony...just his children, and...' Dante swallowed '...his current wife, and then back here for drinks, and no doubt more damn antipasti...' his bile was rising '...then the reading of the will...' He took a belt of brandy and Mia gave up on her suckling pig and stared at her plate in silence.

'I forgot to say—' Dante's voice was now eerily calm '—that I shall be giving the eulogy. Mia?'

She looked up, somewhat startled by the sound of her own name and the question in Dante's voice. 'I have spoken with all my family to ask what they want included, and now I ask you. Is there anything you would specifically like me to add?'

Mia had not been expecting to be offered any input into the eulogy and she did not know how to respond without offending those who had loved Rafael the most—after all, Mia was more than aware that their marriage had been a charade.

'Mia?' Dante invited a touch more tersely.

She could not meet his dark eyes now, even as she spoke. 'I've already said everything I wanted to to your father. I am sure whatever you have written will be wonderful.'

'So there is *nothing* you would like me to add?' Dante checked.

Mia did not know what to say and the silence that seemed to stretch on for ever was broken only when Luigi's chair scraped back and he stood. Luigi looked at her with so much disgust that for a second Mia thought he might fling the contents of his wineglass in her direction, but instead he walked away from the table. 'I am going to the church,' he said. 'I rather think it might be warmer in there, even with the doors open.'

'We shall come too,' Stefano said, gesturing to Eloa to stand as he shot Mia a look and then addressed his brother. 'Are you coming, Dante?'

'I have a few more things to sort out first.' Dante declined his brother's invitation to leave.

'Then I shall come back later and collect you for the vigil.'

The rest of the family all agreed that they too would not wait for dessert and as they headed out she heard someone mutter a distasteful word under their breath. She also deciphered a comment in Italian, about her not even being able to squeeze out a tear, let alone declare her love for her late husband.

Only Dante remained seated.

'Well, that went well…' Mia's voice was high, her burst of mirthless laughter shrill.

'It was never going to go well,' Dante said, and turned those black eyes to her. 'I have no idea what my father was thinking, requesting that we dine together.'

'Neither do I.' She did not look at him and instead wrung a serviette between her hands. 'Dante, I have no issue with your family sitting at the front, either with me, or I can sit further—'

'No.' Dante cut in. 'You will not be seated further back. I will speak with my mother. However—and I'm being frank now, Mia—I can usually give speeches and eulogies with my eyes closed, but I am struggling with what to say in this instance. Should I say how happy you two made each other in his final years? Or should I say that finally my father met the love of his life?' He threw his hands in the air in an exasperated gesture. 'Surely you have something you want me to add?'

What could she say?

What could Dante say?

Anything that he had just suggested would be cruel to Rafael's loved ones, but she knew she sounded a cold bitch when she shook her head. 'No. As I've said, I said all I had to to your father.'

The look of contempt he flashed her was so direct as to be almost physical, so much so that she felt she could have put up her hands and caught it.

There was no question they even attempt dessert.

'Excuse me, please,' Mia said, and put her serviette down.

'You don't need my permission to leave the table, Mia,' he said, 'but please, go ahead and get the hell out.'

She headed up the stairs to her suite where she wished, how she wished, that she had insisted on taking her meal up there.

Damn you, Dante.

Mia was very used to spending her evenings alone in the Suite al Limone. The drapes had been drawn by Sylvia and, having showered and pulled on a slip nightdress, she climbed into bed, dreading tomorrow and the funeral a hundred times more so now.

Of course it brought back memories of her parents' funeral and though she tried to push that aside, the mere thought of being alone in a car behind the hearse made her feel sweaty and more than a little nauseous.

Mia wanted some tea, something hot and soothing, but until Dante left there was no way she would go downstairs and make some.

And though she wanted Dante gone, conversely she was not looking forward to him leaving for that would mean she would be here on her own.

Since Rafael's death, Mia had found it creepy to be alone in this house at night.

In fact, she found it to be terrifying.

Sylvia and her husband had a cottage close by, and she could call them, of course—not that she ever would for something as trivial as tea. Yes, this really was to be her last night here because the very stiff upper lipped Mia was, in fact, petrified of ghosts. There was no way she could stay here, knowing Rafael was buried in the grounds. Her cases were all packed and tomorrow, once the reading of the last will and testament had taken place, she was leaving.

The Romanos wanted her gone anyway, that much she knew.

Well, she'd make it easy on them.

Mia lay there trying to read, but when she heard Stefano arrive to collect Dante for the vigil she put her book down. There was the sound of the main doors closing followed by wheels on the gravel and only then did she pull on a robe and come out of the suite. Turning on the lights as she went, jumping at every creak, gingerly Mia made her way down the stairs. She pushed open the doors to the kitchen and realised then that she wasn't alone, for there, sitting silent and nursing a brandy, was Dante.

'Oh!' Mia exclaimed when she saw him, and clutched the top of her robe, more than a little embarrassed to face him in her night attire. 'I thought you had gone.'

'No. I decided not to go to the vigil.' He rarely explained himself, and found himself questioning why he was doing it now. 'As I just said to Stefano, I saw him the day he died; I don't need to again.'

Mia nodded. Privately, she could think of nothing worse than spending a night in a church with an open coffin. 'I was just getting a drink. Do you want one?'

He gave a slight shake of his head, and then, perhaps

remembering they still had tomorrow to get through, he answered her more politely. 'No, thank you. I am just about to head to the hotel. Oh, and there is a slight change of plans to tomorrow. Stefano insists that Eloa comes to the burial.'

'Of course she should be there,' Mia said, but then frowned because his disapproval was evident as he stared into his glass. 'What, don't you like her?'

'What the hell does that have to do with anything? The fact is he wanted his children there, not some ship that passes in the night.'

'Hardly a ship,' Mia said. 'They're engaged to be married.'

'Let's hope then that Roberto draws up a watertight pre-nup for him.'

'Do you never consider they might be in love?'

'God help them if they are; love causes nothing but problems.'

'You're so cynical.'

'Said the young widow on the eve of her rich husband's funeral.'

Bastard, she wanted to hiss, but turned her back on him instead.

Dante tried not to notice the slight shake of her hand as she prepared a tray and made tea.

It surprised him. Not so much the shake of her hand, more that she made tea and served it herself, instead of summoning the staff.

He rather imagined her sitting up in bed, ringing down for tea to be served, and then he hauled his mind from that for he did not want to think, even for a second, of Mia in bed.

And certainly he did his best not to notice her feminine shape beneath the silk robe.

Something had shifted between them since his father's

death. The self-imposed rules of avoidance, to which Dante had strictly adhered, were starting to crumble and he fought hard to rebuild them.

He looked over towards the vast windows, but so dark was the night that he might as well have been looking at a mirror. Suddenly she turned and met his gaze in the window, then spoke to his reflection. 'Dante, I don't want to travel at the front of the procession.'

'Tough,' Dante said, remembering his rules. 'You are his wife!'

'But I don't want to be in the car on my own.'

'Then where are your family and friends?' Dante asked, but halted immediately because, from the little he had been told by his father, he knew both her parents were dead. Yet he would not be guilted out of pointing out the facts. 'You insist this is a real marriage, so why isn't anyone here to support you in your loss? Or are they tired of the games you play? You have a brother,' Dante pointed out, 'yet he wasn't at the wedding, neither is he here today, though I seem to remember that last year you went home for *his* wedding. Are you worried, if he were here, that he might let slip some of your lies?'

Mia didn't answer him.

Dante stood to go, but he could not leave it there. 'It is not a punishment that you travel alone; it is a courtesy that the Hamilton family have their own car at the front of the procession. It is not my fault you have no one to fill it.'

She turned from speaking to his reflection and faced him. 'Are you hoping that the villagers pelt me with rotten fruit?' Mia asked.

Dante saw a flash of tears in her sapphire-blue eyes. It was her first real display of emotion since he had arrived; in fact, it was her first display of emotion since the day they'd met, and he detested that it moved him. He detested that he wanted to reach out and take her in his arms, and that the sight of her in her pale coral robe would remain with him all night.

Worse, he would be fighting the memory of her all night.

Dante's want for her was perpetual, a lit fuse he was constantly stamping out, but it was getting harder and harder to keep it up. His breathing was ragged; there was a shift in the air and his resistance was fast fading. 'What did you think, Mia, that we were going to walk into the church together? A family united? Don't make me laugh...'

No one was laughing.

'Take your tea and go to bed.' Dante dismissed her with an angry wave of his hand, but even as he did so he halted, for it was not his place to send her to bed. 'I didn't mean that. Do what you will. I will leave.'

'It's fine. I'm going up.' She retrieved the tray.

'We leave tomorrow at eleven,' he said again as they headed through to the entrance.

'Yes.'

She turned then and gave him a tight smile, and saw his black eyes meet hers, and there was that look again between them, the one they had shared at the dining table. It was a look that she dared not decipher.

His lips, which were usually plump and red, the only splash of colour in his black-and-white features, were for once pale. There was a muscle leaping in his cheek, and she was almost sure it was pure contempt, except her body was misreading it as something else.

She had always been aware of his potent sexuality, but now Mia was suddenly aware of her own.

Conscious that she was naked beneath the gown, her breasts felt full and heavy, aware of the lust that danced inappropriately in the air between them. The prison gates were parting further and she was terrified to step out. 'Goodnight,' she croaked, and climbed the stairs, almost tipping the tray and only able to breathe when she heard the door slam.

Tea forgotten, she lay on the bed, frantic and unsettled. So much for the Ice Queen! She was burning for him in a way she had never known until she'd met Dante.

Mia had thought for a long time that there was something wrong with her, something missing in her make-up, for she'd had little to no interest in sex. Even back at school she would listen in on her peers, quietly bemused by their obsessive talking about boys and the things they did that to Mia sounded filthy. Her mother's awkward talk about the facts of life had left Mia revolted. The *fact of Mia's life*: it was something she didn't want! There was no reason she could find. There had been no trauma, nothing she could pin it to. Just for her, those feelings simply did not exist. Mia had tried to ignite the absent fire and had been on a couple of dates, but had found she couldn't even tolerate kisses, and tongues positively revolted her. She couldn't bear to consider anything else.

And while this marriage had given her a unique chance to heal from the appalling disaster that had befallen her family, the deeper truth was that it had given her a chance to hide from something she perhaps ought to address.

A no-sex marriage had felt like a blessing when she and Rafael had agreed to it.

Yet the ink had barely dried on the contract when she had found out that though those feelings might be buried deep, they were there after all.

Mia had been just a few days into the pretend position of Rafael's PA, and the carefully engineered rumours had just started to fly, when Dante Romano had walked in. A mere moment with him had helped her understand all she had been missing, for with just a look she found herself reacting in a way she never had before.

His dark eyes had transfixed her, the deep growl of his

voice had elicited a shiver low in her stomach, and even his scent, as it reached her, went straight to form a perfect memory. When Dante had asked who she was, his voice and his presence had alerted, startled and awoken her. So much so that she had half expected him to snap his fingers like a genie right before her scalding face.

Three wishes?

You.

You.

You.

Except she had been there to execute a business arrangement—one to which even Angela had agreed. She was to marry Rafael.

Yet so violent had been her reaction to Dante that Mia had considered backing out. Of course, that was impossible, for the first instalment had long since been spent.

And so she had cut that moment down to size and decided—a decade too late perhaps—that it was no more than the equivalent of a teenage crush.

Except, despite her constant quashing, it grew and it developed and it hit her in waves of rolling fire that she did not know how to put out.

For right now, as she thought of Dante and the looks they had shared this night, she wanted to close her eyes and imagine his mouth on hers. Right now, she wished Dante were there in his suite on the second floor or, even better, in Suite al Limone with her… She moaned in frustration, actually fighting not to touch herself and think of him, for on so many levels it would be…

Wrong.

Wrong.

Wrong.

He loathes you, she reminded herself.

There was just tomorrow to get through and she could go back to being Mia Hamilton, instead of a For Display

Purposes Only wife, and do everything she could to pick up the threads of her life.

And she would never have to lay eyes on Dante Romano again.

CHAPTER FOUR

THE SKY WAS tinged pink and threatening snow for the day of the funeral as Mia rode Massimo back to the house, carefully avoiding the lake.

Massimo was Rafael's horse, and she had taken over riding him when Rafael had grown too weak to do so. He was a beautiful black Murgese stallion, an Italian breed that Rafael had adored. Despite his size, Massimo was a polite and obedient horse.

And today he was sad.

'They know when something is up,' the stable manager told Mia when she returned him.

'I believe so,' Mia agreed.

The stable manager had the same look of sadness, concern and worry that all the staff had worn in recent months as it had become clear that Rafael's time was nearing.

Later today their fate would be made known.

Mia wasn't privy to the decisions Rafael had made.

She assumed the Luctano residence would go to his children, but could not imagine any of them living here. Mia guessed that it would be somewhere they dropped in on from time to time, like the rest of the Romano residences that were dotted across Europe. It was sad, Mia thought as she walked back to the house, holding a long single orchid she had collected on her ride, because it really was a home that deserved owners who loved it.

Mia headed up to Suite al Limone, to which the pinkish sky outside had given a warm coral hue.

Family members were starting to arrive and she was certain it was for the best that she stay upstairs until the last minute.

Having showered, Mia received updates from Sylvia, who had brought her breakfast.

'The Castellos are flying into Florence then taking a helicopter. They asked to use the helipad here; Dante refused and said it was being kept just for family, but Gian De Luca just landed his helicopter!' Sylvia raised her eyebrows at a slightly bemused Mia. 'He's a duke, you know.'

'I didn't know.'

'He doesn't use his title. The point is, though, that Gian is not family.'

No, that much Mia knew. Gian, though a friend of Dante's, *had* been one of the few at their wedding and was the owner of La Fiordelise, a hotel in Rome where their wedding had been held. Gian had a reputation with women that was worse than Dante's.

'It's a clear snub to the Castellos,' Sylvia further explained. 'Gian's helicopter has the gold insignia of his hotel on the tail and is very recognisable.' She gave a little, much-needed laugh on this very solemn day. 'There is always offence waiting to be taken at an Italian funeral. Still, it's all taking shape; Dante has it all under control.'

Mia, though, despite appearances, was not under control.

She felt shaky and nauseous and rather terrified about what lay ahead.

For the procession around the grounds and through the winding road to the church, Mia took some motion sickness medication and then made herself eat breakfast, recalling how dizzy she had become at her parents' service from both emotion and lack of food. She was grimly determined that no such thing would be happening today.

Of course, today's events were very different from when her parents had died, but with her black clothes all laid out, and sadness permeating the air, she could not help but reflect on that awful time.

It had been March and she had been due to start a new job, but before she did so there had been a family holiday to New York City with her parents and brother. It had been wonderful, taking in a show on Broadway and enjoying the delicious sights. On their final day, her father had hired a car to go a little further afield, even though Mia had advised against it, reminding her father of the dreadful time they'd once had in France when he'd attempted to drive on the opposite side of the road.

Paul Hamilton hadn't listened, though, and her mother, Corinne, had laughed off Mia's concerns.

They'd had a wonderful day, but it had been early spring; the clocks hadn't yet gone forward and dusk had descended as they'd headed back to the hotel. Her father had become confused by some headlights, had drifted across the road and a crash had ensued.

Her parents had been killed instantly, her brother seriously injured, and Mia had felt as if she'd been trapped for hours when really it had been only thirty minutes until she'd been freed.

Mia knew that it had been thirty minutes because she had read the reports, many times.

As well as poring over and over the horrendous medical bills.

She'd had travel insurance, thank God. Meticulous and organised Mia had bought it at the same time as her flight.

Her parents had had annual coverage and so they had been taken care of and their bodies repatriated.

But it had soon transpired that Michael, her brother, had not taken out insurance.

It had been more than horrendous. As well as losing her

parents, the family home had had to be sold. But even that hadn't covered the massive bills, starting with a trauma team callout, followed by three months on a spinal unit—where he had been billed right down to the last dressing—and then there had been the cost of a care flight home for her brother, who had been left paralysed from the waist down.

They had been in debt up to their eyeballs and of course Michael had become severely depressed. The job she had been due to start had been lost long ago, and so Mia had applied for and taken a job at Romano's in London. Though it had paid well and had been a fast-paced, busy role. As well as that, she had been working on improving her Italian in the hope of a promotion, while visiting her brother and dealing with the issue of housing for him.

It had all got too much.

Mia had been grieving, scared and *angry.*

Angry at her father for not listening to her concerns about him driving on the other side of the road, and angry with her mother too for not supporting her when she had voiced them.

And then there was her brother, who had been foolish and selfish enough to travel without insurance—though, of course, he had paid a terrible price, and it would be futile and mean to get angry with him.

So Mia had held it in, and held it in, and on an exceptionally busy day at work—Rafael Romano had been visiting the London office—when another debtor had called, and she had come close to a panic attack. Rafael had seen her distress, stopped and asked, 'My dear, whatever is wrong?'

It still touched her that during his own very difficult time—Rafael had himself just been asked for a divorce while, unbeknownst to his wife, undergoing a health scare—he still had taken the time to ask her what was wrong.

Of course Mia hadn't voiced her anger, just admitted to the hopeless position she was in.

And, because of that conversation, more than two years later, here she was, preparing for dear Rafael's funeral.

But this morning, when surely it should be Rafael and his kindness and the help he had given to her family that should be consuming her, it was memories of being trapped in that car that had Mia literally shaking.

She could still hear her mother's voice from the passenger seat, calling out to her. Telling her to hold on. That help would be here soon and that she loved her.

Except the report clearly stated that her mother had been killed on impact.

Yes, Mia had gone over that report a lot.

It scared her.

More than that, it terrified her.

At the age of twenty-four she was more petrified of the dark than she had been as a little girl, for she didn't just *believe* in ghosts, Mia knew that she had heard one speak.

'Get a grip, Mia,' she told herself, and with breakfast done she dressed for the funeral.

Her underwear was all black and new, and she had black tights that might be considered by some a little sheer for a widow, but she had bought them online. The soft wool dress she had bought in Florence, and from neck to hem it was adorned with little black pearl buttons. A stupid choice for a funeral, Mia decided, because her hands were so shaky, but finally every last button was done up.

She did not darken her fair lashes with mascara, for though she did not cry easily—in fact, she could not remember when she last had—Mia did not want to chance it. Her hair she wore up in a simple chignon and she wore no jewellery other than her wedding and engagement rings, both of which would be coming off tonight.

It was almost eleven and, though reluctant to leave the

warmth of her suite, she picked up the orchid she had collected on her ride this morning and stepped out.

Mia looked down to the foyer below and the family gathered there, all dressed in black. She could hear the sound of low funereal voices.

Thankfully, there was no sign of Angela, who had vowed never to set foot in the house while '*this tramp*' was here. Though Mia was rather certain that Angela would make an exception for the reading of the will!

Mia was less than impressed with Angela, though of course she had kept her opinions to herself. The fact was that it was Angela who had wanted all this, yet *loved* the role of victim and, to Mia's mind, played it a little too well.

Dante turned as she made her way down the stairs, and stood watching her approach.

He even announced it in English!

'Ah, here is my stepmother now.'

Dante heard the cruel ring to his tone and did nothing to temper it, for his loathing of Mia was his final defence. He had to constantly remind himself of the destruction she had caused to his family. As well as that, he had to retell himself over and over that his father's wife was, and would remain for ever, out of bounds.

Her blue eyes, for the very first time, shot him an angry look. It was a mere flash of her building temper, for Rafael's death had released her from the role she had played for the last two years. But then she reminded herself there was still this day to get through.

Just a few hours until she was free.

Ariana very deliberately turned her back on Mia, and Dante saw it.

Worryingly for Dante, he felt for Mia as she stood in the foyer so pale and alone.

He did not want to care about her.

He could not allow himself to care about her.

And so he reminded himself just how much he despised her as he suggested they all head out to the cars.

The funeral of Rafael Romano was to be a huge affair.

The Romano hotel was full, not just with guests who had flown from afar to attend but also with the press, though they were kept back from the very private residence.

Mia walked down the stone steps, doing all she could not to look at the hearse. She saw the door in the vehicle behind it being held open for her and she wanted to turn and run back into the house. She actually thought about doing just that for a fleeting second, but of course knew she could not.

Dante was at the vehicle behind where his siblings were getting in, but he looked over and saw Mia stiffen, noticing how timidly she climbed in.

Despite what he had said last night, the fact that she travelled alone was a clear slur, and everyone knew it. Mia sitting up front and alone made her even *less* than an outcast, for it signalled to all that she had never been part of the theatre of his family.

They hadn't given her a chance.

Dante had no doubt that Mia Hamilton was in it for the money, but what if there had been some measure of love between her and his father?

The flash of tears in her eyes that he had witnessed last night was still capable of moving him, and the strain in her voice when she had said she did not want to be in the car on her own played again in his mind.

'I'm going to go and sit with Mia,' Dante said to the twins and Eloa.

'Oh, please,' Ariana sneered. 'Why on earth would you do that?'

But Dante didn't answer. Instead, he left the car and walked towards the one in which Mia sat.

It was cool this morning and when the car door opened, a gust of wind burst in; Mia looked over and jumped when she saw it was Dante.

'Have I done something wrong?'

'No.' He got in beside her. 'I am sure we can manage a more united front on this sombre day.'

'Thank you,' Mia said, relieved the animosity had been put on hold, and grateful to have someone sitting next to her, for his presence made this just a little less daunting.

As the procession moved off, Dante stared fixedly ahead, rather than witness the tears from the staff.

The car moved slowly and as they made their way towards the stables Dante's hands tensed into fists when he saw that Massimo had been brought out. The stable manager wore a black suit and held Massimo, who pawed the ground as the hearse passed.

And Dante remembered long ago summer treks with his father and tried not to break down.

They passed the groundskeeper's cottage. He wore a black hat, which he removed, and bowed his head. Then on to the vines, and Dante thought back to childhood summers, happier times. He closed his eyes and remembered the last conversation he'd had with his father.

Dante had told him about the board meeting the next day, and that he was embroiled in yet another scandal.

'Hey,' Pa had said, 'at least you're not a Castello.'

The Castellos were from over the valley and had a restaurant chain that had flourished in the UK. The sons used their wealth unwisely and were careless with women.

'Don't let the board dictate your life to you,' Pa had said. 'You have always had your own compass, Dante, just follow that. I'm proud of you.'

Slowly, ever so slowly, they moved out to the perimeter of the estate, edged with poppy fields that were stripped of colour this cold January day. Roberto, his father's lawyer, stood outside his cottage, and with a black handkerchief wiped his eyes as they passed, but Dante himself did not cry. He didn't know how.

Had Pa known? Dante pondered as they made a slow loop around the fields to allow the staff to make their way to the church ahead of the procession.

Dante was sure he had sensed that the end had been imminent and that he might not get home in time.

And they were leaving Rafael's beloved home now.

As the procession turned out of the private property, the curved roads were lined with tall thin cypress trees, like soldiers standing to attention as they passed. Beyond that, a tapestry of bare vines owned by Romano Holdings—thanks to the divisions in his family—and Dante took in a shuddering breath.

They approached the village but even the red terracotta roofs looked dismal today. Mia turned from staring out of the window and looked over at Dante.

He was locked in his own thoughts, his strong, haughty face pale and tinged grey, and she could see from the tilt of his jaw that he was holding it all inside.

Her heart ached for him now just as it would have for anyone burying a parent, or perhaps it was that she wanted comfort of her own, for her hand instinctively reached out and closed over his bunched fist.

Dante did not as much as glance down.

His hand was cold beneath her fingers and she clutched it tightly to impart warmth, but was startled when she heard the black frost of his voice. 'Mia—' her name was delivered in a malevolent tone that caused her to shrivel '—*get* your hand off me.'

Walking into the church, Mia made her way to the front and could feel way more than a hundred eyes drilling into her back.

She took her place in the front pew and knew that she was not worthy of it. Behind her, Rafael's family sobbed, none too quietly.

Despite the cool day, there was sweat trickling between her breasts. She dragged in a deep breath. She sat there, her frozen English self, with her head held high, as the service commenced; later she sat, still rigid and upright, as Dante read the eulogy, wondering what he had come up with to say.

'Rafael Dante Romano was born to Alberto and Carmella, and was the older brother of Luigi...'

Mia could understand most of what was said, but was a step behind, as she had to translate Dante's words in her head.

'His life was a busy one, but then he always said there would be time to rest when he was dead.'

She heard that Rafael had married Angela when he had been nineteen and that she had said it was a marriage full of love, laughter and surprises.

Yes, Dante agreed, his father had always liked to surprise everyone.

Mia struggled to translate the next part, but deciphered that Rafael had moved the small family business beyond Luctano to restaurants in Florence, always, *always*, buying more land with the profits, more vines...

Dante spoke of the time his mother had thought he was building a romantic garden, and of her disappointment when she'd thought it was a bocce ball green, and then her bemusement when she'd realised that it was a helipad.

'There would be no helicopter landing on it for a year,' Dante said, 'but soon he would supply the best restaurants in Florence, Rome, Paris, London...'

Dante paused, for this part was difficult for him. Here he had to paint a picture of the happiest of families, and lying did not come readily to him because Dante was honest to a fault.

His mother and father had fought when he had been little; he could remember hearing the rows and the dread and certainty he had felt that his parents would soon break up. The arrival of the twins had afforded them a second start, though, and so he remembered then the peace that had arrived in his family and pushed on.

Mia saw that slight waver.

Oh, why did she notice everything about him?

Why was she so completely attuned to him?

And why the hell had she touched him?

Even now, sitting there holding an orchid in the midst of her husband's funeral, her hand, where she'd touched Dante's, felt tingly.

Even now, as she sat in the musty church, she felt as if she were inhaling him again, inhaling the freshness of his cologne that she had tried not to notice in the car.

Mia felt tears prick her eyes when Dante spoke of the twins' arrival.

'He had always wanted a daughter.' Dante looked over at Ariana, who wept quietly. 'And he was so pleased to have another son...'

He spoke on until finally it was time for the most difficult part of this eulogy, and she stiffened as Dante switched from Italian to English. 'My father loved his family, yet, being Rafael, there was room for more love in his life and still time for more surprises. Two years ago he married Mia...' He paused again, though certainly not for effect. He was fighting the very private devastation that that chapter of his father's life had caused. Dante forced politeness and made himself look at her as he spoke. 'I know Mia was a great comfort to him, and brought him peace in his last years. I know, because he told me so on the night before he died.'

It was the best he could do, for though he could not say that she had been welcomed into the family, or that Mia and Rafael's love had shone like a beacon, instead he dealt in facts and tried to do so with the respect this day deserved.

Then he switched back to Italian and Mia sat looking down now at the orchid as he finished the eulogy, touched that Rafael had said that about her, and grateful to Dante for sharing it.

'Sadly,' Dante concluded, 'there are to be no more surprises. It is now your time to rest.' His voice finally cracked. 'We shall miss you for ever.'

The burial was awful.

Ariana was sobbing, and Stefano cried too, with Eloa holding him, as Dante stood alone with his hands still fisted at his sides.

Mia stood alone, beneath a huge holm oak, feeling both sick and icy cold as the coffin was lowered into the ground. When it was her turn to throw the orchid, her thighs seemed to have turned to rubber and she was terrified that she might faint.

Mia was sweating in the frigid air, but then an arm came around her and steadied her. Oh, she could have, possibly should have, retorted, 'Dante, *get* your hand off me,' as he had to her, but instead she gasped out, 'Thank you.'

'Come.' He guided her to the edge of the grave and then guided her hand to toss in the single orchid that she held.

It was done.

She closed her eyes in weak relief. 'Thank you,' she said again, as he removed his arm and they headed back to the car.

Dante chose to walk back to the house.

He had none of the damned antipasti and nothing to drink other than water, for he needed to retain every last ounce of sense he had.

And so to the last will and testament of Rafael Dante Romano.

Dove c'è un testamento, c'è un parente!
Where there's a will, there's a relative, indeed!

Luigi had a front-row seat and, as predicted, Angela did indeed deign to set foot in the house. They sat, all frosty and staring ahead, although Dante stood at the French windows in his father's study, for he wanted to see every flicker of Mia's reaction, whatever the will might say.

In the end it was straightforward with no real surprises.

Most of the divisions had taken place at the time of the divorce and following the terminal diagnosis.

The family residence had been left to Dante, the Switzerland residence to Stefano, and it was Paris for Ariana.

There was a property in the city of Luctano that was now Luigi's to squander.

And there was some jewellery and trinkets and portraits from each of the residences left to his ex-wife.

Perhaps there was one slight surprise: for Mia Romano, his current wife—there were two residences in the UK, a relatively minor cash payment, as well as all jewels gifted during the marriage, on the agreement there would be no further claim to the estate. There was also to be a grace period of three months before she left the Luctano residence.

Dante had expected Mia to get more, but then he knew she had been haemorrhaging money from him in the two years they had been together. It was her lack of reaction to the relatively low figures that mystified him.

Mia sat upright, listening to Roberto, and was her usual dignified, inscrutable self.

Of course, there was no doubt in Dante's mind that she would contest the will and he didn't care if she did.

He would simply set his lawyers onto her like hungry

hounds for however long it took, and let her burn through her inheritance in fees.

Roberto continued to speak.

'He hopes his family will continue to represent him at the annual Romano Foundation Ball.' Dante glanced at his mother, whose lips pursed. Well, he could remember her tears at having to miss the glamorous ball, which had always been her night of nights and, as his father would say, Angela was not just the belle of the ball, but the belle of Roma in the lead-up to it.

He looked at Mia who, as his widow, would naturally be hostess each year until she married again, but he saw no reaction in her features. Or possibly there was, because her ears were a little pink. She shifted in her seat, so that she turned her back to him just a little, and he realised she must have felt him watching her.

Yet still he watched.

He looked at her lips, still a touch swollen, and those eyes still devoid of tears. He wanted to take her by the hand, leave the whole sorry mess behind, and carry her up to his suite and lose himself in her.

Instead Dante listened as Roberto spoke on.

'He trusts his children to oversee it with diligence and care...' Roberto put down the paperwork for a moment and took a drink of water before resuming the reading. 'There is to be a personal donation of one million euros to his favourite charity...' As Roberto named it, Dante suppressed a wry smile that retired racehorses would get more than Mia!

Yes, there was black humour in dark days.

When Roberto had concluded the reading of the last will and testament there were drinks for those who wanted them, but most did not.

Stefano and Eloa drove with Luigi and his wife back to their house, and a short while later Dante walked his mother and Ariana out. 'I will be over to Luigi's later,' Dante said to her. 'But first I want to speak with Roberto.'

'Don't come over on my behalf, Dante.' Angela shook her head then addressed her daughter. 'Ariana, tell Gian that I shall just be a moment.'

'Gian?' Dante checked, for his mother did not like Gian, especially since his father's second wedding.

'Ariana and I are heading back to Rome tonight; I asked Gian if he could take us.'

'But my pilot is here. Why didn't you ask me to organise him?'

'I didn't know if you were staying or going.' Angela shrugged. 'I just want to get away, it is too painful to be here. Ariana...' She looked over again. 'Go and let Gian know I shan't be long.'

But first Dante gave his sister a kiss. 'Are you okay?' he checked, troubled, for since the funeral Ariana had been terribly withdrawn.

'I'll be fine.'

'Are you staying with Mamma tonight?'

'I think Mamma just wants to be alone,' Ariana said. 'I might go to Nicki's.'

Nicki was a friend of Ariana's who ran a little wild, and wouldn't be the most calming influence. 'Stay here,' he suggested, but Ariana gave him a wide-eyed look. 'I didn't mean here in the house. I meant at Luigi's, or at the hotel.'

'No,' she shook her head. 'I just want to go back to Rome.'

'You're sure?' he checked.

'Very.'

Dante decided he preferred Ariana feisty and argumentative and was worried as his dejected-looking sister headed off. 'Keep an eye on her, Mamma.'

'Of course.' Angela nodded. 'I am going to go.'

'First hear this,' Dante said. 'As soon as Mia is out and everything has been settled, I shall transfer the house to your name. I am sure he left it to me rather than you so that if she contests the will, as I expect her to, there is less chance she will win. It is rightfully yours and—'

'I don't want the house, Dante,' Angela cut in.

Dante was stunned.

She had wept over this house. Sobbed to Ariana how she missed being at home. Cried at the wake and said she had ached for two years to be back in Luctano.

'Surely you want it. You said—'

Again she cut in. 'Dante, I have done my time here. It is beautiful, yes, but I don't want the headache of the endless staff it takes to run the residence, the grounds, the stables, the vines. This house is a labour of love, and my love for it died long ago. I like my apartment in Roma. I cannot say it more clearly than that. I don't want the house.'

'Did you ever?'

He saw his mother's shock at the question, and he instantly regretted raising the matter today, but his father's death had thrown up so many questions. Though clearly his mother had no intention of answering any of them. 'I shall see you in Roma, Dante.'

Roberto had already left and, with the mourners all gone, Dante stood by the fire and waited for relief to hit, for the day had gone as well as it could have. No drama, no scenes, his father had been laid to rest.

So where was his peace?

Yes, his father's death had thrown up many questions.

His mother didn't want the house?

Had she ever? Dante's question had not been a spontaneous one—the thought had been brewing for some time.

He remembered the rows in their childhood that had stopped when the twins had arrived, but then again, there had been an awful lot of trips by his mother to Rome. She would come and visit Dante at school there, even though he boarded.

Suddenly, Dante *could* place his mother's lover.

Signor Thomas, his English tutor at school.

Dante had always felt lied to.

Never more so than now.

CHAPTER FIVE

MIA HAD LONG SINCE left the family and mourners to it, and was packing up the last of her things.

She took off her wedding and engagement rings and placed them in her purse. She cast a final longing glance around Suite al Limone, feeling torn to leave it behind.

Mia didn't feel completely ready to yet.

When she heard the last of the cars leaving and the drone of voices fade, she rang down for one of the staff to come and take her cases down to the car.

Except there was no response to her summons.

She made her way down the stairs and saw that Dante had stayed till the last.

'Where are the staff?' Mia asked.

'I said they could be finished for the day; the tidy-up can happen tomorrow,' Dante said. 'It has been a long and emotional day for them too. Don't worry,' he added, 'I am going to head to the hotel now. You will have the place to yourself soon.'

'There is no need for you to go to the hotel, Dante.'

His mouth twisted into a smile. 'You have your grace period, Mia, plenty of time to sharpen those claws…'

'I have no idea what you're talking about. I shan't be staking any claim to the house, Dante, and neither shall I be taking the three-month grace period. I am leaving to-night. It's all yours.'

Dante looked at her and waited for more information, but there was none forthcoming. He had expected her to stay, clinging till the bitter, expensive, contested end.

He felt like a prize boxer, primed to fight, yet suddenly without an opponent. As she went to walk off he made what he hoped was the parting shot. 'On to your next one?'

'My next one?' Mia frowned.

'The next foolish old man…'

'You have no idea,' Mia retorted.

Oh, yes, he did! 'The next foolish old man who would blow apart his family and reputation just to be with you.'

'Your father was no fool,' Mia said, because Rafael Romano had known exactly what he was doing when the deal had been made. 'And neither was he old. He was barely in his fifties.'

'But far too old for you,' Dante retorted, though the fact was, his loathing of their union had nothing to do with age; it was that his father had chosen *her*.

Mia.

The woman who drew from him a desire so potent that she had made the last two years a living hell.

'Oh, please…' she sneered, and she could almost hear the prison doors between them clanging open, for duty was done.

Almost.

There was just this final bit to get through and she would be free of the Romanos and never have to lay eyes on them again. Or, more pertinently, never have to put up with the scathing barbs of Dante Romano again.

And though she should retrieve her cases this minute and leave it all behind, foolishly Mia decided that she would have her say, for she could hold it in for not a second more.

Her one final say!

And this was a new version of hell for Dante, watching her step towards him in anger, her curves in her black dress nearing him, her eyes glittering, as she moved closer, ever closer…and finally there was emotion on that unreadable face.

'You have no idea, Dante. You look at me and you see a whore, you stand there and judge me, but even with your assumptions, you're a hypocrite. You think nothing of sleeping with women for money.'

'I've never paid for it in my life.'

'Please! You think they would be with you if you weren't rich, if you didn't shower them in diamonds, or take them to your fancy hotels and give them the full Dante Romano treatment?' Jealousy coursed through her, as it had for two years, hearing from Rafael and then reading herself of his endless trysts, his lavish ways. But it was something else coursing through her as he met her eyes and gave his response.

'Oh, they would still be with me.'

Dante said it with such authority that she began to doubt her case, yet Mia fought to retrieve it. 'No. They want you for your money, the jewels, the gifts; they would hardly want you for your tenderness—'

'I can be tender when I choose to be,' he interrupted. 'And I can be less than tender when *she* chooses that I be.'

As Dante gave her a teasing glimpse of him in the bedroom, the lights went out in her head. His hand took her left one and he examined it for a moment. 'You wasted no time in removing your rings, I see.' He moved the hand he had rejected earlier today to near his mouth and kissed the tips of her fingers.

It was only their second contact ever, and just the lightest touch of his mouth made her want to fold over as his velvet lips brushed skin that felt as if every nerve in her fingers lay exposed and wired to her centre.

'You see, my dear stepmother, I can be tender…'

'*Stop* calling me that!' Her voice shrilled as he took

a finger in his mouth and sucked it. Despite herself, she wanted to press her finger deeper for more of the caress his tongue gave.

He sucked and he kissed, then left her finger cold as he kissed her palm.

'Why?' he said, kissing her palm so tenderly, yet it was painful too as between strokes from his tongue he taunted her. 'Does it embarrass you to be turned on by me?' he asked. He kissed her hand then placed the palm of it on his chest as he continued, 'Did you feel shame when you sat in the dining room last night and wanted me?'

'I did not want you,' she insisted, pushing back at him a little, her voice strained as it forced out the lie.

'And then last night, in the kitchen...'

'I didn't want you,' she choked, but his smile told Mia he knew she lied. 'I *don't* want you,' she begged, though neither believed it.

'Then go, dear Mia. Stop playing with fire.'

She *should* go, Mia knew. She should turn and run, except she had never thought she was capable of such a brutal desire.

Because this desire *was* brutal—an aching, physical want that dimmed regular thought. She was playing with fire and Mia found that she liked the burn.

Their eyes locked and held, and beneath her palm she felt the now rapid thud, thud, thud of his black heart.

His hand came to her face and he traced her cheek, then slid it behind her hair and yet he did not pull her towards him. Instead Dante asked a question. 'What *do* you want, Mia?'

'For this all to be over,' she admitted.

'And me.'

'To never have to see you again.' She shivered.

'Yet here you stand.'

'Yes.'

He kissed her then, slow and deep. His lips were plump as he parted hers with his tongue and she let him. It mattered not that she had rarely kissed a man before, for there was no experience required when Dante claimed a mouth so fiercely, so absolutely.

The thought of tongues had always repulsed Mia.

Now, though, she tasted the cool wedge of muscle and the only thing that repulsed her was her own crippling desire, for she craved more. She danced her tongue with his, tasting him, wanting more, even as she fought to reject his kiss.

It was Dante who removed the pleasure of his mouth and she stood there, running a tongue over her wet lips just to taste him again.

'And yet *still* here you stand.'

She swallowed, and his eyes watched her throat as she did so. He lifted her hair, lowered his head, and his mouth met her tender neck.

Oh, God, Mia thought as he pulled her right into him and kissed her neck, not lightly but deeply.

'Dante…' She was pressed into taut flesh and she could feel his hard length against her stomach. She felt dizzy as his mouth pressed harder against her neck, and something awakened deep inside her.

'Go now,' he told her, even as he undid the little black pearls of her woollen dress and exposed her black bra. 'Go,' he said, 'before we do something we regret.'

'I don't want to go.' So raw was her admission that for the first time that day, tears squeezed out of her eyes.

'We can't go anywhere,' he told her. For the first time he was not warning a lover that he had no desire for a lengthy affair—more, he was reminding Mia that they could never be.

'I know.' She whimpered her response, for he had lowered his head and the feeling of his mouth on her breast brought both tension and relief. He tasted her at great length, and to various degrees; his tongue lathed, his teeth nipped, and his jaw was rough, all of which was a dose of the sublime, and when he lifted his head she only wanted him more.

Need overrode shyness, so it was Mia who removed his shirt, taking in the body that she had ached to see for so long. The dark bruises of his nipples, the fan of hair on his chest and the flat, toned stomach were a feast not just to her eyes but to her mouth as well as she tasted his skin. The sound of him unfastening his belt had her clenching down below. Yet when he had completely undressed, when she saw him so erect, she felt her throat tighten at the sight of him. She couldn't not touch him, yet she was nervous too, and so she stroked first the line of black hair on his stomach, and then trailed her hand down to the jet-black, crinkly curls below.

'Take me in your hand,' he said roughly.

Now it was fascination that overrode shyness. First, she touched him lightly, but feeling the strength behind the soft velvet skin she closed her hand around him and was startled—in a good way—at the low growl he gave.

'Mia.' He sounded like he was on the edge as he put a hand over hers and together they stroked him. To see him grow even more at the touch of her hand made her throat feel as if she were choking, so tense was she with excitement.

'I need to know you,' he said as he undressed her. 'I need to know your scent and your taste...'

She was shivering as he knelt and pulled down her tights, taking her knickers too, and she wept as he held her hips and he kissed her there. 'Dante...' Her hands were in his thick hair, his tongue probing, as his hand moved between her thighs to part them further. He was seducing her on his knees and she was shy but wanting, nervous but needing. She did not know this feeling, this feeling that moved her hips of their own accord into his kiss, and did not know how the stroke of his tongue could make her feel so urgent, so desperate. 'Please, Dante,' she begged, because she was losing control and not sure how to or if she should. His fingers were on a delicious, relentless, creep into where not even Mia herself had been. She clamped her thighs together and forced out her truth. 'I've never slept with anyone.'

Dante halted, unsure if this was a game, but when he looked up and saw her—stunned, frantic and so very unsure; when he felt the press of her thighs on his hand, for the first time, a woman naked and wanting yet resisting—he was unsure how to proceed.

'Virgin?'

One word that raised so many questions.

Or rather it should raise so many questions, but it raised something else instead, to intense proportions. And now they were past caring that they were forbidden.

'Come here,' he said. He pulled her down so she was on her knees facing him. He took her face in his hands, and he looked at her turned-on eyes and swollen mouth. He had but one question. 'Do you want this?'

'Yes.'

And then, for the first time, Mia received the warmth of Dante's smile. It was a caress in itself; it was intimate; it was everything, for it blew away the grief and hell of today. So beautiful was his smile that she returned it, even though she was shivering.

'It's okay,' he told her, then his mouth kissed her hot cheeks and he pulled her into him so that she sat on his thighs. They kissed, wet, slow kisses, her hands holding his head, her breasts splayed against his chest as Dante kissed her deeply. He drank from her mouth and he sucked her tongue as he drew her deeper into his embrace, so that she was pressed against his length and she was mired in desire and frantic with need.

He laid her down on the rug; he was lost in her, relieved to let the grief and the strains of the day disperse as their bodies meshed.

When he first nudged in he was met with resistance, so he pushed in again and then he heard her whimper as he inched into her virgin space.

She bewitched him, she entranced him, and right now he was tender.

So tender that his kiss dimmed her pain, so tender that his hand, warm and firm on the small of her back, felt like a balm, even as he drove into her. 'Stay still,' she whimpered, for she somehow had to acclimatise to the feel of him inside her.

He paused and kissed her softly. His breath was ragged then as he fought the urge to move, but at her signal he started to stretch her again.

'Dante,' she sobbed as his palm in her back guided her to take him in deeper and deeper.

He was dizzy at the sensation but he was also aware of how new this must be for her. He withdrew a fraction and looked down at her pale, tense features, and saw there were tears spilling from her eyes.

He lowered his head and brushed her temple with his lips. He tasted the salt of her tears on his tongue, and then he covered her mouth with his and drove in again, swallowing her sob.

And then they were one.

He started to move, stoking the fire that was spreading within her. He lifted his head to watch the reaction as he ground in, each thrust jolting her, and saw she was wild for the sensations he evoked. She felt wound up, taut from her jaw to her toes, and there was no pause from Dante and no desire to escape. He was relentless and rattling all her senses, and she was arching into him and surely near repletion, and yet he told her that there was more to give… and then he called out her name.

'Mia…' He called it again. '*Mia* Mia…' *My Mia.*

And it just finished her, every nerve shooting arrows to her centre, arching her in tension. His last rapid pummels, the final swell of him brought her release, pulsing over and over. And yet he groaned for more, demanded that she let go further, and even to the end she fought the very climax that engulfed her.

Not even a breath could she take in, so intense was the pleasure he gave as with a breathless shout he shot deep inside her.

Still, even as the flickers of sensation died, he moved slowly, while she panted, still unable to draw a deep cleansing breath.

She was silently shocked—not at what had been done, more at what his touch had revealed, for she was tender and sore yet also spun in a golden glow. She did not know how she had lived without knowing such pleasure.

How she must now live never knowing his touch again.

And that sinking feeling started now, for with a groan he rolled off her and lay with his arm covering his eyes, as he realised the failure of his own self-control on this solemn day.

For a while there he'd forgotten that he was grieving.

The winter that had settled in his soul had faded, but was back now with a vengeance, for it was combined with self-loathing and Dante was well aware he had not taken adequate care. But for now he had but one question. 'What were you doing, married to him, Mia?'

She had been a virgin and what had driven Dante wild with desire before now just saddened him. That knowledge told him there had been no passionate affair between her and his father. It really had all been a lie and one he could not understand. 'Was it just for the money?' he asked.

Mia lay there, listening to the fading crackles from the dying fire. The vast lounge was cooling now and she would give anything to roll into Dante and be held in his arms, yet if she moved even an inch closer, she knew she would shatter and reveal the truth.

A truth she had not only sworn never to reveal but a secret she had been paid handsomely to keep.

And so, instead of rolling into him, instead of drawing closer, Mia returned to her taciturn self and her response was a brittle, 'I don't have to answer that.'

'No,' Dante said, 'you don't.' But how he wished she would.

Dante pulled his arm from over his face, but still they could not look at each other. He had another question for Mia. 'Was it worth it?'

'Which part?' Mia asked, and her voice was hollow as she looked up at the ceiling, knowing he was asking about what had just taken place, while also looking at the sum of the lie she'd been living these past two years. 'Being savaged by the press and called a gold-digger and a whore for marrying your father? Being derided by your family at every turn? Or sleeping with you?'

'All of it?' Dante said. It was an important question, because if she said yes, then he might just take her up to his bed and not give a damn as they breakfasted together in the morning and to hell with the world.

But for Mia, self-preservation had kicked in. She'd been vilified so many times for her marriage to his father that she could not bear the thought of word getting out about a sordid affair with her late husband's son on the evening of his funeral. 'No,' Mia said, for such was her shame right now. 'If I could, I would pay the money back, with interest, just to have avoided this.'

It was the most horrible ending to something so lovely and still neither could meet the other's eyes. She got up and headed to her suite, deciding that Dante could pick up the clothes in the lounge, for she would never be wearing them again.

Mia showered quickly and threw on some fresh clothes, and then carried her cases down the stairs.

It took several journeys, but when she went to call for a car, he appeared, somewhat dressed. Well, he had on his suit trousers and his white shirt but it was untucked and his feet were bare. 'I'll drive you to the airport,' Dante said.

'Please don't,' she replied.

'Mia.' He caught her wrist as she went to walk off and told her what she already knew. 'We didn't use any protection.'

'No.' She felt a bit sick at the thought of that, for she was usually so meticulous and organised and was still reeling that she could have lost control like that.

'You need to go to a *farmacia*…'

Mia stood, still unable to look at him as Dante handed out emergency contraceptive advice as if he were an expert! Though she guessed he was more than used to it.

'You'll take care of it, Mia?' He did not call her *bella*; he would be remembering *her* name. Because Dante always took care, and was aghast at his own lack of thought. 'Mia?' he checked.

'Yes,' she hissed.

'Because you do *not* want to be pregnant by me.'

'I get it!'

'Do you?' he checked. 'It would be a scandal like no other and, aside from that, I never want to have children.'

'I get it, Dante.' She gave a tight smile. Mia was well aware he liked his single lifestyle, without consequences. 'All care and no responsibility.'

'But I didn't take due care.'

She looked at this reprobate playboy. No, she did not want to be pregnant by him. 'Then I shall.'

Perhaps to make up for his lack of assistance in bringing the cases down the stairs, he did help load them into the car, but there was no kiss, no Dante standing on the stairs, waving goodbye.

Of course not.

Before the car door had even closed he was back in the house.

There could be no happy ending to this.

It was appalling, what had just taken place.

And both of them knew it.

CHAPTER SIX

It was Dante who alerted Mia that there might be an issue.

For a few weeks there had been silence from Italy.

After a turbulent flight back to England, Mia had headed to the small flat that was part of her inheritance from Rafael.

Michael's wife, Gemma, had been keeping an eye on it, and, aware of Mia's impending return, the place had been aired and there was bread and milk and suchlike. Mia bypassed all that and had headed to the bedroom where she'd lain, still in her coat, curled up on top of the bed covers, utterly conflicted. A part of her was aghast at what had taken place between Dante and herself, while the other part saw now that it had been inevitable, for she had ached for him for so long.

She was dismayed too at her own lack of regret, for, despite her brave words to Dante when he'd asked if it had been worth it, Mia knew that, given the chance, she would do it all over again.

On the morning after she'd arrived in London, Mia had showered and dressed and sworn to put that one indecent Tuscan night behind her and move on, before heading off to visit her brother and his wife.

Michael had met Gemma on his return to England following the accident. Gemma was a physiotherapist and over hours of rehabilitation they had become friends. Mia had noticed the increasing references to Gemma in online conversations with Michael, and then finally Gemma had appeared on the screen. Not long after that, her brother had told her they were in love. The odds were stacked heavily against this young couple, but Gemma was both motivated and determined, and as Michael came out of the fog of depression he had resumed his more usual 'can do' attitude.

Michael had supported Mia when she had married Rafael, while never—at the time—realising that Mia had actually been supporting him.

Now, though, he was starting to see what his sister had done on his behalf.

'You shouldn't have done this, Mia.'

Mia gritted her teeth rather than point out that had he *bothered* to take out travel insurance she wouldn't have had to have done it. Her anger was still there, but it was permanently suppressed and with no fair outlet, for she knew that Michael had more than paid the price for his foolish decision.

And so she smiled and carried on as yet more outstanding bills were paid. As well as that, Michael and Gemma's home was transferred into their name, and modifications to accommodate a wheelchair and bathroom renovations were soon underway so that the inheritance was all but spent.

Angela Romano had been a Rottweiler while the deal had been drawn up—reminding Rafael over and over that everything he gave Mia he took from his own children, when everyone knew it was but a drop in their gold-plated ocean.

But she and her brother had homes, and were debt-free, and life could finally start again, so Mia set about looking for work.

Had it been worth it?

In the safety of her own head she could answer Dante's question more honestly.

Yes.

She was back to being Mia Hamilton and here in London nobody gave her as much as a second glance. She was yesterday's news and her brother, after his life-altering trauma, was finally embracing life.

And yet...

Had it been worth it?

Mia wasn't so sure.

When an invitation to the annual Romano charity ball arrived in the mail, Mia stared at it for a very long time, unsure what to do.

She felt dizzy with want for Dante and ached to see him again, but when she thought of news of their illicit night ever getting out, of their torrid one-night stand on the night of Rafael's funeral ever being exposed, she felt sick.

That night with Dante had changed her; that one blissful time had set in motion this endless craving for more. She stuffed the invitation in a drawer, much as she suppressed her own wants, and did her level best not to think about a man who, with a crook of his finger, could again unleash her desire.

Mia was just coming out of a job interview, pleased with how it had gone, and was turning on her phone when it rang.

'Pronto,' Dante said.

With one word from him Mia almost caused a little pile-up of suited people as she came to a halt on her walk to the underground.

'Dante.' She tried to keep her voice even, tried not to betray the sheer pleasure that could be brought to her day by the mere sound of his voice. 'How are you?'

'That is what I am calling to ask you.'

'Me?' She was flummoxed, wondering if she had forgotten an important anniversary for Rafael, or if he was chasing her up because she hadn't RSVP'd to the invitation to the Romano Ball. 'Yes, I'm fine, why?'

Dante was brusque, he was up-front, and he *completely* sideswiped her. 'I just wanted to be sure there were no consequences to our time together.'

'No,' Mia said, 'of course not.' After all, she had taken the tablets. 'Everything's fine.'

'That's good, then,' Dante said. 'I just wanted to make sure.'

Only now Mia wasn't so sure herself.

As Dante clicked off, she caused another little pile-up of suited people again as she drew to another abrupt halt, while trying to work out dates.

The pharmacist in Italy had, Mia was sure, said it might delay her period by a week…

She was more than a week late, though.

Damn you, Dante for making me stress, Mia said to herself as she clipped off to *another* pharmacist and bought a home pregnancy test.

Except the little indicator told her that she was pregnant.

And a second test told her the same thing.

Then the doctor told her that, yes, in fact, she was due on the seventh of October.

'But I took emergency contraception…'

During a deeper discussion with the doctor Mia recalled there had been turbulence on the flight home and she had been ill. It was often the case as Mia did not travel well. She could not even sit in the back of a car and her stomach lurched at the mere sight of a helicopter; certainly she would never set foot in one. Usually she took medication when flying or travelling long distances, but on that night she had been too muddled to take her motion sickness pills and had simply accepted the consequence of that when she'd been ill on the plane.

Had she stopped to think about it, the importance of keeping the pills down would have been obvious, except Mia had no experience with contraception and had been flying out of Italy like a bat out of hell, reeling from what she and Dante had done. Of all the things on her mind, avoiding pregnancy had only been one amongst many.

And now she was pregnant.

Had it been worth it?

She asked herself Dante's question again, and for many nights the answer was unequivocally no!

No!

No!

Mia felt terrified, mortified and simply wanted it gone. But then February turned to March and the anniversary of her family's accident, and Mia lay there, not exactly at peace but thinking, on this painful day, how far she had come—from the terror of the accident and the deep lows of grief to being there for Michael; to two years in Italy, which, for the most part, had been healing and restful; and then to Dante, a man who had awakened a side of her she hadn't thought existed, and together they had made a baby.

Had it been worth it?

Maybe…

She was starting to come round to the little life inside her.

Yet, aside from the scandal if it ever came out, if two years with Rafael had taught her anything, it was Dante's reputation that told her he would not take the news well. She knew the board had repeatedly insisted that he tame his ways. She knew that he had absolutely no desire to settle down, or have children; she knew it because she'd heard him arguing with his uncle Luigi. Oh, she knew from *many* sources. Dante himself had told her they could go nowhere and had warned her not to fall pregnant by him.

He'd practically had on a white coat as he'd dished out advice!

Well, it was too late now.

She'd survive, Mia knew, because she always somehow

did, and that thought got her out of bed and dressed for a third-round interview.

This time with the boss!

The other boss, the very good-looking one in Italy, was more than a touch subdued. His mother commented on it when she dropped by the office to say goodbye before heading off on a cruise.

'I'm fine,' Dante insisted.

'Why have you got Ariana so involved in the preparations for the ball?' Angela complained.

'She does have a degree in hospitality.'

'It's her excuse all the time, and I've barely seen her in recent weeks. I am sure she is seeing someone.'

'And?'

'The only function she should be preparing for is her wedding,' Angela sighed.

It was a familiar complaint. While Dante was frequently pressured by the board to marry and settle down, he was confident enough to shrug it off. For Ariana, he knew the pressure to marry from her mother was both relentless and intense, although Angela had more than her daughter on her mind. 'Ariana said you are thinking of putting the Luctano property on the market?'

Dante nodded then checked again if his mother wanted it. 'Have you changed your mind?'

'No, no,' Angela said. 'I just wondered what was going on. You're very quiet, Dante. I haven't seen you since the funeral.'

'Because I've been busy with work.'

But Angela was sure there was more to his pensive mood. 'I know it might seem a little insensitive that I am going on a cruise so soon after your father is gone, but it was booked some time ago.'

Dante said nothing rather than lie. Privately he thought

it was too soon for her to be kicking up her heels, even if they had been divorced. He also found it no coincidence that she was leaving two weeks before the ball, and not arriving back until the day after. When his parents had been married, his mother had loved nothing more than the preparations and the heightened press interest as the date of the lavish event approached.

'Is *she* going to the ball?' Angela suddenly asked, and Dante knew his mother referred to Mia.

'I am not sure.'

'Really,' Angela said, 'Mia should have the decency to stay away. And who would escort her? If she goes it will just make everyone feel uncomfortable.'

'My father was specific in his request that all of his family attend. Technically, Mia is the hostess of the event.'

'You haven't put that on the invitations?'

'No.'

Dante was in little doubt that his mother was envisioning her own return as hostess at future events so he moved to change the subject. 'So, who are you going on the cruise with?'

'Just a friend.' Angela shrugged.

'More than a friend perhaps?' Dante probed.

'I *am* seeing someone,' she finally admitted. 'You might even remember him. Mr Thomas, your old—'

'My English tutor.' Dante pushed out a smile.

'How do you know it was him?'

'I saw you together,' Dante said. 'And I thought I recognised him. He's a nice man, from what I remember.'

'Yes, we ran into each other a few months ago. He asked how you were and we got talking...' She looked worried. 'You're not cross?'

'Why would I be cross? It's time for you to be happy.'

'Thank you,' she said, and stood up. 'Is Stefano here?'

'He's at a very long lunch with Eloa,' Dante said, and rolled his eyes. 'I doubt he'll be back.'

When his mother left he sat a while and, despite the smile he had given, Dante wasn't sure he believed that they had only bumped into each other a few months ago.

He'd always felt lied to and, since his father's death, more and more he was starting to see why.

'Dante.' Sarah knocked on his door and he told her to come in. 'Matteo Castello called and asked to speak with you. I said you were in a meeting.'

'What did he want?' Dante frowned, because the Castellos, though not rivals—not even close—were not his choice of people.

'It's for a reference.'

His frown deepened, because Sarah looked a touch uncomfortable. 'You're not jumping ship?'

'No, no.' She smiled. 'It is Mia he is calling about. Matteo is considering her for the role of his executive assistant in London.'

Well, well, Dante thought. 'Thank you,' he said.

'Oh, and speaking of Mia,' Sarah added, 'she still hasn't RSVP'd for the ball.'

Dante gave a dismissive wave. 'Not my problem.'

God alone knew, though, it was his main problem!

Dante *badly* wanted Mia to come to the Romano ball so he would have the chance to see her again and hopefully...

Yet Mia *still* hadn't responded.

'Right, I'm off,' Sarah said.

'It's only three!'

'Dante!'

Oh, yes, his Christmas present for Sarah had been a long weekend for her and her husband at La Fiordelise and she'd chosen to take it this coming weekend.

'Fine.' Dante sulked.

Everyone was at it.

Everyone except him, since Mia.

Dante could not get her out of his head and the thought of being with anyone else had lost its usual appeal.

He set off his Newton's cradle, and watched the silver balls clack, clack, clack as his own ached.

Ms Prim would disapprove of that, Dante thought, and then the memory of her uptight expressions made him smile.

But the smile was wiped from his face when he thought of her working for Castello.

When Sarah had gone, Dante reached for his phone, but instead of calling Castello it was Mia's number he pulled up. It had been a couple of weeks since their last, brief conversation and she answered promptly. 'Mia speaking.'

'Mia, it's Dante.' He *felt* the tense silence for a moment before continuing. 'I've been asked by Castello to provide a reference for you. Is this some sort of joke?'

'Why would it be a joke?' Mia responded tartly. She had been caught off guard, and had answered the phone without looking, hoping it was news about her job. That it was Dante calling had sideswiped her, but she reminded herself she was no longer Rafael's wife, no longer playing a part. 'I do have to work.'

'Perhaps, but does it have to be for our rival?'

'Hardly a rival. The Romanos are a hundred times bigger. If you must know, I've applied for several jobs.'

Dante sat there, his lips pressed together as another side to Mia was revealed to him. When married to his father she had been rather quiet and, though her presence had sat in the forefront of his mind, she had remained in the background, saying little.

That wasn't so much the case now, Dante thought as she continued.

'While your father gave me an excellent reference, given we were married, it doesn't carry the weight it should, and the woman I worked under in London has left.' Not that Mia had been much good at that time. 'I didn't actually put your name down.' She gave a slightly shrill laugh as if to say, *Perish that thought.* 'Look, if it's going to be an issue I'll pull out of the application.'

'No, no,' Dante said, and blew out a breath. 'Mia, the man's a sleaze, though.'

'He seemed perfectly polite.'

'Trust me on this.'

Mia didn't answer.

The truth was, despite her brusque, matter-of-fact voice, Mia was sitting in her little lounge with silent tears streaming down her cheeks at the impossibility of it all. It wasn't even the prospect of telling him about the baby that overwhelmed her; she still hadn't decided if she would or, if she did, how or when.

No, it was hearing his voice as she tried to haul herself out of the vortex of Dante that had her silently weeping— wanting him so, and not just his exquisite touch but more of him, all of him; the sudden smile he gave to others, which he had but once given to her; the passion and energy of him, a man who, despite their rows, never made her feel unsafe, even on the edge of unleashed passion.

'Mia?' he said to the silence.

'I have to go.'

'Before you do, there is one other thing…' His husky tone warned her about the danger of the subject matter. 'You haven't RSVP'd about the ball…'

'No.' Mia croaked.

'Well?' he said, and his voice had a thick edge to it. 'Are you coming?'

'I don't know,' she said. She Did Not Know. It wasn't just that she was pregnant that mired her, more it was the craving to see him. Tears were streaming down her face and she had to force an affronted tone even as she dreamed of his kiss. 'Why would I put myself in that snake pit?'

'For the sick children, perhaps?'

'Dante!' She actually gave a soft laugh at the glimmer of humour, because they both knew the ball would be a success with or without her there, but that tiny joke had her tummy flip for it told Mia that he wanted her to come, and he did, for he then moved in to persuade her.

'My mother won't be there.'

'I'm not worried about your mother, Dante.'

'If you need a gown—'

'I already have a gown. I couldn't attend last year, remember?'

Oh, he remembered.

Because, though his father had been too ill to attend, which had been a cause for concern, for Dante there had been a sigh of relief that he would not have to see Mia in finery and on his father's arm. 'Roberto would escort you to your table and I can assure you there shall be no animosity. I will have a word with Ariana...'

'Dante, she's the least of my concerns.'

'Okay.' Dante took a breath and attempted to address the elephant in the room. 'Well, if you're worried that there might be a repeat—' He halted, because right now he *should* be promising Mia that there would be no repeat of their forbidden night; he should be assuring her that it had been a mistake and would never happen again. Yet Dante never lied. 'Mia—' his voice was back to controlled and brisk '—I shall leave it up to you. Naturally there will be a suite reserved for you. If you choose to attend you just have to call Sarah, and she will arrange your flights.'

But he could not leave it there. 'Are you sure everything's okay, Mia?'

She was quite positive that he wasn't asking how she was

holding up after the death of Rafael. He was asking again if there had been any fallout from that night.

Mia took a breath to consider her response and knew she was simply not ready to tell him yet. She was just starting to get her own head around things, and certainly she did not want to tell him over the phone. 'I'm fine.' And it wasn't a lie; she felt better about *things* today than she had since she'd found out, and did not want to disturb that fragile ground.

'That's good,' Dante said, except when the call had ended he was left unsure about whether he believed her.

Dante told himself he had no reason to be concerned. Mia had surely taken the emergency contraception.

Yet, despite her assurance, he had heard her brief hesitation prior to answering him and Dante had been left with that feeling he knew only too well: that he was being lied to.

No!

For once Dante tried to quash his eternally suspicious nature and believe the words that had been said. After all, Mia had not contested the will. In fact, she had left Luctano when she could have stayed on for three months. There had been no interviews given to the press, no demands made. If there were consequences to that night, he was more than certain either he or his legal team would have been informed by now.

Perhaps it was time to start trusting her?

And, if he did, then why couldn't they be together one more time? Discreetly, of course.

Yes, Dante wanted Mia to come to the ball.

They were a fire that needed to be put out for, by ignoring the sparks, a real burn had started to take hold.

CHAPTER SEVEN

OF COURSE MIA had no idea that she was about to get the full Dante Romano treatment.

Even as the plane landed at Rome's Fiumicino Airport, Mia did not know if she was right to be here. She had been so unsure, right up to the last minute, whether she would attend the ball that she'd decided against calling Sarah to arrange tickets and had taken the precaution of booking her own. She arrived in Rome somewhat frazzled after her budget flight, and nervous about facing Dante and, despite her brave words, facing the rest of his family too.

Certainly, she was not sure if she was ready tell Dante about the baby. And though she had been spared morning sickness, on arrival in Rome Mia felt drained and nauseous, both from flying and from nerves. She wore a lavender shift dress that she hadn't worn in ages, but it was both loose and smart enough, teamed with her stilettos, for her arrival at the hotel. She added a slick of lipstick before heading out to the waiting taxis, her decision made.

If Dante was back to treating her with that slight disdain and certain contempt then, no, she would not be sharing *her* news. That was the best way she could both describe and justify it to herself—right now, while she wasn't visibly pregnant, it was *her* secret to keep and to reveal when she so chose.

Despite her nerves as she took a taxi to La Fiordelise,

the hotel where the function was being held, she could not help but smile. Mia hadn't been in Rome for a very long time. With Rafael's deteriorating health, they had mainly been tucked away in Luctano. Rome in spring was amazing indeed, and less crowded than when she'd been there a couple of summers ago. The sight of wisteria cascading like a lilac waterfall down the walls of ancient ruins was beautiful indeed and had her craning her neck in the back of the taxi that took her to her hotel.

Mia would have loved to explore, but there simply wasn't time. She had left it too late to get a hair appointment—it would seem that all were booked out on this day—and her make-up she would do herself. There was also an appointment to be had with a razor!

The taxi pulled up outside a most gorgeous white marble building, which was to be her home for the night.

'Signora Romano!' The doorman greeted her as he opened the taxi door and Mia was startled that he knew her name, but then surmised that the staff would have been heavily briefed on the guests for the ball, and she was, after all, Rafael's widow.

Once inside the hotel she saw the opulent surroundings, with deep red carpets and vast marble columns. She swallowed nervously as a worrying thought occurred.

Her gown was red.

Oh, God!

She was attending as Rafael's widow and her gown was red!

But there wasn't time to dwell on it.

Instead of checking in, as Mia had expected to do, she was personally greeted by the exceptionally good-looking Gian De Luca, the owner of La Fiordelise.

Mia was starting to understand that this night wasn't just big, it was huge, and she had forgotten what it was like to be in the Romanos' world!

'We are delighted to welcome you to La Fiordelise,' Gian said, and introduced her to the guest services manager, who, he said, would escort her to her suite.

As she rode the ancient elevator, Mia was having a silent panic about her gown. It was in deep blood-red silk, a halter neck, with a slit at the back that revealed a glimpse of brilliant scarlet silk lining. It had been made with a great deal of skill and care and was sensual and gorgeous, though it showed a little too much of her shoulders and back for Mia's usual taste. It had been absolutely suitable for her entrance, and first real social appearance as Rafael Romano's wife.

She just wasn't so sure it was a suitable gown for Rafael Romano's recent widow!

'I trust you will be comfortable,' the guest services manager said.

Comfortable!

The suite was utterly sumptuous, with stencilled walls dotted with gorgeous oil paintings, and tastefully decorated with antique furnishings. It was like stepping into another world and as she glanced through to the bedroom she saw the bed dressed in rich linens and silk drapes.

And it was all for her!

Rafael had told her the ball was an oppulent affair. In fact, Mia knew that in the divorce negotiations Angela had fought to continue to attend the ball, but Rafael had put his foot down and said, no, it would be too messy; Angela could keep the Romano surname but not her place at the ball.

Mia had never fully grasped the lavishness of the occasion.

She grimaced slightly at her paltry case as it was delivered, and knew it was filled with one silk gown, stilettos, nightwear, underwear, a denim skirt and top and a make-up bag. Never had the usually meticulous Mia felt so vastly underprepared.

'Is there anything we can help with?' the guest services manager asked.

So daunted was Mia by the prospect of tonight she was brave enough to ask for some help. 'Actually, I've probably left it far too late but I wasn't able to book a hair appointment.'

'I shall have the personal stylist come and speak with you now.' He smiled. 'No problem at all.'

It was indeed no problem, for after a *long* conversation with the personal stylist, it was agreed that while Mia took high tea on the balcony, her bath would be drawn and then the hair and make-up experts would come in.

The suite was stunning and looked out at Piazza Navona, a gorgeous public space with grand statues and fountains, and Mia sat sipping tea and trying to quell her nerves while telling herself it would all be okay though she felt terribly rude to have not RSVP'd. Her gown had been taken to be skilfully pressed and she had a host of fairy godmothers on hand to get her ready for the ball.

A little later she lay in a deep bath, terrified about all the night held, still not knowing what would happen between her and Dante.

Would they get a chance to speak?

And, if they did, would she tell him about the baby?

But there was more on her mind than the baby. Just the thought of seeing him was enough to mean the pink hue to her skin could not all be blamed on the fragrant warm water out of which she now stepped.

She was to be given the full treatment, although Mia had declined a massage, unsure if she could while pregnant, and most unwilling to tell the staff her secret. Instead, she applied gorgeous body oil and then put on a fluffy white gown and stepped out to begin her transformation.

'Subtle make-up,' Mia said, her eyes drifting to the very red gown.

'Of course, Signora Romano.'

Her rather short nails were buffed to perfection; even her toenails were treated to the same.

In her time with Rafael she had steered clear of all this, preferring to retreat to the Tuscan hills, but now she was getting a real insight into the lavish lifestyle the Romanos led in Rome and she was finding it unnerving.

There was a knock on the door, just as her hair had been done and her make-up was being applied. There was a slight flutter of panic from all the staff present when it was established that the owner, Gian, was personally delivering a package to the room.

'Un regalo per Mia,' she heard. *A gift for Mia.*

It was a black velvet box, the colour Mia now wished her dress was!

As the staff stepped back to focus on her shoes and dress, Mia opened the card.

It was cream with embossed gold edging but the note was handwritten.

Thank you for attending
Dante Romano

Mia opened the box slowly and was startled at what she saw: a pair of the most exquisite rose-gold drop earrings and on the end of each, twinkling and shining, were briolette-cut diamonds.

No wonder Gian had hand-delivered them for they were surely worth a fortune. They must be on loan for the night, Mia decided, because they were simply divine. Perhaps Dante did not want her looking like the poor relation tonight.

But it turned out that she looked nothing like the poor relation!

Even Mia gasped at her own reflection as she stood before a long mirror, for she barely recognised herself.

The dress was as exquisite as she remembered from last year's fittings, but her bust had filled out a touch, and there was rather more curve to her hips, which made her overall figure seem more voluptuous. Her make-up was not quite as subtle as she'd hoped—though her lips were neutral, her lashes had been darkened and black and winged eyeliner had been applied—but she'd been told the gown required it. And the gown absolutely required the earrings she now put on, because they pulled the whole look together completely.

And soon she would face Dante.

The elevator took her down to the first floor. From there she took the grand stairs down to the reception where the family were gathered before entering the ballroom.

Mia drew on every bit of reserve she possessed in order to at least appear calm while knowing she had completely underestimated the magnitude of this night.

And there Dante was, standing with Ariana and Stefano.

She could feel his eyes on every inch of bare skin as Mia made her slow way down. Ariana must have said something caustic for Dante tore his eyes away and turned to his sister, and it was clear to Mia that he was scolding her.

Indeed, Ariana had failed at first hurdle to put animosity aside. '*Hardly* a grieving widow,' she hissed when she first glimpsed Mia.

'I told you, Ariana,' Dante warned, 'to cut it out.'

He turned his attention back to Mia and all he could think was, *Thank God*!

Thank God his father had been unable to attend last year, for had he seen her like that, he would have been plunged straight into hell. And while Dante knew only too well Mia's beauty, he was simply blown away for in that stunning red she was, to Dante, absolute perfection. He saw she was not wearing her wedding and engagement rings, and when the earrings caught the light and sparkled he felt a certain pride that she wore *his* diamonds tonight. She looked seductive yet elegant, and she had him fighting himself not to walk over and offer his arm for those last few stairs.

'Mia,' Dante said as she joined them, 'you look stunning. Thank you for being here tonight.'

'It's my pleasure.'

'How are you?' he asked.

'I'm fine,' Mia said. Well, apart from being about to spontaneously combust! Dante looked impeccable and wore a dinner suit with utter ease. The jacket was velvet and as dark as his eyes, which were blazing with approval. His scent, that unique Dante scent, had reached her and as his suited arm brushed her bare one lust rippled through her like a stone skimming a pond.

Ariana and Stefano were rigidly polite but soon gave in and drifted off, leaving Mia standing with Dante.

'Where's Roberto?' Mia asked, as he was supposed to be escorting her for her entrance into the ballroom.

'Roberto is unwell,' Dante said. 'It's nothing serious, but unfortunately he's unable to attend.'

'Oh.' Mia blinked, sorry to have missed seeing him.

'I can't escort you in,' Dante said. 'That might be…inappropriate.'

'Of course,' Mia agreed, more than a little relieved because there were practically sparks flying between them.

'However,' he continued, 'I have asked Gian—'

'Dante,' Mia interrupted, 'you don't have to rummage amongst family and friends for someone to escort me. I am perfectly capable of walking in alone.'

'Very well,' Dante said, admiring her greatly, and then, as the MC called his name, he added, 'Oh, and just so you know, I shan't dance with you, Mia. I think you know why.'

He left her standing there, a little breathless, a little

stunned, as if she'd just been thoroughly kissed, and then, as it was her turn to be introduced, Mia entered the ballroom alone.

Heads turned as Rafael Romano's widow made her entrance. There were, Mia was sure, whispers behind manicured hands that the widow wore red. Still, she focussed instead on the gorgeous décor as she made her way to the head table. The ballroom was heavenly and lavishly furnished, with rose-gold brocade walls and ornate arches and a central chandelier that cast endless stars over the many tables, which were adorned with silverware and a centrepiece each of a tall column of fragrant gardenias.

The people seated at her table were all standing and as Mia approached she was grateful to Gian, who politely kissed her on the cheeks, and only when she had taken her seat on a gorgeous Chiavari chair did the rest of her table sit down.

It was going to be a very awkward night, although she had expected no less.

Mia was seated between a minister—of what, she couldn't quite catch—and Gian, which provided somewhat of a buffer for this dinner of discontent. Ariana, looked ravishing in a black ballgown, was seated on the other side of Gian. She was pointedly silent towards Mia. Stefano and Eloa had eyes only for each other, while Luigi and his wife made no attempt to be friendly.

And Dante?

He sat opposite Mia, with the minister's wife by his side and someone Mia didn't know on the other. But she was beautiful and laughed loudly at everything Dante said and gazed up at him with utter adoration.

Would he be so cruel as to bring a date?

Mia truly didn't know.

There was a toast to Rafael to kick off the night, and they were told by the MC that all the champagne was from his private cellar. Naturally Mia raised a glass and took a pretend sip, though the flash of tears in her eyes as she toasted Rafael were genuine as she thought of her dear friend.

They nibbled their way through the antipasti and for the *primo piatto* it was ravioli, stuffed with pecorino, in a creamy white truffle sauce. It was perfection and Mia wished she wasn't too nervous to fully enjoy it.

'This was Rafael's favourite meal,' Mia commented to Gian.

'Indeed.' Gian nodded. 'The whole menu was chosen by Ariana to reflect that; the truffles are from his home.'

'How lovely,' Mia said, and glanced over at Ariana, who refused even the slightest truce, and instead rather pointedly turned her elegant shoulders and spoke to the guest on her other side.

When the main course was served, Mia had *filetto di maiale alla mela*, and it took her straight back to the fragrant scent that had greeted her after a long ride on Massimo, but the gentle reminiscence was soured when she saw the woman next to Dante place her hand on his arm as she vied for his attention. Worse, he turned to her and smiled in agreement at whatever it was she had said.

Oh, Mia was more than jealous. Disappointment coursed through her for no matter how she might deny her reasons for being here, the simple fact was that she wanted time alone with Dante.

She wanted that dangerous dance.

As desserts were cleared away—again a selection of Rafael's favourites all chosen by Ariana and displayed to perfection—Eloa at least made an attempt at conversation. 'Ariana has also been helping us with our wedding preparations.'

'Oh.' Mia smiled. 'When is the wedding?'

'May,' Eloa said.

'It's going to be amazing.' Ariana slipped in a dig. 'Anyone who's anyone has been invited.'

And Mia, given she hadn't been, was clearly a no one to them.

Eloa at least had the decency to blush.

When the meal was over, and before the speeches and silent auction, there was to be socialising and dancing. Of course, out of respect to Rafael, Mia sat out the dancing and thankfully Gian took the poisonous Ariana off to dance.

Yet, despite the tension at the table, despite Ariana's caustic words, despite herself even, Mia found that she had missed them all.

Yes, even if it made perfect sense that she hadn't been invited to Stefano and Eloa's wedding, even if it would be hell to attend, it hurt that she wouldn't be there.

That their lives were all moving on without her.

She was hormonal, Mia decided, sniffing back sudden tears and then doing her best to speak with the Minister of Something, though she had no real idea what was being said. That she could not focus had nothing to do with her less than fluent Italian, for the minister spoke in perfect English. It was more that she was so acutely aware of Dante. Like a black panther, he sleekly worked the room; his beauty was raw and exquisite and accentuated by his stunning attire and she was very aware that she knew the beauty of his body beneath.

But then came the hell of watching him dance with his date.

Mia had never been jealous in her life until Dante, but now she found that it felt like a corkscrew stabbed into her chest, twisting tighter and tighter, making it impossible to focus on what the Minister of Something said. 'Of course we attend every year, but this is special indeed.'

'Yes,' Mia attempted. 'Rafael would have loved it.'

'Yet he didn't attend last year?'

'No,' Mia agreed, though her eyes kept drifting to the dance floor as she tried to fathom how it might feel to be wrapped in those velvet arms. 'Rafael wasn't well.'

'That's obvious now! Although we weren't privy to that information at the time...' On and on he went, clearly affronted that he hadn't been personally informed that Rafael was ill. 'I've done a lot for the foundation...' the minister continued, but it was all white noise to Mia as she watched Dante laugh at whatever his dance companion had said.

Dante *laughed*. Mia had never, ever seen Dante laugh before. The corkscrew twisted again and she gritted her jaw at the exact moment his eyes met hers—another woman in his arms, his narrowed eyes assessing her. She felt them scald her bare shoulders and it was as if his hands were at the back of her neck and freeing the tie, for her breasts felt prickly in the fabric of her gown...and then his gaze came back to her eyes and her cheeks stung as if she'd been slapped.

'Don't you agree?' the minister said.

'I'm sorry?' Mia couldn't even attempt to recall whatever he'd said, for not only hadn't she been listening but Mia was suddenly, embarrassingly, near to tears. 'If you'll please excuse me for a moment,' Mia said. She made her way out of the ballroom and to the powder room, which was as decadent as any she'd seen—not that she had the energy to really take in her surroundings. Instead she gripped a marble bench and looked into a large antique mirror at unfamiliar, made-up eyes that were glittering as brightly as the diamonds that hung from her ears.

'You're doing well, *Signora*,' a middle-aged woman said. 'It must be a difficult night for you.'

'Thank you.' Mia smiled, and after taking a moment to gather her breath she stepped out of the bathroom and walked almost straight into Dante.

'Come with me,' he said, and led her across the foyer.

He took a sheet of paper from his pocket. 'I am running the speech by you, in case we are seen stepping out.'

'Yes.'

Finally, they had some privacy for he had led her to a delicious occasional garden. As the French doors closed on them, she dragged in a lungful of cool night air. It was Mia who spoke first. 'Who is she?'

'Who?' Dante frowned, and then he saw that her neck was not just red but mottled and he could almost *taste* her jealousy. It was such an unexpected turn-on to see the cool and collected Mia anything but that he smiled as realisation hit.

'That's the minister's daughter; she's not my date.'

'You're flirting with her.'

'God, no,' Dante said.

'You were *laughing* with her.'

'I was trying to keep things light,' Dante admitted. He laughed a false laugh, the one he must have used, and for some reason it made her giggle. 'She always tries to flirt with me; it is the same every year, though usually I have a date. She is thoroughly over-excited tonight because I appear to be alone. But I am not alone,' Dante said, and as he stepped closer to Mia her smile faded. 'Am I?'

Mia swallowed, before answering. 'No.'

'Who am I here with tonight, Mia?' he provoked in a low sexy drawl that demanded she answer.

'Me.'

'Pardon?' he said.

Her voice was husky. 'You're here with me.'

'Yes,' Dante said, 'and never forget it. I dance my duty dances, but the only one I want to dance with is you. Know this, Mia: every year that you come to the Romano ball, I will come alone.'

And with those words, Dante moved his own goalposts. He had sworn only one more night, but the thought of meeting each year at this event was tempting indeed. It might be for only one night, once a year, yet it was more of a commitment than Dante had ever made to anyone before.

The thought of them never quite ending was tempting indeed.

He stepped closer still and her world shrank further; even the sounds from the ball faded to nothing, for she could hear her own pulse in her ears.

'You got the earrings, I see,' Dante said, as his finger lightly touched one sparking jewel.

'Thank you,' she said, but her voice came out high, as if owned by a teenage boy, for his hand was warm on her neck. 'Should I leave them in the suite's safe or...?'

'They're yours,' Dante said. 'From me.'

'Oh, no!'

'Oh, yes.'

'Dante, please don't buy me gifts.'

'But I want to,' Dante said silkily.

'We should go back in,' Mia attempted, because *now* things were dangerous. Now, finally alone, there was nowhere to hide the lust that thrummed between them. She shivered, though not from the cold. It was because his hand trailed from her neck, down her bare arm and then to the curve of her waist. The feel of his palm caused sensation to pool at her centre, and the slight dig of his fingers made her sex clench.

'Did you know,' Dante said, and his voice felt like a lick to her ear, 'that this hotel is named after the old Duke's mistress?'

'I didn't know,' Mia responded, and her eyes met his. They glittered with ire—was Dante inviting her to be his mistress?

Or was it desire? For she was so exquisitely turned on now it was as if they danced alone.

'It is said,' Dante continued, his breath on her cheek,

'that the Duke and Duchess were to host a private dinner for the Principe and Principessa in this very *dimora*...' He registered her frown at the unfamiliar word. 'Mansion,' he translated. 'But instead of being here to greet his esteemed guests, the Duke was, yet again, visiting Fiordelise, and so was, yet again, inexcusably late. Always he was late, and so it was decided that Fiordelise would have her own suite next to his...' She knew he could not kiss her and ruin her make up, but his mouth was so close that it almost felt as if he were. 'The Duke was never late again.'

She had to fight her own lips for they wanted to stretch to meet his. 'We can't do this, Dante.'

'Why not?' Dante asked, as his hand slid around to the small of her back. 'I have to have you, Mia.' She recalled how that night his hand had felt like a balm as he'd pushed into her, and possibly he was thinking the same thing for now he pressed against her and her hips fought not to press back.

'Then we can't be seen, Dante.' Mia shivered, as she gave in to the knowledge that tonight they must meet.

'We shan't be,' Dante said, and he took her hand. For a second she thought he was about to kiss her fingers in that decadent way again, but instead he pressed something cold into her palm and closed her fingers over it.

He let her go then and she dared not look at what he'd handed her. But she could feel the cool metal and it took a second to dawn on Mia that he had handed her a key and that they must have adjoining suites.

'If you want me tonight,' Dante said, 'all you have to do is turn the key and you will find that the door on the other side is already open.'

Forget the corkscrew in her chest, Mia thought, for the key she held in her palm now wound her far tighter, albeit somewhat further below. The weeks since the invitation had arrived had caused silent, frantic negotiations with herself, insisting that she did not want to sleep with Dante again, while knowing she really did.

Except there was the pregnancy that Mia had not revealed to Dante—not that she had a chance to now—for the French doors were opening and Dante abruptly dropped contact and stepped back.

'Dante.' Stefano came out to the occasional garden and saw them standing there, grim faced, with Dante still holding the paper. 'There you are.' Stefano took in the very tense atmosphere and thankfully completely misread it, so much so that he assumed they were engaged in a row! 'You told Ariana and me to put the animosity on hold for one night,' Stefano challenged. 'Surely you can take your own advice? The speeches are about to start.'

'I'll be right there.' Dante said, and accompanied his brother back to the ballroom, leaving Mia to slip the key into her small purse and make her own way back alone.

Dante took up the microphone and thanked everyone for coming; he spoke of his father and how important this night had always been to him.

Mia stood there, trying to mimic his calm, trying to laugh when appropriate, trying to concentrate on the rest of the night, while the key in her purse seemed to pulse like a nuclear alarm.

All she could think about was that tonight she would be with Dante.

CHAPTER EIGHT

THE REST OF the ball passed by in a blur, but finally there came an appropriate time for Mia to leave and she headed up to her suite. She found that not only could Dante be tender when he so chose, he could be romantic too. There was champagne chilling and a silver tray of handmade chocolates, as well as a glorious display of roses in the deep blood-red colour of the dress. She doubted the colour choice was coincidental and it told Mia he had taken in every detail of what she wore.

Her breathing was coming a little too fast, as if Dante were actually present. As she took out the key from her purse, Mia truly didn't know what to do.

Oh, she knew what she *wanted* to do—her slightly frantic eyes took in her surroundings and found that the lounge had an adjoining door—and she wanted to turn the key in the lock and be thoroughly made love to by Dante.

But would it be wrong not to tell him about the baby first?

Mia truly did not know how to say the words. Should she just blurt them out?

Or would she chicken out and write a note, slide it under his door, and await her fate?

She sat at the walnut desk, a stack of thick cream paper embossed with 'La Fiordelise' in swirling gold in front of her, and thought of Fiordelise waiting for the Duke to visit as she tried to work out her *I'm pregnant* speech.

Dante, I don't know how to tell you this...
Dante, there was a problem after I took the pills...
Dante...

Her heart was thumping, but more with frustration than fear, because she knew the second she told him about the pregnancy their magical night would end and everything would change. And then Mia made the first truly selfish decision of her life: while she knew she had to tell him, and she would tell him, she wanted Dante tonight.

She abandoned her writing and turned the key in the adjoining door.

He might be ages, Mia told herself. After all, there were many guests to thank and to say goodbye to, but she jumped when a mere moment later the lever on the door slowly lowered. She stood as the door was pushed open and there was no question now if she would tell him.

No questions in her mind at all.

'Mia.' He took a step forward and she stumbled towards him.

And when he took her in his arms, all the fear of telling him, the uncertainty all hushed as if a plug had been pulled and all that was left was the vacuum of them into which he drew her.

Dante pulled her right into him and held her as he had wanted to the entire night, and she revelled in the bliss of being back in his strong, warm embrace.

He kissed her temple, and her eyes screwed closed at his soft touch, then a tiny cry came to her mouth as he kissed her cheeks.

'Dante...' She sought his mouth, but he denied it, and lowered his head to the tender skin on her neck and inhaled her scent.

He could feel her shaking, literally trembling with desire. Dante wanted her naked in bed—his bed, or hers, he cared not which. He just wanted to kiss every inch of her, but then he lifted his head and their mouths met and everything changed.

For both, it was the end of longing.

It was a fierce kiss, when he hadn't intended it to be, but it was a mutual kiss borne of three months of yearning from both of them.

Dante's scent, which Mia had hungered for, consumed her again, and their untamed passion unleashed her and caused her to reveal *other* truths that she'd not intended to share. 'I've missed you,' she panted between kisses. 'Dante, I want you so much…'

The breathless admission was delivered with a wanton edge that surprised Dante, for she was always so pent up that it was delicious to know another side existed.

And he too was unleashed.

There was no thought of bed now, just a craving for skin.

He reached for the zipper but as his hand brushed her breast she moaned into his mouth and he read that moan, the zipper forgotten, roughly handling her breasts through the silky fabric.

It made her feel desperate, frantic even, for more of his touch.

Mia had felt desperate and frantic many times in her life, though for sadder reasons, and she had always hidden it, always held on to her emotions, but when with Dante, when safely locked in his embrace, her reserve tumbled.

His hands were everywhere, roaming her body then deftly hitching up her dress, his hands impatient and delicious. She had never wanted anything so much in her life. She was no longer shy, or guarded. She was grappling with his shirt just to feel his chest, and then his belt— she did not know who this woman was. They were both panting and their foreheads were locked together as he reached for a condom. There was the tiniest moment for Mia to tell him that it wasn't necessary, but she was desperate and wanton and sliding down her panties as that thought dispersed.

The sumptuous lounge was impossible to negotiate because they could not bear to drop contact.

Dante lifted her heavy gown and then he lifted Mia and positioned her and with his hands on her hips pulled her down onto him. But Mia did not know how to move with abandon, how to find her own rhythm, when she had known but one night with him.

Dante searched for a wall, any wall, but as he moved them to it the roses in their vase were knocked to the floor in their haste.

Then she felt the cool wall behind her and she locked her arms around his neck as he took her against it, over and over again.

Mia's legs were wrapped tightly around him and the heel of one stiletto was digging into the back of the other calf. She was vaguely aware that it hurt but she could no more consider moving than flying to the moon, for the feeling of Dante inside her, raw and unbridled, was beyond exquisite.

He thrust into her so deeply and so rapidly that her thighs were shaking, and her neck was arching so that the top of her head met the wall. 'Dante…' She was coming and crying but still he did not relent.

'Di più,' Dante said.

More.

And there *was* more, Mia found, for as he thrust into her, she heard Dante's breathless shout as he released himself into her, which had her clamping all over again, every nerve so tight she could not even scream as, for a moment, she entirely left her mind.

And then he kissed her back into time.

* * *

He carried her through to the bedroom and laid her down, before collapsing beside her to collect not just his breath but his thoughts.

Soon he would undress her, Dante decided. Soon they would start again, but slowly this time. But it wasn't just sex on his mind as they lay together, staring at another ceiling. This time his arm did not cover his face.

'What do we do?' Dante asked, and turned his head so they looked at each other. 'Meet once a year in our decadent palace, or...' He saw her eyes shutter and guessed she wasn't ready to glimpse stepping out and facing the world and to hell with the scandal it would cause. Yet *he* was beginning to glimpse a tentative future, when he never once had before. He was starting to trust Mia, and he knew this was different because in the three months they had been apart he had not been able to get her out of his mind.

'What do you think we should do?' he asked.

'I don't know,' Mia admitted. She looked into those gorgeous black eyes and knew she could hold it in no longer. 'Dante, I'm pregnant.'

Mia waited, for his intake of breath, for his shock, or even his refusal to acknowledge that fact. What she did not expect was the dark chill of his calmness, like a still, deep pond that would silently swallow you, or the weary sigh he gave, as if he had expected no less.

'Of course you are,' Dante said, and he rolled himself off of the bed. That suspicious, contemptuous look that he displayed so well was on her again.

'What's that supposed to mean?' Mia asked.

'It means,' Dante said, as he did himself up, 'that I am not in the least surprised we find ourselves here.' For a moment there he had trusted her, had honestly believed they might stand a chance. 'Has the money run out? How much more do you want?'

'Dante, please…'

'No need to beg.' Dante deliberately misinterpreted her words. 'Just speak with a lawyer. Though, when you do, tell them I want DNA before I respond.'

'Do you really think I want to be in this situation?' Mia asked.

'Yes,' Dante said. 'Absolutely! I think you are exactly where you want to be; in fact, you are where you planned to be.' He stared right at her. 'I told you where and when to get emergency contraception.'

'And I took it,' Mia said.

He gave *such* a mocking laugh. 'You had one job, Mia. Did I have to go and fetch the pills and watch you take them myself? No, I trusted that you would take care of it. Clearly you didn't.'

'Just because you're such an expert on emergency contraception it doesn't mean we all are. I forgot to take my motion sickness medication that night. If you're such an expert, perhaps you should have warned me that if I vomited within three hours—'

'I'm no expert!' he angrily interrupted. 'I was looking it up on my phone while you got the cases. The pharmacist should have told you.'

'She spoke in Italian, Dante, and very fast.' But Dante didn't want to hear it. He was already heading out to the lounge to gather his clothes, and she was shaking and upset as she followed him. 'Yes, I made a mistake, and, yes, this isn't what you want. Well, guess what? I didn't want to be pregnant either. I wanted the Romanos out of my life for good.'

'Yet here you are,' Dante pointed out. 'You never wanted to be gone.'

'Do you think I enjoyed the scrutiny? Being called a gold-digger and a whore by the press?'

'I don't believe you, Mia, and with good reason. You've

been lying to me from the first day we met. You introduced yourself as his PA when you knew you were about to the blow the family apart. You masqueraded as his lover, yet that was clearly a lie, so tell me, why should I start believing what you say now? There hasn't been a word of truth from your mouth from the very start. There's been nothing but trouble since the day you came into our lives.'

He stalked out through the adjoining door, but then returned and took the bottle of champagne. 'You won't be needing this,' he said tartly, and walked out again.

This time, it was Dante who turned the key.

CHAPTER NINE

NEITHER MIA NOR Dante got much sleep.

Mia wasn't angry at his reaction. How could she be, when she had asked the very same questions of herself?

Well, not the DNA one, but even that she understood.

Rafael had once told her about the various paternity suits filed against him, how a woman with whom he had once had a business dinner had announced eight weeks later she was pregnant with his child, and had insisted the same right up to the return of the results. Sadly there were people willing to go to any lengths to get their hands on the Romano fortune.

No, she had never expected Dante to blindly believe and suddenly trust her, of course not.

But it still hurt that he didn't.

Yet Dante was right, Mia thought as she peeled off her gown. Despite the chaos of her personal life, Mia clung to order and hung the dress up. Then, with shaking hands, she returned the gorgeous earrings to their box and put them in the safe, but such was her turmoil that Mia just tapped in the first numbers that came to mind. Yes, she clung to order, even removing her make-up and brushing out her hair. But even with her night-time routine and the sumptuous bed, it was impossible to sleep, for there was no real relief that Dante now knew the truth.

* * *

Dante did not sleep either.

In fact, he paced his way through the early hours of morning, tempted to go to her suite and haul her out of bed so that they could sort this out.

Except the straight black arrows of anger he aimed at her blurred when he thought of Mia flying home after the drama of the last twenty-four hours. He did not easily lean into sympathy, but conceded that he had not taken his usual care that night, for he never had sex without condoms, yet when they'd made love the thought hadn't as much as entered his head.

The champagne went untouched because Dante needed to think. He could not get past her lies, albeit of omission, and so he swung between doubt—one moment believing it had been a simple mistake—and panic.

Yes, sheer panic.

A baby!

He had struggled enough when he had been landed with Alfonzo, but this wasn't a dog, this was a baby, with arms and legs and teeth—well, eventually teeth, he knew that much!

A person.

A whole other person for whom he would be responsible, as if his damned family wasn't already enough.

He would be stuck co-parenting with Mia in London, because the thought that they might parent together never even entered his head. The one thing he avoided was relationships, even if for a brief moment he had considered the possibility of one with her.

That had been before her bombshell, though.

It felt exactly that—like a bomb had exploded in his brain.

At six, just as morning coffee was delivered, his phone buzzed, and when he saw that it was Sarah he took the call.

As she spoke, Dante glanced at the adjoining door as Sarah told him that photographs of himself and Mia had been taken last night in the occasional garden and were being sold.

'Do you know who took them?' Dante asked.

'Not at this stage.' Sarah said. 'Of course, it might have been a set-up. Mia might—'

Sarah was brilliant at her job and possibly as suspicious by nature as he. Of course he would expect his PA, who liaised with his PR people, to consider that Mia might have set him up, yet Dante had to draw a shaking breath in as he fought not to reprimand her.

'It was not a set-up,' Dante said. 'I took Mia out to the garden.'

'Of course, but—'

'Drop it,' Dante said, and quickly realised it didn't matter who had taken the pictures. What mattered was the explosion of interest that would take place the moment the images got out.

He gave rapid orders to Sarah, but when the call ended Dante knew, even as his legal team were being woken, there was no hope of the images being shut down. He made some rapid decisions, before taking a breath, unlocking his adjoining door, and knocking on hers.

'Mia!' There was no answer and after a couple more knocks he pushed down the lever and found himself back in her lounge. It was somewhat chaotic with the remnants from their lovemaking scattered about. There were roses strewn on the floor and he saw a crumpled sheet of paper and rescued it, reading her pained drafts of telling him about the baby.

Dante, I don't know how to tell you this....
Dante, there was a problem after I took the pills...
Dante...

And now he had to tell her this. He made his way to the bedroom and knocked on that door.

'Mia?'

The door opened immediately as his knock on the adjoining door had woken her, and Mia had pulled on a robe and had been about to head out of the bedroom when he had knocked again. 'Is it time for round two?' she asked.

'I'm not here to argue. I want you to pack up your things and get dressed—'

'Don't worry, Dante, I'm leaving.'

'Do you really think I would wake you up to kick you out? Mia, we need to leave now, together. I am taking you back to Luctano where I can control things better. There were photos of us taken last night in the garden. Compromising photos...' He saw the colour drain from her face.

'No!'

'Yes.'

'Have you seen them?' she asked.

'No, though by all accounts they speak for themselves.'

'But we didn't as much as kiss...' Her voice trailed off when he gave her a wide-eyed look, for their lips may not have touched but certainly there had been contact. 'Oh, no...' She could hear the roar of her pulse in her ears and her legs seemed to turn to lead but she pushed them to move and then sat down on a chaise longue by the windows in the vast bedroom.

Dante remained at the doors and watched as she put her head in her hands. Mia was clearly devastated and, surprisingly for Dante, even with Sarah's words lingering, not for a second did he think she might have engineered it. 'We can leave now, unnoticed, as the pictures are not yet out, but I guarantee it is a window that will close very soon.'

He sounded so calm when she was so not. 'Dante, I can't go in your helicopter.'

'That's fine, I will drive.'

'But I'm starting a new job tomorrow,' Mia said, and then cringed at the thought of starting work with the photos coming out and buried her head in her hands again.

Dante looked around the room rather than at her, and saw the dress hanging up neatly and the shoes side by side, so at odds with the chaos that was about to hit. 'Mia, despite what I said last night, it is clear that we need to speak, so let's just focus on that for now.'

It didn't take Mia long to pack and Dante took even less time, for she could feel his impatience from the lounge as she stuffed the gown in her case and pulled on a denim skirt and strappy top.

'Where's your luggage?' Mia asked when she came out.

'Sarah will come and pack for me…' he said, but as he followed her out he saw a fresh blue bruise on the back of her calf. 'What happened to your leg?'

Mia glanced down and then twisted and looked at the bruise her own stiletto had made and gave him her answer. 'You did.'

They drove through a sleepy Rome, bathed in a golden sunrise, the streets more deserted and more beautiful than Mia had ever seen them, but nothing could soothe her now.

'I forgot the earrings.'

'It's fine.'

'I left them in the safe.'

'I'll tell Sarah to get them. She's waiting at my place; I have to collect a few things before we head off,' Dante said, and turned into a lane.

He lived very close to the hotel, in Campo Marzio, in the historic centre of Rome, with everything she loved about Rome on his doorstep.

Not that Dante had a doorstep as such.

He parked the car on a cobbled lane. She got out and followed him through a heavy gate, where they were greeted by a doorman who pulled open the lift. Despite herself, Mia was curious to glimpse his home.

But they were not alone.

Sarah was there and handed him a case, and though she gave Mia a polite nod she clearly had no interest in her and was just sorting things out for the boss, so Mia stood as Sarah and Dante spoke, and took in her surroundings.

The vast lounge with its high walls and ornate ceiling was a stunning marriage of ancient and modern. There were rugs everywhere and heavy leather sofas, and the huge pieces of modern art on the walls clashed marvellously with the picture-perfect view of the Spanish Steps.

The biggest surprise, though, apart from the most delectable view, was a tiny, ancient-looking white dog sitting on the sofa. Dante did not seem the type to have a small dog—or any dog, come to that. His eyes were white with cataracts but whether or not he could see Dante, he thumped his tail when his master arrived. The dog didn't get up, just lay there as Dante stroked his ears while he spoke with Sarah, who had but one question for Mia: 'What is your code for the safe?'

'One, two, three, four,' a blushing Mia admitted, trying to ignore the look that passed between Dante and Sarah that said, *Too stupid for words*.

'We should get going,' Dante said to her in English.

'Are we bringing him?' Mia asked, and pointed to the scruffy little dog.

'No. Alfonzo lives only to lie on my couch; he hates being moved. Is there anything you need?'

'Coffee,' Mia admitted. She had no room in her brain to think of anything else, and there was nothing to be gained from pointing out that she had few clothes with her when the shops weren't even open.

'I'll collect some breakfast from the café.'

He got them some pastries too, and there was an armistice while he drove them out of Rome and they took breakfast on the go.

'It's like being a fugitive,' Mia commented.

'A bit,' Dante agreed, 'though they will soon figure out where we are, but at least you will not be standing at Fiumicino or arriving at Heathrow when word gets out.'

He took a couple of calls on the way, and one was from Sarah.

'Your earrings are now at my apartment.'

'Thank you.'

'One, two, three, four,' Dante said. 'How the hell do you remember that?'

'I wasn't exactly thinking straight last night,' Mia said. 'I'm usually more careful.'

It was what he did to her, Mia thought.

Dante had taken the order she eternally sought and tumbled her into chaos.

Though not now.

For despite the strain in the air and the questions to come, suddenly there was no place she would rather be than with Dante on a Sunday morning with Rome in the rear-view mirror and the baby no longer a secret.

'I didn't picture you with a dog…'

'I didn't picture me with a dog,' Dante responded, and then added, 'Or a baby.'

'How old is he?'

'More than a hundred in dog years. He belonged to the woman in the apartment below, and when she was taken in an ambulance to hospital, Sarah offered to feed him.'

Gosh, that corkscrew in her chest tightened a little as she pictured Sarah and Dante lolling in bed, only climbing out to the sound of sirens.

Dante glanced over and saw the mottled colour on her chest and her pursed lips, and despite his dark mood found that he smiled.

'So, when the old lady died, Sarah said that she would have him, except it turned out her husband was allergic to dogs.'

He glanced over again, and the relaxing of her features had him smiling again.

'I suggested he go to the pound to be rehomed. Sarah insisted he was too old and arthritic and too blind and that they would put him down. I said I thought that might be for the best...'

'Dante!'

'Yes, well, I should have listened to myself, because he's been living on my couch ever since.'

And having his ears stroked, Mia thought.

She looked over at him and now, despite the imminent disaster of exposure, she felt oddly relieved that he now knew and that made her brave enough to ask, 'Are you cross that I didn't tell you last night before we...?'

'No,' Dante said. 'I am cross that you did not tell me when I asked, and I am cross that in the weeks since you found out you did not think to pick up the phone—'

'Of course I thought about it!'

'Yet you didn't do it. Instead, when I asked if there might be an issue, you told me that everything was fine. Twice,' he added.

'The first time I didn't know,' Mia admitted. 'I've had no morning sickness, and there was nothing to make me think that I might be pregnant until you called.'

'And the second time?'

'I was just starting to get used to it myself,' Mia said. 'For the first time in two weeks I hadn't cried myself to sleep and was just coming round to the notion of keeping the baby. I didn't want to rock that fragile boat.'

'You sounded fine on the phone,' Dante pointed out, remembering her brisk and efficient tone. Certainly, she hadn't sounded fragile, or like a woman who was crying herself to sleep at night. Still, there was one thing he wanted to make clear. 'I am *not* cross that you didn't tell me last night.'

'Honestly?' Mia checked. 'I do feel bad about that, because I did think of telling you. When you put on the...' The word 'condom' died on her lips. It was such a revolting word, though it had felt far from revolting at the time.

'Never interrupt sex.' He glanced over and saw her blushing. 'If we are ever having sex and over my shoulder there is a newsflash that the world is ending, please don't stop proceedings to tell me.'

She gave a half-laugh.

'There'll be none of that for now, though,' Dante said. 'We need to sort things out properly.'

They drove in silence for a while, both dwelling on that.

For Mia, the 'for now' offered if not hope then a glimpse of possibility that this wasn't the end of them.

While for Dante he'd simply meant what he'd said: the attraction was there, it was pointless to deny it, and after all it had got him to considering more. Last night he had been thinking along the lines of an occasional affair, while knowing deep down that could never work in the long run.

The debris from the bombshell was settling and he was starting to think with a clearer head.

'Have you seen a doctor?' Dante asked.

'Yes.' She looked at him. 'I'm keeping the baby, whether you want me to or not...'

'That is one thing we are agreed on at least.' He glanced over and then looked away. As to the rest, it was one hell of a mess.

'Whether you believe me or not, I didn't plan this, Dante.'

'Not at first perhaps,' Dante said. He was always honest and so did not amend his thoughts as he vocalised them, 'but I believe that I was your Plan C.' He had done a *lot* of thinking last night. 'I am sure that when you married my father, you wanted your little Romano baby to ensure endless wealth, and when my father was ill and could not...' He blew out a breath as he couldn't both drive and allow his mind to go there at the same time.

'And my Plan B?' Mia asked, curious as to how his mind worked.

'Contest the will.'

'I didn't, though.'

'Because there's no need to if you're carrying my baby.'

'If?' She gave a small mirthless laugh. 'How did you get to be so suspicious?'

'Because everyone lies.' Dante shrugged. 'My perfect family is a nest of liars.'

Mia swallowed because she, perhaps even more than Dante, knew he spoke the truth.

'I think my mother had a long-running affair,' he said, taking the curves in the road with skill, but Mia found she was holding her breath, not just at his driving but as he inched towards the truth.

'Dante, can you please slow down?'

He glanced at the dashboard and then over at her and though he was within the limit, when he saw her pale features he slowed down the car but not the conversation. 'Perhaps my father decided it was his turn to cheat...' He blew out an angry breath. 'And then you came along, dear Mia. Except he was too ill to give you a baby and permanent access to his fortune, and so to Plan B.'

'But I didn't contest the will,' Mia pointed out.

'No, you saw a chance for a Plan C.'

'Which was?'

'A last roll of the dice with me.'

'Oh, please! Are you saying I set out to seduce you that night? Poor Dante...' She scoffed.

'I never said I was a victim,' Dante countered. 'We were

both more than willing. I'm just saying you saw a chance and you took it—or rather,' he added with a jaded edge, 'you *didn't* take your pills.'

'If you think that,' Mia said, 'then you don't know me.'

His temper was building. His theory, now voiced, was growing in momentum as they neared Luctano, where she had lived as his father's wife for two years.

Two damned years!

He ground the gears in place of his jaw and Mia felt not just his tension but her own and she again asked him to slow down.

'I am within the speed limit!'

But all the same he slowed right down, taking the bends like a tourist when he knew these roads like the back of his hand.

Mia stopped pressing her foot on an imaginary break and looked out at the colour-drenched view. The splash of poppy fields in the distance, the tall cypress trees and the sights that had been her home for two years. She had honestly thought she would never see Luctano again, but there was no time to enjoy the now familiar scenery spread before her, for the enormity of them being exposed was starting to hit. She was nervous about facing Sylvia and the staff, and about her brother's reaction too, and panic was building, though she tried to keep it from her voice as she broke the strained silence. 'Dante, can you do anything to stop the photos being released?'

'They're already out,' Dante said.

'How do you know?'

'Because from the buzzing in my pocket I might be forgiven for thinking I picked up your vibrator by mistake instead of my phone.'

'You're disgusting!' Mia spluttered, appalled that he would say such a thing, but Dante was unabashed.

'No,' Dante shot back, 'that title belongs to you.' Their

shameful night would be on stage now for the world to see, and he was furious with himself for his weakness for Mia and the awful feeling that the woman who fascinated him and who he had come to adore might have played him. 'It took two years for you to get a Romano between your legs. You must have needed something to help you along in the interim.'

'Absolutely not!' Her cheeks were on fire, her hands bunched, stunned he would talk about such things. *Such* things she had never done, except for Dante it seemed to be a given that she had.

'Was just thinking of the millions enough of a turn-on then?' he asked.

'Excuse me!' Mia spluttered. 'I didn't know *such* feelings existed until you!' She was embarrassed even to discuss it. 'And,' Mia added, 'it was significantly longer than two years. I was a virgin when we slept together, if you remember rightly.'

Oh, Dante remembered very well indeed.

And he was trying not to do exactly that.

But was Mia saying he'd been not just her first lover but her first orgasm? Dante was considering pulling the car over so curious was he.

So curious!

He looked over and saw her uptight features and for once felt rather chastised as Ms Prim took out her own phone to look at the articles. 'Don't,' he said hurriedly. 'You really don't need to see them.'

'I want to know what's being said.' Mia let out an anguished cry and dropped the phone in her lap as if it was a hot coal.

Oh, it was such an intimate photo.

Mia had barely recognised herself in the mirror before she had headed down to the ball, and she barely recognised herself now, because in the photo she was clearly on fire for Dante for all to see.

There was not a strap or a button undone in the photo, yet she felt as if the world had been invited into her bedroom.

'What?' Dante said.

But she refused to answer him, just sat with that pained expression and with her hand over her mouth. Even though they were only a little way from home, *now* he pulled over the car and retrieved her phone to see what was being said for himself.

They headlines were pretty brutal, but one in particular stood out.

Step-Mamma Mia!

Beneath the headline was a picture of them groin to groin and with his face over hers. It had been taken from inside, probably with a phone, but it was enough to capture her in that red dress, gazing right at him, him holding her tight and close. There was a stirring in his groin as he recalled the feel of Mia in his arms, pressing the key into her hand and the quiet certainty that they were again headed for bed.

'That's not me,' she said, and Dante frowned at her choice of words.

'Oh, that's you all right, Mia,' Dante refuted, but it was dawning on him that this was a side to Mia only he had seen, and though usually this type of picture didn't rattle him, her clear distress had him angry on her behalf. There was no real time to dwell on it, though, as her phone lit up then. 'Someone called Michael is calling you.'

'My brother.' She shuddered. 'He must have seen it.'

Yet instead of declining the call, he was surprised and more than a touch impressed when she took the phone and answered the call with brisk aplomb. 'Mia speaking.'

She listened for a moment and then laughed dismissively.

'Oh, do stop worrying Michael, it's fine,' she told him. 'Just a stupid misunderstanding.'

So she really did have a brother and one she seemed to be close to; Dante blinked when he heard her calm, upbeat tone.

Now she was reassuring him. 'Michael, I'm completely fine. In fact, I'm just heading to Dante's now. I'm going to turn my phone off, but you can call me on the landline if you need me.' If Dante had not seen her pallor and heard her moan just moments ago, he would have believed her when she said, 'Absolutely. I'm fine.'

It took the angry wind from his sails.

Had Mia been like that when he'd called her about the reference and prompted her about the ball?

Who was Mia? he pondered. She was like a chameleon. Seductive, yet reticent and shy, upset at times and the next icy calm. A wife, a virgin...pregnant.

'Let's get home,' Dante said.

Dante drove towards the sprawling Romano residence but as they approached the lake Mia thought of the grave, and knew there was no way she could stay there tonight.

'I want to stay at the hotel.'

'Mia, the whole point of being here is so we can have some privacy. There is no one but my father's— I mean, *my* staff here...' They were his now. 'The hotel has its own helipad, the press will soon be there...'

'You have your own helipad,' she pointed out.

'Yes, but if they dare land on my property they'll be charged with trespassing and they know it. As well as that, the hotel is going to be full of paparazzi—the very people we are trying to avoid.'

'Dante, I *really* don't want to stay here.'

'I've told you, the press can't get to us.' He assumed

that was what concerned her. 'There are guards on the perimeters.'

It wasn't the press that concerned her, though; it was the grave inside the perimeter.

'It's creepy,' she attempted.

But Dante had never known fear and gave a half-laugh. 'If things go bump in the night, you know where to find me...' Then he halted.

No flirting, Dante reminded himself.

Arriving at the residence, Sylvia greeted them warmly, except she flushed a little when she spoke. 'It is good to see you, Signora Romano...' Her voice trailed off and Mia *knew* she had seen the salacious articles. 'How have you been?'

'Very well, thank you.'

'Should I take your case up to Suite al Limone? Or...?' Her eyes flicked to Dante.

'I'll be staying in Suite al Limone,' Mia responded quickly, feeling exquisitely uncomfortable. 'I'll take my own case up.'

'Mia,' Dante suggested, 'why don't you have a rest, then freshen up and get changed for lunch—?'

'Get changed?' Her laughter was slightly hysterical. 'It's this or a ballgown, Dante. I didn't exactly come prepared to be hidden away in Luctano.'

But Luctano was a little more prepared than she was.

'You left a few clothes in the laundry,' Sylvia said as she followed Mia up the stairs to the suite. 'When Dante called, I remembered them, and I have put them in the cupboards and drawers. You can give me any laundry you have.'

'Thank you.'

'What happened to your leg?' Sylvia asked.

'It's nothing.' Mia blushed and glanced down to the foyer where Dante was still standing, but then she caught Dante's eye and he gave her that gorgeous slow smile that said he knew it was hard for the wife of Rafael Romano to be back, mired in scandal with his reprobate son, and he could be kind when he chose.

It helped.

And it helped, perhaps more than it should, to be back in the gorgeous, familiar suite that she hadn't felt quite ready to leave.

'It's good to have you back,' Sylvia admitted.

'How have you been, Sylvia?'

'It's been very quiet since you left,' she admitted. 'Dante has rarely been here. It is a bit of a ghost house really.'

Mia swallowed, for she hated that kind of talk.

'But we are still here, for now at least,' Sylvia said. 'It is good to have someone to cook for. I shall serve lunch at one, if that is okay?'

'That would be lovely.'

Mia took out the little linen bag that contained the dress and things from when she had flown into Rome.

'I'll have these back to you soon.'

'Thank you, Sylvia.'

After she had gone, Mia looked through the drawers and wardrobes. There wasn't much.

Her black woollen funeral dress hung in the wardrobe. And black funeral knickers, which had been peeled off by Dante, sat lonely in the top drawer. There was also a pair of grey capri pants and a cream top, and some espadrilles, so at least, after the long drive, she could get into fresh clothes. And there were also some tatty jodhpurs and her very old, short riding boots, which she'd left, meaning for them to be thrown out. The thought of a ride to clear her head was tempting but a rest was even more so and Mia gratefully closed the drapes.

She stretched out, grateful for the reprieve from Dante's accusations, while understanding his suspicions. After all, she had been married to Rafael for two years, and of course Dante would think it had been for money.

God, how did she tell him the truth without breaking Rafael's confidence? It was an impossible question, and one that often kept her awake at night. Just as she was drifting off, the buzz of a helicopter approaching had her climbing from the bed.

Recalling what Dante had said about no one landing here, she peeled back one of the drapes just a touch. It wasn't the press; it was Gian De Luca's helicopter. Thanks to Sylvia's observations, Mia recognised it and now watched it land, then swallowed when she saw who stepped out.

Yes, Ariana Romano was gorgeous—stunning, in fact.

And she was clearly furious!

Dante had come out, and was walking towards her as Ariana ran towards him.

'Oh.' Mia let out a slight cry as Ariana delivered a vicious slap to his left cheek and then raised her other hand to do the same to the other side, except Dante caught it and words were exchanged.

'That's from me,' Ariana said as she delivered the slap and then raised her other hand. 'And this is from—'

Dante caught her wrist and didn't need Ariana to tell him that the second intended strike would have come from his mother.

'How could you?' Ariana spat, as Dante held her wrists. 'With *her*!'

'Stop this,' Dante demanded.

'After all she did to our family, to Mamma. I hate you for this, Dante.'

'Come inside and sit down and we can speak properly.'

'Is she here?' Ariana's voice contorted with disgust. 'Did you bring that bitch here?'

'God help him!' Dante said by way of response, and his sister's angry tirade was briefly halted.

'Who?'

'Whoever ends up with you!' Dante responded, and then watched as Ariana shook her hands free and with a sob ran back towards the helicopter.

'Damn!' Dante hissed, loathing his sister's anguish, while angry at her too and knowing there was still more hurt to come when she found out about the baby.

The baby!

He still jolted at the very thought he was to be a father.

A father.

He looked towards the holm oaks and knew he needed to speak with his own. He turned and walked towards the lake.

Dante stood at his father's grave and truly did not know what to say.

Sorry for the scandal with your wife?

Sorry that we are having a baby?

Sorry for bringing shame to the family?

Except he wasn't entirely sorry for the scandal. Dante was well aware that he would love another repeat of the *mistake* with Mia.

And as for the baby...

No, he would not apologise for a life made.

But for bringing shame to the family he would apologise. Except even that confused him, because his father had always smiled at Dante's reckless ways and had told him to live his own life, as long as he hurt no one.

Except a relationship between him and Mia could only cause hurt all round.

So he stood, hoping for answers, or inspiration, or a feeling of forgiveness to descend, but there were only more questions.

'I thought you blew up your marriage over Mia,' Dante

said. 'I thought you were drunk on lust and had lost your mind. It would seem I was wrong and for that I am sorry.'

Dante didn't get it.

Perhaps he never would.

'Was it my mother who had an affair?' Dante asked, but of course there was only silence.

'Was Mia supposed to appear as your revenge affair?' He was met with silence again.

CHAPTER TEN

'SHOULD I TAKE lunch up to Signora Romano?' Sylvia asked, when Mia failed to put in an appearance for lunch.

'Perhaps ask Mia what she wants,' Dante said. 'After all, she is not *my* Signora Romano.' He smiled up at Sylvia who, of course, would have seen the news. And such was Dante's smile that when she tried to fire him even a slight look of reproach, she was completely disarmed and instead clipped him over the head with a far friendlier hand than Ariana's had been.

'You need ice on that cheek,' Sylvia said, for she had of course been witness to Ariana's brief visit.

She had always been far more than a housekeeper.

'Always making trouble,' she fondly scolded Dante.

Sylvia had been good to them. When his *mamma* had left for Roma on one of her many trips, Sylvia had taken over the role of *matrona* with the twins.

But then Dante found that he frowned, his good mood tainted with the impossible thought that Sylvia and his father...

No.

Instantly he dismissed that thought. Sylvia and her husband were happy, but though he dismissed it, one unsettling thought as to that scenario remained: his mother had not been happy. Even during long, endless summers, when her husband and children had been here, she would find reasons to flit back to the city…

There was more to it, Dante was sure, and today he intended to find out what had truly caused the demise of his parents' marriage. That meant he and Mia needed to talk.

'Sylvia, why don't you take the rest of the day off once lunch is done?'

'But what about dinner?'

'I'm sure we can manage. In fact, can you please tell all the staff to finish up for the day?'

Dante wanted absolute privacy; he wanted to have things out with Mia.

Lunch was a rather more casual affair when Mia finally descended than the one just before the funeral, but the table had been set up with the same exquisite care. Mia took a seat opposite Dante, her eyes drawn to the livid fingerprints on his cheek.

He looked stunning, even bruised. He wore black jeans and a thin black jumper and was unshaven, and it dawned on Mia she had never seen him in anything other than a suit. Even when he'd used to visit the hospital or drop by the house to visit his father, it had always been on his way back from or headed to work.

It felt odd to see him casually dressed, but in an unsettlingly nice way.

Why did she have to fancy him so? Why couldn't she deal with him in more familiar, practical ways?

'What did Ariana have to say?' Mia asked, as she picked at her starter.

'Nothing that needs repeating.'

'Did you apologise?'

'I never apologise for my sex life.' Dante shook his head. 'It's no big deal.'

'Well, she shouldn't have slapped you.'

'No, though I can't blame her really. She was also here to

deliver a slap from my mother. It probably was my mother who sent her or, if not, who encouraged her.' He dismissed the incident with a wave of his hand. 'I can't be bothered with their drama right now.'

'Have there been any more articles?' Mia couldn't bring herself to look and her phone was still off.

'There have been,' Dante said. 'Though they are all in the same vein.' He brought her up to speed on other things that had transpired while she'd rested. 'An extraordinary board meeting has been called for nine a.m. tomorrow. I am to explain myself, apparently.'

'What will you say?'

'I don't know,' Dante admitted. He had never before felt nervous about facing the board, but he was now—not that he would admit it. 'The photos should never have happened. I should have been more careful.' Then he added, 'Again.' He was weak where Mia was concerned, Dante realised.

Two years spent holding himself back must have worn down all his reserves because, even with the problem they faced, even with his suspicious mind, he wanted her again. But there were serious issues that needed to be faced now. 'The fact is, Mia, there is more that will soon be exposed than whatever those photos suggest.'

'I can't bear it,' Mia gulped, but then fell quiet as their plates were cleared away, only resuming when Sylvia left. 'It was bad enough being picked apart in the papers when I married your dad, but at least they were just implying I was a gold-digger. This is my very private life that's being discussed.'

Dante had to suppress a smile, deciding it would be inappropriate, but by *very private*, he assumed she meant sex. 'I think it is best you stay here for now, for a few weeks at least, and that way when word gets out, you will be shielded.'

'I'm not staying here, Dante, hiding away. My family is in England and I need to work.'

'Please.'

'Oh, that's right,' she retorted. 'I trapped you. Hooray, I never have to work again! Well, guess what, I don't want your millions. I want my privacy, and I do not want my baby's start in life to be some titillating article online. I am going to call work tomorrow and...' Her voice trailed off as Sylvia came in to serve the next course and they switched to inane chitchat.

Their main was chicken, but Mia declined, and just picked at fennel, orange and watercress salad, which, though light and refreshing, seemed at odds with the subject matter, for her own carelessness was weighing heavily on her mind.

Yes, it took two and all that, but her mistake had changed his world and when they were alone again she told him a simple truth. 'Dante, I messed up with the tablets. I'm sorry that I didn't know. And I'm sorry I'm not sophisticated enough to be on the Pill, or carry condoms, or anything like that...'

'It is me who should have taken better care.' Dante halted her. 'I apologise for that.'

They had been utterly lost in each other, Mia knew. 'I was flustered and careless, but I did take the morning-after pill, Dante.'

Was he mad to believe her?

Possibly, but for that part at least, Dante did. 'I know.' He looked at her for a long moment and then gave her a slow smile. 'The baby must really want to be here.'

'Yes,' Mia said, for she had come around to thinking the same, although it had taken her several days to do so. 'But, Dante, I can't just hide away here, waiting for word to get out. I'm supposed to be starting work tomorrow. I can't simply not show up.'

'Is the job with Castello?'

She nodded and when she did so Dante shook his head. 'Castello's a sleaze; I already told you that. He either fancied you or he gave you the job out of curiosity about me.'

'Oh, so I couldn't get it on my own merits?'

'Well, I doubt it was for your excellent Italian, given the predicament we're in. And it can't be based on your reference, because I gave you a shocking one.'

Her mouth gaped. 'You're not allowed to do that.'

Dante shrugged insolently as he held her gaze. 'I am, as long as it's accurate.'

'What did you say?' she asked.

'That you were a poor timekeeper...' He watched her fight not to smile. 'And I said you were a little slovenly in your habits...'

'You're not serious?'

'Well, you did leave your underwear on the floor of my lounge.'

He loved the way she blushed as she asked, 'What else did you say?'

'That in all fairness I could not recommend you to an old family friend.' Yet as nice as this conversation was starting to be, Dante held firm. 'You're *not* working for him Mia.'

'I'll decide that, Dante.'

She was a different Mia without his father or family here.

They were different and the closer they got the more he wanted her. But there was still so much to sort out, for though he believed her about the contraceptive mistake, Dante still felt he was being lied to.

Always.

'Mia, what were you doing, married to my father?'

The sliver of orange on her tongue felt like sand as he asked the inevitable question and she took her time to chew and then swallow as she worked out how best to answer him.

Or rather how not to answer him. 'Dante, I think we have enough to sort out with the press and my being pregnant without discussing your father.'

'There is nothing that can be sorted until I understand what you were doing with him. A torrid affair I might not like, but I could better understand it, yet you never slept together. Were you supposed to be some warped attempt to salvage his pride because my mother was sleeping with my old high school tutor?'

Mia was suddenly reminded of the hot-and-cold childhood game, and had to fight not to blink as she thought, *How warm you are, how warm you are*...as Dante inched ever closer to the truth.

'How did it start, Mia?' Dante persisted. 'How did the two of you…?'

'We met at work.'

'I meant,' Dante snapped, 'how was this sham of a marriage conceived—tell me, Mia, how does a trainee executive assistant, with only passable Italian, get the role as my father's PA, mistress, and then wife?'

He wanted his father's memory to rest, yet these questions were buzzing and swarming and he needed to hear the truth, yet Mia refused to answer him. He was getting nowhere, and Dante pushed back on his chair and stood. 'How the hell are we supposed to sort this when you can't trust me enough to be honest?'

'It's not that.'

'Then what?'

Mia pressed her fingers into her temples. She felt railroaded and unsure how to proceed. All Mia knew was that she had to work out, *carefully*, whether or not to tell Dante the whole truth.

And if she did, how to tell him?

'Mia?' Dante pushed, but when nothing more was forthcoming, exasperated, he strode off. 'I'm going out.'

'Where?'

But Dante didn't answer.

He badly needed some advice.

Dante could have walked to Roberto's; it was just a twenty-minute or so stroll to where he lived, but in case there were any dramas with the press, he took the car. Roberto had given him good advice on a couple of personal predicaments in the past.

Except it didn't look as if Roberto was home.

Remembering that Roberto had been unwell, Dante negotiated the pots of orchids on the porch to peer through a window, but found the drapes were closed.

What if he'd fallen? Dante thought. What if...? But his concern momentarily faded as Roberto came to the door.

'Dante!' Roberto greeted him. 'This is a nice surprise.'

'Hey,' Dante said. 'I thought for a moment you were out.'

'No, no, I was just having a rest.'

'How are you feeling?' Dante asked, troubled by Roberto's complexion.

'Better, though I could not have made it there last night. So, tell me, how was the ball?'

'You haven't heard?' Dante raised his eyebrows because Roberto was usually sharp and the first to know what was going on with the Romanos. 'Roberto, I need some advice.'

'Then come in.'

Dante tried not to frown as Roberto let him in, for the place wasn't in its usual neat order and neither was Roberto, who he was sure was wearing yesterday's clothes, for they were rumpled and less than fresh. The drapes were closed too and there was the smell of stale whisky on Roberto's breath, but Dante made no comment.

'We'll go through to the study...' Roberto said, and waved him through.

It was a little messy with the smell of cigarettes hanging in the air, and the study was rather dusty. 'Excuse the mess,' Roberto said. 'I haven't been in here for a while.'

'It's fine,' Dante said. 'What did the doctor say?'

'The usual.'

'Which is?' Dante pushed, troubled by his appearance.

'I am to take up a hobby.' Roberto gave a wry laugh. 'Start walking, stop smoking, cut down on whisky.'

'And are you going to take his advice?'

'I am pondering it,' Roberto sighed. 'He says it is common for a man to become depressed when he retires. Now, what can I do for you, Dante?' Roberto asked as he took a seat at his desk.

'I'm not sure,' Dante admitted. 'It's regarding Mia.'

'She's not contesting the will, is she?' Roberto frowned.

'No,' Dante said, 'There are bigger issues than that to be faced. I found out last night that Mia is pregnant.'

'No.' Roberto immediately shook his head. 'That is not possible.'

'Well, she's told me that she is.'

'Then she is a fool to play that game.' Roberto angrily thumped the desk. The usually reasonable lawyer was suddenly angry. 'Why will she not let Rafael rest? Tell her from me there will be no quick settlement. A simple DNA test—'

'No, no,' Dante interrupted, 'Roberto, you misunderstand. She is not saying the baby is my father's. The fact is... I slept with Mia.'

'You?'

'Yes.' Dante knew how it sounded, but he never played coy and certainly not with the family lawyer. 'On the night of the funeral.'

'But you used protection?' Roberto checked, confident he had, for Dante was no fool.

'No.'

'Dante!' Roberto let out a long weary breath, but then rallied.

'Then I give to you the same advice that I gave a moment ago. Until there is a report from a doctor stating that she is pregnant, we do nothing. And the same until we get the DNA result. She probably isn't pregnant and just trying for a quick settlement...'

'Mia *is* pregnant.' Dante was adamant in his defence of her.

'Well, it might not be yours. I had a client once where the woman—'

'Roberto,' Dante interrupted angrily, already sick of the inferences and hearing Roberto doubt the baby was his. 'How many times do I have to say it? Mia is pregnant and the baby is mine.'

'Calm down.' Roberto frowned, no doubt unused to seeing Dante like this.

Except Dante was not calm.

'We'll sort it.' Roberto attempted to soothe him.

But his talks of settlements and alimony did *nothing* to soothe Dante.

'Just back off,' Dante said, even though he had been the one to seek out Roberto's counsel. 'I will deal with Mia.' And he would, but for now he had other questions he had come here to ask. 'Roberto, I need to ask you something. Did my mother have an affair?'

'What's this got to do with Mia being pregnant?'

'You tell me,' Dante returned. 'I don't get how the divorce was so quick and so clean when they'd had thirty-three years together.'

'Because both sides wanted a clean break and both sets of lawyers worked hard to facilitate that.'

'But was my mother the one having the affair? Is that why it was all rushed through, in a misplaced effort to save my father's pride?'

'Leave it, Dante.'

'Why? You must have helped arrange this marriage of

convenience between my father and Mia. Was it to save face because my mother was the one who was about to leave?'

'Just leave things, Dante. Please. Let your father rest.'

'No.' Dante was as belligerent as he was frustrated and he pushed back the chair and stood. 'I want answers, and if you refuse to give them to me then I'll go elsewhere.'

'Come back here,' Roberto said, but as Dante stormed off he followed him. 'Just let things be,' he called from his door as Dante climbed into his car.

But Dante wasn't listening. He refused to let things be.

Mia wouldn't tell him, and neither would Roberto.

That only left one person.

His mother was due back from her cruise today.

Indeed, all roads led to Rome.

He would not be driving, though. Dante called Sarah, asking her to send his helicopter, right now, this minute, to return him to Rome.

'There are storms forecast,' Sarah said, though Dante didn't want to hear it. But then Dante, who had never known fear, felt its sudden arrival at speed, for as he drove, he caught a glimpse of a rider in his fields, and slowing down he saw that it was Mia, riding Massimo. Through the poppy fields she cantered and the pair of them looked stunning, the black horse gleaming against the red poppies and a thundery navy sky. But though Mia appeared to be handling him with ease, the fact was she was pregnant.

He halted the car in the middle of the road and climbed out. He could hear his heart pounding in his chest, and feel the sudden dryness of his mouth. Suddenly his fear was laced with fury.

How dared she risk it?

If she fell and the horse bolted, it would take for ever to find her, assuming she wasn't trampled.

He wanted to press on the horn, but he did not want

to startle Massimo, and anyway it appeared as if she was heading back to the stables.

Well, Dante would be there to meet her.

As Mia came into the yard she was tired in that nice physical way, but her head was no clearer and she had no idea how to deal with Dante's questions.

She felt better now, though, and Massimo had ridden like a dream. She praised him as they came into the yard. 'There's no slowing you down, is there, boy?'

She was just getting her breath back, a little elated, and looking around for the stablehand because it was awfully quiet, when she saw Dante come round the corner. She was suddenly breathless again because his face was as thunderous as the sky.

'*What* the hell are you doing?' he asked, and he took the reins.

'What does it look like?'

'Don't be facetious,' he said. 'Get down.'

Mia ignored him and cast her eyes around the yard. 'Where is everyone?'

'I have given the staff the rest of the day and night off, so we can have some decent time to ourselves.' He got back to the issue of her riding. 'What the hell were you thinking, riding Massimo?'

'Dante, I don't know what you're making such a fuss about. My mother rode until two weeks before she had me. I even checked that it was okay with the doctor...'

'You didn't check with *my* doctor,' he snarled.

'Thank goodness for choice, then.'

'Get down, Mia.'

He would not be argued with, and she had the awful feeling he was going to come and fetch her himself, so she took her right foot out of the stirrup and went to dismount. It was a manoeuvre she had made hundreds if not thousands of times, but she had never been more aware of her movements.

Dante was too.

Relief was seeping into him that she was back at the yard and safe, yet it was tempered with anger. Those thousands of questions he'd had were fading with the ache of distraction as she went to dismount.

Mia held Massimo's mane with her left hand and swung her leg over, taking the cantle of the saddle with her right. It was going to be a very long, slow slide to the ground with Dante's eyes trained on her.

Her breathing was difficult but for very different reasons now and when his hands came to her hips, instead of guiding her down, he held her there, suspended.

In fact, he took all of her weight and held her with strong hands that seemed to burn through her. It felt electric, it felt like something she had never known, and her eyes screwed closed.

He lowered her down very slowly and with such utter precision that had they not been completely dressed she might have been forgiven for imagining he was lowering her onto him. A jolt shot through her as her boots hit the stone ground, and there she remained.

His hands were still hot on her hips and pressing in and she did not know how she could go from defensive and defiant to wanting to fold over and be taken, but then slowly he turned her round.

'You are pregnant,' Dante stated, although she took it to be a question.

'Yes!'

'So there is to be no more riding.'

'You can't stop me, Dante.'

'Actually...' he smiled that black smile '... I can and I will have the horses moved this afternoon unless you give me your word that you won't ride again.'

'Very well,' Mia said. 'While I'm staying here, I shan't ride. However,' she added, 'if you question this pregnancy again, I'll walk. It took enough guts to tell you without you accusing me of making it up.'

'I did not accuse you. In fact, I can see now that there are changes.'

He could see the swell of her bust in her T-shirt, and now he held her in his hands he could feel a fleshiness to her hips. It was turning him the hell on.

She was flushed in the face and he wanted to claim that pouting mouth, to slide down the zipper of her jodhpurs and feel her heat, but there was just one thing stopping him: now, when he had her, right in his arms, with her face staring up at his, he would test her reaction and he *would* get to the truth.

And *then* he would explore those changes.

'I just came from Roberto,' Dante said.

'Did he tell you to arrange a DNA test?' She gave a mirthless laugh, while *still* wanting his kiss. 'You're all so predictable.'

'No, no,' Dante said. 'Roberto said there was no way you could be pregnant. In fact, he was most insistent.'

'Dante…' She was getting annoyed, and was about to brush off his hands but stilled when he spoke next.

'You see, he did not know then that I was telling him the baby was mine. He did not know you were just three months pregnant; he did not know anything, in fact, except he stated that the baby could not be my father's.'

'I don't see where you're going with this…' Mia swallowed, and he watched her carefully; he saw too the wary dart in those gorgeous blue eyes as she tried to come up with a response. 'Clearly Roberto knew that the marriage was…' her voice trailed off.

'Was what?' he persisted.

'For money.'

'Why, though?' Dante pushed. 'I don't doubt you were in it to make a quick buck, and I accept that my father was ill, and might have been unable…' He still could not go there either in conversation or in his head. 'But what I *don't* get is why his lawyer would know that.'

She was struggling to breathe and again she thought of that childhood game as Dante veered closer to the truth.

How hot you are, how hot you are…

He loomed over her with the sun behind him, the devil in black, but even as he neared the truth she did her best to divert him 'Perhaps Roberto had to know what might happen if I were to get pregnant. It would have been a messy estate indeed, as we both know.'

'Mia, you're lying to me,' Dante said. 'Over and over you lie to me, and you're doing it again.'

'Dante…' She loathed that she had no choice but to lie. 'I'm not.'

'Then why is your pulse racing beneath my fingers?' he said. 'Why are you trembling, Mia? And not in the way you were a few moments ago?'

'I'm not,' she said again, not knowing what to say to him.

'Will you tell me what you know?'

Mia wanted to.

Oh, how she wanted to, but promises had been made and paid for, and what she knew might well blow this family apart.

'Mia,' Dante said again, his voice low with threat, 'will you please tell me what the hell went on between you and my father?'

'No!' she said, her voice choked with the threat of sudden tears, for she did not know how she could carry this secret and forge any chance of a future with Dante at the same time.

And it was there, at that very moment, that Mia knew a future with Dante was what she wanted.

She loved him.

Not that she could tell him that, for she had to work out what to do with this wretched secret first.

But Dante's patience had long since run out. He would not be waiting for Mia to gather her thoughts, for he could hear his helicopter making its approach. 'If you won't tell me, then I shall find out for myself.' He dropped contact then, turned on his smart heels and stormed off across the yard.

'Where are you going?' she shouted.

'I don't have to tell you things either,' Dante retorted over his shoulder.

'Dante, please...' She was running after him, suddenly frantic. 'Don't leave me here...'

'Don't be ridiculous.' He shrugged her off. 'We're not joined at the hip.'

'But you don't understand,' she begged. 'I don't want to be here at night on my own.' But either Dante didn't hear her or he ignored her, for he was already gunning the car towards the helipad.

A few minutes later Dante's helicopter lifted off, and Mia was alone, with no staff, and no idea when Dante would be back.

If at all.

With rising panic, Mia dealt with Massimo and the rest of the horses, and then on legs that felt like jelly she headed back to the house, starting to run as she saw the darkening sky.

It felt as if shadows were chasing her and all bravado left when she saw that the little car belonging to Sylvia and her husband wasn't there. They must have taken the unexpected night off as a chance to go out.

She really was alone.

'Get a grip, Mia,' she told herself as she went in, flicking on lights and closing the drapes. She had to get over this fear because soon she'd be a mother; soon it would be her chasing away shadows and things, as Dante would say, that went bump in the night.

Except there was nothing soothing about Suite al Limone just before a storm. She stripped off her riding clothes and stood in the shower, willing the water to warm her, yet she felt chilled to the bone.

And as she stepped out of the shower and pulled on her robe, birds were screeching as they came home to roost and to hide from the storm. It was then that a window blew open.

It was the wind, of course it was the wind, but, instead of closing it, Mia gave in to her fear and sank to her knees.

She had never been more terrified in her life.

CHAPTER ELEVEN

DANTE ARRIVED AT his mother's apartment, this time without warning.

His pilot had skilfully dodged the storm and it was a surprisingly sunny Rome evening that Dante looked out on as a driver took him to his mother's apartment. Less of a surprise were the reporters and photographers across the street, waiting for the reappearance of the errant Romano son.

'Hey, Dante!' they called as they snapped away with their cameras. 'Where's Mia?'

'How did you get the bruise, Dante?'

But Dante turned angry eyes straight at them and the questions rapidly faded.

His mother, though, wasn't daunted by his brooding and was suitably furious! Fresh from her cruise but less than relaxed, she hurled open the door.

'Dante, how *could* you?' she shouted. 'I have the press outside, reporters calling, and you are all over the papers with *her*. She ruined my life, Dante! How the hell could you do this to me?'

Dante responded by greeting her lover. 'Signor Thomas,' he said, 'would you excuse us, please?'

Signor Thomas stood tall, but far less imposing than he had appeared to Dante a couple of decades ago, and Angela was adamant that he remain.

'He is to stay. We both want to hear how you defend your actions with the woman who wrecked my marriage.'

When she offered a rather choice word, the bear had been poked enough, and though Dante did not growl, his voice held an unmistakable threat. 'Never, and I mean *never*, speak of Mia that way again,' he warned, and then pulled his mother aside and spoke only for her ears. 'Know this: if he does stay, I shall not be moderating my questions to suit the audience.'

'David and I don't have secrets.'

'You mean he just blindly believes every word that you say?'

His mother took in a breath and, Dante noticed, was not quite so much on her high horse as she had always been before. She walked over to her lover.

'David,' she purred. 'Would you leave us, please?'

'Very well,' said Signor Thomas. 'But, Angela, please call me when you have finished speaking with Dante.' He kissed her cheek and gave her arm a squeeze and then, having nodded to Dante, walked out.

Dante waited until the door had closed, but Angela did not. 'What on earth were you doing with Mia?'

'Exactly what it looks like,' Dante said, refusing to lie. 'But I am here to ask about you and Signor Thomas. You didn't just bump into him after the divorce, did you?'

'Dante, stop.'

'No,' he said belligerently. 'I remember he was here once when I came home. He said he was dropping off school-work…' He gave a scoffing laugh. 'It was you who broke up the marriage, wasn't it?'

His mother had the look of a deer caught in the head-lights. 'Dante, let things rest.'

'Lies never rest,' Dante said. 'They wait and regroup and return. You were having an affair all along, weren't you?'

'I don't have to answer to you!'

'Then I'll draw my own conclusion. You have the audacity to judge me, to judge Mia, to drag Ariana into your hate fest of negativity, when all along *you* were the one having the affair.'

'Your father and I came to an arrangement a long time ago,' Angela said.

'Why involve Mia?' Dante shot out, because he still didn't get it.

'Our marriage was over long before Mia.'

'Did you ever love him?'

'Dante, please…'

'Do you even miss him, or was it all just an act?' He looked at his mother, tanned from her cruise, dressed in the latest fashions with made-up eyes, and then he thought of Mia, who had admitted the marriage had been for money and been hot in his arms, and everywhere he looked his father's memory felt besmirched. 'The only one who actually misses the guy is…' Dante halted.

An impossible thought had occurred in a mind going at a million miles an hour as he thought of the endless orchid pots on Roberto's porch and the sweet scent of the arrangement at the hospital…

Mia, shaking and close to fainting, as she threw an orchid into his grave.

The family lawyer by his father's bedside when he passed, as his new wife walked in the hospital grounds.

And Roberto, who had not missed a Romano ball since its inception, too ill that year to attend.

Depressed, the doctor had said.

Or had he been grief-stricken?

A million tiny pieces flew together and made a star then exploded again as the revelation hit. He thought of Roberto's whisky breath and his sudden frailty, he thought of the tears in his eyes and the unkempt home.

Roberto was the only one grieving as a lover surely would.

Just when he'd thought his father could no longer surprise him, well, it would seem Rafael still could...

'My father was gay, wasn't he?'

Silence was his answer.

'Wasn't he?' Dante persisted.

'He was my Rock Hudson, Dante.' Angela started to cry and finally he had his confirmation.

His head was reeling, but there was also a certain calm, for all his life he had felt he'd been lied to.

And as it turned out, he'd been right.

'Why couldn't he tell me?' It was the question that first came to mind.

'Dante?' His mother helplessly shrugged.

'Why couldn't he tell me?' Dante rasped. 'I thought we were close...'

'You were.'

'Then why?'

'Because I begged him not to. I didn't want anyone to know that our marriage was all a charade and that Rafael could only ever try to love me.'

'Is he even my father?' Dante asked, while knowing it was the most ridiculous question, for they'd had the same build, the same eyes, the same dark humour.

'Of course he's your father. Dante, I am not going to take you into our marriage—'

'Well, I'm very sorry to tell you,' Dante said, cutting her off, 'but I think you have to, because Stefano and Ariana will have the same questions as me.'

'They must never know.'

'Of course they have to know. When did you find out?'

'He told me...' Angela said, and she sat down on the edge of a plump sofa, clearly shaken.

'Tell me,' Dante implored, for he needed the truth.

She pointed to the decanter. He poured her a brandy and he watched as she took a sip and composed herself for a moment. 'Please,' Dante said, and finally she nodded.

'The Romano brothers were the ones all the women wanted,' Angela started in a shaken voice, but then she gave a bitter laugh. 'I was thrilled when my mother said Rafael was to marry me. The Romano brothers were so handsome and everyone knew they were going places. His father, your nonno, felt that Rafael needed a wife. And we were okay at first—well, sort of—but I had nothing with which to compare...'

Dante joined her on the sofa, knowing this was difficult for her, and he took his mother's hand.

'I remember having coffee and biscotti with my friend and she said you have to do it at least once a week to keep a husband happy. I was lost as to what to say. We barely...' Angela swallowed. 'I did get pregnant with you, Dante, but that was it. I was too naïve to even have my suspicions; I was just angry and cross and felt unwanted. We would fight a lot, but then when you were five I screamed at your father that I wanted more babies and finally he told me why he could not give them to me.'

Dante was aching and hurting for his parents and all they had dealt with, yet still curious to know more. 'What did you say to him?'

'Many things...things that I shall regret for ever. But then anger left and we sat at the table. He cried and cried, because in every other way I think your father did love me, at least back then.'

'Why did you stay?'

'What choice did I have? I could not divorce him. Could you imagine our families? We were married with a child. Somehow we had to make it work. And so we talked, and we talked, and we agreed to try IVF. We bought an apartment here and I would stay in Rome for my treatments. I suppose we were happy then, Dante. I got pregnant with the twins and the business took off even more. I would come to Rome at weekends to see my son. I would watch your sport, and I met David.'

'Does he know about my father?'

'Yes,' Angela said. 'I told you, we have no secrets. Dante, I had a life here. I buried myself in my children, in charities, in functions. Your father was happier too, and no more so than when he met Roberto…'

'How long were they together?'

'Fifteen years. More than most marriages, and they would have been together for many more had your father not got ill, although the truth was starting to come out.'

'How?'

'The press has always had an interest in the Romanos, as you well know.' She gave a tired shake of her head. 'A couple of years ago, there were some rumours. Your father and Roberto had been seen in a restaurant in Florence and also dining at La Fiordelise a couple of times. I couldn't bear it, Dante. I told him to stop the rumours in their tracks. As well as that, David told me he could no longer stay on the sidelines; he wanted marriage too…'

Dante frowned as his mother continued.

'My children were grown and I decided it was time for me, so I told your father I wanted a divorce. I asked him to lie one more time for me, to take the blame, but in a more familiar way…'

'An affair with his PA?'

She nodded. 'I did not know, because he kept so much from me, that at the time your father was undergoing tests. He had found out he was dying. Had I waited, we could have avoided so much humiliation with the divorce, so much drama—' She stopped herself from what she was about to say, but it was the same words that had been said on the day Rafael had died.

And Dante could well guess what she meant. 'Had you waited, you would have been his widow?'

He thought of his mother fighting to still be allowed to attend the ball, of her asking the judge to be allowed to still keep the Romano name.

At the time he had thought it was because she'd wanted the same name as her children, but he had never dwelled on it.

'I don't doubt that it was hell for you and my father, and that you had many reasons to stay and for the marriage to appear to work. But those reasons surely ended close to a decade ago…'

'The arrangement worked,' Angela maintained. 'Until David insisted on marriage and brought things to a head.'

'Yet you and Signor Thomas still haven't married,' Dante pointed out, and watched as his mother pressed her lips together, possibly glad now her son had suggested that David leave as he made a very pertinent point. 'The fact is that you love being a Romano and you didn't want it to end.'

'I earned that name!' Angela snarled.

And all the trappings and kudos that came with it, he reflected. Oh, his father might not have loved her in the traditional sense but he had assured Angela an extremely prominent and privileged life.

Dante had always thought it would be Mia clinging to every contested detail of the divorce settlement, but he could see now that it was more likely that it had been his mother. He had often wondered if guilt had made his father so generous; now he was sure that was the case. And he wondered too how life might have been if his mother had been prepared to break the status quo once her children were grown, end the marriage, and let his father live his true life.

While he doubted he would ever get those answers from

his mother, who loved to put herself in a flattering light, there was one more thing he badly needed to know. 'How did he get Mia to agree?'

'Money,' Angela said, as if the answer was an obvious one, and Dante's jaw tightened. He loved his mother, but she had an arrogant air to her. He did not like that part of her, and he saw it far more clearly at this moment.

'How did he get her to agree?'

'She was desperate,' Angela said. 'About to lose her job, but you know your father, he would always fall for a sob story...'

'Stop!' Dante said. 'Stop being so cruel when you speak about her. I mean it. I will call you out on it every time. I don't give a damn if my father was gay, and I don't care if you slept with every tutor in my school, but I will not let you speak about her like that again in my presence. You might feel that disparaging her is part of the act, but to me that was unnecessary and cruel...' He took a breath to calm himself for there was more he needed to know. 'And what do you mean, a sob story?' It was just so unlike the Mia he knew.

'She told him how her parents had just been killed...' Dante frowned. From the way Mia had carried herself, as awful as it was, he had assumed it had happened years ago, but his curiosity turned to horror as his mother spoke on. 'She told him that her brother had spinal injuries and had had no travel insurance...'

'Her brother has spinal injuries?'

'Yes, she had just got him back to the UK from the States. Your father said he would speak to her manager and say that she should keep her job, but Mia admitted she could not do it any more. She could not hold down a job. She was having nightmares after being trapped in the car with their bodies...'

Dante went cold. 'Mia was in the accident that killed

her parents?' The mere glimpse Mia had been trapped in a car with her family appalled him.

He thought of her standing in the yard, pleading with him not to leave her alone, and it made him glance out to the black night sky. He stood abruptly.

'Where are you going?' Angela asked.

'To Luctano,' Dante said. 'To Mia.'

CHAPTER TWELVE

IT WAS A hellish flight back to Luctano and though the pilot dodged the storm cells it was very turbulent.

But it was not the rain or the heavy clouds that had his stomach lurching, it was his own self-castigation. His own impatience and assumptions. He had assumed her brother had not come to the funeral because Mia had secrets she didn't want shared. Just as he had decided her marriage to his father had been for selfish gain.

Mia was right, Dante realised. He did not know her.

But he wanted to.

He did not really know the depth of his feelings for her, just that he had to get back to Luctano and make sure she was okay.

The rain was torrential and falling sideways as he dashed from the chopper to the house and he ran through it, calling out her name.

'Mia!'

There was no sign of her, except that all the lights were on, and he marched up the stairs. 'Mia.' He came to her bedroom door and knocked loudly. 'It's me, Dante. Can I come in?'

'Give me a moment…' came her hoarse reply, but Dante did not have a moment in him left to give and opened the door to the Suite al Limone, and what he saw hollowed him.

Mia, always in control, always so together and composed, was sitting on the floor, bedraggled and wet in her coral robe and hugging her knees, her face bleached white as she looked up at him. A drape was billowing and there were tears streaming from her eyes as she shouted at him to get out. Dante knew this was a private side to Mia that she would prefer no one saw, yet as he witnessed pure terror, he wanted no secrets between them.

Secrets had caused enough damage; secrets were what had brought them to this point.

'God, Mia.' He was appalled at what he had done. 'I'm sorry.'

'Get out,' she screeched.

But Dante refused to leave her. 'It's okay, Mia.'

'It's not okay,' she shouted, and yelled accusingly, 'You left me here and you sent away all the staff...' Her voice was rising, the terrible panic that had floored her when she'd stepped out of the shower was now tinged with relief that he was back, but also loaded with anger. 'How could you leave me here?' she shouted. 'How dared you bring me here just to leave me alone?'

Finally she felt it was safe to be angry.

Dante was across the room in seconds, stunned and horrified to see the pent-up woman finally unleash.

She was ranting about ghosts, about graves, about her brother, and the bastard who had brought her to a house where she didn't want to be, and had then left her all alone.

Dante crouched on the floor and he took her damp, shaking body in his arms. 'You're okay now, you are safe,' he told her over and over.

'But I'm not.'

'You are.' And he sounded so convincing that she almost believed him.

'I'm going mad,' she told him. 'How can I be a mother when I'm like this?'

'You'll be the best mother in the world,' he told her.

Which only made her cry.

'Mia, I'm so sorry.'

'I'm terrified of ghosts…'

'There are no ghosts,' Dante said.

'But there are.'

'There are no ghosts,' he insisted, and even tried a joke to haul her out of her fear. 'It's just the skeletons in my family closet that are rattling.' But that only made her cry all the more. But her tears didn't daunt Dante; in fact, there was an odd relief to meet the real Mia after all this time. 'There's no such thing as ghosts.'

'My mother spoke to me, though.'

To hear this very private woman admit to something so bizarre deserved more than cold common sense and a quick dismissal.

'Come,' he said, and helped her to stand, not knowing quite what to do with her when she was so upset. He did what he could and helped Mia over to the bed. 'Have some water.'

'You don't believe me.'

'I didn't say that,' Dante said, as he helped her into bed. 'I'm not getting in,' he said, and lay on top of the bed and pulled her into him. 'I know about the accident and your brother,' Dante admitted. 'I just found out and I am so very sorry. Now tell me about your mother. Is she talking to you now?'

'I'm not hearing voices, Dante.'

'Good,' he said. 'So tell me.'

'I don't know how.'

'Just say what happened, whatever way you can.'

It all came out then, in a back-to-front way—being trapped with her parents and her injured brother—and Dante listened, aghast at what she had been through. He held her and could feel the frantic hammering of her heart, close to the beat of his own.

'I told my father not to drive. I mean, what was he thinking, driving in a city on the other side of the road?'

'People do it all the time,' Dante said.

'And why the hell didn't Michael get travel insurance? How could he be so damned selfish and reckless?'

'It was a mistake,' Dante said, 'with appalling consequences. Perhaps go easy on him. I am sure he is beating himself up enough without—'

'I could never say all this to him.' Mia almost sat up in an effort to explain, but Dante pulled her back down. 'I'm only saying it to you!'

'Keep going, then,' Dante said. Finally he understood her better; understood that the anger she'd felt had had nowhere to go, for her parents were dead and her brother needed her support, despite her own devastation at the consequences of his one simple mistake.

'When I came to, I knew straight away that things were bad. I thought I was the only person to have made it, but then I heard my mother speak. She said to hold on, that the ambulance would be on its way, that help would arrive and that she loved me. I heard her, Dante.'

'Okay.'

'But when the report came back it said that she'd been killed instantly. Yet I *heard* her speaking to me.'

'Okay,' Dante said, and he thought for a long moment. 'What if it wasn't as instant as they said in the report? I mean, I appreciate science and everything, but they weren't actually there.'

He made her smile just a little. With his arms around her, and his arrogant authority, Dante made her smile about a subject she had never thought she would smile about.

And though he believed his own theory he gave it more thought. 'What if she used her dying breaths to speak to you?'

'Perhaps.' Mia *had* thought of that, but she liked hearing it from him.

'Or what if you were semi-conscious and imagined what you most needed to hear?'

'I don't think so.' She shook her head and then sighed as she conceded, 'But…it's possible.'

'Or,' Dante said—and he put logic aside for Mia—'what if there is *something* that we cannot explain, and she somehow managed to be with you for a little while, even if she was gone?'

She looked up. 'Like her spirit?'

'I guess.' Dante looked down and smiled. 'And, even if—and I am suspending my beliefs here—but even if there are ghosts, surely she wouldn't want to hurt you?'

'No.'

She felt calmer for finally sharing with someone the hell of what had happened.

With him.

'Did my father know all this?' Dante asked.

'Some,' Mia said. 'Most of it, though not the ghost part, but he knew about Michael's injuries and the bills for treatment and how we lost everything getting him home.'

No wonder he had been haemorrhaging money on her, Dante thought, angry with himself again at his own assumptions.

'I wish you could have told me this.'

'You don't think I'm mad?'

'A little bit mad,' Dante said, and he gave her that smile that chased cares away, at least for a little while. 'Mia, you and my father—'

'Please, Dante.' She cut him off. There was more to be said, Mia knew that, though she could not face it now. 'No more questions. At least not tonight. I know we have to speak, I'm just too tired now…' She felt so depleted, yet so oddly calm in his arms, that she could not bear to break the gentle peace.

'No more questions,' Dante agreed, and he lay on the bed with her in his arms. He'd never thought he could be pleased that Mia had been married to his father but, yes, Dante was glad that his father had been able to help when she had needed it so badly. And he was glad, too, that she'd had the benefits of this gorgeous house, and Sylvia, and the horses and things as she'd recovered from a most terrible experience. 'You can ride Massimo,' Dante suddenly said. 'If the doctor says that you can and it helps you relax.'

She laughed at his huge concession. She looked up from his chest into dark eyes and then blushed, though not in the way she usually tended to when she looked into his eyes. 'I'm embarrassed you saw me like that,' Mia admitted.

'Don't be. I'm glad you finally told me what has been scaring you.'

'Really?'

He nodded and then came the balmy comfort of his mouth slow and soft on hers. His clothes were damp from the rain. It was the first time she'd noticed, but as he pulled her into him, she felt that he was damp, and his hair in her hands was wet too.

But it was his mouth, his mouth that brought both comfort and need, and the scratch of his jaw a sublime tiny hurt that chased bigger hurts away.

Until he halted them and moved his face back from hers.

'Don't stop.'

'I am stopping,' Dante said. 'I am not going to be accused of taking advantage...'

'You're not,' Mia grumbled, moving back in for a kiss, but Dante peeled her from him. 'No, I don't want you regretting me in the morning. We still have a lot to sort out and you might not want me any more when you hear what I have to say.'

'What?'

'I'm going to be in the baby's life, Mia. I loved my father very much, but really I only saw him in the summer. I don't want that with my child.'

Mia might not want questions but she had plenty for him. 'So what do we do?'

'What about you stay here?' Dante said. 'You were happy here. Of course I would have to sort out...' He nodded his head towards the window.

'You can't exhume him!' she said in horror.

'No, but I'd think of something and you'd have a nanny and things.'

'Where would you live?'

'Rome,' Dante said, as if it was obvious.

And to Dante it was. 'Half an hour away in the helicopter, so we wouldn't get under each other's feet.'

He offered a very practical, very good solution, but he broke her heart with his absolute refusal to consider the possibility of them.

'Under your feet?'

'Yes.' He was unapologetic. 'I'm not relationship material, Mia. Surely to God you know that about me?'

'I do.'

'So, just think about living here,' Dante said, 'but not now. You need to get some sleep.'

And even with her breaking heart, he could still make her laugh as he checked behind the drapes. 'Nothing hiding there,' he said, and he even checked the dressing room. 'No monsters there...'

'Stop it,' she said. She lay there in bed, thinking how honest and how wretched he was, to simply dismiss any possibility of them out of hand. And also just how gorgeous he was, and how he could make her smile, and just how much better things were when he was near. He was kind, but so cruel too, because he tucked the bedding in around her and was a complete gentleman when she didn't want him to be.

'Goodnight,' he said, but as he opened the door to step out, he added, 'And for the record, Mia, if there was a ghost, I really don't think my father would be rattling around this house. I rather think he'd be over at Roberto's.'

Mia startled. 'You know?'

'I do.' Dante smiled.

'How do you feel about it?' Mia asked,

'We'll talk in the morning. You're too tired now, but if you need anything...'

'Dante—' Except she was speaking to a closed door.

Mia kicked her heels on the bed in frustration and lay there scarcely able to believe not only that he knew about his father but that he was smiling, *and* that he would leave her hanging. But then she started to smile as she realised Dante was giving her a choice.

He always had.

From their first night together, not once had he pushed her, or tried to persuade her.

It was sex, Mia reminded herself.

Nothing more than that to Dante.

Yet he could be hers tonight, if she so chose.

And she so chose!

Mia pulled back the covers and rather gingerly climbed out of bed, because she loathed the house at night, but when she opened the bedroom door she had to smile, because Dante had left the lights on for her.

And there was a shoe at the bottom of the stairs.

A sock too.

Then a shirt.

There was a treasure trail, which she guessed would lead her to his door. She was glad of it, for Mia had never so much as been up these stairs before. There were his trousers halfway down an elegantly lit hallway, and she made her way down it, a little nervous, a little scared, a little cold, but desire propelled her. It was Dante she could accuse of being slovenly now for his black silk boxers were on the floor, leaving no doubt he was naked on the other side.

Pushing open the door, she was met by Dante's smile in the softly lit room as he pulled back the sheet. She ran the last steps to his bed and climbed into his warm, waiting arms.

'You know?' she said, continuing their conversation.

'I do, and I don't care about all that now. Come here,' Dante said, and pulled her not into his arms but up onto his stomach. 'I only care to see the changes in you.'

He slipped her robe off but she fought to retrieve it as she felt very naked and very aware of his stomach on her sex. 'Dante...'

'What?' he asked. 'Are you going to play shy?'

'I am shy.'

'Not with me you're not.'

It was true. With Dante she felt less shy.

'Can I ask you something?' Dante said, as he held her hips. 'And you don't have to answer, only tell me what you want me to know. When you said you'd never known such feelings...' He felt her blush all over, even her thighs on his waist burnt with embarrassment. 'Never?'

She nodded.

'How?' Dante asked, as if life without sex was an impossible feat.

'Just...' she shrugged '...no interest.'

'None?'

'No.'

'So what about that look you gave me the day we met? That come-to-bed look, that get-down-on-your-knees look.'

'I would never do that.'

'Okay. What else won't you do?'

She told him and Dante listened with great interest. 'You have a very long not-to-do list.'

'Yes.'

'So you don't ever want to taste me?'

Mia couldn't believe she was discussing things she had always considered filthy, and, what's more, she couldn't believe that the thought turned her on. 'Maybe that one I do want to try. Look, I don't expect you to get it. You're mad for all of it.'

'I used to be,' Dante said, 'until an uptight girl came along and there's been no one else since then. Waste of a condom last night, wasn't it?'

'You're wicked.' Mia smiled, trying not to show her deep thrill that there had been no one else, but Dante was examining those changes to her body now.

With one finger, he stroked her breast and his light touch had her clench in a heady mixture of frustration and pleasure. Then he upped the pressure and rolled her nipple between his finger and thumb and then with his warm palm he caressed her so softly that she leant into his hand for more.

His hand moved to the back of her head and he pulled her forward. Mia closed her eyes as his tongue flicked her swollen nipple then tasted her slowly and deeply, sucking on her and edging her towards desperation.

'It's going to be okay,' he said, and ran a light hand over her stomach. 'I'll sort this for both of you.'

She gave a slight mirthless laugh because, whatever way Mia looked, there was going to be hell to pay.

'I will. I'll build a canopy over the residence and hide you both away,' Dante said, while knowing that hiding was not the answer. 'Come with me tomorrow.'

Mia tensed. 'I can't face the board.'

'No,' Dante said, and just as she breathed again, he ran a hand over her gold curls and slipped his fingers inside. There was no clamp of her thighs now as she let him explore her.

He stroked her so lightly that it made her quiver and then he amended his request.

'You don't have to face the board, just come with me to Rome.' He knew the press would be outside his apartment. 'I'll book us into La Fiordelise.'

'Adjoining suites?'

'If that's what you want.' Dante said.

'Dante.' She just wanted to focus on the bliss his fingers gave, and she answered through gritted teeth. 'We'd have to drive.'

'Fine,' Dante said, not caring if it meant a five a.m. start.

His fingers were more probing and so insistent now that they brought her up on her knees. 'Dante...' she said, because she was coming undone and he had to stop with the questions, yet he didn't.

'You'll come to Rome?'

'Yes!' She shouted it, scarcely able to believe he could carry on a conversation when his fingers were doing unimaginable things and she was rocking on his hand, just coming to his skilful command. 'Oh, God,' she shouted as he removed the pleasure of his hand and left her frantic and pulsing in the air, but then he took her hips and groaned as he slipped inside her orgasm and delicious tension encased his length.

She rested her hands on his chest as Dante moved her at his whim. It was the most delicious feeling, to feel all giddy and sated while she moved to his tempo. Dante thrust up into her as she screwed her eyes closed.

'Open them,' he told her.

She ignored him.

'Open them,' he demanded, and she looked down at the two of them, to see Dante sliding into her. To both see and feel the passion was dizzying, and it was then that

Mia found her own rhythm and it wound her tighter, ever tighter. But it was the sudden tight grip of his hands and the digging in of his fingers that held her still as Dante started to come, and it toppled her so that she felt as if she was spinning undone as she gave in to the deepest orgasm she had known.

Mia collapsed onto his body, which wanted her, and lay listening to the thud, thud, thud of his heart that didn't. At moments like this, she told herself she didn't care.

Even when she rolled off and they lay both on their stomachs with their heads turned to face each other, all she felt was calm.

So calm that even the hoot of an owl outside didn't startle her as it usually would.

Instead she looked right into his eyes as she spoke, 'I'm really not sure about going to Rome.'

He stared back at her. 'If my father's secret has taught me anything, it is not to hide.'

'That's all very well,' Mia replied, still calm, 'but I won't be paraded by you for a few weeks, until you relegate me to an ex who happens to have had your baby.'

'Fine.'

'So, what is the point of me going with you to Rome?'

It was Dante who blinked. He'd been about to point out that he still didn't know what to say to the board, though the truth was he was very used to winging it. The deeper truth was that tomorrow would be made easier by knowing she was close—not that he told her that. Instead he trotted out his usual line when a woman tried to get too close. 'You're growing more demanding, Mia.'

And still Mia did not react. 'Yes,' she replied, for she would not be his plaything until he grew bored. There was something about Dante that imbued her with confidence and in this little post-coital haze she gave him a slow smile. 'I *am* growing more demanding.'

'You want me to marry you for the sake of the baby, don't you?'

'No.'

'Good, because that is the most ridiculous reason on earth.'

It was now that she turned away, but still he wrapped her in his arms.

Dammit, how could he could be so nice, even while he was breaking her heart?

Married to Dante for the sake of a baby, that was the last thing she wanted to be.

Mia wanted the impossible.

But it was something Dante considered a pointless burden and something he didn't believe in.

Love.

CHAPTER THIRTEEN

Mia did not want to go to Rome!

There was too much music to be faced there and the more she thought about it, the more she felt offended that he didn't so much as consider bringing her to his home!

'Are you sure that I agreed to this?' she grumbled as they headed to the car, with sunrise still almost an hour away.

'Very sure.'

Dante was in jeans and she was in capri pants but she had a dress freshly pressed, thanks to Sylvia, in a suit carrier, and would change at a breakfast stop outside Rome.

And though Mia would dearly love to doze her way there, it would seem that the driver wanted conversation.

'What do you want me to tell them about us, Mia?' Dante asked as they passed the poppy fields.

'Deny, deny, deny.'

'Lie, lie, lie, you mean,' Dante said. 'I'm not going to do that.'

'Then say nothing.'

'That's what you want?' Dante checked. 'Because that I can easily do. I'm more than happy to tell them it's none of their business. I don't need the board's approval.'

'They're your family, though.'

Dante sighed.

Didn't he just know it.

'I should never have agreed to work with family. I knew

it was a mistake to take it on. Hell, if Luigi hadn't been my uncle when I found him gambling profits away I'd have fired him on the spot.' He told her about his uncle's penchant for casinos. 'And bloody Ariana does nothing other than spend, spend, spend...' He ticked them all off one by one, the work-shy cousins, the aunt who spent more time drinking the wine than selling it, the scandals and hidden affairs that further served to prove his point: marriage was completely pointless. 'Yet, because I don't hide my behaviour, they think it gives them licence to judge...'

'Did your father?'

'No.' Dante gave a soft, regretful laugh, missing him. 'He always had my back. I thought he knew I would always have his.'

'He did know that.'

'Then why couldn't he tell me he was gay?'

Finding Mia so upset last night had blown the question straight out of his head. Then the bliss of sex had again chased it away, but he had lain the rest of the night, asking and asking himself why his father hadn't told him.

'I think he wanted to, Dante. In fact, I'm quite sure if he hadn't become ill, he'd been about to come out, despite—' She stopped herself.

Dante, though, finished what she'd been about to say. 'Despite my mother's wishes.'

Mia said nothing, blood being thicker than water and all that.

'Mia,' Dante said, in a rare admission, 'I need your take on this.'

'Yes,' Mia reluctantly said. 'I think he would have come out, despite your mother's wishes, though we're not all like you, Dante. We don't all just shrug and carry on when our sex life gets hauled before an extraordinary general meeting.'

'I guess.'

They spoke some more about his father and Roberto as they left Luctano far behind.

'Was the orchid from him?' Dante asked.

'Yes, I collected it from Roberto on my ride that morning.'

'Poor Roberto,' Dante said.

'Yes,' Mia agreed, 'but as I said to him, he got to spend fifteen years with the love of his life and there's nothing poor about that.'

They chatted some more about his father and Roberto but inevitably the conversation turned back to them and the situation that Mia could not face. She didn't want the slurs in the papers to be read by their child, and how Dante dealt with today would greatly affect that.

'Dante, what are we going to do? If they find out about the baby the papers are going to be merciless.'

'I don't care.'

'Well, I do. I hate how they keep saying that I'm your step—'

She could not even say it.

'You know,' Dante said, 'I am quite sure you could get your marriage annulled.' It was one of the many possibilities he was considering. An annulment would void the marriage and tell the world that it had all been a sham so that Mia would no longer be his stepmother.

'I probably could,' Mia agreed. 'But I would never do that to your father and neither would you.'

'No,' Dante said. 'It was just a thought.'

'I think I should go back to London, and just lie low until it all dies down.'

'You want to live in London?'

'My family are in London.'

'What about my family?' Dante asked. 'Because that is what my child will be. What? Do I have to fly to see him?'

'It might be a her.'

'Well, if it is, I am not living with an ocean keeping me from my daughter! And what about us?'

'What *about* us?' And her foolish heart leapt in hope that he was actually considering them but, of course, this was Dante.

'Well, are we still going to sleep together?'

'What the hell?'

'I'm serious. Sex is important.'

'An actual date might be nice.'

'It might,' Dante agreed, 'except you don't want us to be seen together. So, what, do we come together now and then in our decadent palace?'

'Heaven forbid that you invite me to your home.'

'Ah, so that is what the sulking is about,' Dante said. 'Mia, the press will be outside, and...' he told the truth, though he at least tried to lighten it '... I don't like to bring women back home. I prefer hotels. It's better for Alfonzo...'

'Alfonzo? It's better for the dog if he doesn't meet the women you sleep with?' Her incredulity was topped only by how much she hated his lack of commitment, because it was his commitment she craved.

'We'll go to my home if you really want to, but don't blame me if we're photographed again.'

'No, we'll go to the hotel.'

As the sun rose, of course his phone went off.

'*Pronto!*'

It was Sarah, and he told her he'd be there by nine and that she didn't have to worry about feeding Alfonzo. When he rang off he turned to Mia. 'I'll feed him after I drop you at the hotel.'

God, she was even jealous of his dog!

And then, because it was Dante's phone, the second he ended the call it lit up again.

'*Pronto!*'

It was his mother. Mia struggled to keep up with Angela's

very emotional, very rapid words, but it would seem she wanted to tell Stefano and Ariana before he faced the board.

Mia frowned, and had to sit on her hands when Dante suggested they all meet at Romano Holdings at eight.

There wasn't time.

'There isn't time,' Mia said, because the traffic was already growing. 'You've got to get me to La Fiordelise, and feed Alfonzo. We're already pushing things.'

'Can't you just wait in my office? There's a private entrance to the car park.'

'No!' Mia was adamant, but then checked herself, not wanting to make this harder on him. After all, it was a big thing that Angela was about to be honest with the twins. 'Fine, but as long as I don't have to see any of your family or colleagues, and *then* we go straight to La Fiordelise.'

'Fine,' Dante bit back.

He *loathed* her shame.

As they arrived at the headquarters of Romano Holdings in EUR District they were both simmering with rancour as they slipped into the private entrance. Mia had on dark glasses and carried the suit carrier, more to shield herself, as they took the back stairwell up to the first floor in order to avoid the lobby. But finally, just before eight, she sat in Dante's office.

She sat on a low sofa as Dante dropped his clothes without thought, opened up a panel and produced a shirt. 'Choose a tie for me,' he said, as he dashed into the shower.

What, was she his wardrobe assistant now?

She was rattled and unsettled at being back here. Though they had used the side entrance, she had seen the pack of press outside the main one, and she was nervous too that his family were here.

She chose a gorgeous aqua tie, but as Dante dressed hurriedly, he rolled his eyes at her selection and produced a grey one instead. 'I'm not going to a wedding.'

'I know you're not,' Mia said, 'because you haven't shaved.'

And despite their filthy moods they shared a smile.

'I'd better go up.' He was to meet his family in what had been Rafael's private suite on the top floor. 'You'll be okay?' he checked, and gave her a quick kiss. 'There's the kitchenette...'

'I do know,' Mia said. After all she had worked here, albeit briefly, but her sniping at being back here stopped when she saw his tense features. 'Good luck with your family.'

'Thanks,' Dante said.

'Will you come and tell me how it went before you go to the board meeting?'

'I'll try,' Dante said, and then rolled his eyes, not so much at her, more at the grim morning he faced.

Mia showered and she rolled her eyes when she realised the dress and shoes were the ones she had worn the very first day she had met Dante.

She should have run a mile! Mia told herself, but knew that she lied.

Was it worth it? She asked Dante's question.

Yes, because she loved him.

It was a relief to stand there in the still silence of his office and admit it out loud.

'I love him.'

But she learnt something else as she started his Newton's cradle and watched the balls go clack, clack, clack: love made you brave.

She would not be his casual lover, neither would she be seen on his arm until he grew tired and moved on to the next woman.

Dante Romano had better raise his game.

Love was love.

It hadn't ended because Rafael had died.

If anything, it made it more precious, and Dante watched as his siblings choked out the same regret he held.

'Why couldn't he tell us?'

And love was love, because although he was angry at his mother, Dante chose not to judge or reveal her part in all this. Instead he borrowed Mia's words. 'Perhaps he didn't want his sex life brought up in a meeting.'

'But why go through all that with Mia?' Ariana asked.

'He was dying,' Dante said. 'Mia gave him a chance to hide in the hills and live out his life in some peace.' And he would be grateful for that for ever.

Ariana's heart was torn and she was angry at her mother too, aghast that the perfect image that her family had portrayed had now collapsed like a house of cards.

'So Stefano and I were just produced to keep up the charade...'

'Ariana.' Dante stepped in when again his mother could not respond. 'It wasn't like that. They were different times, and they did the best they could.'

'By lying to us?' She turned accusing eyes on her mother.

Ariana was not, Dante knew, upset about her father being gay. She was upset about the nest of lies and her own part in things, for she turned on her mother. 'You told me how to behave, and I did it. You told me to hate Mia and so I did.' Ariana started to cry. 'You told me we were a happy family until *she* came along...'

'Ariana,' Dante said. 'It is a shock, I know, but now we know the truth we can start over again.'

But it was going to take more than a few words of comfort, Dante knew. Ariana's world had been built on lies, and she was rocked to her very core.

'What about Roberto?' Stefano asked. 'Is that why he was too ill to attend the ball?'

'I believe so.' Dante nodded. 'There is something I want

to run by you.' He didn't have to, given that the Romano residence was legally his, but it was something else he had spoken about with Mia on the drive here. Dante wanted to things put right, hopefully with his family's support. 'I would like the Romano residence to go to Roberto,' Dante said. 'He loves the vines, the stables. Really it was their home. They were together for fifteen years.'

'Yes,' Ariana said after a moment's thought. 'He should have it.'

'I agree.' Stefano nodded.

'But he left it to you,' Angela fretted. 'It's worth a fortune...'

'Not everything is about money,' Dante said, and tried to keep the bitter note from his voice when he spoke to his mother. 'It's about the home going to its rightful owner.'

And, after a long, silent moment Angela nodded. 'Yes...' She cleared her throat before going on. 'I want to apologise to all of you for my behaviour throughout the divorce.' She looked over at Dante. 'And I would like to apologise to Mia too.'

Dante nodded. 'Thank you. I am sure Mia will appreciate it.'

'So do I,' Ariana said, and her eyes filled again with tears.

'Come on,' Dante said as he glanced at the time and saw that soon the meeting was to commence. 'Let's get it over with.' But as they headed out Dante remembered he'd said he'd try to drop in on Mia. 'Tell them I'll be there in a short while. Mamma, do you want to be invited into the meeting as an observer?'

'You're not going to tell them about your father?' Angela asked anxiously. 'I don't think he would want that.'

'Of course not,' Dante said.

'So how are you going to explain the photos?'

'Go,' Dante said without answering, 'I'll be there soon.'

The truth was he still had no idea.

He was worried about Ariana, though not just because of today. He saw clearly now his mother's manipulation of her, and knew Ariana faced it most days. As well as that, with Stefano and Eloa soon to marry, he was sure Ariana felt shut out, and she didn't have the diversion of work to distract her.

But there was far more than Ariana on his mind today.

Mia would bear the brunt of the fallout from the photos so he took the lift down and headed for his office rather than the boardroom.

There was so much riding on this meeting. He'd never given a damn what the press said about him, but Mia did, and she was worried too about the effect the salacious head-lines might have on their baby in later years.

There was a lot to get right.

As he walked into his office, there stood a sight for sore eyes.

Mia, in stilettos and wearing the gorgeous lavender dress she'd had on the day they had met and with her hair worn back from her face.

'Who are you?' Dante said, just as he had on that long-ago day.

'A different person from the one I was then.' Mia smiled. 'How did they take it?'

'Fine.' Dante gave a tight shrug. 'Sort of. Ariana is upset with my mother.'

'It will take time,' Mia said.

'Yes.'

'Say whatever you have to to the board,' Mia said bravely. 'I'll be fine with it.'

'You're sure?' Dante checked.

Mia nodded. 'You're right. It is foolish to try and hide it when I'll soon start to show. We are where we are.'

'You sound like one of Luigi's presentations.' Dante found that he was smiling.

He looked at her sapphire-blue eyes and saw her cheeks flush pink as they had on the day they'd first met.

'I wish we could go back to that day,' Dante admitted. 'I wish you really had been my father's PA, with terrible Italian.'

Mia smiled.

'I'd have given you lessons,' Dante said.

'I'd have learnt a few choice words then.'

'Probably.' Dante smiled.

'Would you have asked me out?'

'Mia, I wanted you on sight. I wasn't thinking about going out, believe me.'

'You're too honest sometimes.'

'I know I am.'

And she loved him for it, Mia honestly did, and so she walked over to him and she looked right into his black eyes and decided that this was the last time she'd be weak. While Dante had been in with his family, Mia had made the only decision she could live with if she had to co-parent with an eternal playboy, and so this might well be goodbye.

And though this was in all likelihood their last ever kiss, she was grateful for this man who had helped her get over her shyness.

It felt so good to kiss him, to slip her tongue between his strained lips and to press herself against his tense body, to hold his head and kiss him as she never had before, for his mouth was barely moving yet she could feel how turned on he was.

'I wish you had done that the first day we met,' Dante said.

'So do I.'

She kissed him again and now he kissed her back, so thoroughly that they were up against his door and making noises that did not sound like just a kiss. And then, because it was Dante, of course there was the intrusion of his phone.

'I hate your phone.'

'I hate it too,' he admitted as he very reluctantly took the call and told Sarah he'd be in shortly.

'Except I can't go in like this,' Dante said. He took her hand and held it there where she could feel him hard through his trousers. But when he released his hand, Mia's remained.

'That's a little more how it goes,' Dante said in a voice that incited disorder, 'when I think of that day.'

'Here?' Mia frowned. 'You want to have sex with me here?'

'No.' He proceeded to give her her first private Italian lesson, and watched her blush and the nervous swallow in her throat as he told her what he wanted, and it served only to further turn him on.

'Here?' Mia checked, a little stunned but feeling sick with excitement too.

Dante could be selfish at times too. He held her eyes as he unzipped his trousers because, yes, he wanted Mia on her knees.

The sound of his zipper, the ragged edge to his breathing had her thighs turning to liquid as she all too readily sank down, but then nerves hit.

'I've never...' she attempted.

'I know.'

Mia wanted to, though.

She kissed the shaft and perhaps did not quite meet the mark, but his moan was one of pleasure, and so she inhaled his soapy scent and tentatively kissed higher.

'Mia,' he said when she reached the top, and breathed on him a while. Now his voice made her feel dizzy and she tasted him with the tip of her tongue and then ran that same tongue over her own lips to know his taste.

She looked up and met his eyes and asked, 'Is this filthy of me?'

He gave her his stunning smile, the one that went straight to her heart. 'Dirty girl.'

And it freed her.

He made her laugh, even as she went down on him.

He turned her fears and shame to small hits of pleasure because he just loved the feel of her mouth so much that it didn't matter that she had no idea what to do. She tasted him slowly at first, taking him in a little way and then, braver, she took him in deep.

He stroked her hair, fighting not to press her head down with his hands.

His phone was ringing but neither cared, for Mia was lost in the moment. And when he started to thrust, Mia felt as if her dress was on fire, so desperate was she to rip it off, and her mouth gaped open, stunned as she started to come.

And for Dante, who was trying to hold back and not hold his hand to the back of her head and thrust harder, the pause in proceedings, the gasping noises of her orgasm tipped him over the edge. 'Mia,' he warned, but then he swelled and she got her wish to taste Dante properly. She knelt back on her heels, heady with the rush of her own lost inhibitions.

He helped her to stand and Mia found there was something about being brave that made her even braver.

'Dante,' she said as he tucked himself in. She checked his tie and he was back to his usual perfect self—apart from the bruise on his cheek. 'You need to come up with something better.'

'What?'

'Better than tucking me away in the hills. I'm past all that and I'll never be your occasional mistress.'

He gave her a smile that said, *We'll see.*

'Oh,' Mia said as he opened the door, 'I meant what I said. I'm no longer hiding.'

'Good,' Dante said, and then frowned, because he wasn't quite sure what she getting at, though there was no mistaking the warning in her tone. 'Is it?'

'It is for me. I've decided that I want to be dated, and I want romance.'

'I bought you flowers,' Dante said, 'chocolates, earrings...'

'Yes, we've established you're a generous lover. I'm quite sure you've bought all your women similar gifts.' Her eyes flashed. 'You give everything you're willing to on the very first night. Well, guess what, Dante? I want a relationship that progresses.'

'I only found out about the baby yesterday.'

'This has nothing to do with the baby,' Mia said. 'It's been three months since we slept together, and more than two years since we met. If you can't give me what I want, then I'll find someone who can.'

'While pregnant.' He gave a slight scoffing laugh.

'I can wait,' Mia said. 'But I won't wait it out in bed with you, and neither am I hiding in the hills on tap for you. I will get the relationship I want.'

'Good for you,' Dante said, for he'd had women make the same demands too many times before and he wouldn't be coerced. 'It won't be with me.'

'I understand that.'

Dante refused to back down. 'So go for it.'

'Thanks,' Mia said. 'I'm glad I have your blessing.'

He turned to go then suddenly changed his mind. 'What was that for then?' He pointed to the door where she'd knelt just moments ago.

'I fancied it.' Mia shrugged, and then gave him a smile. 'I have a *to-do* list now.'

Sarah suddenly called his name from outside the office. 'Dante!'

His face was black as he turned and saw a harried-looking Sarah coming down the corridor towards him. 'I've been calling you; the mood's not exactly great in there.'

The mood wasn't great here either, but Dante shot Mia a look and then strode off to face the hostile board.

'How could you?' Luigi was red in the face and so livid that Dante would not have been in the least surprised if he were to jump over the desk and attempt to strangle him with his tie. 'How could you besmirch your father's memory and shame the Romano name?'

Dante ran a worried hand over his forehead, but it had nothing to do with their angry, reproving faces.

What the hell had Mia been saying?

He could not go there in his head.

He knew she'd been goading him.

Yet it was more than goaded he felt, for he felt ill at the thought of a future without her, and summers and weekends and evenings with his child—minus Mia.

'Dante!' Luigi tried to command his attention. 'He is barely cold in the ground. You disgust me, Dante. There is no coming back from this. We are a family business...'

'Perhaps...' Ariana offered a suggestion. 'Perhaps you can say you were comforting Mia.'

'Yes,' Angela said, completely incapable of simply observing and clearly liking the sound of Ariana's suggestion—anything to cover up the truth. 'You could say Mia was crying for Rafael, and you were merely offering support.'

'By pressing her against a column with his hips?' Stefano said with a generous dash of Romano sarcasm. 'No, I think we just have to ride it out.'

There had been no innuendo meant, but when he glanced up at his brother both men did share a slight smile.

And when the rest of the board had had their say, when they had all vented their emotions, and given their exceedingly low opinion of him, Dante stood and walked to the window, sorely tempted to say, *To hell with the lot of you,* for he knew he could walk away right now and be completely fine.

But, *famiglia, famiglia, famiglia…*

No, they weren't the perfect family, but they were his and he loved them.

He gazed out towards the dome, to the Basilica dei Santi Pietro e Paolo, only he wasn't searching his mind as to how to answer the board.

Mia had just warned him she *would* be dated and if not by him, then…

'Go for it,' he had said, as he always did, refusing to be railroaded or backed into a corner, refusing even to consider a future. Yet here he stood, in the middle of a board meeting, and was deeply considering one.

'Dante!' Luigi said, but to Dante his uncle's voice sounded like it came from underwater; instead it was Mia's voice that rang clearly in his head, and her response to his suggestion that she annul the marriage.

'I would never do that to your father and neither would you.'

That was having someone's back.

That was family.

And at that precise moment the idea of love crystallised for Dante, and instead of a burden pressing even more heavily down on him, it felt as if one had been lifted.

It was more than just a thought, it was more certain and real than anything he had felt in his life.

All that he had for more than two years denied and resisted flew into him now. He turned and faced the board and offered his response.

'I'm not going to discuss our relationship with you.'

'Relationship?' Luigi thundered. 'Since when did you do relationships?'

But Dante refused to clarify. 'I give enough of myself to the company without having to explain my personal life.' But this time he did not give his usual rant about being single and sleeping with whoever he chose. 'I will tell you only this: nothing took place while my father was alive, and it is my belief that I would have his full support.'

Dante turned in surprise as his mother then spoke. 'You would have Rafael's support, Dante.'

His mother could be difficult and self-serving at times, but she had his back now and he was grateful for that. 'Thank you,' Dante said. 'Do I have the board's support?'

'You have mine,' Ariana said.

'Thank you.'

'You always have mine,' Stefano replied, and Dante thanked him too.

There was silence from everyone else.

'Feel free to walk,' Dante offered, though of course no one did. Instead, they sighed their passive-aggressive sighs and nodded their judgmental heads because the fact was they needed him, far more than he needed them, and they knew it.

'Then that's that,' Dante said. 'And from now on, if you can't be nice to Mia, you will be polite or God help you when you have to answer to me.

'Now,' Dante said, 'if you'll excuse me, there is somewhere else I need to be.'

And that somewhere wasn't his office, though of course he headed there first. 'What did they say?' Mia asked the second he came through the door.

'The usual,' Dante said. 'Come on, I need some air. We can leave by a side exit if you prefer not to be seen with me.'

'I already told you, I'm not going to hide.'

'Good,' Dante said as he guided her out.

'Have you been fired?' Mia asked as they took the lift down.

'Fired!' Dante gave a wry laugh. 'They can't fire me. They could ask me to step down, but of course they won't. No, I will still be ensuring their pockets are lined for years to come...'

'Do you hate your work?' Mia asked as they headed through the foyer.

'No, I love my work,' Dante contradicted her. 'It's just a pain at times that I work with family members who think they have a say in every aspect of my life, when they don't. Anyway, enough about work. I have given myself the rest of the day off.'

'Where are we going?' Mia frowned, for they stepped out to bright blue skies and fresh spring air and Dante said a few choice words to the reporters all waiting to hear how the meeting had gone.

He seemed buoyant, yet tense, and she trotted to keep up with him, her stilettos sinking into the grass, as he walked with purpose through the stunning Giardino delle Cascate—the Garden of the Waterfalls.

They were exquisitely beautiful, a lush green haven in the business end of the city, with a cascade of waterfalls and arches of water. It was such a tranquil oasis that Mia stopped trying to keep up with Dante for a moment in order to drink in the spectacular sights and sounds.

And Dante stopped too.

'Amazing, isn't it?' he said. 'I come here sometimes to kick a stone and scream.'

'Really?' Mia said, smiling at the very thought.

'But not today.'

'Dante, what happened in there?'

'Not much,' he admitted, and then contradicted himself. 'Everything.'

'I don't understand.'

'I want to marry you, Mia,' Dante said. It wasn't Mia he wanted on her knees, it was himself, down on one, and he did just that. 'Mia, will you marry me?'

'Dante!' She covered her mouth and gave an embarrassed laugh, sure he was just making a show, or saying it for effect to appease the hungry press and the board. 'Stop it. You don't have to do this.'

'But I want to.'

'What the hell did you say to the board? Dante, I don't want to be another mistake you're taking on and I do not want you marrying me just because I'm having your baby.' She couldn't bear that, but Dante immediately corrected her.

'No, it's not that. I cannot stand the thought of you with someone else. It makes me want to spit.'

And me, she wanted to cry.

'You're the best thing that's ever happened in my life. You wanted romance, Mia, well, you're getting it. I love you and I want nothing more than for you to be my wife.'

She was scared to believe him, too stunned at the turn-around, and so she reminded him of his firmly held views. 'You don't believe in marriage.'

'I'll believe in ours.'

His voice told her he was serious, his eyes told her this was true, and Dante, she reminded herself, was honest to a fault. Except that fault made him perfect now, for she was hearing his absolute truth. She was starting to believe that absolutely this was Dante on one knee, telling her that finally he believed in the beauty of love.

'I think I loved you the day we met,' he told her, 'but I've spent more than two years denying that I did. I *had* to deny it, and I think I got so used to doing that, I never let myself consider this might be love. But it is. It absolutely is.

'So, Mia, will you marry me, please?'

She was embarrassed, laughing, humbled and thrilled, just a jumble of emotions as she looked at the man she wanted to be with for ever, and to tell him that she felt the same. 'Yes,' she said, 'Dante, I would love to be your wife.'

He stood, and their kiss was a mix of breathless laughter and tears, and sheer elation for all that was to come.

'I'm going to take you this morning to Via Cola di Rienzo,' Dante said, 'and buy you the nicest ring we see, but first...'

'We have to feed Alfonzo.'

'We do,' Dante said. 'And I want to show you your new bedroom.'

'Sounds like a perfect morning,' Mia said.

And she kissed her perfect man.

CHAPTER FOURTEEN

MIA STOOD IN Suite al Limone and gazed out at the sparkling lake and the guests all gathered for the wedding, just three weeks after the ball.

A whirlwind wedding, some said, but Mia and Dante felt as if they had been waiting a long time for this moment to finally arrive, when they could stand together and announce their love to the world.

Dante had asked where she wanted to spend her wedding night, and with her vow to never to set foot in a helicopter, Mia had chosen the Suite al Limone. She wanted one more night in this gorgeous space, being made love to by Dante, and then...

She would be ready to leave it.

The wedding was being held in the grounds and then the residence would go to its rightful owner, the love of Rafael's life.

Roberto had cried when Dante had told him that the place was his. Everyone knew the house and grounds would be cared for and tended. Of course, she and Dante would return and visit, for they were family really.

But now, for the second time, though for the right reasons, Mia was about to become Signora Romano.

She wore the palest green velvet, with a soft tulle overlay, and her hair was in loose curls. On her head there was a small crown of Romano vine leaves and her posy was of wild, freshly cut poppies from the land they loved so.

Her sandals were flat and gold and she felt beautiful and confident and very, very ready to marry the man she loved as she walked down the grand stairs.

'Oh, Mia.' Michael sat in his chair, elegant in his wedding suit, and so proud of his sister. 'You look stunning.'

'Thank you.' She smiled at her brother, who had been through so much and had finally come to a place of peace with his situation, helped by the gorgeous Gemma, who loved him so very much.

A helicopter was hovering overhead, no doubt to get a shot of the wedding, and Mia, finally, could not care less.

Instead, Mia walked towards Dante with her brother by her side and with her head held high, to the smiles of family and friends.

Angela was there, smiling proudly, and Luigi with his wife.

Stefano was the best man and so Eloa, who would be a bride herself in a couple of weeks, stood with Ariana, who was both smiling and crying on this emotional day.

There were no doubt a few wide eyes amongst the guests. And perhaps there were again whispers behind manicured hands. Dante had specifically said, after all, that nothing had taken place between them before Rafael died, yet the bride was *clearly* in the family way!

Mia could almost hear the clacking of rosary beads as they counted it to be less than four months since the funeral!

Roberto was there, of course, looking handsome, polished, and smiling at the bride as he dabbed at his eyes.

Then Dante turned to see his bride and the smile on his face was slow, stunned, delighted, and it made everything all right. Not a soul present could doubt that they were about to witness the marriage of two people who were deeply in love, for as he stepped forward towards her, everyone laughed when Stefano put a hand on Dante's arm and told him to wait, that she would be by his side soon.

'You look beautiful,' Dante said. He took her hand and kissed the tips of her fingers and they shared a smile.

'So do you,' Mia said, as she looked at her very handsome groom. He wore a stunning grey morning suit with a silver-grey waistcoat, and he looked so elegant and *so* clean shaven she wanted to reach out to stroke his cheek.

She resisted, but the bride was blushing fiercely as they faced each other and made the vows that would bind them for life.

They were in English because Dante wanted her to be sure she understood every word.

'I, Dante Rafael, take you, Mia Jane…' And he put his hand to her cheek as he gave her his promise to be faithful always, in joy and pain, in health and in sickness, and then his voice became husky as he gazed into her eyes and vowed that he would love and honour her for the rest of his life.

Mia started to cry, then made her vows to Dante in English. 'I, Mia Jane, take you, Dante Rafael…' They were similar vows to his, except she ended them with, 'To love and to cherish, all the days of my life.'

And then it was time for Dante to kiss his bride, and Mia closed her eyes to the bliss of his lips, the smoothness of his cheek, and the fragrance of pure Dante.

It was a gorgeous wedding and Dante, of course, made a wonderful speech, with one more surprise to come.

Actually, two more surprises to come, for there was a reason that Mia was rather big for her dates.

'My wife and I are thrilled to share the news with family and friends, that we found out, last week, that Mia is having twins.'

Yes, their forbidden night had come with two delightful

consequences and there were congratulations, dancing and celebrations all around, though for a little while the happy couple slipped away for some private time together.

'Are you sure you want to do this?' Dante checked.

'Very,' Mia said, and in the sunset they walked hand in hand towards the lake, then stood beneath the holm oaks.

They saw they weren't the first to visit. There were beautiful orchids that had been lovingly placed there this wedding morning by Roberto, and beside them Mia placed her gorgeous bouquet of poppies on dear Rafael's grave.

There was nothing to fear, Mia knew now. In fact, it felt as if he was smiling down on them.

With Dante by her side, she was no longer scared.

* * * * *

THE TERMS OF
THE SICILIAN'S
MARRIAGE

LOUISE FULLER

For my wonderful husband, Patrick.
Still impossibly handsome,
and still pressing all the right buttons…

PROLOGUE

THE BAR WAS starting to empty.

Across the room, the blonde sitting at the counter with her friend looked over and gave Vicenzu Trapani a slow, lingering smile. A smile that promised a night, or quite possibly more, of unparalleled, uncomplicated pleasure.

Under normal circumstances he would have smiled back and waited for her to join him. But nothing was normal any more, and he wasn't sure he was ever going to smile again.

Picking up his glass, he stared down into the dark gold liquid. He didn't normally drink bourbon, particularly when he was back in Sicily, but it had been Ciro who had caught the bartender's attention. Ciro who had snapped out the order before Vicenzu's own numbed brain had even fully registered where they were. Ciro who had commandeered the table in the corner and pushed him into a seat.

They had left the meeting and come straight to the bar. Vito Neglia was their lawyer, and an old family friend, but today he had also been their last hope.

A hope that had been swiftly and brutally extinguished when Vito had confirmed what they already knew.

There was no loophole. Cesare Buscetta had acted within the law.

He was the new and legitimate owner of both the Trapani Olive Oil Company and the beautiful, beloved family estate where Vicenzu and Ciro had spent an idyllic childhood.

Vicenzu's fingers tightened around his glass. The family estate he still called home.

Home.

The word stuck in his throat and, picturing his mother's expression as he'd handed the keys over to the agent, he felt his stomach lurch.

It had broken his heart, having to do that to her, and the memory of her bewildered, tear-stained face would be impossible to forget. The reason for it impossible to forgive.

'We must fix this.'

Ciro's voice broke into his thoughts and, looking up, he met his brother's gaze—and instantly wished he hadn't.

Ciro's face was taut with determination, his green eyes narrow with a certainty he envied...eyes that so resembled their father's that he had to look away.

His stomach tightened. Ciro was his younger brother, but he was his father's son. Whip-smart, focused, disciplined, he could have taken over the business and run it with his eyes shut—hell, he could have turned it into a household name overnight. And, had their father been cut from different cloth, that was exactly what would have happened.

But Alessandro Trapani had not been a cut-throat man. To him, family had mattered more than global domination.

Or had it?

Vicenzu felt his stomach lurch again and, pushing away the many possible but all equally unpalatable answers to that question, he lifted his glass to his lips and drained it swiftly.

Meeting his brother's gaze, he nodded.

'We have to get it back. All of it.'

Ciro's voice was quiet, but implacable, and Vicenzu nodded again. His brother was right, of course. Cesare Buscetta was not just a thief, he was a bully and a thug. But it was too soon...feelings were still too raw.

He'd tried to explain that to his brother—had reminded him that revenge was a dish best served cold. Only Ciro couldn't wait—*wouldn't* wait. His need for vengeance was white-hot, burning him from the inside out. He wanted revenge *now* and he needed his brother to play his part.

'Vicenzu?'

For a moment he closed his eyes. If only he could turn back time. Give his father back the money he'd borrowed. Be the son his father had needed—wanted.

But regrets were not going to right the wrongs that had been done to his family and, opening his eyes, he leaned back in his chair and cleared his throat. 'Yes, I know what I have to do and I'll do it. I'll take the business back.'

His chest tightened. It sounded so simple—and maybe it would be. After all, all he had to do was get a woman to fall in love with him.

Only this wasn't *any* woman. It was Immacolata Buscetta—the daughter of the man who had hounded his father to death and robbed his beautiful, always-laughing mother of her husband and her home.

There was not much to go on. Cesare was a protective father, and by all accounts his eldest daughter was a chip off the old block—as ice-cold as she was beautiful. Who better than her to pay for the sins of her father?

He felt a sudden rush of fury. He would make her melt. Seduce her, then strip her naked—literally and metaphorically—and make her his wife. He would take back what belonged to his family and then, finally, when she was his—inside and out—she would discover why he had really married her.

A fresh round of drinks arrived and he picked up his glass.

Ciro's eyes met his. 'To vengeance.'

'To vengeance,' Vicenzu repeated.

And for the first time since his father's death he felt alive.

CHAPTER ONE

'OH, MY, DOESN'T she look beautiful?'

Without changing the direction of her gaze, Immacolata Buscetta nodded, her insides tightening with a mixture of love and sadness.

'Yes, she does,' she said softly, addressing her response to the Sicilian matron who was standing beside her, clutching her handbag against her body with quivering fingers.

Actually, privately she thought 'beautiful' was too mundane a word to describe her younger sister. Her stunning, full-skirted traditional white wedding dress was beautiful, yes, but Claudia herself looked beatific.

Not a word Imma had ever used before, and she would probably never use it again, but it was the only one that remotely came close to capturing the blissful expression on her sister's face.

Imma's heart gave a small twitch and she glanced over to where Claudia's new husband was greeting some of the one hundred carefully selected guests who had been invited to celebrate the marriage of Claudia Buscetta to Ciro Trapani on this near-perfect early summer's day in Sicily. There would be another hundred guests arriving for the evening reception later.

Of course Claudia was in a state of bliss. She had just married the man who had stormed their father's citadel and declared his love for her like some knight in a courtly romance.

But it wasn't Ciro's impassioned pursuit of her sister that was causing Imma's insides to tighten and her heart to beat erratically. It was the man standing next to the newlyweds.

Ciro's brother, Vicenzu, was the owner of the legendary La Dolce Vita hotel in Portofino. Like pilgrims visiting a shrine, members of royalty, novelists looking for inspiration, divas and bad boys from the world of music and film—all eventually made their way to his hotel.

Her throat tightened. And Vicenzu was the baddest of them all.

His reputation as a playboy and pleasure seeker stretched far beyond the Italian Riviera and it was easy to see why.

Reluctantly, her gaze darted towards him again, drawn like a moth to the flame of his absurdly beautiful features.

He was standing slightly to one side, taking advantage of an overhanging canopy of flower-strewn greenery, which made him both screened from view and yet still the most conspicuous person there.

With dark hair, a teasing mouth and a profile that would grace any currency, he stood out among the stocky Sicilian and Italian businessmen and their wives—and not just because he was a head taller than most of them.

Glancing up through her eyelashes, she felt a cool shiver tiptoe down her spine. In their formal suits and dresses, quite a few of the guests were perspiring beneath the heat of the sun, but he looked effortlessly cool, the impeccably fitted white shirt hugging his lean, supple body and perfectly setting off his dancing dark eyes.

At that moment he turned, and those same dancing eyes met hers, and before she had a chance to blink, much less move, he was sauntering towards her, a lazy smile pulling at the corners of his mouth.

'Immacolata…' He made a disapproving face. 'You don't play fair, do you, Ms Buscetta.'

'Play fair?' She stared up at him, her pulse beating with fear and fascination, trying to look calm and unaffected. How could he talk about being fair, looking like that? 'I don't understand.'

Up close, his beauty was so startling it felt like a slap to her face. His eyes, that beautiful, curving mouth, the clean-cut lines of his features… All made her mind go completely blank and made her feel bare, *exposed*, in a way that no other man ever had.

'Playing hide-and-seek without telling me...' He shook his head. 'That was sneaky.'

'I wasn't hiding,' she lied, desperately wanting to turn and walk away and yet held captive by the soft, baiting note in his voice. 'I was looking after my guests.'

'Not all of them,' he countered. 'I was feeling very neglected. Quite light-headed, actually. In fact, I think we might need to go somewhere quiet so you can put me in the recovery position.'

She felt her cheeks go red and, hating this instant and—worse—visible response to the easy pull of his words, she lifted her chin and glanced pointedly past his shoulder. 'There are cold drinks on the terrace, and plenty of seating.'

He grinned. 'Don't you want to know why I'm feeling so light-headed?'

'No, thank you. I'm perfectly fine as I am.'

'I couldn't agree more,' he said slowly.

As he spoke his eyes meandered over her body in a way that made her feel breathless and on edge. Fighting to keep control she glanced down at the lapel of his jacket. 'Vicenzu, I—'

His eyes glittered. 'It's okay. I get it. You thought I was just a pretty face, but now we've got to know each other a bit better you're starting to like me. It happens all the time. But don't worry—I'm not going to tell anyone.'

Her face flamed. 'Actually, I was just going to tell you that you've lost your boutonnière,' she said stiffly. 'Now, if you'll excuse me, I need to check on—on something. In the kitchen.'

Before he could say anything she turned and began walking blindly away from his mocking gaze, her panicky response to him echoing in her ears.

Panicky and prim and gauche.

Gritting her teeth, she smiled mechanically as people

greeted her. What was the matter with her? She was an educated woman, had been top of her class at business school, and she was the daughter of one of the most powerful men in Sicily, soon to be CEO of her father's latest acquisition. So why had she fled like a rabbit from a fox?

But it hurt to look at him—and hurt even more to look away, even though that was what she'd been doing her very best to accomplish ever since he'd arrived at the church.

Only as they were maid of honour and best man, there had been no avoiding his laughing dark eyes during the service.

It had been equally impossible not to be swept along by the beauty and romanticism of the ceremony, and as a shaft of sunlight had gilded his extremely photogenic features she had briefly allowed herself to fantasise that it was her wedding, and Vicenzu was her husband...

Her pulse twitched. It was nearly five years since she'd been remotely attracted to anyone, and her response to him was as shocking as it was confusing.

Three times she'd lost her place in the order of service, distracted by his gaze—a gaze that had seemed never to leave her face, making her tremble inside.

But no woman—particularly one who had zero actual hands-on experience of men—would consider Vicenzu Trapani husband material. Unlike the rumours about her father's links to organised crime, the stories about him were not just idle gossip. On first impressions alone it was clear he'd earned his flirtatious reputation.

Not that it mattered, she told herself quickly as she skirted around the chattering guests. She had absolutely no intention of falling in love with anyone ever again—and especially not with a man whose behaviour was as provocative as his smile.

All she had to do was ignore her body, and him, for the next couple of hours and concentrate on what really mattered today: Claudia and her new husband.

Plucking a chilled mimosa from a passing waitress, she fixed her gaze on Ciro.

He certainly looked the part. Like his brother, he was tall, dark and handsome, but the resemblance was superficial.

Where Vicenzu was all languid grace and rolled up shirt-sleeves, Ciro wore his suit like custom-built armour, and the imperious tilt of his jaw hinted at an inner confidence and determination that had clearly driven the stratospheric rise of his retail empire.

It was that business success which had persuaded her ultraprotective Sicilian father, Cesare, to agree to the swiftness of this marriage. That and the fact that Ciro came from exactly the kind of respectable background her father craved for his daughters.

The Trapanis were a good, solid Sicilian family, trusted and respected, with a good, solid Sicilian family business to their name. A business that Alessandro Trapani, Ciro's father, had just sold to her father, along with his beautiful home.

Imma felt her shoulders tense. She didn't know all the details of the sale. Despite having groomed her to follow in his footsteps, Cesare was both controlling and secretive about many areas of the business he had built from the ground up.

In his words, old man Trapani had 'got into a mess financially' and wanted a quick sale. Probably it was those same money worries that had led to Alessandro's collapse and tragic, untimely death two months ago.

Her eyes were drawn to the petite woman talking to Claudia. Ribs tightening, she felt an ache of sympathy for her.

With her cloud of dark hair and almond-shaped eyes, Audenzia Trapani must have been exquisite when she was younger, and she was still a beautiful woman. But there was a fragility to her now, and a stillness—as though she was holding herself tightly inside.

Her gaze was still hovering on the older woman when she suddenly became aware that she was being watched. Looking up, she felt as if her skin had turned inside out. Vicenzu had joined his brother and was staring at her again, his eyes locked on her with an intensity that almost made her flinch.

'Immacolata!'

She turned, relief battling with regret. Her father was bearing down on her, and she felt a familiar rush of love and frustration.

Like a lot of Sicilian men of his generation, Cesare was compact—a solid-bodied barrel of a man. The muscles of his youth were turning heavy now, and yet it would never do to underestimate him on the grounds of age. Cesare was a force of nature. Still handsome, vigorous and uncompromising, a powerful and some thought intimidating presence at any occasion.

'Papà.' She smiled, hoping to deflect the criticism she knew was coming. As he kissed her on each cheek she inhaled the potent mix of cigar smoke and citrusy aftershave that remained in every room he visited long after he'd left.

'Why are you not with your sister?' He frowned. 'Today of all days I want to show both my beautiful daughters off to the world.' His dark eyes softened. 'I know it's hard for you, *piccioncina mia*, watching your sister leave home, and I know you think it's all been too quick, that she's a little young to be married…'

Imma felt her smile tighten, and her father's voice seemed to fade into the hum of background chatter. It wasn't just Claudia's youth that made her feel anxious about the speed of her marriage. It was something more personal: a promise made…

Only neither her father nor her sister wanted to hear her tentative reservations about how fast everything had moved. Cesare had pursued and married their own mother at the age of seventeen, and as for Claudia—she was a dreamer.

And now her dreams of love and a handsome husband and a beautiful home had all come true.

But what about my dreams? Imma flexed her fingers

against her cool glass, trying to ignore the pulse of envy beating inside her chest. *When will they come true?*

Hard to say when she actually had no dreams. No idea what she wanted. No idea who she even was.

For her, there had never been any time for thinking about such things. She had always been too busy. Trying to be some kind of mother to Claudia, studying hard at school and then university, and always mindful of the wishes of her father. For without a son to fulfil *his* dreams Cesare had made her the focus of his ambitions.

All his ambitions—including having his say on her choice of future husband, and that was never going to be some local boy made good, like Ciro Trapani, or his rakish older brother.

Not that Vicenzu would ever be interested in her, she thought, her gaze fluttering fleetingly over the perfect angles of his profile. Being in charge of her father's household and a mother figure to Claudia had made her seem far older than her years. And, although she actually shared her sister's shyness, her brief, disappointing interactions with men—she couldn't really call them dates—had left her so wary that she knew her shyness came across as remoteness or disdain.

Hardly qualities that would tempt a man like Vicenzu who, if the internet and the tabloid press were to be believed, was like catnip to women.

But why would she even want to let anyone get close to her? She was tired of being hurt and humbled. Tired of men running a marathon from her when they realised her surname was Buscetta. Tired of never being good enough, pretty enough, desirable enough for them to face up to her father and fight for the right to be with her.

But her sister's beautiful, romantic wedding was not the time to be letting such thoughts fill her head and, taking a quick, calming breath, she looked up at her father.

'Just at the beginning, Papà.' She took his hand and squeezed it.

Cesare smiled. 'You've been like a mother to her, but marriage is right for Claudia. She doesn't have the temperament for studying or business.'

Imma nodded, her momentary stab of envy instantly swamped by remorse. More than anyone Claudia deserved to be happy, for although their father indulged his youngest daughter, he also found her easy to ignore. Now, though, for the first time in her life, she was in the spotlight.

'I know,' she said quietly.

Cesare grunted. 'She's a homebody and he's a good man for her. Strong, dependable, honest.'

Her father's chest swelled and she could tell he was almost bursting with satisfaction that his daughter had made such a good match socially.

'Come.' He held out his arm. 'Let's go and join your sister—it's nearly time to eat.'

'Where have you been?' It was Claudia, hurrying towards her, clutching the hem of her dress. 'I was just about to send Ciro to find you.'

There was a slight unevenness to her voice, and Imma felt her heart squeeze. She might be a married woman now, but Claudia was still and would always be the little sister she'd comforted whenever she was sad or hurt. Papà was right. Today of all days Imma needed to be there for her—because tomorrow she would be gone.

Pushing back against the ache in her chest, Imma took her sister's hand.

'I just wanted to check in on Corrado,' she said quickly.

Corrado was the Buscettas' Michelin-starred chef, and he had been extremely put out by Cesare's insistence that other Michelin-starred chefs must be flown in at incredible cost from all over the world to help him cater for the wedding breakfast.

But Cesare had been unrepentant. It was his daughter's

wedding, and no expense would be spared. He wanted the whole of Sicily—no, make that the whole of Italy—rendered speechless with envy and awe and so, as usual, it had been left to Imma to pour olive oil on troubled waters.

'No, there's nothing wrong,' she added as Ciro and Vicenzu joined them. 'It's just difficult for him, having to share his kitchens, and I didn't want him sulking in any of the photographs.'

'If he does that he'll be looking for a new job,' Cesare growled. 'And he can forget about references. In fact, he can forget about working, full stop. If he doesn't have a smile pinned on his face every second of today I'll make sure he never works again.'

A short, stunned silence followed this explosion. Claudia bit her lip and Ciro looked confused. Vicenzu, on the other hand, seemed more amused than unnerved.

'Of course he won't be looking for another job, Papà,' Imma said firmly. 'Corrado has been with us for ten years. He's one of the family—and we all know how much you value family.'

'And we share those same values, Signor Buscetta.'

Imma glanced sharply over at Vicenzu. For a few half seconds she had been distracted by her father's outburst, but now she felt her stomach swoop down like a kite with a broken tail.

He sounded and looked sincere, and yet she couldn't help thinking he was not. Quickly, in case her father began thinking along the same lines, she said, 'Isn't that how we all ended up here today?'

As she pasted a smile on her face, her father grunted. 'Forgive me. I just want everything to be perfect for my little girl.'

'And it is.' Ciro took a step forward, his deep voice resonating in the space between them. 'If I may, sir, I'd like to thank you for making all this so special for both of us.' He turned to Claudia, who was gazing up at him, her soft brown eyes wide with adoration. 'I promise to make my marriage to Claudia equally memorable.'

Beaming, his good humour restored, Cesare slapped him on the shoulder and then, flicking his ostentatious gold watch free from his cuff, he glanced down at it.

'I'll hold you to that. And now I think we should go and eat. *Ammuninni!*'

Her father held out his arm to Imma, but as she moved to take it Vicenzu sidestepped her, his dark hair flopping over his forehead, his mouth curving into a question mark.

'May I?'

Imma felt her father tense. She knew his opinion of Ciro's older brother. Vicenzu's hedonistic lifestyle and his reputation as a *donnaiolo*—a playboy—had been her father's one and only real objection to Claudia's marriage.

Before she could reply, Cesare said stiffly, 'I think I would prefer to escort my daughter myself.'

There was a short silence, and then her heartbeat accelerated as Vicenzu's teasing dark eyes rested on her face.

'But what would Immacolata prefer?'

Imma froze, his words pinning her to the ground as if he had cast a spell rather than asked a question. Around them the air seemed to turn to stone, and she could sense Claudia's mouth forming an *O* of shock.

No one, certainly not her father, had ever asked about Imma's preferences before, and she had no idea how to respond. But she did know that her father was expecting her to refuse Vicenzu, and maybe it was that assumption, coupled with a sudden longing to indulge in a little impulsive behaviour of her own, that made her turn to Cesare and say calmly, 'I think you should escort Audenzia, Papà. That would be the right and proper thing to do.'

More importantly, it was exactly the right thing for her to say. When he was a young man, her father had just wanted to be rich and powerful, but now what he wanted most was to be accepted in society on an equal footing by people like the Trapanis.

'Of course—you're right,' he said, and Imma felt her heart begin to beat faster as Vicenzu held out his arm.

'Shall we?' he said softly.

Her heart bumping into her ribs, she wondered how he managed to imply so much in two little words. And then, doing her best to ignore the hard swell of his bicep, she followed Claudia and Ciro towards the circus-tent-sized marquee, where the wedding breakfast was being held.

Inside it was impossibly romantic, and Imma felt her stomach flip over as Vicenzu led her to their flower-strewn table. She was already regretting defying her father. Vicenzu Trapani probably flirted in his sleep and she needed to remember that—not let the emotion of the day or his dark eyes suggest anything different.

'So, Vicenzu,' she said quickly, before he had a chance to speak, 'I've heard so much about your hotel. Tell me... how many people work at La Dolce Vita?'

Dropping down next to her, he frowned. 'Well, Immacolata, that's a tricky one. Let me see... I guess, on a good day, probably about forty percent of them.'

The smile tugging at his mouth was impossible to resist, and of their own accord her lips started to curl upward, like the sun rising in the morning sky.

'I know—you think they should all be working. And you're right. I need to crack the whip a bit.'

As his smile slowly unfurled, she felt her stomach flicker like a flame in a breeze. 'I meant—' she began.

He was grinning now. 'I'm just teasing. The answer is I don't know or care. All I know is I get to enjoy your company for the foreseeable future. And, as you're the most beautiful woman in this tiny, unassuming tent...' he glanced mockingly around the vast marquee '...that makes me the luckiest man on earth.'

A cool shiver ran over her skin. Her heart was suddenly beating so fast she felt it might burst free of her ribs.

'Really?' She met his gaze calmly, even as his words resounded inside her head.

'Really. Truly. Absolutely. Unequivocally. Did I say that right?'

She saw his eyes light up as she smiled. 'Yes, only that doesn't make it true.'

'But why would I lie?'

His tone was still playful, but he was staring at her intently.

'Look, I'm not good for much—just ask anyone who knows me...'

He leaned forward so that he was filling her view, and she felt her skin grow hot and tight as he stared down at her steadily.

'But I am a connoisseur of beauty, and you are a very beautiful woman.'

For a second or three the world seemed to stop—or at least the hubbub in the tent faded to a dull hum beneath the uneven thump of her heartbeat. He probably said that to every woman he met, and yet she couldn't stop herself from hoping that he was telling the truth.

He took her hand and she felt her stomach flutter. But he didn't kiss it. Instead he turned her arm over and examined the skin on her wrist.

'What are you doing?' she asked.

'Looking for chinks in your armour,' he murmured.

There was a brief shifting silence, and then he glanced up as waiters began filing into the marquee.

'Great—it's time to eat.'

His eyes met hers, soft and yet intense in a way that made her breathing knot.

'Let's hope the food is as delectable as my hostess,' he said. 'I don't think I've ever been hungrier...'

* * *

The food had been incredible. Seven courses accompanied by a note-perfect string quartet. Then there had been speeches, and now Claudia was leaning into Cesare as they slowly circled in the traditional father-and-daughter dance.

But Imma had barely registered any of it. Not the food, nor the music or the toasts. Of course she had gone through the pantomime of raising her glass to her mouth and smiling and nodding, but inside she had been too busy trying to work out the enigma that was Vicenzu Trapani.

She'd expected to like him—*obviously*. A man didn't get the kind of reputation he had for no reason. And this must be how he was with every woman. She was no different in her response to his easy charm and lush beauty.

And yet although she had wanted to find him shallow and spoilt, flirtatious and flippant—and he was all of those things—she felt she might have misjudged him.

Particularly in those moments like now, when he seemed to forget that she was there and his eyes would seek out his mother at the far end of the table.

Her breathing lost its rhythm. Of course she missed her own mother, but his loss was so recent…still raw.

Glancing over at him, she said hesitantly, 'It must be difficult.'

'Difficult?' He raised one perfect eyebrow.

'Today. I mean, without your father. I know Papà wishes he'd come to him sooner.'

Vicenzu's handsome face didn't change, but she could sense an immediate tightening beneath the surface of his skin.

'It's no harder than any other day.'

The lazy amusement had left his voice and her cheeks grew warm. Wanting to kick herself, she glanced across the dance floor to where Ciro had taken over from Cesare. Watching him gaze down into Claudia's upturned face, she felt an ache of the loss to come.

'I'm sorry, Vicenzu—'

'It's Vicè—and, no, *I'm* sorry.' He frowned, his face creasing without impairing its beauty. 'You're right. It is hard without him, and I should have expected it to be, but I'm an idiot.'

Maybe it was the bleakness in his eyes, or perhaps his earlier defiance of her father, but she felt suddenly protective of him.

'You're not an idiot for missing your father. I miss my mother every day.'

They were so close she could feel his warm breath on her face, see the stubble already forming on his jaw. For a full sixty seconds they stared at each other, wide-eyed, mesmerised by the bond they seemed to have formed out of nowhere, and then, standing up, he held out his hand.

'Maybe not,' he said slowly. 'But I will be an idiot if I leave this wedding without having at least one dance with you.' He hesitated. 'That is if you'll dance with me?'

Her mouth felt dry and her blood was humming in her ears. She could feel a hundred pairs of eyes on her. But her eyes were fixed on his and, nodding slowly, she stood up and took his hand.

CHAPTER TWO

BREATHING OUT, VICÈ pulled Imma against him, keeping his beautiful face blank of expression. It was all part of the plan, he told himself. The first step in his great seduction of Immacolata Buscetta.

But inside his head a war was raging between the man he was and the man he was trying to be and needed to be.

No change there, then, he thought irritably.

Except this time there would be no second chances.

It should be easy—and had it been any other woman it would have been. Women liked him. He liked them. But Imma wasn't like other women. She was the daughter of his enemy—and as such he'd expected to hate her on sight.

Everything he'd seen and heard about her in advance had made that seem likely. He'd expected her to be cool and reserved, less overtly aggressive than Cesare, but still her father's daughter. And she was definitely a princess. Watching her with her staff, it had been clear to him that her quiet words and the decisive up-tilt to her jaw held the same authority as a royal command.

Her dark, demure dress seemed to confirm the message that she wanted to be taken seriously—only it couldn't hide her long, coltish legs.

He felt his chest rise and fall.

And as for that long dark hair… It might be neatly knotted at the nape of her neck but he could all too easily imagine running his fingers through its rich, silky length, and her bee-stung parted lips definitely seemed to contradict the wariness in her green eyes.

In short, she was beautiful. Just not the cold, diamond-hard beauty he'd anticipated.

And that was the problem.

He'd wanted to go in for the kill—do it quickly and cleanly like a shark—only it was turning out to be so much harder than he'd anticipated. Particularly with Imma's smooth, supple body pressed against his.

His chest tightened and, catching sight of his mother's face again, he closed his eyes, wishing it was as easy to shut out the confusion he felt on the inside.

Could he do this? Could he actually pull this off?

They were the questions he'd been asking himself for weeks now—ever since he and Ciro had sat in that bar drinking bourbon.

Ciro was his brother and his best friend. There was less than a year between their birthdays, so he couldn't remember a time when Ciro had been smaller, weaker, slower than him.

Maybe he never had been.

It had certainly felt that way for most of his life.

Opening his eyes, he watched his brother dance past, his hand wrapped around Claudia's waist, his face gazing down into hers.

He looked every inch the devoted husband—and he would look that way right up until the moment when he told his new wife the truth and her world came tumbling down.

And, even though he would have preferred to take things more slowly, when the time came he would do the same to Imma. He wanted vengeance every bit as much as Ciro.

His heart stilled.

His father had not been a critical or judgemental man, but he remembered once as a child they had been in Palermo, and a stocky man with a sneering smile had got out of a car and Alessandro's eyes had narrowed.

Sensing his son's curiosity, his father had told him he was a man 'without honour'. He had never forgotten the man's name or his father's words. Coming from his mild, gentle father, they had shocked him.

Now they choked him.

Cesare Buscetta had hounded and humbled Alessandro to death. He needed to pay for his crimes, and it was Vicenzu's job—*his duty*—to make that happen.

'Excuse me, Imma...'

It was Ciro, a small apologetic smile playing around his mouth. His eyes met momentarily with his brother's.

'It's time for Claudia to go and change, and apparently you said you would help her—'

Imma was frowning, and she seemed dazed—almost as though she'd been woken from a dream. 'I'm so sorry...of course I did. Would you mind?'

'Vicè?' His brother frowned too. 'Imma's talking to you.'

'Yeah, I heard, bro.' Feeling Ciro's gaze on his face, he softened his voice and stared down at Imma until he saw a flush colour her cheeks. 'I mind tremendously, but I'll forgive you as long as you come right back.'

As she lifted her face and looked up at him his chest tightened painfully. He'd sworn an oath with Ciro and he was going to keep it—but it would be so much easier if she had eyes of a different colour.

Watching her walk away, he gritted his teeth.

It wasn't fair. Why did her eyes have to be *green*? And not just green but the exact lush green of the Nocellara olives that grew so abundantly on his family's estate. Olives he had helped pick as a child. Olives his father had nurtured and loved almost as much as he had nurtured and loved his family.

It was one of his earliest memories—that first time he'd been allowed to join his father and the other estate workers for the harvest.

He had been so proud when he'd shown his father his haul, and Alessandro had not so much as hinted that the fruit he'd picked was too small and not ripe enough.

It had been that way for his entire life—his father covering up his mistakes, never holding him accountable, always giving him another chance. He couldn't even pinpoint when it had first started.

Had it been at school? When he'd got into trouble for trading tips on how to kiss girls in exchange for getting his homework done? Or when he'd got drunk and driven a tractor around the olive groves? He'd written off the tractor, and some of the estate's oldest trees—but, just like on all the other occasions when he'd messed up, Alessandro had simply sighed and shaken his head.

Something bitter rose in his throat—the burning anger that had been swirling inside his chest since his mother's distraught phone call.

If only his father had told him the truth about Buscetta he would have been able to help. It could have been his chance to make amends. It wasn't as if he was still a child. He didn't need protecting from the truth.

And then, just like that, he felt his anger drain away swiftly, like water spiralling down a plughole.

To his father he had still needed protecting.

That was why Alessandro had kept both his financial and his health worries to himself. Vicenzu glanced over at his brother. And that was why Ciro was so insistent that they seek revenge on Buscetta.

Unlike him, his brother had always been independently successful on a scale that far surpassed their father, and the idea that Alessandro hadn't thought Ciro man enough to take on his father's problems had incensed his younger brother.

The truth was actually the opposite, he thought numbly. His father had known that he'd be able to rely on Ciro, but he hadn't wanted to confide in one son and not the other, so he'd sacrificed himself so that *he*, Vicenzu, wouldn't feel inadequate.

It was yet another reason for him to feel guilty.

'How's it going?'

Glancing up at his brother, he shrugged. 'It's going fine,

I think.' He leaned forward and picked up a *confetti* from a nearby table. It was a traditional gift for the wedding guests. His mother still had hers from her own wedding. Five pastel-coloured sugared almonds—a reminder that married life was both sweet and bitter—and five wishes for the new husband and wife.

Health, wealth, happiness, children and a long life.

His shoulders tensed. Now, thanks to Buscetta, his parents' wishes had withered like olives exposed to a hard frost.

He sensed Ciro's impatience even before he heard it in his voice. 'You *think*? What does that mean?'

He felt a flicker of irritation—and envy. Ever since he could remember people had wanted to make his life easy. Not just his parents, but his friends and pretty much every woman he met. Ciro too. Until now. Now his brother was so on edge, so picky and demanding all the time.

But Claudia had always been the easier sister to seduce. She was younger, naive in the extreme, and had clearly been groomed for marriage. All Ciro had had to do was get past her monstrous father. Okay, that had sounded tough on paper, but in reality Cesare had laid out the red carpet for him.

Obviously.

His brother ticked all the boxes, whereas Vicenzu just owned a hotel. It might be the most celebrated hotel in the Western hemisphere—part sanctuary, part crash pad for its hard-partying, glamorous A-list clientele—but still...

And, of course, there was his reputation—

'Vicè!' His brother's voice tugged him back into the present. 'I thought seduction was supposed to be your area of expertise?'

'It is.' He turned towards his brother, his hands itching to both hit him and hug him. As usual, he went down the path of least resistance. '*Scialla*—just chill, Ciro, okay?' Grabbing his brother by the shoulders, he pulled him into an embrace. '*Festina lente*, bro.'

'There's no time for chilling, *bro*,' his brother said irritably. 'And quoting Latin at me doesn't change the facts. We agreed—you agreed—'

'Yeah, and I'm doing it.'

'Do it faster.' They were facing each other and their eyes met. 'I don't want to be stuck in this marriage for any longer than I have to be.'

'I know.'

Ciro held his gaze. 'Look, ever since I was a teenager I've watched women climb over each other to get to you. Immacolata Buscetta will be exactly the same. So just do this for Mamma, and for Papà, and then everything will go back to how it was before.'

Except it wouldn't.

They would have avenged their father, but nothing could bring him back to life. They would have the business and their home, but their mother still wouldn't have her husband.

He glanced over to where Audenzia was sitting, sipping coffee. His parents had been so devoted to each other they had never spent a night apart during their forty years of marriage. He'd always feared falling short of their ideal, and now he was having to seduce a woman he hated into marrying him.

'I can't help feeling that Papà wouldn't like this,' he said quietly.

Ciro stared at him. 'Maybe not—but he's not here to ask, is he? And if you're having second thoughts, maybe you should ask yourself why that's the case.'

The pain was sharp and humbling. And just what Vicenzu needed to clear the confusion from his mind.

He had made and broken enough promises in his life.

This time he would do whatever it took to keep one.

It was dark when Ciro and Claudia finally left.

'He will take care of her, won't he?'

Vicè was standing next to Imma at the edge of the marquee. Having waved off the happy couple, most of the guests had already gone back inside, but she had wanted to wait until the car had disappeared.

He felt a rush of anticipation—like that moment on a rollercoaster ride just before the track dropped down. Now that it was close, he just wanted to make it happen.

'Yes, of course,' he lied.

She nodded. 'You don't have to wait with me,' she said, glancing back at the distant car, her green eyes tracking its progress. 'I know it's silly, but it's the first time she's gone away without me.'

'I want to wait.' He hesitated. 'And there's nowhere I'd rather be than here.' Taking her hand, he gently pulled her closer. 'With you.'

Her eyes lifted to his face, and there was a faint frown on her brow as she tugged her pashmina closer to her body. He felt his blood start to hum. He'd bet his last sugared almond that she was trying to hide how aroused she was by his words.

'I don't think we know each other well enough for you to say that,' she said quietly.

'So let's get to know each other better.' He took a deep breath. 'Let's go somewhere more private.'

She looked up at him, her green eyes wide with confusion and a curiosity that made his groin turn to stone.

He nodded. 'I know it's sudden, and I'm guessing you think I do this kind of thing all the time. But I don't. Usually I'm just looking for fun—but not today. Not with you.'

She bit her lip, and for a moment he thought he'd gone too far, too fast.

'Look, forget it,' he said quickly. 'I must be crazy, suggesting something like that—'

She nodded slowly. 'Yes, you are.'

He felt her fingers tighten around his.

'But maybe it's about time I did something crazy too.'

His heart gave a leap, and he felt shock mingling with confusion. He couldn't believe she was agreeing with him.

'I should say goodbye to Papà first—'

'*No.*' He squeezed her hand. 'Don't go back in—please.' There was no way he was going to let her talk to Buscetta before she left. 'My driver's out front. We can call your father on our way to the airport.'

She stared at him for a moment, and then she smiled. 'Or we could go completely crazy and take my father's helicopter...'

Leaning back into the cream leather upholstery, Vicè breathed out slowly. The Buscetta helicopter was rising up into the dark sky, its rotor blades whipping up the discarded *coriandoli* so that for a moment he felt as if he were in a snow globe—a sensation exacerbated by the feeling of his world being turned upside down and shaken vigorously.

He could hardly believe it.

That Imma had agreed to his impulsive suggestion that they get to know one another seemed fantastical enough, but for her to more or less commandeer her father's helicopter in order to make their escape seemed too preposterous to be true.

And yet that was exactly what was happening.

At that moment Imma turned and smiled at him, her eyes bright with eagerness and pleasure at her part in the adventure, and he felt his heart jump, his body responding to her sudden and thrilling abandonment of the normal expected preliminaries.

Well, perhaps not all of them.

Remembering that this was supposed to be a seduction, he lifted her hand to his mouth, feeling her pulse dart under the skin like a minnow in a pond.

'Will this thing make it to the mainland?' he asked softly.

'The mainland?' she repeated.

He held her gaze, his eyebrow curving upward at the question in her voice.

He and Ciro had accepted that Buscetta would never countenance Vicenzu courting Imma. Plus, the second brother falling in love with his other daughter was so implausible it would almost certainly hint at some kind of plot, so they'd decided that it would be better to present him with a fait accompli.

His shoulders stiffened. Of course before he'd even thought about how he was going to make that happen Ciro, being Ciro, had already proposed to Claudia and started the process of arranging the paperwork for their marriage.

But seducing a woman was not something Vicè consciously did—normally it just happened. He had no idea how to cold-bloodedly reproduce that organic process, so he'd left it to the last minute—like he did everything else in his life.

Not that he'd told his uber-efficient brother that.

Arriving at the wedding, he'd decided to seduce Imma and then use his reputation as leverage for their marriage. It would be a delicate balancing act. She'd know he wouldn't be Cesare's choice for her husband. But nor would her father want her to be viewed as just another notch on Vicenzu's bedpost. And obviously his plan wouldn't work if they kept their liaison private, which was why he needed it to play out in public.

And where better to find maximum publicity than at his celebrity-studded hotel with its inbuilt entourage of photographers?

'I thought I was taking you back to mine,' he said.

'To the Dolce Vita?' She looked confused. 'I thought you wanted to go somewhere private.'

Good point, he thought, his shoulders tensing.

It was a rookie error—except he wasn't a rookie. As Ciro had so pointedly remarked earlier, this was supposed to be his area of expertise.

Glancing out of the window, he felt his pulse slow as he realised he'd made another error in assuming he was calling the shots. Imma might not be planning to go back to his hotel, but they were clearly not just flying in circles so...

'I do,' he said. He let his gaze linger on her face. 'And I should have realised that totally rules out my hotel. But ever since you walked into that church behind your sister I haven't been able to think straight.'

Watching her chew at her lip, he felt his heart kick against his ribs.

'I'm guessing you have somewhere in mind,' he said softly.

He felt her fingers move against his and, glancing down, was almost shocked to see her hand entwined with his. Holding hands was not his thing, but his parents had always done it and his ribs tightened as he pictured his mother sitting alone at the wedding. That was another crime to chalk up to Cesare Buscetta's relentless greed.

But as he felt the ever-present trickle of anger start to rise and swell he pushed the memory away. His anger would wait. Right now he needed to focus on the task in hand.

Closing his grip around her fingers, he gently pulled her closer. 'So where are you taking me?'

No doubt Imma had some favourite boutique hotel in mind—somewhere quiet, intimate—and actually that might work for him. They could lie low until he had her eating out of his hand, and then he could discreetly tip off the paparazzi.

He felt her gaze on his face.

'Papà has a villa on Pantelleria...'

Pantelleria. Unlike most people in the world, he'd heard of the island—but, like most of the population, he'd never set foot on it. Why would he? It was basically a black volcanic speck in the Mediterranean between Sicily and Tunisia.

'Right...' He nodded, holding his easy smile in place. 'Your father isn't going to have a problem with that?'

She hesitated, her face tensing a little as though she was weighing up what to say next.

'He bought it as a kind of hideaway, somewhere to get away from work—only he's not very good about handing over the reins, so he never really goes there. But Claudia and I love it. It's just so beautiful—and very private.'

Her eyes seemed to grow even more opaque.

'But if you've changed your mind I can get Marco to—'

She was close enough that he could feel her small, firm breasts through the thin fabric of his shirt, and the tiny shivers of anticipation scampering over her skin. Seducing Imma at a hideaway on a remote island owned by Buscetta himself was about as far away from ideal as it could get, but he didn't want to jeopardise this mood of intimacy between them.

The time for talking was over.

He looked down at the pulse beating erratically at the base of her beautiful throat, feeling his body harden to stone for the second time in as many minutes. Reaching up, he caught her chin with his hand, tilting her face to his. 'Nothing's changed.'

He could make it work—he *would* make it work.

Needing to defuse any indecision she might still be feeling, he did the first thing that came into his head. Lowering his mouth to hers, he kissed her.

Whatever he'd been expecting when his lips touched hers, it wasn't what actually happened. For a brief second or two she stilled against him, her mouth softening beneath his, lips parting on an intake of breath, and then her hand slid over his neck, fingers pressing lightly against his skin as though she was reading Braille.

Barely breathing, he moved his lips over hers, teasing her with the whispering heat of his mouth, the firm tip of his tongue, stirring her senses, tasting her, all the while telling himself that he hated this woman, that she was guilty by association.

But then she moaned softly, shifting against him. Her fingers curled through his hair to grasp his skull, her tongue pushing between his lips, and hunger, hot and powerful, punched him in the gut.

Her scent enveloped him and, breathing in sharply, he made a rough, incoherent sound against her mouth, trying and failing to still the blood pounding through his veins, almost idiotically stupefied by the strength of his desire and hers.

He was hard—very hard—and, framing her face with his hands, he kissed her fiercely, pulling her closer so that she pressed against him, wanting more of her, needing more of her—

'Miss Buscetta?'

Imma jerked back and they stared at one another dazedly as the pilot's voice filled the cabin.

'We'll be coming in to land in about five minutes. There might be a few crosswinds, but nothing to worry about.'

With a hand that trembled slightly, Imma pressed the intercom. 'Thank you, Marco.'

Vicenzu breathed out unsteadily, blindsided by her response, and utterly floored by his own.

He had wanted so much more than just her mouth. And, judging by the dull ache in his groin, he still did.

His heart beating out of time, he struggled to pull his brain back online. 'Imma—'

Her green eyes fluttered to his face, wide and startled. The curves of her cheeks were flushed with desire, or embarrassment, or maybe both.

He swore inwardly. 'I'm sorry. I didn't expect—I didn't mean for that to happen—'

Actually, what he hadn't expected was for it to feel like that—for her to be so gloriously responsive, so fierce, so sweet, so everything he'd ever wanted in a woman.

But how was that possible?

He was only supposed to be seducing this woman to avenge his family.

'I understand.'

She inched backwards, slipping her hand free of his. He watched her fold it back into her lap, his heart beating as violently as if he'd just sprinted for a finishing line. Only for once—incredibly—he didn't appear to be on the winner's podium.

'Imma—'

'Please.' She held up her hand and her beautiful mouth no longer looked soft and kissable but pinched, as though she was trying to hold something in. 'I don't need to hear it.'

'Hear what?'

Her face was pale and set, and there was a tension to her body he recognised. It was as though she was bracing herself for bad news.

'I've heard it all before,' she said, staring past him. 'Let me guess. You're worried things are moving too fast. Or maybe you respect me too much? That's always popular.'

He frowned. Her words made no sense. 'I don't understand—'

She ignored him. 'You know, back at the wedding I thought you were different. But I guess when it comes to the crunch you're just like everyone else.'

The bitterness in her voice was unmistakable now.

'I'm sorry for taking up so much of your time, Signor Trapani. But don't worry. You can go back to your precious hotel and the rest of your "sweet life" now. Just tell Marco where you need to go and he'll take you.'

There was a slight judder as the helicopter touched down, and before he had a chance to respond, even to absorb her words, she'd pulled off her seat belt and was out of the door and gone.

He stared after her, shock and outrage swirling up inside him, and then he was wrenching himself free and following her into the warm night air. She was moving fast, and he found himself having to run to catch up with her.

He'd never run after a woman metaphorically, let alone in reality, and the fact that he was having to do so made his irritation intensify with every step.

'Imma!'

She carried on walking and, frustrated by the sight of the smooth, untroubled knot at the nape of her neck, he caught her arm, jerking her round to face him.

'Where's all this coming from? All I said was—'

Her eyes narrowed and she shook his hand off. 'I heard you the first time.'

Watching the bow of her mouth tremble, Vicè felt his breath hitch in his throat. Before her anger had been crimped, confined by a forced politeness, now she was clearly furious.

'Look, I get it. It was a wedding. You were bored, or curious—maybe both. But I do have feelings and I am done with being picked up and dropped like some toy.'

She glared at him, her hands curling into fists. 'But I suppose I should be thankful that at least one Trapani brother has the courage of his convictions.'

His jaw clenched. Being compared unfavourably to Ciro was such a frequent occurrence he rarely even reacted any more, but Imma's criticism, delivered in that clipped, dismissive manner, somehow got under his skin, so that suddenly he was having to rein in his temper, usually so slow to rise.

'Meaning?' he said.

Her lip curled with contempt. 'I mean, unlike you, Ciro's not scared of my father.'

Listening to her words echo in the silence, Imma felt slightly sick.

She hadn't meant to say that out loud, only there was no real point in continuing with this farce.

Vicenzu Trapani was a beautiful liar, and she was an unforgivable idiot.

What was worse, for just a few short hours she had actually started to hope…started to think that Vicè was different—that, incredibly, like Claudia, she had met a man who was prepared to stand proudly beside her.

And not just any man—a man who was in a class of his own. Cool, glamorous, and with a smile that made her body ache and a mouth that turned her inside out.

Remembering her uninhibited response to his kiss, she felt her skin grow warm. She had kissed men before—three, to be precise—but Vicè's kiss had been like nothing she'd ever experienced, and if Marco's disembodied voice hadn't interrupted she would have gone on kissing him forever.

Her cheeks burned as she replayed that sound she'd made when he'd pulled her against his hard body. It had felt so good, so right—but clearly not good or right enough for him to want to continue.

She hung on to her temper as he took a step towards her, his eyes narrowing like chips of volcanic rock.

'*Scared?* Of your *father*? Let me tell you something, Imma. I feel many things for your father, but fear isn't one of them. I'm no more scared of him than Ciro is.'

Gone was the handsome easy-going playboy. The skin across his cheekbones was tight, like a ship's sail in a strong wind. But it was the rawness in his voice that convinced her that he was telling the truth.

And just like that her own anger turned to air.

'I thought you'd changed your mind.' She swallowed. 'Like all the others.'

There was a beat of silence and she heard him breathe out unsteadily.

'I panicked,' he said.

His dark eyes found hers, and the naked heat in them sent a jolt through her body.

'But not because I wanted to back out. I thought I'd come

on too strong.' He hesitated, and then, reaching out, took her hand and pulled her closer. 'I meant what I said earlier. I want to get to know you better.'

As he gazed down at her she felt her pulse begin to beat a little faster.

'And if you still want that too then I won't let anything or anyone—including your father—get in the way of that happening. Do you understand?'

Her heart was pressing against her ribs. It was what she'd wanted to hear for so long—and, more importantly, it was clear he meant it.

Nodding slowly, she let him pull her into his arms.

CHAPTER THREE

'So, WHO ARE these "others"?'

Glancing up at Vicè, Imma frowned. Neither of them was hungry, but they were drinking wine on the vast terrace next to the pool. Or rather he was drinking. She was too jittery to do anything but clutch the stem of her glass. Besides, just looking at him made her tongue stick to the roof of her mouth.

Watching him languidly stretch out his long legs, she felt knots form in her stomach. He was so perfect, with his dark poet's eyes and panther-like grace...

Trying to stay calm, she gazed past him. It was a bad idea. Somebody—probably Marianna, the housekeeper—had lit some candles, and the twitching flames made the curves of his face even more dangerously appealing.

Accompanying the darkness was the lightest of breezes—a whisper of dry air from Africa—and on it came the scent of the roses and jasmine that Marianna cherished in the garden that surrounded the villa on all sides.

The undiluted romance of it all sent a tremor through her blood.

She cleared her throat. 'Others?'

He picked up his wine glass, lounging back in his seat, his dark eyes roaming her face. 'Earlier, you said something about me changing my mind "like the others".'

'Oh, that...' She felt a prickle spread over her skin and down her spine. 'It's nothing, really.'

How could someone like him truly understand? But he held her gaze.

She sighed. 'Just that my dates were always ever so keen on me—until they worked out who my father was. And then—'

'Oh, I see,' he said softly.

She nodded. 'Papà has a reputation. Friends in low places. I'm sure you've read the stories about him?'

He shook his head, his eyes gleaming. 'Too busy reading about myself.'

The teasing note in his voice made her skin sting. Pulse quickening, she glanced away. What was he thinking when he looked at her like that? And why did her body like it so much?

Reaching across the table, he took her hand. 'Look, what they can't find out they make up. It's not important.'

His voice was gentle but his dark eyes were burning into her, the intensity of their focus accelerating her already racing pulse. He was everything she wanted, but everything she feared. Compelling. Confident. Curious about her.

She had never talked like this to anyone. Her father's moods were too changeable and Claudia was so young and innocent.

She felt his fingers tighten around hers.

'Those men had no right to judge you, *cara*.' His beautiful mouth twisted. 'Believe me, I know. People think because they read about you that they know you, but they don't.' His eyes met hers. 'They really don't.'

Remembering the stories she'd read about him, she felt a twinge of guilt. How could she complain about being judged when she was guilty of doing the same to him?

'And those people don't know you,' she said, her words tumbling over themselves. 'The real you. You're funny, and smart, and kind, and sweet…'

Her voice petered out. Beside her, Vicè leaned back a little, his expression midway between surprise and amusement—unsurprising, given that she'd sounded like some teenage fangirl.

Cringing inwardly, she frowned. 'Look, maybe this wasn't such a good idea. I'll get Marco to drop you back to your hotel—'

Reaching over, he tugged her towards him. Then he smiled…a slow, flickering smile like a candle being lit that made a pulse of excitement beat beneath her skin.

'*Cara*, forget about my hotel…you're the sweetness in my life.'

Oh, she liked him so much—and she'd almost ruined everything with her stupid accusations. But this was all so new and different. She was different with him. More impulsive and open. Bolder.

Her body tensed. Only not so bold that she was looking forward to facing her father.

Picturing Cesare's outburst, she shivered. He would be angry enough about her leaving the wedding early, but his fury would be visible from space when he found out she had left with Vicè and come here. Particularly as he'd hinted that he was finally ready to talk about her role at Trapani.

'How mad is he going to be?'

Her chin jerked up. 'How did you know what I was thinking?'

'Just a guess.' He sighed. 'Come on, let's go inside. I think you need something stronger than wine.'

Inside, he poured two glasses of grappa and, dropping down beside her on the sofa, handed her one. 'Look, I feel like this is my fault. Why don't I call him? Explain—'

'No, absolutely not.' She shook her head. She could think of nothing that would antagonise Cesare more.

Leaning forward, Vicè stroked the curve of her cheekbone with a tenderness that made her skin melt.

'I'm not scared of him, Imma.' His face stilled as though something had just occurred to him. 'Are *you*?'

She shook her head. 'Of course not. Papà just doesn't like surprises. He has plans for me. Expectations. Your father's business—he wants me to run it.'

He lifted his glass. 'And you don't want to.'

It was a statement, not a question. And just for a moment

his eyes seemed to narrow. But when he lowered his glass she realised he was just curious.

'Yes, I do. It's a wonderful business. And it's the least I can do for Papà. I want to be there for him.'

Her pulse skipped. Her father was going to be apoplectic, but it was the aftermath of his rage she was dreading.

He would become even more controlling—particularly regarding her matrimonial choices. Claudia could have her Ciro, but Cesare wanted Imma to marry well—and by 'well' he meant to a man nearer his own age, whose wealth was equal to the GDP of some small country.

Love hadn't been mentioned.

She shivered inside. She couldn't disappoint her father. He needed her to fulfil his dreams.

All she wanted was just one night for herself.

An experience that was hers and hers alone.

An experience she would remember forever—an encounter that would imprint on her body and mind to help her through years of dutiful marriage to a man she didn't love.

Tonight she wanted fire and ecstasy. She wanted to understand her own needs and desires…be in charge of making that small but important change from sheltered, uninformed virgin to a woman who had experienced the storm of passion.

Picking up her glass, she saw her hand was shaking a little. Her body was humming…fear mingling with desire. Fear of missing out. Fear of giving in to what she wanted.

And she wanted Vicè.

Her hunger, her need for him, was like a tornado inside her, upturning everything in its path so that her skin could barely hold it in.

And by bringing Vicè here she had already sealed her fate. Her father was going to come down on her hard and fast. So shouldn't she make sure it was for something that mattered?

And what mattered more than choosing your first lover?

This might be her last opportunity to make that choice and she was choosing Vicè. Because he was handsome, charming, and most importantly she trusted him.

'But I want to be here with you too,' she said slowly. 'And I don't care how angry that makes him.'

Their gazes locked.

'He has no reason to be angry.'

His dark eyes held her fast and heat shivered down her spine.

'Nothing's happened.'

Something stirred deep inside her, and she took a steadying breath.

'Nothing's happened *yet*,' she said softly.

Her hunger for him was like the lick of a flame. Only he could put out the fire.

The glass in her hand was shaking. Reaching over, he took it from her.

'Are you saying you want something to happen?' he asked.

His eyes were steady on her face, his expression intent, as though he was trying to read her mind.

She didn't know where to start, or how to ask for what she wanted. But she knew that she wanted to share it, feel it, with him—with this man. With Vicè.

She nodded. 'Yes, that is what I'm saying.'

Her belly clenched. She sounded so formal, so uptight, but she couldn't help it. Her body was just so wound up, so hot and tight with hope and need and anticipation. And fear of rejection.

Her stomach was a ball of nerves. 'It's just that I'm scared—'

'Of being hurt?' He gave her a crooked smile. 'It's a risk, and I guess it's a particularly big risk with someone like me...someone with my history.' His dark, mocking face was suddenly serious. 'But if it makes you feel better I think I'm the one in danger here. You make me feel things I've never felt, want things I've never wanted before—'

Heat surged over her skin, lifting the hairs on her arms, making her breasts tingle and tighten. So many choices had been made for her already. So much decided and dictated. This night with Vicè would be hers, and hers alone.

'I want them too,' she whispered. 'I want you.'

But he was gorgeous and sexy, and he had his pick of beautiful, experienced women. Would he really want someone so inexpert and gauche?

For a moment she thought about telling him the truth. Only what if it changed things between them?

Vicè might be a playboy, but he was also a Sicilian. What if beneath the languid posturing he retained an old-school Sicilian attitude to taking a woman's virginity? What if he backed off?

She made up her mind.

Being here with him was straight out of a fantasy, and raising the topic of her virginity would introduce a cool reality she wasn't ready to face yet.

'Shall we go somewhere even more private?' she said softly. 'More intimate...'

Vicenzu stared at her in silence, a pulse beating in his throat, her voice replaying inside his head.

Intimate.

He felt his belly flip over.

Intimate.

The word brushed against his skin. It made him think of subdued lighting, soft laughter and naked bodies.

His own body turned to granite as she bit her lip.

'Imma, are you sure?' Holding her gaze, he softened his voice. 'I know my reputation, and I don't want you to think that's why I'm here.'

She shook her head. 'I don't think that.'

She was staring up at him, her face expressionless, but

he could hear the nervous edge in her voice and knew she
was trying to sound calmer than she felt.

It was understandable. Given how protective Buscetta
was about his daughters, it was unlikely she did this kind
of thing very often—and certainly not under her overcon-
trolling father's nose. Clearly being here, in her father's lair,
was spooking her.

Her cheeks were flushed and her dark hair was coming
undone from the knot at her neck. He studied her face, lost
momentarily in the delicacy of her features and the flame in
her eyes. He felt his pulse accelerate. He could do this, but
he needed to take charge, keep it light—not let her beauty
get in the way of what was really happening here.

'I'm happy to wait, *cara*. Well, maybe happy is pushing it.' He grimaced. 'Obviously I'd be in a lot of pain—'

She laughed then, and for a moment he almost forgot
why he was there. It was such a lovely sound. All he could
think about was how to make her laugh again.

But then he blanked his mind as she stood up, pulling
him to his feet.

'I might just freshen up.'

She seemed more nervous now they were in her bedroom, and he kissed her softly on the mouth.

'Good idea. I'll wait here. Take all the time you need.'

Actually, he was the one fighting for time. He needed to
put some distance between himself and Imma otherwise...

As the door closed he began unbuttoning his shirt, and
then, frowning, he pulled out his wallet. He was checking
he had condoms when he noticed he had a notification on
his phone. It was a voicemail from Ciro.

*Vicenzu, it's me... Look, I can't do this for much longer.
I've fulfilled my part. She's going to sign the house over
to me today. You need to get your side done, and quickly.
Whatever it takes to get the business back, do it. Because
I don't know how much longer I can keep the pretence up.'*

He thought about the edge to Imma's voice.

Then he pictured his mother sitting alone at the wedding. Taking back his father's business and their family home would go a long way towards making her smile again. And it would wipe the smile off Buscetta's face at the same time.

He knew what his mother would say. That two wrongs didn't make a right.

His jaw tightened. No, they didn't. On this occasion two wrongs would make two rights.

Hearing the door to the bathroom open, he texted Ciro quickly, then tossed his phone onto a chair. Composing his face, he looked up—and his breath stalled in his throat.

Imma was standing in the doorway, her long dark hair hanging loose over her shoulders.

Her naked shoulders.

Actually, she was entirely naked except for a tiny pair of cream lace panties—a fact that his groin had apparently registered several moments before his eyes.

His body hardening to stone, he stood hypnotised by her small rounded breasts and rose-coloured nipples. Her skin was the colour of the purest cold-pressed virgin olive oil, and just looking at it made his ribcage tighten around his chest.

He was used to nudity, and blasé about beauty, but there was a vulnerability to her pose that had everything and nothing to do with sex.

His pact with Ciro was forgotten. And his anger and grief and guilt—everything that had propelled him to this softly lit room—was swept away by a need he had never experienced before.

He stared at her, dry-mouthed, feeling the blood throb through his body.

She took a step forward, reaching out to touch him.

'Wait,' he said gently. 'Let me look at you first.'

She looked up at him, and he took his time absorbing her beauty.

Expression shuttered, he stepped closer and stroked the curve of her cheek. 'Don't be shy. You're beautiful.'

'So are you.'

Heat flared inside him as she touched his chest, her warm fingers sending shock waves over his skin. Leaning forward, he brushed his mouth lightly over hers, sliding his hand through her hair.

It wasn't a kiss—more a prelude to a kiss. She drew a quick breath and her eyes met his. Then, taking his hand, she led him to the bed.

He stripped quickly and slid in beside her. As he ran his hand lightly down her arm, she shivered against him.

'Are you sure about this?'

Heart pounding, Imma stared up at his beautiful face. She had never been surer about anything. Her whole body felt as though it was clamouring for him.

But as he shifted closer she felt a rush of panic. Up close and naked, there seemed to be even more of him than before. His limbs seemed more solid, and—she glanced down at his erection—he was very hard, and bigger than she'd imagined.

Her pulse accelerated. This wasn't going to work. Vicè had a wealth of sexual experience. No doubt he was expert at all kinds of lovemaking and used to sophisticated, skilful lovers. But beyond the mechanics of sex she knew absolutely nothing.

'Yes, I'm sure. Are you?'

'Am *I* sure?' He seemed to consider her question, frowning. Then, 'Yeah, of course.'

His hand moved to cover her hip, his fingers gliding over the crest of bone in a way that made her skin tingle.

'I mean, as long as you respect me in the morning...' he added.

His eyes gleamed and she started to laugh.

Dipping his head, he brushed his mouth against her. 'Tell

me what you want.' His voice was warm with desire. 'What you like.'

She didn't know what she liked. She didn't know where to start. Where it would end.

'I like this…' Her finger trembled against the curve of his jaw. 'And this…' She touched his chest, the smooth contours of his muscles. 'And this.' She flattened her hand against the trail of fine dark hair that ran down the centre of his stomach.

He sucked in a breath, his pupils flaring.

'I like that too,' he said unsteadily and, lowering his mouth, he kissed her.

He kissed her lightly, then more deeply, slowing the kiss down, slowing her pulse and her breath, kissing her so that she forgot her doubts, forgot his past—forgot everything except the touch of his mouth and the heat of his skin and the unchecked hunger in his dark eyes.

He cupped her breasts, gently thumbing each nipple, and then, taking his weight on his knees and elbows, he grazed the hardened tips with his mouth, his warm breath sending shock waves of desire up and down her body so that her stomach clenched around the ball of heat pulsing inside her.

She arched against him, pressing herself closer, wanting more of him. His fingers were sliding over her skin now, in slow, measured caresses that made a moan of pure need rise up in her throat.

Would it be like this on her wedding night? Would her husband make her feel like this? That nameless man who was yet to be chosen for her. She took a breath, fighting panic, and instantly felt him still against her.

'Cara…' He shifted his weight. 'Is this okay? Do you want me to stop?'

'No.' She splayed her hands on his chest, feeling his quickening heartbeat through her fingertips. 'I don't want you to stop. Please, don't stop.'

She couldn't admit the truth. It would be crazy to admit

that she wanted this to last forever—for him to be that name-less man, to be her husband.

Reaching up, she brought his face down to hers and kissed him slowly, deepening the kiss as he pushed against her.

His hand moved across the outside of her leg, then be-tween her thighs. Shivering, she shifted closer, lifting her hips, pressing against the hard contours of his knuckles, seeking him, wanting him to ease the ache inside her.

'Your skin is like silk,' Vicè murmured.

He pulled her closer, moulding her body against his, his mouth finding hers—and then he felt her hand enclose the heavy weight of his erection.

He cut off a groan, catching her hand in his, blood thun-dering in his ears.

'Not yet…not me.' Pushing her gently back on the bed, he leaned over her, kissing her deeply. 'This is all about you.'

Hooking his thumbs into her panties, he slid them down her legs. Now she was completely naked.

'Look at me,' he said softly.

Her eyes locked with his and he felt his heartbeat ac-celerate.

His breathing staccato, he began again at her face, trac-ing the outline of her lips with his tongue, kissing the curv-ing bones of her cheeks, and then he lowered his mouth to her throat, tracking the pulse beating frenetically beneath the smooth skin, moving with deliberate, sensuous slow-ness down to the swell of her breasts.

Her hands slid through his hair and she pushed his head against her nipple, moaning softly as she arched her body up to meet his lips.

His heart missed a beat. He was desperately trying to centre himself. Trying to stay detached. But she was just so beautiful, so eager and responsive. He couldn't stop himself from responding to her. His need for her was like a fever in his blood.

Her nipples were taut and he sucked first one and then the other, nipping the swollen ruched tips, his erection so hard now it was almost horizontal.

Ignoring the ache in his groin, he found her mouth again, kissing her slowly, sliding his hand down over her waist and through the triangle of curls, gently probing the slick heat between her thighs.

Imma felt her head start to spin. She had never felt anything like this before. His fingers were moving inside her, his thumb brushing the nub of her clitoris, sending oscillating tremors over her skin.

Shivering, she moved against his caress, chasing the pulse beating in his hand, wanting, needing something *more* to fill the urgent hollowed-out ache inside her.

'You're killing me,' he said hoarsely.

She reached again for his groin. This time he didn't stop her, and as her fingers wrapped around his hard, swollen length, he groaned against her mouth.

'Ti voglio,' she whispered. 'I want to feel you inside me. *Ti prego.'*

Gritting his teeth, he shifted his weight and reached over to the bedside table. She heard a tearing sound. Dazed, she watched him slide a condom on.

He gazed down into her face and the dark passion in his eyes made hunger rear up inside her.

Lowering his mouth, he kissed her breasts again, licking her nipples and drawing them into his mouth, and then she felt the blunt head of his erection pushing between her thighs.

It was too big. She tensed. It would never fit inside her.

Her hands pressed against his chest, and he stopped moving, shifting his weight minutely.

'It's okay,' he murmured. 'Take your time. You just need to get used to me.'

His voice calmed her, but it was the hunger etched on his face that made her start to move against him.

Taking a breath, she parted her legs further. She arched upward, straining for something she didn't understand, something just out of reach, something that would satisfy the insistent clamouring of her body.

He moved above her and instinctively she opened her legs wider, her breath jerking in her throat as he rubbed the tip of his erection against the bud of her clitoris. Curling her arms around his shoulders, wanting to feel all of him inside her, she lifted her hips and he pushed into her.

There was a moment of sharpness and she tensed—must have tensed, because he stilled above her. Not wanting him to suspect her virginity—or, worse, stop—she pulled him closer and began to move against him, trying to regulate her breathing as her body stretched to accommodate him.

He was fully inside her now, and his mouth found hers as he matched himself to the rhythm of her breathing. As he started to increase his pace she felt the pulse inside her accelerate in time to his movements.

She was panting now, lunging up towards him. Muscles she hadn't known she had were straining, pulling apart, fraying, and she gripped his shoulders as her whole body suddenly splintered in a rush of pleasure so intense she could have wept.

And then he was thrusting into her, clamping her body to his, his groans mingling with her ragged breathing as he tensed, shuddering helplessly against her.

His hands tightened in her hair and he kissed her face, murmuring her name against the damp skin of her neck. *'Sei bellissima,'* he said softly.

She smiled, suddenly shy beneath his dark gaze. 'Was it okay for you?'

'Was it okay for me?' He laughed. 'I've never been asked that before. It was more than "okay", *cara*. It was incredible.'

'I didn't know it could be like that,' she said slowly.

How could she have imagined such dizzying pleasure was right there, at her fingertips? Her cheeks felt warm. Or rather at *his* fingertips. She had wanted it to be amazing but she had completely underestimated how it would feel, the bliss of being touched, the heat of his mouth...

His eyes roamed her face. 'What's it been like before?'

Her heart gave a jump. She could lie, but it was done now. They had made love. There was no need for secrets between them.

'It wasn't like anything.' She took a breath. 'There was no "before". You're my first—my first lover.'

Her first lover.

Vicè stared at her in silence, made mute by shock and disbelief.

She'd been a virgin.

He couldn't have been any more stunned if she'd thrown a bucket of cold water in his face.

His head was spinning. With an effort, he replayed the time they had just spent in each other's arms.

When he'd entered her—he gritted his teeth, *her actual first time*—her body had been tight, and there had been moments when she'd tensed, moments when he had felt her hesitate.

But he'd put it down to nerves over having sex with somebody new. He hadn't thought she had no experience whatsoever.

Suddenly his skin could barely contain the chaos inside his body.

He was frustrated with himself for not realising, and he felt guilty for not taking it more slowly, more gently—he would have done if he'd known. He was angry too, incomprehensibly. Angry with Ciro, for putting him in this position, but mostly with Imma.

He swallowed against the rush of questions rising in his throat.

Why hadn't she told him?

Why hadn't she said anything?

It made no sense.

But there was nothing he could do about it now. No magic spell to turn back time.

'I am?' He frowned. 'Sorry, I thought… I mean, I know you went to university, so…'

She shrugged casually, her hands trembling as she spoke. 'I didn't live in halls. My father bought me an apartment and insisted on my bodyguards going everywhere with me.'

'So those "others" you mentioned…you didn't…?'

Imma shook her head. 'I never wanted any of them in that way. Not like I wanted you.' She hesitated. 'Is it a problem?'

She was staring up at him, and the expression on her face made him swear silently. He needed to make this all right, and fast, or risk blowing everything.

Shaking his head, he touched her cheek. 'Quite the contrary.' His face twisted. 'I can't believe I'm saying this, but I like it that I'm your first.'

Imma stared at him, her pulse beating out of time.

'Actually, I'm a little embarrassed by how happy it makes me feel,' he added.

Her stomach clenched and blood rushed into her pelvis. Her body was rippling back to life as he pulled her closer.

Breathing out unsteadily, he buried his face in her neck. 'Imma, do you think it's possible for two people to fall in love in a single day?'

Her heart lurched against her ribs. His dark eyes were soft and steady on her face, but she could hear the shake in his voice.

She took a deep breath. 'I do,' she said softly.

'And could you maybe see yourself saying *I do*?' He stared down at her. 'If I asked you to marry me.'

'You don't have to marry me,' she said shakily. 'It was my decision not to say anything. I should have told you I was a virgin—'

'That's not why I want to marry you.'

His arms tightened around her, and she knew he was telling the truth.

'I know it sounds crazy, but I have to marry you—there's no other option for me.'

The poetry of his words made her heart swell.

She was too choked to speak, but as he lowered his mouth to hers she leaned into him, her hands threading through his hair, and kissed him fiercely.

They made love again, and afterwards she fell asleep in his arms.

She was still wrapped in his arms sometime later, when she woke in the early hours, and for a moment she lay on her side, watching Vicè sleep.

There were no words to describe how she was feeling. She was happy—had never been happier—but 'happy' felt too ordinary, too small a word to describe what had just happened.

It was everything she'd wanted for her first time. He had wanted her for herself, just as she had wanted him, and his desire had made her feel sensual. Confident. Powerful. Even when her body had dissolved into hot, endless need.

She still felt as if she was glowing inside.

And it wasn't just the sex.

It was Vicè.

She had fallen helplessly in love with him. And, incredibly, he felt the same way about her. He must do to have proposed.

Her heart trembled.

She might not have his experience, but she had learned

enough about the world to know that a man like Vicè didn't propose marriage after every sexual encounter.

Given his track record with women, he must have been hoping simply to seduce her. It had probably never crossed his mind that he would fall in love any more than it had hers.

Glancing over at him, she felt her throat tighten.

He was so beautiful, so gorgeously masculine, all muscle and smooth golden skin, and he'd been so generous. Remembering how his body had felt, on hers and in hers, her muscles tensed.

Suddenly she was hot and damp and aching.

It had been so good.

Felt so right.

His weight and the press of his mouth…the rush of his heartbeat.

Could she wake him?

She bit her lip. Would that be greedy? Too forward?

He shifted in his sleep, turning his face into the crook of his arm, and she breathed out unevenly.

She was so, *so* happy. The only thing that would make it even more perfect was if she could share her happiness with Claudia. But it was too early—and anyway it was her sister's wedding night.

She frowned. Across the room, she could hear her phone ringing. Slipping out of bed, she picked it up, her heart fluttering with joy. It was Claudia. But of course it was—they had always had the ability to communicate almost telepathically.

She tiptoed out of the bedroom, closing the door softly behind her. 'Hey, you! I was just—'

'Oh, Immie, something terrible has happened.' Claudia's voice was high and trembling.

Imma's breath scrabbled inside her chest. 'Don't cry, *mia cara*. What is it? Tell me.'

'It's all a lie, Immie. He doesn't love me.'

Her heart pounded fiercely. 'Of course he does—'

'He doesn't. He didn't know I was there and I heard him talking on the phone—'

'That can't be right…' The phone felt slippery in Imma's hand and she clutched it more tightly. 'Ciro loves you.'

'No, he doesn't, Immie. He doesn't. He just married me to get revenge on Papà. And Vicenzu is planning to do the same to you.'

The room swayed. For a moment she couldn't breathe. Her lungs felt as though they were full of sand.

It couldn't be true. Claudia must have made a mistake. Vicè wouldn't do that—

But as her sister began to cry she knew that he had.

CHAPTER FOUR

ROLLING OVER ONTO his side, Vicè shifted against the pillow, his hand reaching across the bed for—

His eyes snapped open.

For Imma.

But the bed was empty.

He raised himself up on his elbow, his pulse accelerating as he heard the sound of running water from the bathroom. He glanced at the clock by the bed, realising how late in the day it was. She must be showering.

Only it wasn't the thought of a naked Imma with water streaming over the soft curves of her body that was making his pulse beat faster. It was the sharp, shocking realisation that he had been reaching out for her—for the daughter of his enemy.

Except she hadn't felt like his enemy—not when she'd been moving on top of him with her hair tumbling over her shoulders and a dazed look in those incredible olive green eyes.

When she'd walked out of the bathroom last night, naked except for that tiny wisp of underwear, he'd forgotten all those weeks of anger and doubt. In that moment he had simply been a man swept away by lust.

He gritted his teeth. But now his feelings were less simple—they were downright confused, in fact, and for one very obvious reason.

He hadn't signed up for taking her virginity.

In fact, he'd never slept with a virgin before, and if he'd been going to start it wouldn't have been with *this* woman.

Taking Imma's virginity felt like a bond—a connection between them that didn't fit well with the task in hand. And yet...

He might have made a joke of it earlier, but almost against his will—flying in the face of everything he knew to be logical—he liked being her first lover.

His skin felt suddenly hot and taut. Even to admit that privately to himself blew his mind. When had he turned into such a caveman?

But there was no point in pretending. Satisfaction that he had been her first still resonated inside him.

And affected him on the outside too, apparently.

Gritting his teeth, he lifted the sheet away from his erection. He didn't understand what was happening to him. Imma was very beautiful, and she felt even better than she looked. But he was remembering how she'd fallen asleep, with her body curled around his. He let go of a breath he hadn't realised he was holding.

No matter how attractive the woman, or how intense his desire, he had never felt even the slightest impulse to hold any of his lovers in his arms while he slept.

It must have been finding out she was a virgin. There was no other explanation.

Rolling onto his back, he frowned up at the ceiling. He was irritated at having to feel anything but his usual sense of repletion. He certainly hadn't planned on dealing with all this complicated stuff.

But was it really that complicated? So she'd been a virgin? So what?

She was an adult, and she had wanted sex as much as he had. Getting fixated on being her first lover was making him lose sight of what mattered—the fact that for once he'd done what he'd set out to do.

It had been a playbook seduction. He'd used his hands, his mouth, his body expertly to turn her on, touching her and tormenting her until she had melted into him, her moans of ecstasy filling the silent room.

Agreed, her virginity had added a layer of confusion—

but surely it would make the likelihood of her marrying him and therefore getting back the business a shoo-in.

He was going to push for the soonest date possible for their wedding. After that, all that would remain would be for him to persuade her to sign the paperwork.

Then it would be done.

Revenge would be theirs.

But he was jumping ahead of himself. His moment of triumph would need to be savoured properly with Ciro, over a cigar, and probably some of that bourbon his brother loved so much. Right now there were other things to savour.

His pulse twitched and he felt hunger course through his veins like a caffeine rush.

So why not simply enjoy the ride?

He glanced over at the bathroom door. Maybe he would join her in that shower, after all...

But just as he was about to throw back the sheet, the door to the bathroom opened. Remembering her entrance last night, he felt his gaze narrow—but this time Imma wasn't naked. In fact—disappointingly—she was fully clothed.

His eyes drifted lazily over the simple white cotton dress she was wearing and he felt a pulse of heat bumping over his skin. He wasn't averse to watching her take it off.

Sprawling back against the pillows, he lifted his eyes to hers and smiled. 'Hi.'

'Hi,' she said quietly.

She didn't move, just stood in the doorway.

'Did you sleep well?'

She nodded. 'Yes, thank you.'

'Are you okay? I mean—'

She nodded again. 'Everything's fine.'

He felt relief slide over his skin. He'd been a little worried that, having had time to think, she might want to do some kind of post-mortem. Clearly, though, she had other things on her mind.

She took a deep breath. 'Vicè, last night you asked me

to marry you. I wondered if you meant it? Or if you just got carried away in the heat of the moment?'

'Of course I meant it.' Throwing back the sheet, he got up and walked swiftly around the bed to where she stood in the doorway. 'I want to marry you. I want to do it as soon as possible. Only...'

He hesitated, a rush of triumph sweeping over his skin as her eyes searched his face. *He had done it.* She was hooked. His father's business was as good as his.

'Only what?'

'Only I don't remember you actually saying yes.'

'Oh!' she gasped in a rush. 'Then, yes... I will marry you. But first there's something I want to do.'

There was only a sliver of space between them. Her gaze dropped to his naked body and he felt his groin harden again in time with his accelerating heartbeat. *Really? She was going to...?*

She slapped him across the face.

He swore. 'What the hell—'

'You are a *monster.*'

The softness in her voice was gone, and it was gone from her eyes too. She looked and sounded coldly furious.

'You and that despicable brother of yours.'

She slapped his other cheek, equally hard.

'How could he do that to her? How could you both be so cruel?'

Stunned, his face stinging, he caught her hand as she lifted it to strike him again. A flush of panic and confusion swirled in his chest.

'I don't know what—'

She struggled against his grip. '*Basta!* Enough!' She tugged her hand free. 'I've had enough of your lies. I know none of this is real, Vicenzu. I know because I've read the texts you sent your brother. And I've heard his voicemail.'

She pulled his phone from her pocket and he stared at it

in silence. A cold, dull ache was spreading over his skin, turning his blood to ice.

'You didn't bother locking it—but then I suppose you didn't think you needed to. I mean, why would you be worried about *me*? A woman who was stupid enough to gift-wrap her virginity for you.'

'That's not fair!' he snarled. 'If you'd told me, I would have—'

'You would have what?' She folded her arms across her chest, her green eyes wide with contempt. 'Given up? Gone home? *Yeah, right*,' she jeered. 'And forgotten all about taking back your precious olive oil company. I think not. You might be careless about most things—like the truth…' She paused, her expression not just hardening, but ossifying. 'But clearly you care about that.'

He flinched inwardly, the truth of her words slicing through him to the bone.

But this conversation was always going to happen, he told himself quickly. It wasn't as if he and Imma had ever been going to celebrate their ruby wedding in forty years, like his parents had.

The memory of the last time he'd visited his parents' home made his spine tense painfully. At the time he'd vaguely registered that his father looked a little tired and seemed a little quieter than usual, but it had been easy—shamefully easy—to just tell himself that his dad was getting old.

Except now Alessandro would never get old. That was on him, even more than on his brother, but the person really responsible for this mess was this woman's father: Cesare Buscetta.

She held up his phone. 'Perhaps you've forgotten what you wrote? Perhaps you'd like me to read your text to you? Just to remind you.'

'I know what I wrote, Imma,' he said coldly. He met her

gaze and then, reaching down, picked up his clothes from last night, pulling them on with deliberate unconcern.

Her eyes were sharp, like shards of broken glass. 'You know what makes all this so much worse? I already *knew* about your reputation with women. I *knew* you couldn't be trusted. But then we talked, and you made me believe that people had been wrong about you. That you weren't some spoilt playboy with nothing in his head except living *la dolce vita.*'

She shook her head, and even though he was angry he couldn't stop his brain from focusing on the way her still damp hair was turning her white dress transparent.

'And I was right.' She stared at him, contempt mingling with loathing in her green eyes. 'You're not just a spoilt playboy—you're also a vicious, unprincipled liar.'

'Says the woman who didn't bother telling me she was a virgin,' he snarled, feeling the dam inside him breaking.

A part of him knew that he was only angry with her because he was in the wrong. He had seduced her. Methodically, cold-bloodedly pursuing her at the wedding, gaining her trust, then using all his charm to woo her into bed.

And all the while he'd told himself that she deserved it. He'd thought he had her all figured out. Thought she was a silent witness to her father's behaviour.

Only then she'd told him she was a virgin, and for some reason that had changed everything. It had made him feel responsible, guilty, and that wasn't fair.

'You should have told me,' he said.

'About my virginity?' Her eyes narrowed. 'Why? What difference would it have made?'

He was in a blind fury now. 'It would have made a difference to me!'

She was either incredibly naive or disingenuous if she thought that any man wouldn't want to know whether a woman had ever had sex before.

'Oh, and this is all about you. You and your stupid vendetta.' Her lip curled. 'You were lying to me, Vicè. And you would still be lying to me now if I hadn't confronted you. Tossing a few rose petals on the bed and lighting some candles wouldn't have changed anything.'

Porca miseria! Vicè stared at her, hearing her words pinballing around inside his brain. He wasn't talking about rose petals and candles. He was talking about the rules of interaction between couples.

'So what if I lied?' he asked. 'You lie all the time. To me. To other people. To yourself—'

'Excuse me?' Her voice was a whisper of loathing.

'All that garbage about your father wishing he could have "helped" mine sooner.' *Helped!* The word curdled in his mouth. 'Turning a blind eye to his arm-twisting doesn't absolve you. It was your monstrous father hounding him, breaking him down month after month, that sent my father to an early grave—as you very well know.'

'That's not true.' She spat the words at him. 'Papà told me what happened. How your father had overstretched himself. How he came and asked to be bought out. Maybe he didn't want you and Ciro to know the truth.' She gave him a withering glance. 'I mean, why would he? He clearly knew neither of his sons had what was needed to save his life's work.'

Vicè flinched inwardly. One son certainly hadn't.

A stiletto of pain stabbed him beneath the ribs. Pain followed by rage. With her, for seeing what he was so desperate to hide, and with himself for not having been the son his father had needed.

Instead he had been an additional burden in Alessandro's time of need. For in trying to protect him, his son, his father had been left with nobody to turn to.

'Your father is a thief and a thug,' he said slowly. 'He stole the business my great-grandfather founded and the house where my parents lived their whole married life. Thanks to him, my mother lost her husband and her home all in one day.'

Her face turned pale, but then she rallied, lifting her chin so that her gaze was level with his. 'And is your mother in on this too?'

The tightness in his chest was unbearable. *'What? No. My mother is a saint. She's the sweetest person on earth.'*

'I thought so.'

Her eyes hadn't left his face, and now there was something unsettling in her steady, stinging gaze.

'That's why we're going to get married,' she said.

He stared at her in confusion. *Get married? She still wanted to marry him?* Surely she was joking?

As though she could read his mind, she gave a humourless laugh. 'What's the matter, Vicè? Have you had a change of heart?' Her eyes narrowed. 'Oh, sorry, I forgot—you don't have a heart.'

Imma swallowed past the lump in her throat. It hurt to breathe. It hurt to speak. It hurt to look into his eyes and see nothing but hatred and hostility where only hours earlier she had thought she'd seen love.

She was such a fool. Had she really believed that this beautiful angry man could see past her defensiveness and gauche manner to what was inside? To value and desire what he saw there?

Their night together had been perfect, unrepeatable, miraculous—so that even when he had pulled her closer, or she had reached out for him, it had felt illusory...like an all too vivid dream.

And now she was living in a nightmare of her own making, and no amount of daylight was ever going to wake her up.

If only she could go back in time—back to before Claudia had called her, back to that moment when she had been held in the muscular warmth of his arms. When her heart, her pride, had still been intact.

But it was too late for regrets. All that mattered now was

making him pay. And she was going to keep telling herself that until it felt true.

His face darkened. 'And you, like the rest of your rotten, corrupted family, have no soul.'

Her eyes blazed into his. 'You are nothing to me now—just as I was nothing to you.'

She'd felt something—something real—but for him it had all been a trick, a con, a hoax.

The pain made her want to throw up.

He took a step forward. 'Great reason to get married.'

'It's about on a par with yours.' Pushing past the pain, she filled her voice with contempt. 'You slept with me under false pretences, Vicè. You faked your way into my bed. At least now we both know what's real and what isn't.'

He shook his head. 'What happened last night in your bed *was* real. You wanted me as much as I wanted you.'

Oh, he was good. He was so convincing—so plausible. Even now, when they both knew the truth, he made it sound as if he really believed what he was saying.

She shook her head. 'Actually, you *wanted* my father's business.'

Breathing out raggedly, she watched his face darken.

'No, I wanted *my* father's business.'

'Then you should have approached me with an offer.'

'I'm not going to pay for what was stolen from me.'

The hardness in his voice pressed against the bruise on her heart. The pain of trying to pretend spread out inside her like a rain cloud. Tears pricked behind her eyes and she blinked them away furiously, determined not to show any weakness in front of him.

'No, *I* paid. With my virginity.'

She felt a rush of shame and misery, remembering how her body had softened and melted from the heat of him.

His flinch was small, fleeting, but she saw it.

'Is that the going price for an olive oil company these days?' she taunted.

A flush of colour crept over his cheeks, but his eyes were cold. When he spoke his voice was colder still. 'For the last time, I didn't know you were a virgin.'

'Don't try and pretend you have a conscience, Vicenzu.' Her simmering pain gave way to an even hotter anger. 'You wanted to marry me and you will. Only it will be on my terms. Not yours. And if you refuse then I will find your mother and tell her exactly how you and your brother have behaved,' she said, her voice shaking slightly. 'I will tell her what kind of men the boys she raised have become.'

Her threat was empty. She wouldn't do it. She didn't want to marry him, and nor would she do anything to hurt Audenzia.

But she wanted to hurt him like he'd hurt her, and this was the only way she could think to do it.

His face hardened and the look in his eyes made her want to weep.

'I thought your father was a monster, but you...you are something else.'

And she had thought Vicenzu was the kind of man who crossed any number of boundaries, but not ruthlessly or with wanton cruelty.

Jabbing his phone into his chest, she met his gaze head-on. 'Yes, I am. I'm your nemesis, Vicenzu.'

Her face was aching with the effort of blanking out the beauty of his high cheekbones and full mouth... the mouth that had so recently kissed her into a state of feverish rapture.

His eyes narrowed. 'You really are Daddy's little girl, aren't you? Except that he uses threats and then violence to get what he wants.'

Smiling bitterly, she shook her head. 'What happened to *"what they can't find out, they make up"*?'

He stared at her incredulously. 'I wasn't talking about your father.'

'Well, you couldn't have been talking about yourself. Nobody in their right mind could make this up.' Her voice rose. 'How could you do this to me? How could you be so cruel?'

'You think *I'm* cruel?' He took a rough breath, his face hardening. 'Me? No, I'm just an amateur, *cara*.' He typed something into his phone, scrolled down the screen. 'This is the real deal. Here—' Letting his contempt show, he pressed the phone into her hand. 'You like reading my messages? Read these and then tell me who the bad guy is.'

She stared at him. Her lungs felt as if they were on fire. 'I don't need to. *You* are the bad guy, Vicenzu.'

And, sidestepping past him, she walked quickly away— going nowhere, just wanting, needing, to get as far away as possible from his cold-eyed distaste and the wreckage of her romantic dreams.

She half expected him to come after her, as he had last night. But of course last night he'd been playing her. Last night he'd only come after her because he'd been playing his part, doing whatever it took to get the family business back.

Whatever it took.

Like having sex with her.

The thought that having sex with her had been one step en route to the bigger prize, a means to trap and manipulate her, made her feel sick.

She had wanted her first time to be perfect. To be her choice and not just an expected consequence of her marriage vows. Had wanted it to be with Vicè, because in her na- ivety—idiot that she'd been—she had liked and trusted him.

And when he'd walked towards her at the wedding, his dancing eyes and teasing laughter trailing promises of hap- piness, she'd fallen in love with him.

As she reached the terrace tears began to fill her eyes and she brushed them away angrily.

She had been stubborn and vain. Ignoring and defying her father's words of warning and letting herself be flat- tered by Vicè's lies. Her pain was deserved. But Claudia's...

Her eyes filled with tears again, and this time she let

them roll down her cheeks. She had let her sister down. Worse, she had broken her word.

She had been eight years old when she made that promise—too young to understand that her mother was dying, but old enough to understand the promise she was making. A promise to take care of her younger sister, to protect her and keep her safe in the kind of cruel, unjust world that would leave two young children motherless.

She had always kept her word. Protecting Claudia at school, and at home too. Shielding her from the full force of Cesare's outbursts and trying to boost her confidence by encouraging her love of cooking and gardening.

Only now she had broken that promise.

Remembering her sister's stunned, tearful call, she felt another stab of guilt. Claudia was her priority. She would do whatever her sister wanted—help in any way she needed. Then she would face her father.

But first…

Her fingers tightened around the phone in her hand—Vicè's phone.

She found what she was looking for easily—an email from the family lawyer, Vito Neglia, to Ciro and Vicenzu, plus further emails between Alessandro and Neglia.

She scrolled down the screen, her eyes following the lines of text.

It made difficult reading.

Alessandro Trapani had been unlucky—machinery had broken and mistakes had been made. He had taken out a loan with the bank and then his troubles had begun to escalate. There had been accidents at work, then more problems with machinery, and he had started to struggle to meet the repayments.

Her heart jolted as her father's name leapt out from the screen. But she had been right, she thought with a rush of relief. Cesare had offered cash for the business with the proviso that the sale would include the family estate. She took a steadying breath. It was just as her father had told her. Papà had only been trying to help.

She glanced back down at the screen and some of her relief began to ooze away.

Alessandro had refused her father's offer. But then he hadn't been able to pay one of his suppliers—and, with the bank putting increasing pressure on him over the repayments, he'd gone back to Cesare.

This time her father had offered twenty percent less.

With no other options left, Alessandro had had no choice but to accept.

But that was just *business*, she told herself, trying to push back against the leaden feeling in her stomach. Probably if the circumstances had been reversed Alessandro would have done exactly the same.

Clearly Neglia didn't agree with her.

He had done some digging around and, although he had found no direct link to her father, there was clearly no doubt in the lawyer's mind that Trapani employees had been bribed to sabotage the machinery.

And her father had been behind it.

Imma's throat worked as she struggled to swallow her shock. She felt sick on the inside. Her skin was cold and clammy and her head was spinning.

She didn't want it to be true.

But the facts were stark and unforgiving.

Cesare had used bribery and intimidation to ruin a man's business and steal it away from him. The fact that he had also demanded Alessandro's home made her heart break into pieces.

Hot tears stung the back of her eyes. No wonder Ciro and Vicè hated him. But, whatever her father had done, it didn't give them the right to punish her and Claudia, and she hated both of them for that.

Only despite everything she had read, she couldn't bring

herself to hate her father. It wasn't an excuse, but she knew he would have done it for her and for Claudia.

Cesare was not stupid. He'd heard the rumours about his 'friends' and his shady dealings. And she knew that he wanted something different for his daughters. That was why they had been educated at the convent. That was why they'd been raised like princesses in a tower.

And that was why he had used every trick in the book to acquire a 'clean' business and a beautiful family estate—as gifts for his beloved girls.

The world suddenly felt very fragile.

She forced air into her lungs, tried to focus.

She couldn't hate her father, but she couldn't face moving back home either. She needed space, and time to think about all of this—about her part in it and her future.

Her future.

She sank down in one of the chairs, wrapping her arms around her stomach. She felt incredibly, brutally tired. Tired of not knowing who she was or what she wanted.

Her heart pounded. She had thought she wanted Vicè—that he had wanted her. She had been wrong about that too. And yet on one level she didn't regret what had happened. Having sex with him had unlocked a part of herself she hadn't known existed.

She had discovered a woman who was wild and alive and demanding, and she liked that woman. She wanted to find out more about her, and that was another reason she needed time and space.

Time and space—those words again.

She wouldn't have either living at home with Papà. But sooner or later she was going to have to tell him that she had slept with Vicè, and then he would insist on her marrying someone of his choosing.

Her pulse slowed and she sat up straight, biting her lip, listening to the distant sound of the waves.

Maybe, though, there was another option...

* * *

Clenching his jaw, Vicè stared around the empty bedroom.

He was still in shock. The script he'd planned for today had unravelled so fast, so dramatically, and in a way he could hardly believe possible.

Just when everything had been falling into place so beautifully.

Everything.

She'd even agreed to marry him.

So how come he was standing here with his face still stinging and her ultimatum ringing in his ears?

Behind him the tangled bed sheets were like a rebuke or a taunt and, feeling as if the walls were starting to shrink around him, he crossed the room, yanking open the door and stepping through it in time with his pounding heartbeat.

It was his fault.

Actually, no, it was hers.

If she had told him the truth about being a virgin in the first place he might not have been so distracted, so caught off balance.

He might even have locked his phone.

His chest tightened. How could he have been so unforgivably stupid and careless? When Ciro found out he was going to go ballistic. He might never speak to him again.

The one consolation in this whole mess was that Ciro had already managed to get the house back. He knew his brother: Ciro was a fast worker. Claudia had agreed to sign over the house before she'd learned the truth, and those documents would be signed and witnessed by now.

But what did he have to show for himself?

Niente, that was what!

He had nothing.

He gave a humourless smile. He was trapped on an island with a woman who basically wanted to cut off his *palle* and fry them up for brunch.

Glancing back into the bedroom, he ran a hand over his

face, wishing he could as easily smooth over the last few hours of his life.

The shock of being unmasked had shaken him more than he cared to admit—as had Imma's threat to speak to his mother. Although now he'd had a chance to cool off he knew she'd been bluffing.

But what had really got under his skin was the sudden devastating loss of the woman who had melted into him just hours earlier.

Gone was the passion, the inhibition of the night, when she had arched against him, her body moving like a flame in the darkness. Now in her eyes he might as well be something that had crawled out from under a particularly dank and slimy rock.

And, even though he knew logically that it shouldn't matter what Imma thought about him, he didn't like how it made him feel. Didn't like being made to feel like he was the bad guy.

There was only one bad guy and that was her father.

From somewhere nearby a phone buzzed twice. Glancing down, he saw that it was his.

It was sitting on a small table and he felt his stomach tense. Imma must have left it for him. Feeling a sharp stab of guilt and misery, he picked it up, swearing under his breath.

His stomach dipped. It was Ciro.

His brother's message was short and to the point.

I can't talk now, but it's all gone belly-up here so you need to pull your finger out.

For a moment he let his finger hover over his brother's number, and then, swearing loudly this time, he pocketed the phone.

He couldn't deal with his brother right now. He had to get his head straight first.

He was clenching his jaw so tightly that it ached.

Nine weeks ago he would have walked away.

But nine weeks ago he still had a father.

Tilting his head back, he closed his eyes. He still couldn't believe that he would never see Alessandro again. His father had been his mentor, his defender—more than that, he had been his hero. He had been the best of men…fair, kind, generous and loving.

Opening his eyes, he breathed out unevenly. He'd given up any hope of ever being his father's equal a long time ago, but he could do this one thing and do it right.

He had let down Papà in life; he would not do so now.

Imma was not going to have everything her own way.

He'd sat around listening to his father and Ciro talk business enough to know that she had overplayed her hand with him, and let her emotions get the better of her. In her anger, she had threatened the very thing he had wanted all along.

He *would* be her husband—but he was not going to walk away empty-handed. He was going to take back the Trapani Olive Oil Company and there would be nothing his future 'wife' could do about it.

He found her out by the pool, staring down at the smooth turquoise surface of the water. In her white dress, and with her long dark hair flowing over her shoulders, she looked as young and untested as her name suggested, and her slender body reminded him of the delicate honey-scented sweet peas that were his mother's favourite flowers.

It was hard to believe she was the same woman who had threatened to tell Audenzia the truth about everything he and Ciro had been doing. He gritted his teeth. Hard, but not impossible.

She turned towards him, folding her arms high across her ribs. But even without the defensive gesture he would have known that she had looked at the emails on his phone.

Her eyes were slightly swollen and she looked pale, more delicate. He felt a pang of guilt, but pushed it away. The truth hurt—so what? His mother had been widowed and forced to leave her home. That was real suffering.

'I read the emails,' she said quietly. 'I don't know what to say except that I'm sorry for how my father acted, and for what I said earlier about talking to your mother.' She took a breath. 'I was angry, and upset, but I want you to know that I would never do anything to hurt her. I know she had nothing to do with this.' Her eyes met his, steady, accusatory. 'I would never punish an innocent bystander.'

Her words stung. No doubt she'd intended they should. But he was surprised by her apology. He hadn't expected that—not from anyone bearing the Buscetta surname. Only if she thought that was somehow going to be enough...

He took a step towards her. 'And the marriage proposal?' he said softly.

Her green eyes narrowed. 'Yours or mine?' she shot back.

'Does it matter?'

'I suppose not.'

He heard the catch in her voice, and before he could stop himself he said, 'So tell me, Imma, if you're not looking for revenge then why exactly do you want to marry me?'

Her arms clenched and, watching the fabric of her dress tighten over her nipples, he felt his pulse snake, remembering how just hours earlier they had hardened against his tongue.

She shrugged. 'My father is a traditional Sicilian male. Very traditional. Now that you and I have had sex he'll expect us to marry, and if we don't he'll find another husband for me.' Lifting her chin, she twisted her mouth into a small, tight smile. 'Essentially you're the lesser of two evils, Vicè.'

Chewing her words over inside his head, he felt his gut tense. *Wow!* That was a backhander. It certainly wasn't something he'd ever been called before.

She took a quick breath. 'If we marry, then obviously I'll be your wife legally. But in reality you'll just be there. In the background.'

In the background.

He wasn't sure if it was her disparaging description of his upcoming role or her haughty manner, but he felt a pulse of anger beat across his skin.

'Sounds relaxing. Will I need to get dressed?'

That got to her. She wanted him still. He could see it in the flush of her cheeks and the restless pulse in her throat. Watching her pupils flare, he felt his own anger shift into desire.

Ignoring his question, she said coolly, 'Before we go any further, you should know that I have a condition.'

A condition?

'Is that so?' Taking a step towards her, he held her gaze.

She nodded. 'The marriage will last a year. That's long enough for it to look real. If we manage our diaries, then we shouldn't have to intrude into one another's lives beyond what's necessary.'

He stared at her in silence. All his life women had fawned over him, flattered and chased him. But now Imma was basically treating him like a footstool.

'I have a condition too,' he said silkily.

Seeing her swallow, he felt a flicker of satisfaction.

'I will stay married to you for a year. But I want it in writing now that you will sign the Trapani Olive Oil Company over to me at the end of that year.'

She searched his face. Probably she thought he was joking. When she realised he was being serious, she started shaking her head. 'You can't expect me to—' she began.

He cut her off. 'Oh, but I do. I find managing my diary very dull, so I'll need *some* incentive.'

He enjoyed the flash of outrage in her eyes almost as much as the way she bit down on her lip—presumably to stop herself from saying something she'd regret.

'Is that going to be a problem? Maybe you'd rather go back to bed and thrash all this out there instead.'

Silence followed his deliberately provocative remark,

and he waited to see how she would respond, his body tensing painfully in anticipation of her accepting his challenge.

Two spots of colour flared on her cheeks and he saw her hands curl into fists. She wanted to thump him. Or kiss him. Or maybe both.

And, actually, either would be preferable to this tight-lipped disdain.

But after a moment she said stiffly, 'No, I would not.'

'Shame,' he drawled. 'Still, there's always the wedding night to look forward to.'

'Yes, there is.' She lifted her chin. 'But we'll be enjoying it in separate rooms. Just to be clear, this marriage is purely for show, Vicè. You won't be sharing my bed. Or having sex with me.'

Vicè felt his smile harden.

He'd already had to be celibate in the run-up to his brother's wedding. Not out of choice, but Ciro had insisted, and in the end he'd grudgingly accepted that any hint of scandal would ruin his chances of seducing Imma before he had even got to meet her.

Those nine weeks had left his body aching with sexual frustration. And now she was suggesting that that sentence should be extended to a year.

'Obviously you won't be having sex with anyone else either,' she added coldly. 'I won't have my family's name dragged through the mud by your libido.'

Their eyes met. 'I wouldn't worry about that, *cara*. Your father wallows in something far nastier than mud.'

His words drained the colour from her cheeks, but he told himself that a woman who was prepared to enter willingly into this kind of marriage deserved no compassion on his part.

'That's rich, coming from you,' she said shakily. 'The man who seduced a virgin for revenge.'

He felt his gut twist. But he wasn't going to feel guilty

about that. She should have told him—given him a choice about whether to do things differently.

She lifted one slender wrist and gazed down at her expensive gold watch. 'If you're done insulting me, then a simple yes or no will suffice.'

No. Absolutely not. Never. Not if my life depended on it.

He thought about his life before…*la dolce vita.*

A life of leisure and pleasure. A sweet life.

And then he thought about his mother, and his father, and the promise he had made to his brother.

'Yes,' he said.

CHAPTER FIVE

So SHE REALLY was going to go through with this.

Glancing out of the window of the taxi, Imma felt her fingers tighten around the small posy of lilies of the valley in her lap. Beside her, his dark eyes shielded behind even darker glasses, his fingers pointedly entwined with hers, Vicè sat in silence.

To anyone else he would seem the perfect groom. Young, handsome, intent on marrying the woman he loved.

She swallowed past the ache in her throat. But of course he was good at pretending.

They had left the island and returned to the mainland, 'borrowed' Cesare's private jet and flown to Gibraltar. They had arrived in late last night, and booked into a discreet hotel on the edge of town, near the Botanic Gardens.

Separate rooms, obviously.

Not that it was really necessary. He might be almost painfully attentive in public, but as soon as they were alone he barely lifted his eyes to meet hers, choosing instead to stare at his phone.

And it hurt. Hurt in a way that seemed utterly illogical.

Or just stupid.

Yes, 'stupid' was the only way to describe this hollowed-out feeling of loss for something that had been so fleeting and false.

It didn't help that all the preparations had been so rushed and furtive, but she couldn't risk Cesare finding out and intervening.

Thinking about her father made her chest ache. She loved him still, but right now she didn't trust him—and she didn't trust herself to be around him. She was too angry and confused about everything she had found out, and her desolation and the sense of betrayal were still too raw.

She had no idea what to say or do next. But she did know that she didn't want anything to do with what he'd done to Alessandro. Which was why she'd agreed to hand over the business to Vicè in a year's time.

If she hadn't needed a bargaining chip to get some space and time away from her father she would have handed it over today. She hated owning the thing he wanted—hated knowing that it was the only reason he was here, sitting beside her in the car, on their way to a register office.

Her chest tightened. If they had been other people, or if the circumstances had been different, then maybe all this haste and secrecy would be exciting, impulsive and romantic. But instead it just felt sneaky.

Even though she had texted her father to say that she was at the villa, she kept expecting him to call, demanding to know when she was coming home. Obviously she hadn't told him she was in Gibraltar, and that made her nervous too.

But, judging by the long, rambling and gleeful voicemail Cesare had just left her, she had been worrying for no reason.

He hadn't been fretting over her absence at all; instead he had been shooting boar on the Di Gualtieri estate.

A shiver scuttled down her spine. Stefano di Gualtieri was a fabulously wealthy local landowner and the great-grandson of Sicilian nobility. He was her father's age, and in her opinion he was a bore of a different kind—and a snob. But, despite her hinting as much, she knew Cesare saw him as a possible suitor for her hand in marriage.

Imma exhaled softly, trying to still the jittery feeling in her chest. If her father knew what she was about to do…

But his prospective anger was not the only reason she wanted to keep off his radar for as long as possible. Since reading those emails, her world—everything she had taken for granted about the man who had raised her—had begun to look as fragile as the tiny, delicate bell-shaped flowers in her hand.

She'd thought she knew her father so well. His moods, his brusqueness, his maddening and stifling overprotectiveness. Now, though, she felt as if she didn't know him at all.

Obviously she'd heard the rumours about him, but her father had always brushed them off: yes, some of his friends were a little rough. You had to be tough where he'd grown up—that was just how it was. And he wasn't going to turn his back on his mates. What kind of friend would do that?

'That's why people say these things about me. They're jealous, piccioncina mia. *They hate me for dragging myself up out of the gutter so they scrape over my past...invent stories.'*

It reminded her of what Vicè had said about people making up what they didn't know, and the thought that he had this, of all things, in common with her father made her want to leap out of the car while it was still moving.

Finding out that Cesare had behaved so ruthlessly made her feel sick. But finding out that he'd lied to her had been the reason why she'd finally decided to marry Vicè.

Okay, maybe at first she'd wanted revenge. Part of her still did. And she hadn't been lying when she'd told Vicè that he was the lesser of two evils. Her father would find her a husband, and she shuddered to think who he might choose.

But all her life she had struggled to know herself, and this revelation about her father made her feel she knew herself even less. Marriage to Vicè would at least give her the freedom to think about what she wanted to happen next.

And so this morning they had met with a notary, to complete the necessary paperwork. And now they were on their way to the register office.

Shifting in her seat, she glanced down at her dark blue polka-dot dress. It was the same one she'd worn to Claudia's wedding. And she hated it.

Not because it was a little boring, and cut for an older, more mature woman. But because it was so tied up with the now crushed romantic dreams of her little sister, and those few hours when Imma had mistakenly, humiliatingly, believed that Vicè was interested in her.

She could have bought another dress, but that would have defeated the object. She needed this reminder of where vanity and self-delusion led. And anyway she wouldn't have known what to buy. What was the correct dress code for a marriage of convenience?

Her stomach clenched—doubt gripping her again. She could stop this now. Tell the driver to pull over... tell Vicenzu to get out.

Only then what?

Go back to the life she'd had?

Pretend that none of this had happened or mattered?

Blanking her mind, she sat up straighter. She didn't know if she could go back to her old life. And where could she go, what could she do, if she didn't return to it?

She didn't know that either. And that was why she would go through with this ceremony.

That way, at least she would have time to find the answers to all the questions swirling inside her head.

Feeling Imma shift beside him, Vicè felt his body tense. She was a good actress. Not for one moment would anyone guess that she was marrying him out of spite.

The solid rectangular shape of his phone pressing against his ribs reminded him of the brief but reassuring message his brother had sent.

Have secured the house. Keep your promise.

He should be pleased—and he was. And yet it would be such a relief if, just for once, his brother messed up. But of course—Ciro being Ciro—he had turned everything around. So now it was just him hurtling towards a broken bridge on a runaway train.

In the street, a group of young men jostled against the car, shoving each other and laughing at some shared joke. They looked so happy. And free.

He bit down on a sudden rush of envy. A week ago that would have been him. Now he was marrying a woman he hated. And she hated him.

But it would be worth it. For in a year the Trapani Olive Oil Company would belong to his family again.

'We're here.'

She turned to face him and smiled, and even though he knew it was for show his breath stuck in his throat. She shouldn't be marrying him like this. Where was her father now? Her bodyguards? Didn't anyone care that she was doing this?

He thought back to the way her face had changed when he had taken her that first time. The directness of her green gaze had clouded over, transforming her from sexy to vulnerable. And in that moment, he'd forgotten about her father, forgotten about his. There had been nothing but the whisper of pleasure skimming over his skin and the white heat building between them.

'We could do this with a bit more style, you know. Take some time,' he said.

'We don't *have* time.' Her voice was clipped. 'My father is binary in the way he approaches life. It's his way or no way. We need to present him with an irreversible fact—like a marriage certificate.' She met his gaze, her green eyes narrowing. 'I know this is a little basic, but unlike you I didn't have a couple of months to work everything out in detail. Shall we go in?'

The ceremony was short and functional.

The registrar, a pleasant woman in her fifties, spoke her lines clearly, turning to each of them as she waited for their responses.

They had agreed to use English for the ceremony. But although they were both fluent, to her, the unfamiliar words made everything feel even more remote and pragmatic.

'Immacolata and Vicenzu, with your words today, I can now pronounce you husband and wife.' The woman smiled. 'And now you may seal the promises you have made with a kiss.'

Imma's expression didn't change, but Vicè felt her go still beside him. Glancing down, he saw that her green eyes were huge and over-bright, and her slim body was trembling like a wild flower in the wind.

It's just a kiss, he told himself.

And he lowered his head, assuming it would be nothing more than a passing brush of contact. But as their mouths touched he felt her lips part and instantly his body tensed, his insides tightening as a jolt of desire punched him in the gut.

Instinctively he slid his hand over her hip, tilting her face up to meet his and deepening the kiss.

Oh, but he hadn't meant to do that.

It was insane, stupid—beyond reckless—only he couldn't seem to stop himself.

He wanted her...wanted her with an urgency and intensity that was beyond his control.

He heard her breath hitch in her throat and was suddenly terrified that he would lose her—that he wouldn't be able to satisfy his hunger for her sweet, soft lips—but she didn't pull away.

Instead she leaned into him, her body moulding against his, and then he was pressing her closer, one hand sliding down her body, the other threading through her silky, dark hair.

His heart was pounding and his blood was surging through his limbs as an ache of need reared up inside him, pulsing and swelling, blotting out everything but the softness of her body.

From somewhere far away he heard a faint cough and, still fighting his drowning senses, he broke the kiss.

Imma was staring up at him, her green eyes unfocused, her lips trembling, and it was only the presence of the registrar and the two witnesses that stopped him from pulling her back into his arms and stripping that appalling dress off her body.

The registrar cleared her throat. 'Now, if you'd like to join me, we have the register here, all ready and waiting. Once that's signed, we're done.' She smiled. 'I'm sure you have plans for the rest of your special day.'

Vicè nodded. He did. But unfortunately for him, his marriage strictly forbade those plans being fulfilled.

Watching Imma sign the register, his shoulders tensed. It didn't matter that they had just come close to ripping off each other's clothes in public. Judging by the look on his new wife's face, that wasn't about to change any time soon.

Leaning back in her seat, Imma tilted her head sideways, gazing through the window at the cloudless blue sky. Her posture was determinedly casual, but her ears were on stalks and every five seconds or so her skin tightened and her stomach flipped up and over like a pancake in a skillet.

She felt on edge and distracted. And, even though wild horses wouldn't have dragged it out of her, she knew she was waiting for Vicè to walk back into the cabin.

After the ceremony they had taken a taxi back to the private airfield, Vicè's hand still clamped around hers. But as soon as they had got on board the plane he had excused himself on the pretext of wanting to change into something less formal.

In reality, they had needed to give one another privacy to tell their respective families.

There was the sound of footsteps and instantly her nerves sent ripples of unease over her skin. But it was only the steward, Fedele, bringing a pot of coffee.

'Congratulations again, Signorina Buscetta—I mean Signora Trapani.' The steward smiled down at her. 'Would you like anything to go with your coffee? We have pastries and fruit.'

She shook her head. 'No, thank you, Fedele. But would you please thank the crew again for their kind words.'

It had been easy to tell the cabin crew that she was married, to receive their polite and no doubt genuine congratulations. Sharing the news with her father had been far less pleasant.

As predicted, Cesare had roared. For a good ten minutes he had threatened, reproached her, ranted and railed against her, his frustration and displeasure flowing unstoppably like lava from a volcano.

On any other day she would have tried to soothe him, to be the eye of calm at the centre of his storm.

But not today.

Maybe it had been the strain of the last few hours catching up with her, or perhaps she'd just been worried about letting the truth slip out, but she simply hadn't had it in her, so she had just let him rage until finally he'd registered her silence and said gruffly, 'So this Trapani boy—he loves you, does he?'

'Yes, Papà, he does.'

She'd heard her father grunt. 'And you love him?'

'I do—I really do.'

He'd sighed. 'Well, what's done is done. And if he makes you happy...'

It had been easier to lie than she had thought. Maybe it always was—maybe that was how her father managed to lie to her about Alessandro's business.

It hurt to think about all the other lies he might have told her. Only not as much as it had hurt having to stand next to Vicè at that dismal parody of a wedding and hear him repeat his vows knowing that he meant not one word of them.

She had heard him speaking, heard herself respond. She

had watched the registrar smile and watched the witnesses sign the register. But she had felt totally numb, as though her veins had been filled with ice.

Until Vicè had kissed her.

Her heart bumped against her ribs as she remembered.

It had been as if he'd struck a match inside her. His mouth had tasted of freedom, and the warmth of his body against hers had seemed to offer danger and sanctuary all in one.

And just like that she had leaned into him, her body softening like wax touched by a flame. And all she knew was his closeness. And he had been all she wanted.

She shivered as a jolt of heat shot through her and shifted in her seat, pressing her knees together, trying to ignore the flood of want.

Her cheeks felt hot. Yes, want. She wanted him.

Only how could she?

How could she still want Vicè after everything he had done? The lies he had told... The manipulation... The pretence...

But it didn't matter that it made no sense. It was the truth. And although she might be lying to her father, and to the cabin crew and to the rest of the world, she wasn't going to lie to herself.

The truth was that, even hating him as she did, with every fibre of her being, she still wanted him.

Kissing him should have been complicated.

Except it hadn't felt complicated.

It had been easy. Natural. Right. *Facile come bere un bicchiere d'acqua*, as her father liked to say when he was boasting about some deal he'd made.

But it was clearly just some kind of muscle memory kicking into action. It wouldn't happen again, of that she was certain. She might have been swept along in the moment, captivated by the swift, intoxicating intimacy of that kiss in an otherwise colourless ceremony, but—like the misplaced desire she had felt for Vicè yesterday—it had been just a blip.

'So how did it go? Am I going to be swimming with the fishes? Or did you manage to sweet talk him into accepting me as his son-in-law?'

A shadow fell across her face and, glancing up, she felt her pulse trip. Vicè was next to her, his dark eyes gazing down into her face, a mocking smile pulling at his mouth.

He was wearing a pair of jeans and a slim-fitting navy T-shirt—the kind of low-key clothes that would make anyone else look ordinary. But Vicè didn't need logos or embellishments to draw the eye. His flawless looks and languid grace did that all on their own.

Dry-mouthed, she watched wordlessly, her heart lurching from side to side like a boat in a storm, as he dropped into the seat opposite her.

'It was fine. How about you?'

Ignoring her question, he picked up the coffee pot. 'How do you like it?' he murmured. 'Actually, no, don't tell me... I already know.'

Her stomach muscles trembled. She knew he was just talking about the coffee, but that didn't stop a slow, tingling warmth from sliding over her skin.

'I'm going to go with no milk and just a sprinkle of sugar.'

He held her gaze, his eyes reaching inside her so that for a moment she didn't even register what he'd said. Or that he was right.

Since agreeing to the terms of their marriage he'd been distant, cool, aloof... Sulking, presumably, at having the tables turned on him. Now, though, he seemed to have recovered his temper, and his dark gaze was lazily roaming her face. She knew it wasn't real but, try as she might, she couldn't stop herself—or her body anyway—from responding to him.

Annoyingly, she knew that he could sense her response

and was enjoying it. The hairs on her arms rose. She had dictated the terms of their marriage. She was the one in control. So why did it feel as if he was playing with her?

Suddenly she wondered if she had done the right thing.

'Marianna told you,' she said quickly. She knew her face was flushed, and as he shook his head she frowned.

'She did not,' he said. His eyes hadn't left her mouth. 'But you're my wife, so I assume you want your coffee like your husband. Dark, firm-bodied, and with a hint of sweetness.'

He poured the coffee and held out a cup.

For a fraction of a second she hesitated, and then she took it. 'Thank you,' she said stiffly.

His eyes gleamed and, reaching across the table, he picked up his own cup. He seemed utterly at ease, and she wondered if he was still acting or if his mood really had changed.

It was impossible to tell. Up until a few days ago he'd been a stranger. Yet in the space of those few days so much had happened between them. Big, important, life-changing things.

'Sorry I took so long.' He lounged back in his chair, his dark lashes shielding the expression in his eyes. 'I needed to clear my mind. You know—' he made a sweeping gesture with his hand '—so much emotion after that wonderful ceremony. It was simple and yet so beautifully romantic.'

Hearing the mocking note in his voice, she gave him an icy glare. 'It's all you deserve.'

His gaze locked on hers. 'All I deserve?' He repeated her words softly. 'That's a missed opportunity.'

The glitter in his eyes made her nerves scream. 'What do you mean?'

Tilting his head back, he smiled slowly. 'Just that if I'd known you were trying to punish me I would have suggested something more exciting. Mutually satisfying.'

Her muscles tightened and she felt heat creep over her cheeks. Stiffening her shoulders, she forced herself to look him in the eye. 'I wasn't trying to punish you. It was the only option under the circumstances. And I don't see why you even care about the ceremony anyway. You seduce virgins under false pretences. You don't do romance.'

Something flared in his eyes. 'I don't care, *cara*. But I can't believe a convent girl like you had that kind of ceremony pinned on her wedding board.'

Without warning he leaned forward and brushed her hair lightly with his fingertips. For a heartbeat she forgot to breathe. And then, as heat rushed through her body, she jerked backwards. 'What are you doing?'

'You have *coriandoli* in your hair,' he said softly, holding out his hand.

She gazed down at the rose petals, felt her pulse slowing. Vicè was wrong. She'd never planned her wedding day. In fact, she'd blocked it from her mind. Why would she want to plan a day that would so blatantly remind her that her life choices were not her own?

No, it had been Claudia—her sweet, overlooked little sister—who had dreamed of marriage and a husband and a home of her own.

Remembering her sister's tears, she curled her fingers into her palms. 'It's sweet of you to be concerned, Vicenzu,' she said. 'But I can have my dream wedding with my next husband.'

Vicenzu stared at her, her words resounding inside his head. *Seriously?* They had been married for less than two hours and she was already thinking about her next wedding? Her next husband?

His chest tightened. The thought of Imma being with another man made him irrationally but intensely angry. And as his gaze roamed over her tight, taunting smile and the defiance in her green eyes, he felt his body respond to the challenge. To her beauty.

But his response wasn't just about the swing of her hair

or the delicacy of her features—the dark, perfect curve of her eyebrows, the full, soft mouth, those arresting green eyes. There was something else…something hazy, elusive… a shielded quality.

Looking at her was like looking through a kaleidoscope: one twist and the whole picture shifted into something new, so that he couldn't imagine ever getting bored with her.

He felt his body harden. It had been a very long time since he'd got an erection from just *looking* at a woman.

Containing his temper, and the ache in his groin, he smiled back at her. 'But I'll always be your first, in so many ways, and that means something—don't you think?'

Watching colour suffuse her face, he knew he had got to her.

Leaning back in his seat, he glanced out of the window. 'So which godforsaken rock are we heading to now?' he asked tauntingly. 'Hopefully one with fewer monkeys and more beaches. I mean, this is our honeymoon, after all.'

'This is *not* our honeymoon.'

She leaned forward, her blush spreading over her collarbone, her narrowed green eyes revealing the depth of her irritation.

'This is business. We need to convince everyone, particularly our parents, that we are in love and that this marriage is real.'

Her mouth twisted.

'Otherwise you won't get your father's olive oil company back. And we both know that's all you're interested in.'

His pulse twitched. *Not true.* Right now he was extremely interested in whether the skin beneath the neckline of her dress was also flushed.

He forced his eyes to meet hers. Had she been inside his head on the flight over to Gibraltar, and in the car on the way to the register office, she would have found herself to be right. He had been furious at having lost the upper hand—

having thrown it away, more like—and it had only been the thought of the family business that had kept him going.

Marriage to Imma was just a means to an end. In a year's time he would have his reward and he would have fulfilled his promise to Ciro. Vengeance would be his.

But a year was a long time. And right now, with Imma sitting so close, the business seemed less important than the way the pulse in her throat seemed to be leaping out at him through her skin.

'Fine…whatever.' He shrugged, lounging back and letting his arm droop over the back of his seat with a languid carelessness he didn't feel. 'But I meant what I said about monkeys and beaches.'

She gave him a look of exasperation.

'*Fine…whatever.* If it's such a big deal to you, then you can choose where we go.'

'Okay, then—let's go to Portofino. Let's go to my hotel.'

He'd spoken unthinkingly. The words had just appeared fully formed on his lips before he'd even realised what he was saying. Only now that he had said it, he knew that was what he wanted to do.

She was looking at him with a mixture of shock and confusion, as if he'd suddenly announced he wanted her to sleep in a bath of spaghetti. He felt nettled by her reaction.

For some inexplicable reason—maybe a desire to be on his home turf, or perhaps to prove there was a whole lot more to him than just a pretty face—he wanted her to see La Dolce Vita.

'Is that a problem?' he asked quietly.

But before she could reply, the steward appeared beside them.

'Signora Trapani—Chef would like to know if you're ready for lunch to be served?'

Imma nodded. 'Yes—*grazie*, Fedele.'

The steward began clearing the table.

'*Scusa*—I'm in the way. Here, let me move.'

Moving smoothly, Vicè swapped his seat for the one next to Imma. Taking advantage of Fedele's presence, he slid an arm around her waist, one hand snaking out to clasp hers firmly.

'That's better—isn't it, *cara*?'

She must have had a lot of practice in hiding her feelings, he thought, watching her lips curve into a smile of such sweetness that he almost forgot she was faking.

'You can let me go now,' she said quietly, her smile fading as Fedele disappeared.

'Why? He'll be back in a minute with lunch.'

He pulled her closer, tipping her onto his lap and drawing her against his chest. The sudden intimacy between them reminded him vividly of what had happened in her bedroom.

'Don't be scared, *cara*...' His heart was suddenly hammering inside his chest. 'This is just business...'

'I'm not scared,' she said hotly.

But she was scared. He could feel it in the way she was holding herself. Not scared of him, but of her response to him. Of this tingling insistent thread of need between them.

'Good,' he said softly. 'Because, as you so rightly pointed out, we need to convince everyone this is real—and that's not going to happen if we're sitting on opposite sides of the room. We need to practise making it look real.'

He stared down into her eyes.

'We need to act as if we can't keep our hands off one another. As if we want each other so badly it's like a craving. As if, even though it doesn't make sense, and it's never happened to us before and it's driving us crazy, we can't stop ourselves...'

That pretty much described how he'd been feeling ever since they'd met. How he was feeling right now, in fact. His blood was pounding in his ears and his body was painfully hard. He felt as though he was combusting inside.

Instinctively he lowered his face, sliding his hand into her hair.

'Vicè, stop—'

Stop? He hadn't even started!

Longing and fierce urgency rose up inside him, and as her fingers twitched against his chest it took every atom of willpower he had to stop himself from pressing his mouth to hers.

With an effort, he leaned back, smoothing all shades of desire from his voice. 'So, are we going to Portofino, or not?'

There was a beat of silence, and then she nodded.

He kept his face still. 'I think ten days should be about right for a honeymoon. Or are you thinking longer...?'

'No.'

She shook her head, and he felt his stomach flip over at the sudden hoarseness in her voice.

'Ten days sounds perfect.'

Yes, it did, he thought, his body tensing as she slid off his lap.

Ten days.

And if he had his way every minute of all those days would be spent in bed...

CHAPTER SIX

IT WAS LATE afternoon by the time they arrived in Genoa. At the airport Vicè picked up his car—a surprisingly modest black convertible—and they drove south.

It wasn't just the modesty of his car that was surprising, Imma thought as they left the city's outskirts. Vicè was actually a good driver.

He was certainly nothing like her father. Cesare drove as he lived. Rushing forward aggressively and raging when he was forced to slow down or, worse still, stop.

Vicè drove with the same smooth, fluid grace as he did everything else.

She glanced over at him. They had barely spoken since setting off, but maybe that was a good thing. Every time they talked she seemed to start the conversation feeling in control but end it feeling he had the upper hand.

It didn't help that, despite everything she knew about him, her body persisted in overriding her brain whenever she was near to him.

Remembering exactly how near he had been earlier, on the plane, she felt a coil of heat spiral up inside her. She could tell herself it had been the plush intimacy of the plane or the glass of champagne that had affected her judgement. But it would be a lie to say she hadn't wanted him in that moment.

Only it was going to stop now. It had to.

This marriage might be a lie, but she couldn't lie to herself for a whole year.

She might have agreed theoretically with what Vicè had said on the plane, about making their marriage look real, but she knew she was going to find faking it far more difficult and painful than he would.

For him, those hours in her bed had been a necessary step in his plan to win back his father's business. A trick, a trap, a seduction.

For her, ignorant in her bliss, it had been something more.

He'd taught her about sex. About the sleek warmth of skin, the melting pleasure of touch and the decadent ache of climax.

It didn't matter that he'd been lying to her; her feelings for him had been real. And, even though she knew the truth now, the memory of how she had felt that night remained, overriding facts and common sense.

Admitting and accepting that would stop her repeating the reckless intimacy between them on the plane. But she needed to set some ground rules. Make it clear to him that she *would* play her part—but only in public, and only when absolutely necessary.

Feeling the car slow down, she glanced up ahead. The road was growing narrower and more winding. The palms of her hands were suddenly clammy.

Were they here?

As though he'd read her mind, Vicè turned towards her and, taking one hand off the wheel, gestured casually towards the view through the windscreen.

'This is it. This is Portofino.'

She wasn't ready, she thought, her heart lurching. But it was too late. They were already cruising past pastel-coloured villas with dark green shutters, some strung with fluttering lines of laundry, others decorated with *trompe l'oeil* architectural flourishes that made her look twice.

The town centre was movie-set-perfect—a mix of insouciant vintage glamour and stealth wealth chic. Beneath the striped awnings of the cafes hugging the *piazzetta*, women in flowing, white dresses and men wearing linen and loafers lounged in the sunlight, talking and drinking Aperol spritz.

It was all so photogenic, so relaxed and carefree. A part of the world where *dolce far niente* was a way of life.

She swallowed, her throat suddenly dry. No wonder Vicè chose to live here. And now she would be living here too. Living here as Signora Trapani.

A shiver wound down her spine. Up until that moment she had been so focused on getting married she hadn't considered what being married would mean for her day-to-day life.

But here in Portofino, with Vicè, she would be free. For the first time ever there were no bodyguards tracking her every move, no Cesare dictating her agenda.

No rules to follow.

No rules at all.

Her stomach flipped over.

It was nerve-racking—like stepping from the safety of a ship onto new, uncharted land—and yet she wasn't scared so much as excited.

She let go of a breath. So much of her life had been spent feeling unsure about who she was, being scared to push back against the weight of duty and expectation. But without noticing she *had* pushed back, she realised with confusion. She had already changed, something shifting tectonically inside her.

How else could she be here with Vicè?

Her stomach knotted.

Much as she might want to flatter herself into believing that she had done so alone, incredibly—unbelievably—he was part of it. He had backed her into a corner and she had come out fighting. She had found another side of herself with him.

Feeling his gaze on the side of her face, she turned. 'It's beautiful,' she said simply.

His expression didn't alter, but she could sense he was pleased with her reaction.

'I'll save the guided tour for another time.'

His lip curved, and she felt his smile curl its way through her pelvis.

'I'm sure you'll be wanting to get out of those clothes.'

Refusing to take the bait, she lifted her chin. 'So what happens at the hotel?'

Shifting in his seat, he changed gear, his smile twitching at the corners of his mouth. 'Well, there are people who come and stay and use the rooms—I call them guests—'

She clenched her jaw. 'I meant what's the plan for us?'

'Relax, *cara*.' He was grinning now. 'We'll just play it by ear.'

'That's not a plan,' she snapped.

Back on the plane, she had told herself that it was a good idea to come here. La Dolce Vita was a magnet for Hollywood actors, rock stars and rappers, so there was bound to be a bunch of paparazzi hanging around the hotel. Obviously they would be hot news for a couple of days, but it would all die down pretty quickly and then their lives could go back to normal.

'Normal' with the occasional necessary public display of affection.

Now, though, she was starting to see flaws in the plan—the major one being that Vicè didn't appear to have a plan.

'It'll be fine,' he said.

They were heading up a hill now, along a road edged with cypress trees and pines. Away from the town it was quieter, the air heavy with the scent of honeysuckle and lemon trees, and there was a surprising lushness to the greenery around them.

She felt the car slow again, her heartbeat accelerating as he turned between two scuffed pillars.

'Don't worry—I can do all the talking.'

He made it sound so easy. But then, of course, he was good at painting castles in the air.

Remembering how effortlessly he had persuaded her to believe in him, she gritted her teeth. 'As long as you keep to the script and don't contradict me—'

'Spoken like a true wife,' he said softly, stopping the

car. Pulling off his sunglasses, he glanced over his shoulder. 'We're here.'

Her heart gave a startled leap and, blinking into the sunlight, Imma looked up and felt her mouth drop open. She'd seen photos, but nothing did justice to the building in front of her.

Surrounded by palm trees, flecked with sunlight, the peaches-and-cream-coloured hotel oozed Italian Riviera style. But this was more than just a playground for VIPs, she thought, watching a flurry of petals flutter down from the wisteria-draped facade. It was magical, and the knowledge that Vicè was the man behind the magic made her heart hammer in her ears.

She jumped slightly as Vicè opened her door.

'It used to be a monastery, would you believe?'

He gave her one of his pulse-fluttering smiles and she bit her lip. In this mood he was impossible to resist—just like the hand he was holding out to her.

'No, I wouldn't.'

His fingers threaded through hers and she stepped out of the car, her muscles tightening as he slid an arm around her waist.

'It's true. The monks kept getting overrun by pirates, so they abandoned it. Moved further inland.'

'What happened to the pirates?'

'Oh, they're still here.' He smiled, his dark eyes glittering in the early-evening sunlight. 'One of them, anyway.'

The heat of his body matched the heat in his eyes. For a moment he stared down at her, and the pull between them she'd been trying so hard to ignore flared to life inside her.

'*Ehi, capo!* You're back!'

Swinging round, Vicè raised his hand, his smile widening as a young man with streaked blond hair, sleepy brown eyes and an equally wide smile strode towards them.

'Matteo. *Ciao!*'

'I was expecting you two days ago.'

'What can I say? I got distracted.'

As the two men embraced Imma watched in confusion. *Capo?* Was Vicè his *boss?*

She tried and failed to picture any of her father's employees talking to Cesare in such a casual, effusive manner. But all she could think about were those emails she had read and his treatment of Alessandro.

She felt her stomach clench. She still wasn't ready to go there, and she was almost grateful when Vicè turned towards her, reaching out for her hand.

'Come here, *cara.*'

He pulled her closer, his dark gaze on her face.

'This beautiful woman is the reason I got distracted. Imma, this is Matteo, the hotel manager here and a good friend. Matteo—this is Imma, my wife.'

Her pulse jumped. Vicè was looking at her—really looking at her—so that it felt as if he was reaching inside of her, claiming her for his own.

'My wife,' he repeated softly.

It was an act, she told herself. It was all for show. Only she couldn't stop her stomach from turning over in an uncontrollable response to the intimacy of his words and the flame in his eyes.

For a split second time seemed to end. Just stop.

She forgot where she was and why she was even there. Around her the air seemed to thicken into an invisible wall, and inside the wall was Vicè, his skin dappled with sunlight, his dark gaze pulling her closer...

'You got married!'

She blinked as Matteo grabbed Vicè in a one-armed hug.

'*Che bello!* That's fantastic news. I'm so pleased for you both.'

'Thank you, bro. It was all a bit *di impulso.*' Glancing over at Imma, he grinned. 'What can I say? She swept me off my feet.'

Imma forced her mouth into a smile. Vicè made it all

sound so plausible—no wonder Matteo was beaming at them in delight. But his congratulations were warm and genuine, and it felt wrong accepting them under such false pretences.

She felt a flash of anger. How was she going to do this for a whole year? Smile and lie to every single person she met? It was a daunting prospect, and the wider implications of what she'd agreed to do made her heart cramp.

She felt Vicè's hand tighten around hers.

'Matteo, can you get the bags brought round?'

'Sure, boss.'

'Come on.'

He turned and, still holding her hand, led her away from the hotel to a narrow path that disappeared into the lush undergrowth.

'I'll show you to the villa.'

She let him lead her between the citrus trees and beneath the boughs of myrtle and laurel, but as soon as they were out of sight she jerked her hand away.

'That's enough,' she snapped.

Vicè stopped. His pulse was racing.

In that moment when he and Imma had been talking to Matteo he'd forgotten that their marriage wasn't real. More confusingly, watching her face soften, he'd wanted it to be real.

Pulse slowing, he thought back to when he'd agreed to marry her. At the time he'd been too stunned by her conditions, too determined to get back his father's business, to think about what it would mean to live this particular lie. He'd been lying for so long, to so many people, why would one more matter?

Except now it did.

He wanted to stop, to erase the past and start again.

And not just his marriage to Imma. He wanted to go

back—way, way back, to before his father's death—and live his whole life differently.

He turned to face her, his expression benign, one eyebrow raised questioningly. 'Enough what?'

'I don't want you touching me,' she snapped.

'Really?' he said, one eyebrow raised sceptically. 'You didn't seem to have any objections on the plane. You know, when you were sitting on my lap...'

Watching the pink flush rise over her face up to her hairline, Vicè held his breath. Was it embarrassment or desire? Maybe it was embarrassment at her desire?

Briefly he wondered what she would do if he pulled her closer and kissed her. Kissed her until she melted into him and she was his again. Beneath the overhanging greenery, he saw her eyes had darkened but, glancing over at her taut, flushed face, he pushed back against the heat rising like a wave inside his body.

Sadly this wasn't the right time or place.

'In fact, things seemed to be getting quite...*cosy.*' He drew the word out, elongating it deliberately until the colour in her cheeks grew darker.

She ignored his remark and, tipping her head back in the manner of a queen addressing a commoner, she gave him a glacial stare. 'Are you going to show me where we're going or do I have to find my own way?'

He sighed. 'Isn't it a little early in our married life to start with the nagging, *cara*? Could we at least get to our one-week anniversary first?'

Whistling softly, he sidestepped, moving past her furious face.

Coming to Portofino had been a whim. But, watching her reaction as they'd pulled up in front of the hotel, he had felt his stomach grow warm. She had obviously been expecting some seedy 'no-tell motel', but he could tell she was surprised. And impressed.

He breathed in on a rush of pleasure. Was it impressive? He tried to see it through her eyes.

To himself, and to everyone else too—especially his family—he'd always downplayed how much he cared about the Dolce, making out that it was more of a hobby than a business so nobody would suspect that it mattered to him. But Imma's open-mouthed wonder made him want to stop pretending and tell her how he really felt.

At the villa, he unlocked the door, feeling the usual rush of conflicting emotions.

He loved the spacious rooms. The polished hardwood floors, high ceilings and antique Murano chandeliers all captured the glamour of a bygone era, and the tall windows caught the gentle sea breeze and offered mesmerising views of the serene cerulean bay.

It was the perfect backdrop for his *dolce far niente* life-style. But it was not home. Home would only ever be his family's estate in Sicily.

Turning, he found Imma standing at the entrance, one foot over the threshold. He felt his breath catch. With her dark hair tumbling over her shoulders, and anger mingling with apprehension in her green eyes, she looked some like a woodland nymph who had stumbled across a hunter.

It took him a moment to realise that he was the hunter. Another to realise that he didn't like how that made him feel.

He felt something pinch inside his chest. Revenge was supposed to be sweet, but he hated the guarded expression on her face—*and* knowing that he was the cause of it.

'Okay, this is it. I'll give you a tour of the house first, and then we can just chill for a bit. Maybe have an *aperitivo* and then—'

Distracted by the various and all equally tempting versions of 'and then' playing out inside his head, he broke off from what he was saying and headed towards the kitchen.

He kept the tour brief and factual, opening doors and listing rooms.

'That's it for this level.' He gestured towards the stair-case. 'Shall we?'

For a moment she stared warily back at him, as though he was Bluebeard, inviting her to see where he kept his other wives, and then, averting her gaze, she stepped past him. His chest tightened first and his groin next, as he caught the scent of her perfume, and he took a moment to steady himself before following her upstairs.

'There are no guest rooms,' he said. 'Not that we need any.' He gave her a slow, teasing smile. 'Guests on a hon-eymoon would be a little de trop, don't you think, *cara*?'

'Not on this one,' she said sweetly.

Touché, he thought, holding her gaze. He liked it that he could get under her skin—metaphorically speaking. Of course, what he'd like more would be to actually strip her naked and lick every centimetre of her smooth, satiny body.

They had reached the top of the stairs.

The large, beautiful bedroom stretched the whole length of this floor, and it was filled with light and the scent from the honeysuckle that grew prolifically in the gardens below. Strangely, though, he could still smell Imma's perfume.

He watched as she stopped and turned slowly on the spot, stilling as she caught sight of their bags sitting side by side at the end of the bed.

'What did you say about the other bedrooms?'

'There are none.'

Catching sight of the vibrant aquamarine sea, he walked towards the French windows and opened them, blinking into the sunlight as he stepped onto the balcony.

'You know, sometimes you can see dolphins swimming in the bay. When the Romans came here there were so many of them they named it Portus Delphini—that's why it's called Portofino.'

Imma came and stood beside him. She was frowning.

'Say that again?'

'Portus Delphini—it means Port of the Dolphins—'

'I meant about the bedrooms.'

He dropped onto one of the chairs that were scattered casually around the balcony, extending his legs and stretching his arms above his head. He was fully aware that she was watching him, waiting for his reply, and the tension in her body made his own body grow taut.

'Oh, that...' he said casually. 'I said this is the only one. This is *our* bedroom.'

'No.' She shook her head, her green eyes narrowing. 'This is *your* bedroom. I will take a room at the hotel.'

Now he frowned. 'At the hotel? How is that going to work?'

She was looking at him as if she wanted to take off her shoes and throw them at his head.

'Very simply. You sleep *here*. I sleep *there*.'

He shook his head. 'You're not making sense, *cara*. We're supposed to be crazily in love. People who are crazily in love don't sleep in separate beds—never mind separate rooms in a different building.'

Eyes narrowing, she put her hands on her hips. 'But we're not in love, Vicè.'

Her voice was tense, and he heard the depth of her hurt and anger.

'Oh, I'm sorry—did you start to believe your own lies? I suppose that's what happens when you never tell the truth.'

His jaw tightened. 'You don't get to lecture me about the truth. Not after that show you put on in *your* bedroom the other night.'

For a moment he thought she was going to slap him again and knew on some level he would deserve it. Knew also that he didn't like this version of himself. Worse, he knew his father would be appalled. Alessandro had been a *gentiluomo*. He had treated everyone with the same quiet courtesy, but had reserved a special respectful tenderness for his wife.

'At least it was only one night,' she said acidly. 'Your whole *life* is a show, Vicè.'

Her blunt words felt like the waves that battered the coastline during winter storms.

He stared at her in silence.

Probably ninety-nine percent of what was written about him was untrue, or at best vaguely based on the truth, but he never bothered demanding a retraction. There was no point. His 'bad' reputation was good for business. And, as Ciro's brother, he had grown so used to unfavourable comparisons that he hardly registered them or even knew how to resent them.

But this woman seemed to know exactly which buttons to press. She made him feel things—good and bad—that no one ever had before. Somehow she'd sneaked under the barriers he'd built against the world, so that he was finding it harder and harder to maintain his usual couldn't-care-less attitude.

With an effort, he tethered his temper. 'I'm well aware we're not in love. But what matters is that we appear to be.'

'In public,' she countered. 'Look, we made an agreement—'

'Yes, we did,' he agreed. 'It's called marriage.'

Her chin jutted forward. 'A marriage that I made clear would not include our sleeping together.'

He shrugged. 'Okay, so go back to your father,' he said.

It was an idle threat. She had already made it clear that was not an option. But as her eyes darted towards the staircase he felt his heart jolt, his mind tracking back to the way she'd looked at him when Matteo had been there.

Her smile had felt like the sun breaking over this balcony in the afternoon. Warm and irresistible and real.

He didn't want her to leave.

In fact, he was determined that she should stay.

Obviously he wanted her to stay, or he wouldn't get his father's business back, but for some reason that seemed to matter less than getting her to share that soft, sweet smile with him in private.

'Let him find you another husband,' he said softly. 'Shouldn't be a problem. There must be a queue of men wanting to marry a woman who walked out on her wedding night. And, if not, I'm sure your *papà* will persuade someone to step up.'

Watching the colour leave her face, he knew she was cornered.

'You did this on purpose—didn't you?' she prompted, her incredible green eyes flashing with anger and resentment. 'You knew there was only one bedroom. That's why you wanted to come here.'

'Me? I'm just a passenger, *cara*,' he said disingenuously. 'This is your itinerary. I go where you tell me.'

Her green eyes flared. 'Well, in that case, you can go to hell!'

'Maybe later.' He glanced at his watch. 'Right now, we need to get ready.'

'For what?'

'We have dinner plans. At the hotel.'

Was he being serious?

Imma gaped at him. They were in the middle of an argument—*no*, scratch that, they were in the middle of a power struggle—and he wanted them to just wrap it up and have dinner together.

As if!

Fury rose up inside her and, lifting her chin, she folded her arms. 'I'm not feeling hungry.'

His eyes met hers, and the sudden dark intensity of his gaze made her breath stall in her throat.

'Oh, I wouldn't worry... I'm sure I can find something on the menu to prick your appetite,' he said softly.

The air between them seemed to thicken, his words making her heart miss a beat in such a maddening and all too predictable way that she wanted to scream. He'd tricked her into coming here. He was vile. Manipulative. Duplicitous.

So why was her stupid body betraying her like this?

Her pulse jolted as he began unbuttoning his shirt.

'What are you doing?'

'Getting changed.' Catching sight of her face, he sighed. 'We have to eat. Well, I do, anyway. And we're going to have to face people sooner or later. So let's get it over with. We'll show our faces, smile, look loved up and then it's done.'

'Fine. Since you put it so nicely,' she said stiffly. 'But just because I'm going to dinner with you it doesn't change anything.'

He looked at her for a long moment. Probably it was a new experience for him. No doubt most women would move continents to have dinner with Vicenzu Trapani.

'Of course not,' he murmured. 'The bathroom's through there. I'll see you downstairs.' His dark eyes met hers, then dropped to her mouth, then lower still. 'Call me if you need me to zip you up. Or, better still, unzip you. I'll be happy to help.'

In the bathroom, she washed quickly and changed out of her dress.

How had this happened? At home, when she wanted space, she'd run a bath and lie back, closing her eyes and losing herself in the steam and the silence. And now she was here, hiding in another bathroom from another man.

Only wasn't that the reason she had agreed to marry Vicè? To change all that? To be someone different?

It wasn't the only reason.

Her pulse twitched. Did he know the effect he had on her?

Of course.

Vicè was an expert on women—he knew exactly what to look for. He probably thought he had her all worked out, and that when he clicked his fingers she would come running. But he didn't know her at all.

She glanced down at her dress, her pulse beating unevenly. It was new. Her sister had chosen it for her on a shopping trip in Milan. It had been a rare day of freedom for them. Her mouth twisted. Freedom that had included a posse of bodyguards, of course.

She'd been planning to wear it at the evening function after Claudia's wedding. Only in the end she hadn't had the guts to put it on in front of her father.

Glancing down, she felt her skin tighten. The dress was green, a shade brighter than her eyes, and to say that it was 'fitted' was an understatement. Had it looked this clinging in the shop? Probably. But after two glasses of Prosecco she hadn't noticed or cared.

It wasn't her usual style, any more than the black patent skyscraper heels were. But her sister was always wanting her to dress up, and she'd been so excited, so eager for Imma to buy it.

She lifted her chin and met the gaze of her reflection. She would wear it tonight—for Claudia—and prove to Vicenzu that he knew nothing about her at all.

But as she walked downstairs her bravado began to falter with every step.

Catching sight of him standing with his back to her, his eyes fixed on the sunset lighting up the bay, she felt a rush of panic. Perhaps she should change.

But before she had a chance to retreat he turned and her heart lurched. Suddenly she wasn't thinking about what she was wearing any more. She was too busy marvelling at his blatant masculine beauty.

He was wearing black trousers, a dark grey polo shirt and loafers, and she liked how he looked. *A lot.*

Her throat tightened. She liked how he was looking at her even more.

'Is it too much?' she asked quickly as his dark gaze skimmed her body.

'Not at all.' He hesitated, then took a step forward. 'It suits you.'

His voice was cool, and she wasn't sure what he meant

by that remark, but she didn't want to get inside his head to find out. Right now she just wanted to go somewhere, anywhere there were other people—people who would prevent her from doing something stupid.

Even more stupid than marrying him.

Maybe he felt the same way. Or perhaps he was just desperate for company, she thought as he escorted her swiftly and purposefully towards the hotel.

They entered through a side door. 'We'll deal with the paps later,' Vicè said, his hand locking with hers.

It was lucky for him that he was holding her hand so tightly, otherwise she would have scuttled back to the villa. Even without the paparazzi, the experience of walking into this hotel was intimidating. The beautiful decor was the embodiment of relaxed chic, a perfect mix of retro glamour and contemporary cool, but it was still overshadowed by the fame of the guests.

In the space of a minute she counted at least five A-list film stars, two motor racing drivers, a tennis champion and a disgraced former Italian prime minister—and all of them seemed to know Vicè and wanted to offer their congratulations. Even those who didn't were nearly falling over to catch a glimpse of him.

'They're bored with me,' he murmured.

'What?' She glanced up at him in confusion.

'It's you they've come to see.'

Wrong, she thought as they sat down at their table in the restaurant. He was so devastating you could gaze at him for several lifetimes and not get bored.

He was a gracious, natural host, and a master of *sprezzatura*—that ability to make things happen seemingly without effort or any apparent thought. And he liked people… accepted them for who they were.

Watching him stop to speak to a middle-aged couple who were celebrating their wedding anniversary, she felt her pulse slow. Vicè was turning out to be an enigma. And, even though she knew that feeling this way wasn't clever, he was a mystery she found herself wanting to solve.

The view from the panoramic terrace was legendary, and she could see why. In the fading light of the setting sun the curve of the town's pastel-coloured houses looked like something from a dream.

But if the view was enchanting, the food was sublime. She chose *paté di seppia* followed by *zembi au pesto* and savoured every mouthful.

'So you've found your appetite?'

Looking up, Imma blushed.

'It's fine,' he assured her. Leaning forward, he took her hand. 'It's been a long day. You need to eat.'

Watching him kiss her hand, she wondered if it would feel different if he meant it. 'The food is delicious,' she said.

'I'm glad you like it.'

She met his gaze. 'I didn't think it would be so...'

'So what?'

His expression hadn't changed, but she could sense the tension around his eyes.

'So magical here. You've made something remarkable, and you've done it on your own. Your family must be very proud.'

He nodded. 'Of course.'

'So why did you choose Portofino?'

He shrugged. 'I didn't. It chose me.'

It was a perfectly reasonable reply, but she couldn't shift the feeling that there was more to it than what he was saying. But if there was, he wasn't sharing it. He talked easily and amusingly about anything and everything except himself. Then he either made a joke or changed the subject.

When the meal was over Vicè caught her hand.

'Let's get this done.' He eyed her sideways. 'You know we're going to have to kiss? Nothing beyond the call of duty—just enough to make it look real. Are you okay with that?'

She nodded. 'For the cameras, yes.'

She had been expecting a couple of photographers, but as they walked down the steps of the hotel a crowd of paparazzi rushed forward.

'Vicè, is it true you two only met twenty-four hours ago?'

'Give me a break. I'm good—but not that good.' He grinned. 'It was at least forty-eight.'

There were yells of laughter.

'Aren't you going to kiss your wife, Vicè?'

Her heart leapt as he turned and looked down at her.

'I think I should,' he said softly, his eyes dropping to her mouth.

His hand moved to her back. She felt her stomach disappear as he tipped her head back and stared into her eyes, and then he leaned forward and kissed her.

It was the lightest of kisses, fleeting and gentle. But, staring up into his dark eyes, she felt her brain freeze and her body begin to melt. Pulse jumping, she leaned into him and pressed her mouth against his.

For a fraction of a second she felt his surprise, and then his hand caught in her hair and he was pulling her closer. Her head spun. She could taste his hunger...feel her own hunger flowering with a swiftness that shocked her. Blood was roaring in her ears.

Her fingers slid over his chest, curling into the fabric of his shirt, and she couldn't stop herself from slanting her body against his.

His lips were still moving slowly, deliberately over hers, drawing out the heat that was tightening her stomach so that she was shivering, shaking inside, her body melting with a raw hunger that was as torturous as it was exquisite. And then she was kissing him back, fusing her mouth with his.

The roar of the photographers' voices filled her head. For a few moments the world turned white. Then she felt his swift indrawn breath, and as he lifted his head she dimly became aware of her surroundings again.

'Okay, that's it for now.' Vicè smiled, and seconds later he was leading her back down the path to his villa.

Her heart was hammering against her ribs and her cheeks felt scalded. It had been supposed to be for show, but as he'd drawn her into the half-circle of his arms she had never wanted anything to be more real.

Had Vicè sensed her unbidden response beneath the performance? The thought made her throat tighten and as they walked into the villa she spun round to face him. 'I can't believe you just did that.'

He arched an eyebrow. 'What did you expect? A peck on the cheek?'

Her voice was shaking. 'That kiss was *way* "beyond the call of duty"!'

And she had kissed him back. Her teeth clenched. She was furious with herself. But to reveal that would reveal her vulnerability, and so, as he dropped down onto the sofa, she directed her anger towards him.

'You love this, don't you? Playing your stupid games—'

His eyes narrowed, and then he was on his feet and moving towards her so fast that she only just had time to throw up a defensive hand.

'*Me* playing games?' He shook his head, an incredulous look on his handsome face. 'I'm not the one playing games here, Imma.'

'What is that supposed to mean?' she hissed.

'It means all this fighting and flirting. You *do* know that eventually we're going to end up back where we started? Naked. In bed.'

Her eyes clashed with his. 'In your dreams.'

'In yours too,' he taunted.

His words made her breathing jerk. She shook her head in denial. 'You are impossibly arrogant.'

'So I've been told. But that doesn't change the facts— which are that you want me as much as I want you. So why don't we skip the fighting and go straight to the sex?'

Cheeks flaming, she stared up at him angrily, the truth of his words only intensifying her need to deny them.

'You didn't want me before—you wanted your father's business. And you only want me now because you can't risk having an affair and blowing our deal. As to what I want—do you really think I'd sleep with you again after everything that's happened?'

'Why not?'

His eyes were fixed on her face, hot and dark, and as she caught the intense heat in them her body began to tremble.

'We're adults. We're both getting what we want from this arrangement. Except each other. But I'm willing to forget the past if you are.'

Forget the past.

For a second she couldn't trust herself to speak. 'Excuse me.' She stepped past him.

He frowned. 'Where are you going?'

'To get some bedding. I'm going to sleep on the sofa.'

For a moment he clearly thought she was joking, and then he swore softly. 'Fine. I'll sleep down here.'

She stumbled slightly, caught off guard by his sudden acquiescence.

'Fine. And, just so you know, from now until we leave, there won't be any more public appearances for the two of us. Show's over, Vicè.'

CHAPTER SEVEN

ROLLING ONTO HIS BACK, Vicè savagely punched the pillow behind his head and gazed up at the ceiling.

Newsflash: this sofa might look great, and lounging on it with a Negroni was fine, but it was definitely not designed for sleep.

Not that he was going to sleep any time soon, he thought. Even if his neck hadn't been in agony, his body was wound so tightly he doubted he would ever sleep again. In fact, it had been on high alert ever since Imma had sashayed downstairs earlier and he'd forgotten to breathe.

Gone had been the absurdly staid mother-of-the-bride navy dress and in its place had been a silk number the colour of absinthe that had clung to her body without a ripple, exposing her slim curves and shimmering biscotti-coloured skin.

And then there had been those shoes…

A muscle pulsed in his jaw. It was a toss-up as to whether that dress or her parting shot had rendered him more speechless.

Remembering Imma's words, he felt his muscles tighten. *Show's over.*

Wrong, he thought. It wasn't over. This was just an intermission.

Scowling, he shifted onto his side. Just an intermission that was longer than necessary and extremely uncomfortable.

He scowled. How had he ended up here? Spending a night on the sofa while his new wife slept alone in *his* bed?

He couldn't work out what had happened. So he might not be a business tycoon like Ciro, or even his father, but if there was one thing he understood above all others it was women.

He gritted his teeth. Make that all women except Imma.

Take tonight: she had been spitting fire over their sleeping arrangements, storming off into the bathroom when he'd told her about their dinner reservation. But then she'd seemed to calm down and relax over dinner, eating and enjoying her meal even though she'd claimed earlier she had no appetite.

Her mood had shifted a little when they'd walked out of the hotel. She had been jittery—understandably. Like oysters, the paparazzi were an acquired taste. And, unlike him, Imma had very little experience of facing a phalanx of photographers. But he'd warned her that they would have to perform for the cameras and she'd seemed to be up for it.

His pulse began to beat thickly in his blood.

Had he meant to kiss her like that? As if a clock had been counting down to the end of the world and only by kissing her could he stop time and stay alive?

No, he hadn't—and he hadn't expected her to respond like that either.

He'd thought she would play coy, do her 'duty'...

But then she'd leaned into him, her lips parting. And, lost in the sweetness of her mouth and the pliant heat of her body, he had kissed her back.

His groin tightened at the memory.

It had not been a duty kiss. But, *mannaggia alla miseria*, he was only human, and when a beautiful woman was in his arms, kissing him, what was he supposed to do?

He felt his shoulders tense. She thought he'd planned it—that it had been yet another example of him lying to her about his intentions. The truth was that his arousal had been so fast, so intense, he'd lost the ability to think, much less contemplate all possible interpretations of his actions.

In the time it had taken for her to part her lips he'd forgotten about the paparazzi, forgotten their marriage wasn't real. His breath, his body, his whole being, had been focused on the feel of her mouth on his and he had been powerless to stop.

Only there was no way to prove that to her. Not that she would believe him anyway. And could he really blame her?

His chest tightened. Never before had he treated anyone quite so unfairly as he'd treated Imma.

He'd lied to her repeatedly and manipulated her, using every smile and glittering gaze in his repertoire to lure her away from her family and seduce her. Of course she wouldn't believe him.

Sighing, he stared across the darkened living room.

And that was why he would be sleeping on this sofa for the foreseeable future. Or rather *not* sleeping.

He sat up. There was no point in just lying there. Glancing out of the window, he caught sight of a flicker of light reflected from the surface of the pool and felt a rush of relief, as if someone had thrown him a life jacket. A swim was just what he needed to clear his head and cool his body.

Outside, the warm air clung to his skin. For a moment he stood on the edge of the pool and then, tipping forward, he executed a flawless dive into the water.

For the next forty minutes or so he swam lengths, until his chest and legs ached in unison. Turning over, he floated on his back, his lungs burning.

A huge pale moon hung over the sea, and above him the inky blue-black sky was crowded with stars. The air was heavy with the scent of cypress and honeysuckle and vibrated with the hum of cicadas. It was all impossibly romantic—the perfect setting, in fact, for a wedding night.

All that was missing was his beautiful bride.

He was back where he started.

Grimacing, he turned towards the pool's edge, his limbs stretching through the water. As he pulled himself out and draped a towel around his neck, a tiny speckled lizard darted between the shadows.

But that wasn't what made him catch his breath.

Beyond the shadows, her green dress luminous in the moonlight, her long dark hair hanging loosely over her shoulders, was his wife.

Imma felt her body tense.

Upstairs in the bedroom she had felt trapped. The windows on to the balcony had been open to the sea breeze, but still she had felt hot and panicky.

Back on Pantelleria, marrying Vicè had seemed like a good idea. She had thought she needed time and space to deal with the consequences of her actions—and his. She'd also naively believed that she could play him at his own game.

But the truth, as she'd so humiliatingly discovered this evening, was that she was out of her depth and floundering.

He was too slick, too good at twisting words and situations to his advantage. And for someone who was so poor at telling the truth he was remarkably good at pointing out dishonesty and hypocrisy in other people—namely herself.

She had known that sleep was beyond her, so she hadn't bothered to undress. Instead she had slipped off her shoes and tried to rest.

Even that, though, had been impossible.

How could she rest in his room? On his bed? And it *was* his bed. She'd been able to smell him. His aftershave and something else...a scent that had made her stomach grow warm and her head swim. Clean, masculine...like salt or newly chopped wood. She had felt it slipping over her face like a veil.

Veil. Her throat had closed around the word like a vice.

With Vicè's denials and accusations still echoing in her head, she had forgotten that this was supposed to be her wedding night.

Some wedding night.

She had never felt more alone, so she had crept downstairs, past the sofa, and gone out into the heavy night air.

She had thought Vicè would be asleep. But he was not only very much awake, he was standing in front of her. In boxer shorts. Extremely wet boxer shorts.

Her stomach flipped over and for a heartbeat she couldn't move. She no longer seemed to know how to make her legs work. But she did know that no good would come of her staying there.

'Imma. Please, wait—'

Against her will, against every instinct she had, she made her body still. With an effort, she turned to face him. 'Why? So you can make me feel stupid? You don't need to bother, Vicè. Really. I'm already doing a great job of that all on my own.'

He took a step towards her. 'I don't want to make you feel stupid. I just want to talk.'

She looked away, swallowing against the ache in her throat, feeling trapped again. 'Well, that's a lovely idea, but we don't talk. We argue. And I'm tired of arguing.'

'We do talk,' he said quietly. 'That first night at your father's villa we talked a lot.'

She stared at him in confusion. But he was right. They had talked that night about lots of things. Actually, *she* had talked—and that in itself was remarkable.

Usually, she was the listener. When it was just the two of them, Claudia would always be the one chattering on about some recipe she was going to try, and at work, with her father's shadow looming large over everything, her opinions were politely ignored. As for Cesare himself—like most rich, powerful men, he was far too convinced of his own rightness to invite other viewpoints.

A lump of misery swelled inside her. She was getting distracted. *At her father's villa, Vicè had a reason to listen to her.*

'That wasn't real,' she said flatly. 'None of this is real.'

'I am—and you are.' His eyes held hers. 'And so is this thing between us.'

She shook her head. 'There *is* no thing between us, Vicè.'

But of their own accord her eyes fixed on his chest. For a few half seconds she stared at the drops of water trickling down over his smooth golden skin, and then she looked away, her breathing ragged, her denial echoing hollowly around the empty terrace.

She had taken him back to her father's villa thinking that one night with him would give her the answers she needed. Instead it had simply raised more questions. Like what kind of woman could still want a man like him? And how—*where*—was she ever going to find another man who would override the memory of his touch, his kiss?

'Even if there is, we're not going to do anything about it.'

His eyes were steady and unblinking. 'We already have. So why are you still denying how we both feel?'

'Because it doesn't make any sense,' she mumbled.

'Does it have to?'

She looked up at him, made mute by the directness of his words and the complicity they implied.

He was silent for a moment, and then he sighed. 'Look, Imma, I don't want to argue any more than you do, so could we call a truce? Please?'

Her heart contracted. 'Forget the past, you mean?'

He stared at her. 'Not forget it—just put it on hold.'

She frowned. 'We're not talking about a nuisance call. This is my sister's life—her heart.' *My heart.* Her eyes were filling with tears. 'She doesn't deserve what your brother has done to her.'

'Oh? But my father *did* deserve to be hounded in the last few months of his life?'

His voice was suddenly hard, his eyes even harder. *So much for a truce*, she thought.

'And my mother? She deserved to lose her home? Her husband?'

His tone made her shiver.

'Of course not.' She hesitated. 'Is that why you want the business back? For her?'

For a moment he seemed confused, as though he didn't understand her words.

'I want my father back—so does my mother. There's only one reason I want the business, and one reason I want you as my wife—and that's so your father gets a taste of his own medicine.'

She flinched, the scorn in his voice biting into her flesh. This was exactly why she should have turned and walked away when she'd had the chance.

There was a tense, expectant silence, and then Vicè ran a hand over his face.

'I didn't mean that.' He was breathing unevenly. 'What I said about wanting you... I was angry—I *am* angry—but I don't want to hurt you.'

Glancing up, she tensed. His eyes were filled with a kind of bewildered frustration. He was hurting, and his pain cut through her own misery.

Without thinking, she reached out and touched his arm. 'I wish my father hadn't acted like he did, and if I could go back and change one thing in all of this it would be that.'

There was a silence. He stared at her, but he didn't shake off her hand.

After a moment, he said slowly, 'Not what happened between us? You wouldn't go back and change that?'

He sounded confused, disbelieving, and his dark eyes were searching her face as though he was trying to read her thoughts.

Her mind turned over her words. She was suddenly confused herself. But it hadn't occurred to her to regret that night they'd shared. She wouldn't exchange those beautiful, sensual hours in Vicè's arms for anything. And it hadn't been just the heat and the hunger, or even the fact that for those few short hours she had believed he wanted her for herself.

That night with him had been the first time she had consciously defied her father's wishes—not to his face, maybe, but it had felt like it. The first time she had made decisions about her own life.

'No, I wouldn't change that,' she said quietly.

'I wouldn't change it either.'

His eyes held hers and, catching the heat in his dark gaze, she felt a rush of panic. Last time she had willingly walked into the fire. But she couldn't do so again, knowing what she did now.

'I can't do this,' she said. And this time she acted, turning and running swiftly back into the house.

He caught up with her in the living room, his body blocking her escape. 'Where are you going?'

'Anywhere you're not.' She spoke breathlessly.

'For a year?' He looked and sounded incredulous. 'You're going to keep running away from me for a whole year?'

'I'm not like you, Vicenzu. I can't just switch it on and off for the cameras.'

'What cameras?' Holding out his arms, he gestured to the empty room. 'There are no cameras here. There is you, and me—just like there was at the villa on the island.'

Remembering her shock and misery the morning after, she shook her head. 'But you weren't really you. Or maybe you were, and I just thought you were someone else.'

She had been someone else that night too. Someone reckless and uninhibited. And gullible.

His gaze rested intently on her face. 'I don't understand…'

Tears pricked her eyes. 'You don't need to.'

He frowned. 'We're married. I'm your husband.'

Her chest rose and fell as she struggled to breathe. 'I can't believe you can say that with a straight face.' She gazed at him, her heart racing. 'But I suppose it's not surprising you think this is normal. Your whole life is a charade. Why should your marriage be any different?'

Vicè stared at her, a muscle working in his jaw.

'My life was just fine until I married you,' he said slowly.

If she didn't like charades then why was she making him act like some lovesick puppy in public and then relegating him to the sofa when they were alone?

'How is this my fault?' She seemed almost to choke in disbelief.

He stared at her in frustration, her words replaying inside his head. He *didn't* think this was normal. For him, 'normal' had always been his parents' relationship. Normal, but unattainable.

He was suddenly conscious of his heart hammering against his ribs.

They had been so happy together, so comfortable, and yet still sweetly infatuated like the teenagers in love they had once been. Whereas he—

His body tensed. The idea that he would ever be capable of replicating his parents' marriage had always seemed too ludicrous to contemplate. So he had done what he always did—he'd pushed the possibility away, deliberately choosing a way of life that was the antithesis of theirs.

And his parents had done what they always did too, indulging him even though he knew that they'd longed for him to fall in love and settle down.

Remembering his mother's reaction when he'd called to tell her he was married, he felt his heartbeat slow. It had been a bittersweet moment. She had been so happy for him, but also sad that Alessandro hadn't been alive to see his eldest son finally find love.

What would she say if she knew the truth?

Looking over at Imma, he pushed the thought away, guilt

making his voice harsher than he'd intended. 'This "charade", as you put it, wasn't my idea.'

She lifted her chin. 'True. But if you'd had your way I'd have signed over the olive oil company the morning after we slept together and you and your vile brother would probably still be toasting your victory in some bar in Palermo.'

Her description was just about close enough to his last meeting with Ciro for colour to stain his cheekbones.

Shaking his head, he took a step back, his jaw tightening. 'I don't need this, and I certainly can't live like this for a year.'

'This isn't just about you.'

There was a tautness in her voice, and her mouth was trembling slightly. He realised that she was close to tears.

She sucked in a breath. 'For once I don't want to have to think about what someone else wants or needs. I thought with you—'

As she glanced away he felt his spine stiffen. The events of the last few days must be starting to catch up with her. Or maybe she had been in shock all along.

'You're right. This isn't just about me.' He flattened the anger in his voice, picking his words very carefully, suddenly afraid that the wrong ones would make her run again. 'So tell me what *you* want—what *you* need.'

There was a moment of silence.

'I don't know.' She shook her head. 'I really don't know. I've never known. Maybe if I had none of this would be happening.'

Her shoulders tightened, making her look smaller, wounded, like a bird with a broken wing. Seeing her like that—so diminished, so vulnerable—made him ache inside.

'I doubt that,' he said gently.

He sat down on the sofa, and after a moment, as he'd hoped she would, she sat down beside him.

'There are a lot of reasons why this has happened, *cara*, but you're not one of them.'

She stiffened. 'I know you hate him. My father, I mean. But he's not all bad. He used to be different before...when my mother was alive. He's just been on his own for too long.'

His pulse stalled. He did hate her father—and yet right now the reason for that hate seemed irrelevant. What mattered more was Imma's pain.

'How old were you when she died?'

'Eight.'

Her stark single-word answer made his heart kick against his ribs. Watching the flicker of sadness in her green eyes, he felt the ache in his chest spread out like a dark rain cloud.

His father's death had felt like something tearing inside him—and he was an adult, a grown man. Imma had had to deal with the loss of her mother as a child.

'He hated not being able to help her,' she said quietly. 'I think that's why he's like he is now. He can't bear the idea of something happening to me and Claudia—something he can't control.'

Vicè felt his stomach clench. In that case he and Ciro had already had their revenge. And just like that his hunger for retribution was gone—diluted and washed away by the tears in her eyes.

'He's your father,' he said. 'Of course he doesn't want to see you hurt.'

It was meant to be a generic response, only for some reason he found himself thinking about his own father. Right up until his death Alessandro had spent his life protecting him, constantly levelling the playing field so that he wouldn't have to compare himself unfavourably to Ciro. In fact, it had been that need to protect his eldest son that had ultimately caused his death.

Something jarred in his chest, as if a depth charge had exploded. He'd made this about Cesare, but it was actually about him. It had always been about him and his failings as a son, as a man.

He forced himself to look over and meet her gaze. 'He loves you.'

She nodded slowly. 'But he still misses my mother. That's why he works so much. Only now he's become obsessed with building up the business, and…' She hesitated, her face tensing. 'It matters to him—his name, his legacy. He's never said anything but I know he wishes he'd had a son. Instead, he's got me. Only I can't ever be good enough. He wants me to be tough and ruthless, but he also wants me to be a dutiful daughter. And then there's Claudia…'

The sudden softness in her eyes cut through him like a blade. 'You're close?' he asked.

She nodded. 'She was so little when Mamma died. We had nannies, but they didn't stay long. Papà was so angry, so exacting. Anyway, she always preferred me. And I didn't mind. I *wanted* to look after her.'

Her voice sounded scraped and bruised. It made something hard lodge in his throat. 'You *have* looked after her.'

'How?' She bit her lip. 'I let her marry Ciro and now he's broken her heart.' A tear slid down her cheek. 'I was supposed to take care of her—'

He caught her hands in his. Her whole body was rigid, braced for disaster. 'You did—you are. But she's not a child any more, *cara*—'

'You don't understand. I promised Mamma, and now I've broken that promise.'

She was crying in earnest now and he pulled her onto his lap, wanting and needing to hold her close, to hold her for as long as it took to make her feel whole again.

His skin burned with shame as he realised the mistake he'd made. Imma wasn't her father's daughter at all. She was just a little girl who had lost her mother and had to grow up fast. A little girl who had been so busy trying to be a daughter and a mother and a proxy son all at once that she had never had time to be herself. He couldn't bear picturing her little face, her anxious green eyes.

Gently, he stroked her hair. *'Va tutto bene, cara,'* he murmured. 'It's going to be okay. I've got you.'

He understood now how her family had pushed their needs ahead of hers. And he had been no better. In fact, he had been worse. Deliberately and ruthlessly using her as a means to punish her father.

His arms tightened and he kept on smoothing her hair until finally she let out a shuddering breath.

'None of this is your fault, Imma,' he said quietly. 'You're a good sister, and a loyal daughter, but you're way more than the sum of your parts. You're an amazing woman. You're beautiful and sexy and strong and smart. You can be anything you want.' Pulling the towel from around his neck, he gently patted the tears from her cheeks. 'And I'll be there, remember? In the background...'

Her lips curved up, as he had hoped they would.

For a moment they stared at each other in silence.

'You didn't sign up for this,' she said quietly.

'Oh, I signed up for everything, *cara*. Kiss-and-tell interview, miniseries, film franchise...'

He was trying to make her relax, maybe enough to trust him. But he was surprised to find that he was also telling the truth.

Her smile flickered. 'I want to be there for Papà and Claudia, but I want to be myself too. I thought if I could break free just for one night, lose my virginity to someone I'd chosen, then it would all become clear. Who I am. What I want. And maybe somebody would want me for being me.' She screwed up her face. 'It sounds stupid, saying it out loud.'

He shook his head. 'It's not stupid at all.'

He'd left Sicily to do much the same. Not to lose his virginity, but to put as much distance as possible between himself and his parents' carefully managed disappointment—and, of course, Ciro's effortless success.

'I thought it would be so easy.' Her eyes found his. 'And then I met you.'

'You deserve better,' he said slowly. 'You deserve better than me.' He hesitated. 'How is she? Claudia? Is she okay?'

Her smile faded a little and for a moment he didn't think she was going to reply, but finally she nodded.

'She will be. I'll take of her.'

'I know.' His eyes met hers and he was suddenly conscious of her warm hands on his chest. 'And what about you?'

There was a beat of silence.

'Me?' She seemed stunned by the question. 'I don't— It's not—'

'I want to look after you, Imma.' He stopped. 'Look, I messed up. Ciro too. We were wrong. We made this about you and Claudia and that was wrong,' he repeated. 'Our fight is with your father—not you.' His heart began to beat faster. 'I want to make it up to you. What I'm trying to say is… Could we start this year over?'

Her face didn't change, and nor did she reply.

'If you need more time—' he began.

'I don't,' she said quietly.

He felt a rush of misery and regret, but then his pulse leapt as her hand splayed across his chest.

'But if we start again it has to be different. No more lies, Vicè. No more games. Agreed?'

At that moment, with her body so warm and soft and close to his, he would have agreed to just about anything.

'Agreed,' he said hoarsely.

There was a short silence.

Finally, she cleared her throat. 'You should probably get out of those damp clothes…'

Nodding, he made as though to slide her off his lap, but she didn't move. Instead, her eyes met his.

'Or I could help you…' A little shakily, she ran her fingers down his body to the waistband of his shorts. 'Unless you've changed your mind?'

He stared at her dazedly. *What mind?* Like the rest of him, his mind had melted at the feel of her fingertips on his skin.

A flicker of hope went through him like an electric current and he swallowed, his eyes dropping to her mouth, then lower to the swell of her breasts.

'Is that— Do you— I mean, are you saying what I think you're trying to say?'

His usual effortless eloquence had deserted him. He couldn't remember ever feeling so awkward. But he was shaken by the intensity of his desire, paralysed with fear that he had misunderstood her gesture and words.

'Yes,' she said simply.

It was as if a starter gun had gone off in his head.

Framing her face with his hands, he pulled her closer, his mouth finding hers, and he felt a shiver running over him as her fingers stroked across his skin.

'I've been thinking about this for days...' he groaned against her mouth.

Shock waves of desire were slamming through his body.

'I've been thinking about it too.'

Her breathing was decidedly unsteady now, and she was pushing him back, back onto the sofa.

'Wait, wait... No—not here. Not on this damn sofa,' he muttered.

It was his last conscious thought as, reaching down, he scooped her up into his arms and carried her upstairs.

As he dropped her gently onto the bed Imma sat up, pulling him closer, her mouth seeking the outline of his arousal through the still damp fabric of his boxer shorts. He grunted, his body jerking forward as her fingers slid over his hip bones and she began to move her lips over the swell of his erection.

His hand caught in her hair. 'Imma...' He swore softly.

* * *

Imma felt her stomach clench. Her power to arouse him was shockingly exciting, and he was fiercely aroused. Fingers trembling slightly, she tugged at the waistband of his boxer shorts, heat flaring in her pelvis as she slid them over his hips.

She watched his jaw tighten, the muscles of his arms bunching as she ran her tongue around the blunt, rigid tip, taking it in her mouth. The feel of it jerking and pulsating in her mouth made her head swim.

He groaned, his fingers twisting in her hair, and then he jolted backwards, lifting her face and lowering his mouth to hers, kissing her with a hunger that made liquid heat flood her pelvis.

As her hands reached for him, he batted them away. 'My turn,' he said hoarsely.

His eyes were dark and molten with heat. Pulling her to her feet, he dipped his head, kissed her again, taking his time, running his tongue slowly over her lips then between them, tasting her, slowing her pulse.

She felt his hands on her back and then he was unzipping her dress, sliding it over her body, his hands moving smoothly around to cup her breasts, his thumbs grazing the already swollen tips until she was shaking inside.

And then he was nudging her back onto the bed, his mouth on hers, dropping his head to take first one and then the other nipple into his mouth, rolling his tongue over the tight, ruched skin as her hands clutched his neck and shoulders.

She reached for him again and this time he caught her hands, pinning them to her sides. Deliberately he slid down her body. A shiver of excitement ran through her.

'Let me taste you,' he whispered, and her head fell back, her whole body quivering as he parted her with his tongue.

Her body arched, pressing against his mouth. She had never felt anything like this. She was moaning, shifting restlessly against him, desperately seeking more, her body no longer her own. There was nothing except him...nothing but his warm, firm mouth and the measured, insistent press of his tongue.

Helplessly, she pushed against him, chasing that fluttering, delicate ripple of pleasure, and then her pulse quickened and she felt her body tighten inside, tensing as the ripple became a wave and she cried out, shuddering beneath him.

Releasing her hands, he moved up the bed, licking his way up her body to her mouth. 'I want you, Imma.'

She wrapped her arms around his neck. 'I want you too. Inside me.'

He rolled onto his back, taking her with him so that she was straddling the rigid length of him, hard and hot against the ache between her thighs. Reaching over, he fumbled in a drawer, lifting her gently as he rolled on a condom.

Squirming against him, she moved her hands across his body, over his stomach and down lower, taking him in her hand. He pulled her against him, his fingers tightening around her waist as he lifted her up and pushed into her slowly, easing himself in, inch by inch.

His face was tight with concentration and with the effort of holding back. 'Look at me,' he whispered.

Their eyes met and, gripping her hips, he began to move. She moved with him, and their bodies sought and found a steady, intoxicating rhythm that sent arrows of heat over her skin.

Reaching out, he cupped her breast, squeezing her nipple, and then his hand moved to the swollen bud of her clitoris, caressing her in time to his body's thrusts, his dark eyes never leaving hers.

She rocked against him, feeling the heat rising up inside her again, gripping him with her muscles, holding him as the friction grew. Her skin felt hot and tight. She was hot and tight inside. And suddenly she flexed forward, as though she was trying to climb over him.

He pulled her back, his eyes locking with hers, and then he pushed up one more time and she felt her body arch as he tensed, his hands clamping around her waist, her gasp of pleasure mingling with his groan.

CHAPTER EIGHT

IT WAS LATE when Vicè woke, the distant sound of a motor-boat in the bay dragging him reluctantly from his cocoon of warmth. For a moment he clung on to the last shreds of sleep, and then slowly he opened his eyes and turned his head towards the open French windows.

He had forgotten to draw the curtains, and outside the sky was a marbled swirl of the palest blue and gold, as beautiful as any Renaissance ceiling. But no sky, how-ever beautiful, could compete with the woman lying be-side him.

Imma was asleep, her face resting against his shoulder. Her left hand curled loosely on his chest, the other was resting on the pillow, leaving one rosy-tipped breast bared to his gaze.

His heart began to beat faster. With her tousled hair and long dark lashes brushing her cheeks she looked like a paint-ing. There was a softness to her in sleep, a hint of the vul-nerability beneath the poise that made him want to pull her close and hold her against him.

He tensed. It was the first time in his life he had felt that way about any woman, and yet even though it was new and unfamiliar he didn't feel panic or confusion. Instead it felt completely natural, like smiling.

But was that so surprising, really?

He might have acted unfairly—ruthlessly, even—but he wasn't a monster, and seeing her cry had horrified him. Naturally he had wanted to comfort her.

His pulse quickened. What had happened next had been completely natural too.

Natural and sublime.

He swallowed, his groin hardening at the memory of how

Imma had moved against him. Illuminated in the moon-light, her body had looked like liquid silver—felt like it too.

It had been different from that first time—slower, less frantic, more like riding a wave…an endless, curling wave of pleasure.

But then last time there had been other things in play. Obviously he'd needed to seduce her, but the intensity of his attraction had caught him off guard, made him question his motives so that it had all got tangled up in his head.

Imma had had her own agenda then too. Sleeping with him, losing her virginity, had been her first small act of independence.

Last night, though, it had been far less complicated for both of them.

It had been lust. Pure and simple and irresistible.

There had been no agenda.

He had wanted her and she had wanted him.

Of course they had been fighting it for days—fighting each other for days. But it had been too strong for both of them.

His chest tightened. They had come together as equals and Imma had made him feel things no other woman had—driven him to a pitch of excitement that had subsumed everything that had happened between them.

Including getting even with her father.

She stirred in his arms and he stared down at her, replaying that thought, turning it back and forth inside his head. Yesterday, when she had been so upset, he'd felt something shift inside him, but he hadn't articulated it quite so bluntly before. Putting it into words seemed to make his thoughts move up a gear, give shape to his feelings.

He felt a rush of relief. Getting even with Cesare didn't matter any more. His father's business was as good as his already, and that meant he was free to enjoy this year with Imma.

Watching her eyelids flutter open, he felt his body grow even harder.

And he didn't want to waste a second of it.

'Hey,' he said softly.

She stretched her arms, the movement causing the sheet to fall away from her naked body, sending a jolt of heat across his already overheated skin. For a moment she stared up at him, her green eyes widening with confusion, and then she met his gaze.

'Hey...'

Imma stared up at Vicè, her heart pounding. She had absolutely no idea what to do. Last time she'd been in the same situation Claudia had called, so she had never got to this moment of acknowledgement. It had got lost, swept aside by her sister's revelation. But now there was nowhere to hide from the truth of what they had done—what she had done.

Remembering her hoarse, inarticulate cries of pleasure, the way she had pulled his body and then his mouth closer as he'd addressed that relentless ache between her thighs, her cheeks felt suddenly as if they were on fire.

His touch had been electric, every caress sending her closer to the edge, straining for that elusive *something* that would douse the swirling heat at the centre of her body, until finally it had been in her grasp and she had shuddered to stillness in his arms.

She had never felt like that before—not even that first time. It had been beyond anything she'd ever experienced.

As the moonlight had spilled through the windows she had demanded and given pleasure in equal measure, surrendering to the passion he had unleashed. Now, though, in daylight, she felt a little embarrassed.

Understandably.

She had cried all over him, told him things about herself and her life that she had never shared with anyone, and then she'd had sex with him.

Her heart skipped. She'd expected the sex to be incredible—Vicè was a generous, gifted lover. But apparently he was also a good listener. Talking to him had been easy—even about things she had held so close and kept secret from others.

'If it's any help, I don't know how to do the morning-after bit either,' he said quietly.

Swallowing, she looked up into his dark eyes. Her whole life she had been a complicated, contained girl, equal parts fear and ambition, always wanting to push back, but too scared to refuse, to demand, to ask.

But she wasn't scared any more.

'What do you usually do?' she asked.

'That's just it.' Leaning over, he stroked her cheek. 'I don't do anything. Spending the night with someone isn't my thing.' His mouth twisted. '*Wasn't* my thing.'

She stared at him uncertainly, trying to ignore the way her stomach was turning over and over in response to the implication of his words.

'But it is now?' she whispered.

A curl of hair had fallen over her breast and, reaching out, he wrapped it around his fingers, drawing her closer so that her mouth was under his.

'Yes, it most definitely is.'

Was that true? Or was he simply saying what she wanted to hear?

There was a moment of silence.

'You don't believe me?' His eyes searched her face.

'I want to...' She hesitated. There was a coldness in her chest, the chill of doubt. 'It's just that before this—you and me—it wasn't real. You had an agenda—'

Vicè hadn't wanted her for herself then. He'd *needed* to seduce her. Only she'd had no idea. So how could she trust her instincts, her senses, now?

'And you think I had one last night?' He grinned. 'What can I say? I had to get off that sofa somehow.' He glanced down, his smile fading. 'I'm joking, *cara*. That wasn't why—' His face stilled. 'Is this about what I said before? About only wanting you to get at your father?'

He stopped, his jaw tightening.

'Look, maybe right at the beginning, at the wedding, it *was* about getting back at him and getting the business back. But when you came out of the bathroom—' He grimaced. 'I promise you I wanted you so badly I wasn't thinking about your father or my father's olive oil company. Actually, I wasn't thinking, full stop.'

Imma bit her lip. She wanted to believe him, but it was hard. Her father and Claudia both needed her. For support, for protection. She had never felt desirable before—just necessary.

His hand covered hers, and the warmth of his fingers thawed the chill in her chest.

He shook his head. '*Lo so, cara.* I know I haven't given you any reason to trust me, but I meant what I said last night. I can't get you out of my head—you're all I've been thinking about.' His mouth twisted. 'Watching you walk downstairs in that dress, those heels... I actually thought I was going to lose control. I was desperate to get to the hotel, so I didn't make a fool of myself.' He gave her the ghost of a smile. 'Although being a fool is what I do best.'

It was the kind of teasing remark that was typical of him, and yet she couldn't help feeling there was something beneath the banter.

She stared into his eyes. 'You're not a fool.'

'I'm a fool for you,' he said lightly.

She smiled at that and, lifting his hand, he stroked her hair away from her face. 'You know, I think I'm getting pretty good at this morning-after bit,' he murmured.

'Is that right?' Her lips curved upward, caught in the honeyed trap of his gleaming dark eyes and teasing smile.

'Yeah...'

Their eyes met, and then his mouth dropped, and then

he kissed her. She felt something stir inside—a flickering heat that made her body ripple to life and tighten in response.

Tipping his head back, he stared down at her, and then he ran a finger slowly along the line of her collarbone. 'Although I might just need a little bit more practice...'

His voice was warm with desire, and she felt an answering warmth start to spread over her skin as he took her face between his hands and bent his head to kiss her again.

She wanted him, and she was willing to act on that want. She was making a choice and she was choosing Vicè.

It was a feather-light kiss. But then his mouth fused with hers and she whimpered softly as he moved his tensile muscular body over her.

Gripping his hips, she stretched out beneath him. He entered her slowly, giving her time to adjust, inching forward in time with her soft sighs of pleasure. But she needed him *now*—all of him—and she arched upward, pressing herself against the smooth, polished heat of his skin, wrapping her legs around his hips.

She was already aroused, and soon she was growing dizzy, intoxicated by the hard, steady rhythm of his body. A moan of pleasure climbed in her throat, and then a fierce heat blossomed inside her as her muscles tightened around him and she let go in time to his thrust of release.

Later—much later—they sat outside beneath the canopy of wisteria, enjoying a late brunch on the terrace.

'What are you thinking?' Vicè asked.

Turning, Imma smiled. He was staring at her across the table, his dark eyes fixed on her face.

Her pulse skipped. The shock of his beauty never seemed to fade. Any other man would have been eclipsed by the decadent glamour of the Dolce, but in his cream linen trousers, short-sleeved shirt and loafers, he looked like a poster playboy for the Italian Riviera.

With effort, she pulled her gaze away to the view past his shoulder, where huge white yachts floated serenely on an aquamarine sea. 'I was thinking how lucky you are.'

He raised an eyebrow. 'That's crazy—so was I.'

Smiling, she glanced past him at the panorama below. 'You have such a beautiful view here.'

'No, that's not what's beautiful here,' he said softly.

She shook her head. 'Do you ever stop?'

'You made me, remember?' He rolled his eyes. 'You said we had to eat food. Or get dressed or something...'

Their eyes met. She and Vicè had taken a shower together. Her cheeks felt suddenly warm. At first they had just washed one another, but then the soap had got dropped, and then he had shown her other, more inventive and thrilling ways to pass the time beneath the warm, tumbling spray.

'Somebody was knocking at the door. You were naked.'

'It was Matteo,' he protested. 'And he's seen me naked hundreds of times...' He paused. 'You know, at the orgies.'

Her mouth dropped open. 'The orgies—'

'At the hotel. Surely you've read about them?'

He was grinning.

'Oh, very funny, Vicè.'

He got up, moving smoothly around the table to grab her, laughing softly when she tried to bat him away.

'*Cara*, come on. I'm sorry. I couldn't help it. You just look so sexy when you're outraged.'

'I wasn't outraged. I was—'

'Jealous?'

His dark eyes were watching her intently and she felt her pulse jump.

She lifted her chin. 'Curious.'

'Well, you're going to have to stay curious, I'm afraid,' he said softly, and his calm tone was at odds with the slight tightening of his jaw. 'You're mine, and I'm not about to share you with anyone.'

Leaning forward, he kissed her fiercely, parting her lips to deepen the kiss until her head was spinning.

'Vicè...' Closing her eyes, she whispered his name, her voice trembling, her stomach flipping over in frantic response to his words as much as to his mouth, her body screaming in protest as slowly he released her.

Opening her eyes, she found him still watching her, his face impassive again.

'So,' he said. 'How would you like to spend the rest of the day?'

He shifted against her, and as his arm grazed her shoulder blade her heart jerked. Earlier, she'd been worried this wasn't real. Now, though, she could see that a far more likely scenario was her letting it get real in her imagination. Getting ahead of herself, making connections that simply weren't there and never would be.

For her, every soft word and dark glance might feel meaningful, but the truth was Vicè liked to flirt. It was his default setting. He liked sex too, and it was great that sex had unlocked this wild, uninhibited woman hiding inside of her. But the year was supposed to be about discovering who she was, and sex was only a part of that.

Essentially, the facts hadn't changed. Theirs was a marriage of convenience and in a year it would be over. She needed to remember that. And until it was over she was going to have to set some rules.

First rule: take a step back. Stop allowing the passion she found in his arms to mislead her and make her forget why she had agreed to this marriage in the first place.

Second rule: get out there and do and try everything at least once. How else was she going to work out who she was?

Smoothing her sundress over her knees, she said offhandedly, 'I know I said I didn't want the two of us to go out in public again, but I'd really like to take a proper look around.'

If he noticed the forced casualness in her voice he didn't acknowledge it. Instead he leaned back in his seat and gave her an approving smile. 'Of course, *cara*. It would be my pleasure.'

Imma found the hours that followed both enjoyable and enlightening.

The hotel was larger than she had realised, but still small enough to feel like a private sanctuary, with a decor that cleverly blurred the lines between vintage and contemporary, homely and hip. Chequerboard floors sat alongside huge gilt mirrors and faded hand-painted frescoes of the Dolce's guests and staff.

'My friend Roberto painted them in exchange for my letting him have a room over the winter,' Vicè explained as they wandered out into the lushly beautiful tiered gardens.

There were grander, more opulent, more glamorous hotels, she was sure. But there was something special about the Dolce.

She glanced over at where Vicè stood, joking with Edoardo, the hotel's legendary seventy-year-old pianist, who played everything from show tunes to swing for the guests sipping *aperitivi* on the terrace.

Unlike most hotels, everything felt authentic, rather than staged to create a certain vibe. But then not many hotels so closely embodied the personality of their owner. The Dolce *was* Vicè, and so, like him, it was effortlessly glamorous, flirty and cool.

'Do you want to dance?'

Vicè had stopped in front of her.

'Edo can play anything. Although I'd steer clear of rap or thrash metal.'

Biting into her smile, she shook her head, feeling suddenly conspicuous as around them everyone seemed to sit up straighter and glance covertly in their direction.

'Maybe later.'

Grinning, he took her hand. 'I'll hold you to that. Come on, I want to show you my favourite view. *Ciao*, Edo.' He turned and waved at the older masn.

'*Ciao*, boss. Maybe catch up with you and Signora Trapani later? At the party!'

Imma frowned. 'There's a party?'

'Not here—on the yacht.' When Imma raised her eyebrows, he shrugged. 'I have a yacht—the *Dolphin*. I keep her down in the bay for guests who like to cut loose. There's a party on board tonight, but obviously I wasn't going to go.'

She felt a ripple of relief—and then, remembering her refusal to dance, she stiffened her shoulders. What had happened to rule number two?

'Why not?' she said quickly. 'I'd like to go.'

'You would? Okay…well, if that's what you want to do, great.' He shook his head. 'You are full of surprises, *cara*.'

She gave him a quick, tight smile. Full of fear, more like. How did you even 'cut loose'?

'You're very quiet,' he said a moment later, as he led her along a shady path. 'If you've changed your mind about the party—'

'I haven't.' She stared up at him. 'I was just thinking that you're full of surprises too.'

He eyed her sideways. 'Then you're in a minority of one. Most people think they can read me like a book.' His eyes met hers. 'At a guess, I'd say a well-thumbed easy read—a beach blockbuster, maybe.'

He was smiling, but she had that same feeling she'd had before—that there was something more than what he was saying. And suddenly there was nothing she wanted to know more than what he'd left unsaid.

'That's what you *let* them think.'

He'd let her think that too, at first. Now, though, she could see that there was more to him—a whole lot more.

Take the Dolce. She might have limited hands-on business experience, but she understood enough to know that running one required more than charm and a sexy smile.

His guests loved him. His staff too. She could sense real affection and admiration, and they worked hard for him. He seemed to bring out the best in people. Or at least reveal their untapped potential.

'You have a gift, Vicè,' she said slowly. 'You've made this like a wonderful private club that's open to everyone. And you did it on your own.'

He shrugged. 'It's a living. It's not exactly in Ciro's league. He's Mr Midas.'

They had reached the villa now and, frowning, she followed him upstairs. 'Maybe. But some things are more important than money—and I know you believe that or we wouldn't both be here.'

It felt strange, putting it that way, but it was true. Vicè cared about his father's legacy enough to put aside his distaste and marry the daughter of his enemy. He had wanted revenge on her father, but he had also thrown her a lifeline by agreeing to marry her for a year.

And if revenge was all he was after he certainly wouldn't have agreed to sleep on any sofa.

'You care about your staff, your guests, your family. And it shows. You should be proud of that—of everything you've achieved. I'm sure your family is.'

'Careful, *cara*. I'm already "impossibly arrogant".'

She recognised her own words, but she didn't smile. 'Actually, I don't think you are,' she said quietly.

His eyes locked with hers.

'You're very smart, Imma.' Lifting a hand, he stroked her dark hair away from her face. 'Way too smart for me.'

Her heart began to beat faster and she felt heat break out on her skin. Vicè was wrong. If she was smart she would follow her own rules and stop her body reacting to his lightest touch.

'Not always.' Glancing round the bedroom, she frowned. 'I thought you were going to show me your favourite view?'

'I'm looking at it,' he said softly. He hesitated, his eyes never leaving her face. Then, 'Although I might need to make one small adjustment...'

He took a step towards her and, hooking the thin straps of her dress with his thumbs, he slipped them down over her shoulders. A muscle flickered in his jaw as it slid down her body, pooling around her feet.

Her mouth dried. Caught in the beam of his dark, shimmering gaze, she felt herself melt.

'Perfect,' he said hoarsely.

He leaned over to kiss the bare skin of her throat, and then she was pulling him backwards, onto the bed, all rules forgotten and broken.

'I hope you don't mind, but I bought you something for tonight.'

Leaning forward, Vicè planted a kiss on Imma's lips. As she stared up at him dazedly he sat down on the bed, handing her a large cardboard box wrapped in ribbon.

'I'm going to go and get changed, and then I've got a couple of things to go over with Matteo. Come down when you're ready.'

Ten minutes later he was downstairs, pouring himself and Matteo a glass of wine, his eyes dutifully scanning the guest list.

But his mind was elsewhere.

After they had made love Imma had fallen asleep, but he had been too restless to doze off. Lying next to her soft, naked body had been impossible too, so he'd got dressed and wandered down to the town for the early-evening *passeggiata*.

He'd been wandering through the square, past the cafes and bars, stopping occasionally to greet people, when he'd seen it.

It was the first dress, the first anything, he'd ever bought for a woman.

His mother didn't count.

He hadn't blinked—just walked in through the door of the boutique and walked out again five minutes later, with the box under his arm and a stupid grin on his face.

It was only now that he was wondering why he'd felt the need to get her a gift. Why he was suddenly so keyed up, so desperate to see her happy.

But wasn't it obvious?

She'd been upset, in tears, and he'd felt guilty. *Great*. He could add it to the teetering pile of guilt he already carried around.

His breath scraped his throat as he remembered their conversation.

Imma thought he was an amazing businessman. A self-made man. The pride of his family. *What a joke*. She'd been closer to the mark when she'd accused him of living a charade.

His whole life was a charade. And the worst part was that his father—the one person who had known his weaknesses, his flaws—had lost his life playing along with it.

He wanted to tell her the truth, but he couldn't bear the idea of losing the respect and trust he'd gained. So now he was trapped in yet another charade.

Only how long would it be before he messed up and she saw him for what he really was? It was only a matter of when, and how, and in the meantime there was nothing he could do but wait for things to fall apart.

'Any problems, boss?'

Glancing at Matteo, he shook his head. He'd barely looked at the names on the guest list, but frankly he didn't care who was going to the party as long as Imma was there.

His stomach knotted.

He wanted to show her that he wasn't just a playboy who used his hotel as a private clubhouse. Okay, it was true that if Ciro had been running the business he would have already turned it into a global chain of luxury hotels. But his business was about more than world domination.

It was about people. Treating people like VIPs. And tonight he wanted to make Imma feel special.

He wanted her to enjoy herself. To relax, to laugh, to smile. More specifically, he wanted her to turn that sweet, shy smile his way.

'It all looks great, Matteo.'

The two men stood up and Vicè clapped his manager on the shoulder.

Matteo grinned. 'Okay, *capo*. I'll catch up with y—' He stopped midsentence, his mouth hanging open.

Turning, Vicè did the same. Imma was hovering in the doorway, biting her lip. Her hair was in some kind of chignon, and with her smoky eye make-up and glossy lips she looked as if she'd wandered off the set of a Fellini film.

And then there was her dress.

Beside him, Matteo whistled softly. 'I'll leave you to it, boss.'

He skirted past Imma, smiling, and Vicè heard the soft click of the door.

She turned, the smile she had given Matteo still on her face. 'Could you finish zipping me up, please?'

'Of course.' Finding his voice, he crossed the room. 'There—done.'

He couldn't stop himself from dropping a kiss to the column of her throat, his body hardening as he felt her shiver of response.

'Thank you for the dress,' she murmured.

'You look beautiful.'

Glancing down, he swallowed. The heavy satin looked like freshly poured cream, and his groin clenched as his brain feverishly rushed to bring that image to life in glorious 3D Technicolor.

'It fits perfectly.'

She smiled. 'You look pretty perfect too.' Her eyes skimmed appreciatively over his dark suit.

Recovering his poise, he made a mocking bow. 'This old thing?' As she started to laugh he held out his arm. 'Shall we go?'

Gazing across the water, Vicè breathed in the fresh, salt-tinged air.

The blunt outline of the motorboat was skimming easily over the indigo waves, the hum of its engine lost in the vastness of the bay. Behind him the glittering bracelet of lights along the Portofino seafront was starting to fade.

He glanced over to where Imma sat beside him. Her green eyes were wide with nerves or excitement or both, her cheeks flushed already from the rushing breeze.

They were on their way to the yacht, and he was still slightly surprised at her eagerness to go. But then nothing should surprise him about this woman who had agreed to be his wife. She had been surprising him ever since she'd walked into that church and refused to meet his eye.

Leaning back against his seat, he studied her profile.

Immacolata Buscetta. Prized eldest daughter of a notorious bully and a thief and a chip off the old block. But Imma was most definitely not what she seemed. The clues had been there. He'd just been too blinkered with anger to do anything more than focus on the obvious.

He had believed what he'd wanted to believe, and the fact that she was not the woman he had thought her to be was unsettling enough. More unsettling still was the fact that had she just walked away he would never have known his mistake.

Never got to know her.

The thought of that happening made his stomach clench.

Or maybe it was the sudden swell of the sea as the motorboat slowed alongside the yacht.

'Party's started,' he remarked as they stepped on board.

He felt a rush of exhilaration beat through his body in time to the music drifting down through the warm evening air. Here, he was king. This was his world. And he loved it. He loved the laughter, the pulsing bass notes and the waiters with their trays of champagne. He loved the buzz of energy and the beautiful women with their sequins and high heels.

His eyes roamed slowly down over Imma's body. Actually, make that one specific woman…

His heartbeat stalled. But who said anything about love?

Turning towards her, he caught her hand and pulled her towards him. 'Let's join in.'

Imma felt her heart start to pound.

As they made their way through the crowded yacht she felt even more exposed than when they'd first walked into the hotel together.

Everyone was so beautiful. Particularly the women. All of whom were looking at Vicè with naked longing. She knew what they were thinking. It would be like seeing a peahen with her mate. They must all be wondering how such an ordinary bird could attract this glittering peacock.

'It's okay,' she said quietly as someone called out Vicè's name. 'I think everyone here believes we're married. You don't need to stay glued to my side all evening.'

His brows locked together. 'I couldn't care less what they believe, *cara*. I'm staying glued to your side because I want to. I like being with you, okay?'

She stared at him, her doubts suddenly losing shape, growing hazy next to his muscular solidity and the steady focus of his dark eyes.

'Okay then…'

It took them some time to actually get anywhere. People kept coming over to talk to him, and every person needed introducing.

'Do you know *everyone* here?' she asked as finally they

made their way out into the deck, what seemed like several hours later.

'I suppose I do.'

Glancing back into the crowded saloon, he made a face. 'I know that must seem crazy, but it's what I do—it's who I am.'

She smiled. 'You have a lot of friends.'

And yet he still seemed to prefer her. The thought made warm bubbles of happiness rise inside her.

He smiled down at her. 'They're your friends too now. Now, how about that dance?'

'You took the words right out of my mouth.'

Swinging round, Vicè grinned at the lanky dark-haired man standing beside him. 'Is that the best you've got, Roberto? Really?'

'I'm a starving artist. I'm used to humbling myself.'

'You're an artist?' Imma frowned. 'Are you the Roberto who painted those frescoes in the hotel?'

'One and the same.' He made a small bow. 'But I would much prefer to paint you, *bella*.'

Groaning, Vicè slipped his arm around Imma's waist. 'Get your own wife and paint her.'

'This is your *wife*?' The other man raised an eyebrow appreciatively. 'Lucky man.'

'Yes, I am,' he agreed.

Imma felt a blush suffuse her cheeks as he stared down into her eyes.

'Very lucky...'

Roberto shook his head. 'I think I need to come up with a reason to get you alone, Signora Trapani. Then I can give you the low-down on this guy.'

'She already knows.' Vicè shook his head. 'Now, go and stretch some canvases, or whatever it is you do when you're not bugging me.'

Imma glanced up at him. 'Are you okay?'

'Of course.' He smiled. 'I just want to dance with my wife.'

* * *

She looked so beautiful. A little nervous but she was hiding it well, so that only he would have known. His spine tensed. He liked knowing that he could see beneath her poise, but it made him feel responsible.

Only how could he be responsible for Imma? He could barely manage his own life, let alone someone else's.

Taking her hand, he drew her away from the dance floor.

She frowned. 'I thought you wanted to dance.'

'I do. But I want it to be just the two of us.'

He thought back to when she'd said he had a lot of friends. Were they friends? He stared at the faces, feeling suddenly confused. Tonight none of them seemed even the slightest bit familiar. Nor did he feel like talking to any of them.

Normally he liked being at the centre of the crowd, surrounded by happy, smiling faces. But tonight the music was too loud, the lights too bright.

Turning, he led her through a door marked *Private*, up a spiral staircase and back outside.

'That's better,' he said softly. 'I can hear myself think.'

'You need to *think*? What kind of dancing are you planning?' she teased.

He smiled and pulled her closer. He thought about the party downstairs. And then she leaned forward, her cheek pressing into his shoulder, and he forgot about everything but the feel of her body against his and his hunger for her.

He cleared his throat. 'Are you having fun?'

Looking up at him, she nodded. 'Yes, but I'm happy to leave whenever you are.'

Her lips were parted and her eyes looked dark in the moonlight. Without replying, he took her hand and led her back downstairs, his self-control unravelling with every step and turn.

CHAPTER NINE

RAISING A HAND to shield her eyes from the sun, Imma put down her book and gazed across the terrace. It really was very hot today—far too hot to read anyway.

Totti, Matteo's French bulldog, lay panting beneath the wilting shrubs, and down in the bay even the motorboats were still, smothered into silence by the heat haze shimmering above the blue water.

She was lying on a lounger, half shielded from the sun by the trailing wisteria that overhung the terrace. And for the first time since arriving in Portofino she was alone in the villa.

Vicè was dealing with something at the hotel—she wasn't sure what. After a night of making love she had been too sleepy to do more than mumble when he'd said goodbye.

At first she'd been glad to have a few moments to herself. To think back to last night…to how he'd held her close as if she was precious to him. She knew he had held her because he liked her, and in his arms all those years of wondering who she was had dissolved.

But, much as she might have liked to daydream about those blissful hours when he had chosen her over everyone else, she was still Claudia's big sister and after a few days of just texting she needed to check in with her properly.

Feeling guilty, she had called her, expecting her to be tearful and crushed and needing reassurance.

She had been wrong on all counts.

Claudia had been quiet, but calm, and instead of wanting to talk she had been the one to end their conversation.

Imma shifted against the cushions. Of course she was glad that her sister was coping so well, and yet it was a shock. Claudia had always been so sweet and shy. But she had sounded focused, determined—like a different person, in fact.

'There you are.'

She jumped slightly as a cool hand slid over her shoulder and a shadow blocked the sun. Dropping down onto the lounger beside her, Vicè leaned over and kissed her softly on the mouth.

Her heart bumped against her ribs and she tensed, her breath hitching in her throat, her body taut and aching. Surely she should be used to his touch by now? But she was already melting on the inside, her limbs and her stomach dissolving into a puddle of need.

For a moment her lips clung to his, and she was lost in the warmth and the dizziness of his kiss, and then she shifted back, blinking into the light as he lifted his mouth from hers.

'Was it okay?' she asked quickly. 'At the hotel?'

'It's fine. The guests in Room Sixteen decided to record some new songs. At three a.m. Then they got upset when someone uploaded them to the web.' He grinned. 'Here— I thought you might need a drink. I know I do.' Squinting into the sun, he handed her a glass. 'One perfect Negroni.'

She raised an eyebrow. 'At ten o'clock?'

'It's pretty perfect at any time.' The ice clinked as he tipped his glass up to his mouth. 'Come on, *cara*, this is supposed to be your year of living dangerously.'

As she took the drink, he glanced up at the flawless sky. '*Accidenti*, it's hot today! If you want we can take the yacht out later. It'll be cooler at sea. We could head down the coast to the Bay of Poets.'

With his shirt hanging loosely open and his dark hair flopping into his eyes he *looked* like a poet, she thought. She felt her stomach clench. He might not be as bad or as mad as Lord Byron, but he was certainly dangerous to know.

Dangerous to her self-control.

'Does that mean you're going to write me a poem?'

His eyes gleamed. 'I might. What rhymes with Imma-colata?'

She smiled. 'Poetry doesn't have to rhyme. Free verse doesn't follow any rules.'

'That sounds more like it.'

His dark eyes rested on her face, the corners of his mouth curving up into a smile that was so unapologetically flirta-tious that she burst out laughing.

'You're impossible.'

'So I'm told.' He frowned. 'You're not getting too hot in the sun, are you?'

She felt her pulse accelerate, and a shivery pleasure danced down her spine as he leaned forward and ran his fingers lightly over her stomach, stopping at the triangle of her bright yellow bikini bottom.

'Maybe I should rub in some oil,' he said softly. 'Just to be on the safe side...'

That might work for her skin, she thought, but no amount of oil was going to appease the heat inside her.

She lifted her chin. 'Or I could just go for a swim.'

He grinned. 'Chicken.'

Ignoring his teasing gaze, she stood up and walked down the steps into the pool. He watched her as she did a slow length, and then, downing his drink, he stripped off his shirt and dived in, slicing through the water without a ripple and surfacing beside her.

His hands circled her waist.

'You don't need to hold me.' She held his gaze. 'I can swim.'

'That's not why I'm holding you.'

He pulled her closer and her eyes widened with shock as she felt the thickness of his erection through his shorts.

'If I pass out, I'm relying on you to get me to safety.'

His voice had a huskiness to it that made her heart thump out of time.

'So you see me as some kind of lifebelt?'

His eyes dropped to her mouth, then lower to where the water was lapping at her breasts. 'If that means you're going to wrap yourself around my waist, then yes.'

'I think it's you that needs cooling off, Vicenzu,' she teased. And, grabbing hold of his head, she pushed him under the water, then turned and swam away.

He came up, spluttering, and swam after her, snatching for her ankles and making her scream with laughter and terror until finally he caught her in the shallow end.

Laughing down at her, he scooped her into his arms and carried her out of the pool, his dark eyes glittering. 'You are going to pay for that, Signora Trapani. With interest.'

Her hands gripped his bicep as he lowered his mouth to hers...

'What the—' He swore softly, his face creasing with irritation. On the other side of the terrace his phone was ringing. 'I won't answer it.'

'It's fine. Honestly.' Her body twitched in protest but she managed to smile. 'It might be important.'

Grimacing, he put her down and strode over to his phone. Picking it up, he glanced briefly at the screen, and her throat tightened as he immediately turned away to answer it.

It was Ciro. It must be. There was a tension to his body that hadn't been there before and he clearly didn't want her to hear his conversation.

Moments earlier she had been laughing in his warm arms. Now, though, she felt as if someone had slapped her in the face. For the last few days she had all but forgotten how he and Ciro had plotted together against her family. Now here was a blunt reminder.

Her body stiffening with misery, she watched him pace back and forth, his head bent over the phone, and then, picking up her book, she walked quickly back into the villa.

Inside it was dark and cool and she felt some of her panic recede.

Nothing had changed.

So why did she feel as if it had?

'Imma?'

She turned. Vicè was standing behind her, a frown still touching his handsome face.

'I'm sorry, but I won't be able to take you down the coast today.' His eyes avoided hers. 'Something's come up—'

'What's he done now?' Her heart was suddenly thumping so hard she could hardly speak. Claudia had sounded fine earlier, but—

'Who?' He stared at her uncomprehendingly.

'Your brother.'

'Ciro?' His eyes widened. 'I don't know. I wasn't talking to him. That was my mother.'

Her pulse slowed. She saw that his face had none of its usual animation, and something in the set of his shoulders made her hold her breath.

'Is she okay?'

Vicè had told her very little about his mother. All she knew was that Audenzia had moved to Florence, to live with her sister and brother-in-law.

He shook his head. 'She's had a fall.'

'Oh, Vicè…' Reaching out, she touched his hand. 'I'm sorry.'

'She's okay—just a bit shaken up. She's not alone. My aunt and uncle are with her. But—'

'She wants you.' She finished his sentence. 'Of course she does. We can leave right now. I'll go and get changed.'

'You want to come with me?' He looked confused.

'Of course. You can't go all that way on your own.' Now it was her turn to look confused. 'And besides, won't it look odd if I don't go with you?'

He didn't reply and she stared at him, suddenly mortified. Earlier, in bed and when they'd been laughing by the pool, she had been lulled into forgetting that this was just a mutually convenient arrangement.

But clearly Vicè hadn't forgotten. For him, this was still

about sun and sex and drinking cocktails by the pool. It was obvious—*should have been obvious to her*—that his mother would be off limits. He didn't need or want her there for reasons that were glaringly self-evident.

She felt his fingers tighten around hers.

'I'm sorry,' he said slowly. 'I'd love you to come with me. It just didn't occur to me that you'd want to.'

'No, *I'm* sorry.' She tried to smile. 'I mean, why would you want me there? After everything my father's done?'

'I don't care about what your father did.' A muscle flickered in his jaw and he pulled her closer. 'Look at me, Imma. I don't care—not any more. I told you that's over. Done. Finished. Forgotten. I just didn't want you to have to lie to my mother that's all, to pretend that you love me—'

Her arms tightened around him. 'This isn't about me. It's about your mother. So if you want me to be there, I'll be there.'

Tipping her face up to his, he kissed her softly. 'I'd like that very much.'

They were about an hour away from Florence when steam began swirling up from the bonnet of the car. Swearing softly, Vicè pulled off the road and switched off the engine.

'What's the matter?'

'It's overheated. Wait here. I'm going to flip the bonnet and check the radiator.'

Imma leaned back in her seat. Without the air-conditioning the car began to grow warmer immediately, and she was opening the window when he returned.

'Sorry about this. It'll be fine. We just need to wait about half an hour for it to cool down a little, and then I can add some water. It gets a bit moody when it's hot.' He gave her a wry smile. 'Which you'd probably worked out already.'

'Actually, I don't know anything about cars,' she admitted. 'I can't even drive.'

'What?' He was staring at her in disbelief. 'Why not?'

She felt her cheeks grow warm. 'There was no point. Papà wouldn't have liked me going out on my own, and anyway I have a driver.'

Her heart began to thump. Why had she mentioned her father? The confusion between them back at the villa seemed to be forgotten, but reminding him why his mother was now alone had been stupid and insensitive.

But after the briefest hesitation his eyes met hers. 'I'll teach you to drive, if you want. Maybe not in this one—like I say, she's a bit moody. But I've got other cars.'

'You'd do that?'

'Of course. A year's plenty long enough.'

She kept on smiling, but the implicit reminder that this was a temporary arrangement stung a little more than she knew it should. Not liking the way that made her feel, she searched her mind for something neutral to say.

'So why did you drive this car today if it's so moody?'

His face stilled. 'My mother likes to see me using it. It was my father's car. His pride and joy. We used to work on it together when I was a teenager.'

She felt her stomach knot. He seemed distracted by the memory—wistful, even.

'I bet he loved spending man-time with you and Ciro.'

He hesitated. 'Ciro wasn't there. He couldn't see the point in wasting half a day getting covered in oil. It was just me and Papà.'

The ache in his voice made that knot tighten.

'You must miss him so much.'

This time there was a definite pause before he answered. 'Every day.' His mouth tensed. 'I'm sorry you didn't get to meet him. You would have liked him and he would have liked you.'

'I wish I'd met him,' she said truthfully. 'From everything I've heard he was a true gentleman and a good man.'

Alessandro Trapani's reputation was, in fact, the antithesis of her father's.

Vicè smiled, but the expression in his eyes was bleak. 'He *was* a good man. He had no failings, no flaws.' His mouth twisted. 'Actually, that's not true.'

He glanced away, and now the knot in her stomach was making her feel sick.

'He had one major flaw. Me.'

She stared at him in silence, shocked and distressed by the pinched lines around his eyes as much as the brutality of his statement.

'I don't think that's true,' she said slowly.

'Yeah, you do.' A muscle pulled at his jaw. 'You saw right through me.'

Slowly, she shook her head. 'If that were true then I would never have slept with you.'

'Oh, you would still have slept with me, *cara*. You would have told yourself that I needed saving, or maybe that I was misunderstood,' he said calmly. 'That's what you do, Imma. You take care of people…you protect them.'

'And so do you. You take care of people. That's why they like you.'

Now he shook his head. 'They like me because of how I look and how I make them feel about themselves.'

'Your father didn't feel that way.'

'No, he didn't. My father knew everything about me. He saw my weaknesses and he loved me anyway. He loved me completely and unconditionally and that was his weakness—like I said, I was his flaw.'

He smiled at her crookedly.

'You asked me why he didn't come to me and Ciro for help. Do you remember? You said that neither of his sons had what was needed to save him.'

'I was angry.'

'But you were right. Almost right.' His shoulders tensed.

'He couldn't come to me. He knew I didn't have any money because I'd just asked him for a loan. Another loan.'

The tension was spilling over into his shoulders now. And his spine was so taut it looked as though it might snap.

'He could have gone to Ciro. But he didn't. He wouldn't— he didn't want to do that *to me*. And that's why he's dead. Because he wanted to protect me—my ego, my pride. Just like he did my entire life.'

Imma felt sick. 'That's not true, Vicè.'

'It *is* true.' His voice cracked. 'You were right about me. My whole life is a charade and my father played along with it until it killed him. And, you know, the worst part is that since his death I've had to just get on with it—and I have. So I could have done it all along. I could have been the son he wanted…the son he needed. Maybe if I had he'd still be alive.'

Tears pricked the back of her eyes. The pain in his voice cut her like a razor.

Reaching out, she took his hand. 'You *were* the son he wanted. The son he loved. And if he protected you then it's because he was your father and that was his job,' she said, her longing to ease his pain giving emphasis to her words. 'And I don't think that's why he didn't ask you for help. With his reputation he could have gone to any number of people. But good men have their pride too.'

His fingers squeezed hers. 'You're a wonderful person, Imma. And I hate how I've hurt you.'

'That's done. Finished. Forgotten.' Lifting her hand, she stroked his cheek. 'You've forgiven my father and I've forgiven you.'

'I don't deserve to be forgiven. I should have made Ciro wait. Let his anger cool. Then probably none of this would have happened. But I felt guilty—guilty that we'd lost our father because of me.' His face creased. 'And then I messed it up anyway.'

Imma shook her head. 'You didn't mess it up. *He* did. Claudia heard him leaving you a message. I checked your phone afterwards, just to be certain. It was Ciro who messed up. Not you.'

Vicè stared at her in confusion.

Ciro had messed up? He almost wanted to laugh.

But then he caught sight of Imma's face. Her green eyes were wide and worried, and—his heartbeat stalled—she was worried about *him*.

'It doesn't change anything.' His chest felt tight. 'It's still on me, Imma. I was ashamed and angry with *myself*. But it was easier to blame your father, and that's why I went along with everything. And now I've hurt you, and you're having to live my charade too.'

'Okay. But if you're to blame, then so is Ciro,' she said firmly. 'And your father. And my father. They're all responsible for their actions.' She frowned. 'And so am I. I'm not just a victim, and you're not the villain.'

Her eyes met his, and he felt something inside him loosen.

'Everyone is a work in progress, Vicè. Every new day is a chance to start again and do better. And it's being with you that's taught me that. Maybe you need to accept that too, and let go of the past?'

He stared at her, her words replaying inside his head, the rhythm of her voice soothing him. For the first time since his father's death, maybe even before, he felt calm. The heaviness inside him that he hid so well was lifting.

She was right. Before, everything had always seemed so fixed, so definite—his failings, his relationship with his father and Ciro—so that for years he'd just been blindly following the script. But already he knew that he had changed, and was still changing.

Leaning forward, he tilted her face up to his and kissed her softly. 'I've never met anyone like you, Imma. You're a remarkable woman, and I am so very sorry for how I hurt you.'

Her eyes were bright. 'I know. But I meant what I said. I really have forgiven you.' She hesitated, her fingers trembling against his arms. 'And that's why I want you to have the business *now*. I don't want to wait a year. When we get back to the villa I'll sign it over to you.'

He stared at her in stunned silence. It was the reason he had married her. He had turned his life upside down to pursue this very moment. Only now that it was here he realised he no longer cared about it.

'I don't want it.'

As the words left his mouth his body loosened, his shoulders lifted free of some invisible burden. Ciro could rage all he liked. He was done with revenge.

Now it was her turn to stare. 'I don't understand.'

He pulled her closer. 'Getting even was never really my thing, *cara*. And anyway, I'm too good-looking to be the bad guy.'

Watching her mouth curve into a smile, he felt a rush of relief. He'd hurt her, and he couldn't change the past. But if he let her keep the business then he could at least look her in the eye.

Only what did that mean for their 'arrangement'?

His pulse slowed. Theoretically, there was no reason for them to stay married. Or rather for him to stay married. But the thought of not waking up next to her made something tighten in his chest for one very obvious reason.

He hadn't finished with her, and he knew from the pulse beating in her throat that she felt the same way.

His eyes locked with hers. 'But I still want you to have this year. Actually, I want us both to have this year. We can work on ourselves.' He smiled. 'Or, better still, each other.'

And at the end of the year she would leave and, having had his fill, he would go back to the life he loved. That, after all, was what he wanted—wasn't it?

Reaching into the back seat, he grabbed a bottle of water.

'I'm going to top up the radiator—and then I think we should probably go and see my mother.'

Following his uncle Carlo through the beautiful fifteenth-century apartment, Vicè felt his heartbeat speed up. Carlo had reassured him that Audenzia was doing well, but after what had happened with his father he wanted to see her with his own eyes.

'This way.'

Carlo pulled open a door, stepping aside as a uniformed maid scurried past, blushing as she caught sight of Vicè.

'They're in the salon, and I should warn you that emotions are running high,' he said dryly to Imma. 'They both dote on Vicè—'

Vicè grinned. 'Understandably...'

'Inexplicably was the word I was seeking.' Carlo winked at Imma. 'But when you walk in the room, *mia cara*, I fear that things could get quite out of hand.'

'It's what always happens to me,' Vicè said softly, pretending to wince as Imma punched him on the arm.

He glanced sideways into her beautiful face. He still couldn't quite believe he'd had that conversation with her in the car. He had never talked about his relationship with his father to anyone. Never admitted his worst fears. Not even to Ciro or his mother.

Especially not to Ciro or his mother.

But talking to Imma had been so easy. She had listened and she hadn't judged. She had talked gently and calmly, almost as if he'd been in some kind of accident.

He certainly felt as if he'd been in one—except there were no physical injuries...just the pain of grief and the ache of loss.

But now he felt lighter. She had helped reconcile the past for him, and for the first time in months he could think about his father without a suffocating rush of guilt or rage or misery.

'Vicenzu, my darling boy. And Imma too—this is so wonderful!'

The room was suddenly filled with noise, laughter and tears.

'Come on, Mamma, don't cry. I'm here now. These are for you, Zia Carmela.' Kissing his aunt, he handed her some flowers, and then, crouching down, he kissed his mother on both cheeks. 'And these are for you, Mamma,' he said gently, his heart swelling with love and relief as she took the huge bunch of palest pink roses.

Her ankle was a little swollen, and she looked pale, but she was still his mother—and she was smiling now as Imma stepped forward, also smiling shyly.

'And here is my beautiful *nuora*. Imma, thank you so much for coming to see us. I really am so glad you came.'

'Thank you, Signora Trapani—'

'*Mia cara*, call me Audenzia, please. Now, come and sit next to me. Both of you. And you, Carmela. I want to hear all about your beautiful wedding, and of course see the photos. Carlo, will you take these flowers, *per favore*, and put them in water?'

Lazing back in his seat, Vicè watched his mother scroll down through the pictures on his phone, clutching Imma's hand and occasionally wiping away a tear. He felt relaxed, calm and happy. Life had never felt sweeter.

'I would like a copy of this one, Vicenzu.'

His mother was holding up his phone and, glancing at the photo, he felt his pulse stumble. It was a beautiful picture—a close-up, not a selfie. The registrar must have taken it. They were gazing into each other's eyes and there was a sweetness in Imma's face that made him want to pull her into his arms right now and hold her close.

And apologise. Again.

How could he have married her in that two-bit way?

He'd let her wear that same dress she'd worn to her sister's wedding and exchanged vows with her in a ceremony that had lasted only slightly longer than it would have taken to open a bottle of Prosecco.

That photo was a beautiful lie, and he was ashamed of being a part of it, but he was even more ashamed of having made her part of it too.

'And this one, too. You look just like when you were a little boy. I have a photo in one of my albums…'

'Maybe after lunch, Mamma,' he said, smiling mechanically at Carlo's expression of despair.

As Carmela led Imma away, to show her the rest of the apartment, his mother took his arm and gave it a quick squeeze.

'I know you must have wanted to give her a more special day, babà. But you were in a rush—I understand.'

But she didn't. Not really. He'd seen his parents' wedding album and, although their day had clearly not been as over the top as Ciro and Claudia's, it had been undeniably romantic.

He felt sick with remorse. For a fraction of a second he was glad for the first time that his father was not alive to bear witness to his incompetence and insensitivity.

'I'm sorry, Mamma—' he began, but his mother shook her head.

'For what? Falling in love and wanting your life with Imma to start as soon as possible?' Her eyes were gentle and loving. 'You will make every day from now on special. And you are so simpatico together. I wish your father was here to see the two of you. He would be so very happy, and so proud of the man you have become. A man who can love and be loved in return—isn't that how the song goes?' She patted his cheek. 'He loved that song.'

He smiled down at her, but inside he could feel something tearing. It was crazy, but he kept forgetting that he and Imma were not a real couple. Watching her with his mother and aunt, he'd almost forgotten that theirs was a marriage of convenience not love.

Only now his mother was praising him for something he hadn't done, something he wasn't capable of doing, and he felt guilt and panic unfurl inside him.

He knew what his father had wanted him to be. But he wasn't that man and nor could he ever be him. And besides, in the long-term Imma wanted her freedom. They both did.

'Oh, Carlo, you clever man! How perfect!' Audenzia looked up at her brother-in-law, her eyes sparkling like the glass of Prosecco he had handed her. 'A toast to my darling son and his beautiful bride. To Vicenzu and Imma. *Cent' anni!*'

A hundred years.

It was just a toast, Imma told herself, glancing at the hibiscus flower at the bottom of her glass of Prosecco. But every time she remembered Audenzia's joyful words she felt a sharp nip of guilt. And something else—something she couldn't quite place.

They had just finished lunch on the balcony overlooking the garden. The food had been sublime and the view was incredible, but she kept losing concentration, her mind returning like a homing pigeon to that moment when Vicè had held up his glass and toasted their marriage.

As his eyes had met hers she'd forgotten to breathe, much less raise her glass. But it wasn't those few shared half seconds that were making her heart pound—it was the memory of that half hour in the car, when he had let his mask slip and needed her for something more than sex.

Audenzia reached out and took her hand. 'Now, Imma, I love my boy, but he has a few tiny faults. He can't have too much red wine. It makes him grumpy.'

Vicè rolled his eyes. 'I'm still here, you know!'

'And he puts too much of that product in his hair.'

Imma giggled.

'And I'm *still* here.' Shaking his head, Vicè grimaced.

'Well, you shouldn't be. Go with Carmela and get my albums. We must show Imma *all* the photos before you leave.'

'Must we?' Groaning, he stood up. 'This is just a ruse to get me out of the room, isn't it?'

'Of course.' His mother smiled. 'We want to talk about you in private. Now, go.' She turned to Imma, her eyes sparkling. 'It's important to keep a man on his toes.' She sighed. 'If only I could show you the garden.'

Imma followed her gaze. 'It's beautiful.'

'Oh, it's not my efforts. Carlo is the gardener—the same as my Alessandro. He could grow anything. That's why he bought the estate on Sicily.'

Imma managed to keep smiling but her chest felt tight, and maybe something of what she was feeling showed in her face, because Audenzia reached over and patted her hand.

'Oh, child, don't be upset. I loved my life there, but Florence is where I grew up, and I'm happy to be back here. It was different for Alessandro. It was in his blood...in his heart. Vicenzu feels the same way.'

Imma stared at her in confusion. *Did he?* He had never so much as hinted that was how he felt about the estate. On the contrary, he seemed to love his life at La Dolce Vita.

'Did he ever want to take it over?'

'When he was a little boy it was all he talked about. And of course Alessandro wanted that too. But he didn't want to put pressure on him.' Her smile faded. 'Vicenzu idolised his father, only I don't think he ever believed he could step into his shoes so he stopped trying. But Alessandro would be delighted to know the business is still in the family. And to know that Vicenzu has met and married you.' She squeezed Imma's hand. 'You've seen who he really is and you love him.'

Imma nodded. 'Yes, I do.'

She had agreed automatically but her heart swelled as she spoke, opening like the petals of the hibiscus flower in her glass, and with a shock she realised that she wasn't lying or pretending.

She loved Vicè.

Stunned, disbelieving, she repeated the words in her head.

It was true.

Her heart beat a little faster.

And maybe…possibly…he might feel the same way about her.

Okay, he had never said he loved her, but perhaps, like her, it hadn't occurred to him. Perhaps all he needed was someone to point it out to him.

The drive back to Portofino was quicker and quieter than the trip down.

Fixing his eyes on the road, Vicè was aware that he wasn't saying much. But Imma hadn't noticed. In fact, she seemed distracted, wrapped up in her own thoughts, and that was fine.

There had been enough drama for one day.

The villa felt quiet, almost subdued after the laughter and chatter of Florence, and it fed into his mood so that he felt oddly flattened as he walked up to the bedroom. Maybe a swim would help. Or a drink.

'Do you want some wine?' He turned towards Imma, smiling. 'You look like I feel, *cara*. What we need is a couple of late nights.'

She smiled, but it didn't reach her eyes, and the heaviness in his chest seemed to swell and press against his ribs.

'I'm teasing. I know you're tired. I am too. It was a long day.'

She shook her head. 'It's not that. I want to go back to Sicily with you.'

He felt a rush of relief. *Of course.* That was why she was on edge. Seeing his mother had made her homesick. But it was easily fixed. He wasn't willing to see Cesare, but he could visit friends while she saw her father.

'That's fine. We can fly back tomorrow. We can stay for a couple of days—'

She hesitated. 'I don't mean for a visit. I want to move back. To live there. With you.'

'That would be a hell of a commute,' he said lightly.

Glancing down, he saw the tension, the hope in her eyes, and felt his stomach clench.

'What's brought this on?'

'I suppose it was seeing your *mamma*. It made me think about things...about what we're doing...'

He felt suddenly short of breath. 'I know it's hard, having to pretend. I hated lying to her too.'

'But that's just it. I wasn't lying,' she said slowly.

His heart was beating out of time. 'I don't understand—'

Except he did. He knew what she was saying even if she hadn't said the words—he could read it in her eyes.

Looking down into her face, he felt a sudden rush of panic. Her eyes were wide with hope, with trust.

With love.

'You said you'd give me a year so I could find out what I wanted. But I don't need a year, Vicè. I already know what I want. I want us to go back to Sicily together.'

He held her gaze. 'I have a business here—a life. I can't just go back to Sicily.'

'I thought we could run your father's business together.'

Once upon a time that had been his dream. For a fraction of a second he saw the warm olive groves in his head... could almost feel the dry ground beneath his feet. And then he pictured his father's face, the reassuring smile that hid the disappointment in his heart. He couldn't face seeing that same disappointment on Imma's face.

'I don't want to do that, *cara*. That's why I live here.'

She looked confused—no, more than confused… crushed.

'But… I just… I thought you— We— Your mother—'

He shook his head. 'My mother misses the past. She misses my father. But I'm not my father.'

He felt suddenly furious with Imma. Why was she doing this? Saying these things. Everything had been just fine. Why did she have mess it up?

'I love my life as it is,' he said stiffly.

She jerked back, as though he had hit her, and he knew that her pain was as real as if he *had* hit her. He knew because the pain in his chest hurt so badly it was making him feel ill.

'This year is about helping you. I wanted to do you a favour, that's all,' he lied.

For a moment she seemed too stunned to speak, and then slowly she frowned. 'I don't think I need your help, actually. I can manage just fine on my own.'

The hurt in her voice made his body tense. 'I'm sorry, Imma.'

'Don't be.'

She lifted her chin and he saw the sheen of tears in her eyes. 'We said no more lies, remember? I don't think there's any point in my staying now, do you?'

In the silence that followed her question, her hurt was palpable. But what could he say? *Yes, I want you to stay so we can keep on having sex?*

With an effort, he shook his head, and after a moment, she said quietly, 'If you really don't want the business then I'll sign it back over to my father.' When he didn't respond, she gave him a small, sad smile. 'I'll go and pack.'

He watched her walk upstairs. He'd never known a feeling like this—not even when his mother had called to tell him his father had died. His heart was like a living, struggling creature trapped inside his chest.

Only what choice did he have? He couldn't do to her

what he had done to his father. He couldn't be responsible for her love. Nor was he worthy of it. Not when he was so flawed, so imperfect, so bound to mess up.

CHAPTER TEN

'GREAT PARTY, VICÈ!'

Vicè turned, flicking on his hundred-kilowatt smile automatically as the pop-star-turned-actress who was standing in front of him tilted her head in provocation.

'Thanks, Renée—and congratulations on the nomination.' He raised the glass of champagne he was holding. 'There's a bottle of Cristal at the bar with your name on it.'

'Care to come and share it with me?' she invited, her mane of auburn hair falling into her eyes and the hem of her shimmering red minidress riding high on her thighs as she pouted up at him. 'We could have our own private party.'

His pulse accelerated. She was beautiful, willing, and she had booked a suite, and yet...

He shook his head slowly, pretending regret. 'I need to make sure this party keeps rolling, Renée.'

He had never been too hung up dotting the *i*'s and crossing the *t*'s, but mixing business and pleasure was one rule that should never be broken, no matter how much pleasure was being promised.

His chest tightened.

What a load of sanctimonious drivel!

He liked Renée—she was sweet—but he wasn't going to sleep with her, whatever the circumstances. There was only one woman he wanted, and he had let her slip through his fingers just over five weeks ago.

His mouth twisted. Actually, he'd driven her to the airport.

Way to go, Vicè. Drive the woman you love to the airport and wave her off.

His heart was suddenly thumping so hard against his

ribs he was surprised the shock waves didn't shatter the glass he was holding.

He *loved* her?

For a moment he turned over his words in his mind, waiting for the denial that would surely follow. Instead, though, the echo grew louder, rebounding and filling his head.

He loved her.

But of course he did.

Only he had pushed her away rather than admit it to himself. Or to her. And now she was gone. And he was going to have to live without her in an agonising charade of his own making for the rest of his life.

'Sorry, Renée. I didn't mean to sound so pompous.' Holding up his hand, he tapped the ring on his finger. 'It's just that I'm missing my wife.'

A flush of colour spread over her face. 'I'm sorry… I didn't know you were—'

'It's fine.' He pasted a smile on his face. 'Look, you have a great night.'

'You too, Vicè.'

She blew him a kiss from her bee-stung mouth and he watched her sashay off on her towering heels.

Eyes burning, he turned away from the laughing, dancing mass of people. Last time he had been on the yacht Imma had been by his side. Now, without her, he felt empty. Without her all of this—his life, his much-prized *dolce far niente*—was literally nothing.

It was ironic, really. She had told him that she wanted to find herself, and he had blithely told her that he would give her a year, never once realising that *he* was the one who didn't know who he was or what he wanted.

But he did now.

And pushing her away hadn't changed a thing. Wherever she was in the world, she had his heart. He belonged to her. He would always belong to her.

Only it was too late.

Even though all the dots had been there in front of him he had been too scared to connect them—too scared of the picture they would make. So he had let her leave. Worse, he had let her end it. He hadn't even had the courage to do that.

He was a coward and a fool. For in trying to play it cool he had simply succeeded in making his own world a lot colder.

The ache in his heart made him feel sick, but he didn't care. He couldn't lie to himself any more and pretend he felt nothing for Imma. His 'sweet life' tasted bitter now. The pain of loving had been replaced with the pain of loss, as bad as when his father had died.

Closing his eyes, he pictured Alessandro's face. He still missed him—probably he always would. And yet it didn't hurt quite as much as before. The tension in his shoulders eased a little.

Now it wasn't the funeral he remembered, but happier times. Meals round the table. Stories before bedtime. And watching his father dance with his mother, her head resting against his chest and Alessandro singing softly.

Now he could think about his father without flinching, and that was thanks to Imma. She had helped him grieve and had put words to his unspoken fears so that they had stopped being the terrifying larger-than-life problems he had always refused to face.

Like the words of another of his father's favourite songs, he had let her get under his skin and found he was a better person with her. Or at least good enough for her to confide her own fears.

His heart began to beat a little faster.

Imma had drawn strength from him too. Holding his hand, she had leapt into the unknown. That night on Pantelleria she had even trusted him to take her virginity, and then later entered into a marriage of convenience with him.

She had even trusted him enough to love him.

Staring out across the dark sea, he felt his fingers tighten against his glass.

Maybe it was time he started trusting himself.

Pushing her sunglasses onto the top of her head, Imma stopped beside the market stall. For a moment her hand hovered over a crate overflowing with lemons, and then, changing her mind, she selected a couple of peaches.

Once—a lifetime ago—this would have been her dream. The freedom to wander alone among the colourful stalls, to linger and to chat to people without the continual unsmiling presence of her security team.

But that dream felt childish now, in comparison to the loss of her dream of love with Vicè.

Smiling politely at the tiny, leathery old woman who ran the stall, she took her change and made her way back past the boutiques and ice-cream parlours.

She had chosen the small town of Cefalù in northern Sicily on a whim, but after nearly five weeks of living here she liked it a lot. It would be a good place to stay while she worked out what to do next.

The villa she was renting was outside the town, a good ten-minute walk away from the noisy hubbub of the market. It was quiet—isolated, even—but right now that was exactly what she wanted. Somewhere quiet, away from the world, where she could lick her wounds.

Thinking back to those horrific last hours with Vicè, she felt a rush of queasiness. She'd been so excited, so caught up in the thrilling realisation of her own love for him, that she'd completely misjudged his feelings. And in the face of his less than enthusiastic response to her suggestion that they take over his father's business together she'd had no option but to face the facts.

He didn't need or want her.

He certainly didn't want her love.

And, to be fair, he hadn't ever offered her a real relationship. As he'd said, he'd only been doing her a favour.

She had wanted to call a taxi, but he had insisted on driving her to the airport. She would never forget that silent, never-ending journey to Genoa.

As they'd left Portofino he had asked her if she wanted to listen to the radio. Then he had asked if she wanted him to turn up the air-conditioning.

At no point had he asked her to stay.

At the airport he had offered to go in with her, but her nerves had been in shreds by then and she had simply shaken her head.

Her throat tightened. He hadn't used his legendary powers of persuasion to convince her otherwise. Maybe he had been daunted by her silence.

The other, more devastating but more likely explanation was that he had been desperate for her to be gone so that he could get back to the sweet, easy life he'd had before meeting her...

Walking into the villa, she forced herself to unpack her shopping and put it away before checking her phone for messages. At first she had checked it obsessively, but as the hours had turned into days and the days had become weeks she had forced herself not to look.

Before leaving, she had agreed with him that they would say nothing to their families. She couldn't remember who had suggested it, but she was glad. There was no way she could face her father's I-told-you-so reaction—or, worse, his clumsy attempts to try and make amends. Nor did she want to confide in Claudia. She was doing so well right now, and she feared offloading her problems on to her sister would ruin the fragile peace Claudia had found.

Peace, and happiness at the discovery she was having a baby.

Her breath twisted in her throat.

She had wanted to go to her, of course, but Claudia had

been firm and, hearing the flicker of determination in her voice, Imma had understood that her sister needed to prove she could cope alone.

So she had carried on speaking to both of them every couple of days, acting as if nothing had happened, making sure that the conversation merely touched on Vicè.

Her stomach clenched. Against her will she was living another charade, and it was only through sheer effort of will that she dragged herself out of bed each morning, got dressed and made herself eat breakfast.

Incredibly, the one person she found herself wanting to talk to was Audenzia. During those few hours in Florence she had found herself admiring her quiet strength and love of life.

Under other circumstances she would have liked to get to know her better.

But now, of course, that was impossible.

Almost as impossible as stopping all these incessant what-if and if-only thoughts.

Glancing out of the window, she felt her heartbeat slow. She couldn't see Portofino from the villa, but that didn't stop her from closing her eyes and imagining. *What would he be doing right now?*

Opening her eyes, she pushed the thought away before it could spiral out of control. Each morning she promised herself that she wouldn't think about Vicè until lunchtime, and today she had almost managed it—that was something to celebrate.

In fact, she *was* going to celebrate. She was going to take her lunch to the beach and have a picnic. Even though the 'beach' was not really a beach at all—more a patch of sand in a rocky alcove.

After she'd finished eating, she watched the Palermo to Naples ferry heading off towards the mainland. It made her feel calmer, thinking about all those people on board, with all their hopes and dreams buzzing inside their heads.

Her heart might have been broken by Vicè but that didn't mean her life was over. She was going to be all right. He might not love her, but she couldn't regret the time they had spent together. He had taught her to be brave, to take risks.

Yes, she loved him still. Maybe she always would. But she was ready to face the world. On her terms.

Standing up, she brushed the sand off her legs and began to walk carefully across the rocks and back up to the house. But as she reached the villa her feet suddenly faltered.

A man was waiting for her.

Her heart began to pound.

Not because he was a stranger.

But because he wasn't.

She stared at him, stunned and furious. Even if she wanted to run—and she did—nothing seemed to be functioning. Instead she stood woodenly while Vicè walked slowly towards her.

How had he found her? And, more importantly, why was he here?

He had no right to come here—not when she was finally beginning to get him out of her head, if not her heart, she thought as he stopped in front of her, his dark hair blowing in the breeze.

He was dressed incongruously, in a dark suit and shirt, only it wasn't his clothing that made her throat tighten. But she had learned from her mistakes, and she wasn't ever going to let herself be distracted by his beauty again.

'Hi,' he said softly.

She lifted her chin. 'How did you find me?'

'With great difficulty.' He smiled, and then, when she didn't smile back, he shrugged. 'My lawyer Vito knows some people who keep their ears to the ground. He uses them to find clients that skip bail.'

'And I thought it was my father who had the shady friends.'

His expression didn't change—but then why should it?

If he had ever cared what she thought of him, he certainly didn't any more.

'Why are you here, Vicè? I mean, I take it this isn't a social call?'

'I had a meeting with Vito this morning.' He stared at her steadily. 'I had some paperwork to complete.'

Inside her head his words were bumping into one another in slow motion, like a train and its carriages hitting the buffers. Glancing down, she saw that he was holding an envelope. Her heart shrivelled in her chest.

Paperwork. In other words, he wanted a divorce.

Pain seared every nerve. 'I thought you were giving me a year?'

He glanced away. 'I can't wait that long.'

She wanted to scream and shout and rage—at the unfairness of life and at the unknowable cruelty of loving someone who didn't love you. But she had laid enough of her feelings bare to this man.

'Fine. Just give me the paperwork and I'll sign it.'

'It's already signed.'

He took a step closer and she backed away from him, not caring that he could see her pain, just wanting him gone.

'Your father signed it this morning.'

She stared at him in confusion—and then suddenly she understood. 'You came back for the business. That's why you came to Sicily. For your father's business.'

He stared at her, his gaze steady and unflinching. 'He signed it over to me this morning.'

Why did it hurt so much? She'd known right from the start that he'd only ever wanted that. Whatever he'd said in the car on the way to Florence and then at the villa, it obviously was still.

Her chest tightened.

But why had her father agreed to hand it over? Had Vicenzu told him the truth about their marriage? Even though he knew what it would mean for her.

'Did you tell him about us?' she asked slowly.

He shook his head.

'Then how—'

His eyes met hers. 'I threatened him. I told him I had enough on him to make sure he'd lose everything he cared about. Just like my father did.'

On one level she knew her father deserved it, but it hurt hearing Vicè talk in that way.

'Blackmail and extortion? That sounds more like my father than you.'

'I said all that afterwards.' He ran an agitated hand through his hair. 'First I met him for breakfast. I told him that I wanted to buy back the business and that I would pay what he thought was a fair price.'

'What...?' Imma felt as if she was in a daze.

'I'm not like your father, *cara*. I don't bully or blackmail people into doing what I want. I paid him what he asked— twice what he paid my father—so that you and I can start with a clean sheet.'

Her heart was in her mouth. 'I don't understand...'

'You asked me why I was here.' His eyes found hers. '*You're* why. I've bought the business back. For us.'

She shook her head. 'There is no us.'

'There is. Only it took you leaving for me to see it.' He took another step closer. 'I love you, Imma. And I want to be with you. Not for the cameras, or for the business, but because you're in my heart.'

His voice was shaking now, and she could see tears in his eyes.

'You helped me find out what and who I want to be. And I want to be your husband. For real. Forever.'

Reaching out, he took her hands.

'I'm sorry I didn't stop you leaving, but when you said you wanted us to run the business together I panicked. I mess up all the time, *cara*—with family, with work, with you. And I've hurt people, you especially, and I didn't want to hurt you any more. I don't ever want to hurt you.'

He shook his head.

'I should never have let you go. But I thought that making you stay would have just been me being selfish—that it was what the old Vicè would have done. And I wanted to be a better man. So I let you go and I pretended everything was cool.'

His mouth twisted.

'Only it wasn't. I missed you like crazy. So I went and saw Mamma and I told her everything.'

'*Everything?*' Her eyes widened with shock.

'Everything. I was sick and tired of lying to everyone. To her…to you. To myself.'

Screwing up his face, he shook his head.

'I think it's the first time she's ever lost her temper with me. *Cavolo*, she was mad at me. Like, furious. Every time I thought she'd finished she'd start up again. She told me she was ashamed of me, that my father would be ashamed of me, and then she told me I had to put it right.'

Imma bit her lip and, reaching out, placed her hands against his chest, feeling his heart beating into her fingertips. 'Did you tell her about what my father did?'

He pulled her closer. 'A bit.'

'Is that why you threatened him? For your *mamma*?'

'No. I wanted him to know what it felt like to be cornered and helpless.' He gave her a small crooked smile. 'And then I made him donate a lot of money to my mother's favourite charity. Weirdly, it was the difference between what he paid my father and what I paid him.'

She smiled. 'That won't have helped his heart.'

'*What* heart?'

He gazed down into her eyes and she felt her own heart flutter inside her chest.

'I thought I wasn't worthy of your love, *cara*. Probably I'm not. But I'm going to do whatever it takes to be worthy.'

'So you don't want a divorce?' she asked softly.

'*No.*' He stared down at her, his arms tensing around her. 'Do you?'

She shook her head and, breathing out unsteadily, he buried his face in her hair.

'In that case, I have something for you.' Reaching into his jacket, he pulled out a small square box. 'You never had an engagement ring, so I thought I'd get you an eternity ring instead.' His eyes were bright. 'That's how long I want to be with you. For eternity.'

Tears slid down her cheeks as he opened the box and slipped a beautiful emerald ring onto her finger. 'Oh, Vicè…'

Laughing softly, he wiped her tears away with his thumbs. 'I had some change left over…it was that or blow it all in a high-stakes poker game—'

'Change from what?' She looked up at him in confusion.

He hesitated, and she felt the muscles in his arms tighten.

'I sold the Dolce.'

She gaped at him. 'You *sold* it? But why?'

'I needed the money to buy the business back. It was that or go to Ciro.' He grimaced. 'So, as I say, I needed the money.'

'But you love the Dolce.'

'I did—I do. And I've kept a stake in it. But I don't need it any more.'

His gaze rested on her face, and his love was there for anyone to see.

'You're the sweetness in my life, *cara*.' His eyes dropped to the ring sparkling on her finger. 'Now and for eternity.'

EPILOGUE

IT WAS A hot day in late September—one of the hottest on record, according to Manfredi, the Trapani estate's longest-serving member of staff. But the weather was the last thing on Imma's mind as she walked slowly through the olive trees.

She had spoken to Claudia that morning, and her sister's news had pushed every other thought out of her head.

Almost every other thought.

But right now that would have to wait.

Breathing in the scent of warm earth and grass, she replayed her conversation with Claudia.

Claudia and Ciro were together. They were in love. Both of them this time.

It was a lot to take in—too much for one person on her own.

A tremble of happiness ran over her skin.

But she wasn't on her own any more.

Her eyes fixed on the group of men standing beneath the trees at the other side of the olive grove. Or rather on one particular man.

Vicè was gesticulating energetically, his dark eyes moving over the other men's faces as he spoke, and she felt a sharp, almost unbearable urge to push them all aside and drag him back to the villa and upstairs to their bedroom.

'Imma!'

She looked up at the sound of his voice, her heart leaping as it still did, maybe three, five, sometimes ten times a day, whenever she remembered that Vicè was her husband 'for real' and 'forever'.

Pulse jumping, she watched him excuse himself, and then he was walking towards her, his long legs making short work of the uneven ground and a slow, curling smile pulling at the corners of his mouth.

She felt her stomach flutter. She had thought that he couldn't look any more desirable than he did in a suit, but she'd been wrong. In scuffed work boots, faded chinos, and with the sleeves of his denim shirt rolled up he looked impossibly sexy.

'Signora Trapani...'

He pulled her against him, his mouth seeking hers with an urgency that made her whole body twitch with desire.

Behind them, a cacophony of approving whistles and shouts filled the air.

'Vicè, everyone is watching us,' she whispered.

'So let them watch. I'm just saying good morning to my wife.'

His voice was warm, and she felt an answering warmth across her skin.

Her eyes met his. 'You did that already.'

The corner of his mouth tugged upward. 'I'm thinking that was more of a *ciao* than a *buongiorno*.' His dark gaze drifted slowly over her face. 'How do you feel about going back to the villa and brushing up on our greetings?'

'It wouldn't hurt,' she said softly. 'I mean, just because we're married it doesn't mean we should take each other for granted...'

Watching the flush of colour suffuse her cheeks, Vicè felt his body harden. That she should want him at all still felt like a miracle, but that she loved him...

There were no words that could adequately capture how that made him feel. All he knew was that he was the luckiest man in the world.

The doubts and regrets of the past were forgotten now. Imma loved him, and he knew that her love and the efforts he'd made to deserve it would have earned his father's respect.

Life had never been sweeter.

Uncurling his arm from around her waist, he took her hand and led her back across the field.

'I like this dress.' His eyes ran over the curve of her breast. 'Although I think it will look even better once you've taken it off.'

She smiled, hesitated, then said, 'Claudia called.'

Cavolo. He swore silently.

'Yeah, Ciro called me too.' He'd been so caught up in this morning's meeting he'd actually momentarily forgotten about his brother's call. 'He sounded pretty happy. Is that how Claudia sounded?'

She nodded. 'It's all she's ever wanted, but—'

'But what?' Turning towards her, he caught her chin. 'What is it, *cara*?'

Her green eyes were so open, so unguarded, and he felt a sudden urge to tell her how much he loved her, how necessary she was for his own happiness. But he didn't need to say anything. She already knew, and that made him love her even more.

'You can tell me.'

She bit her lip. 'It *is* real, isn't it? This time? He does love her? I mean, he's not just saying it because your *mamma*—'

He hated seeing her so worried—hated that he had something to do with her doubts.

Pulling her closer, he shook his head. 'Mamma didn't speak to him until after he and Claudia had sorted it out between them. You don't need to worry, *cara*. Honestly, I've never heard my brother sound like that before. He's crazy about her.'

Ciro had been so emotional. For once, he had actually felt like the big brother.

His fingers tightened around hers. 'I promise it's real, *cara*. As real as you and I. All of what happened—it's in the past for Ciro, for me.'

It was a past that didn't feel so much like another country to him as a different planet.

'I feel the same way,' she said.

He stroked her cheek. 'Have they told anyone else?'

'Claudia told Papà.' Her eyes met his. 'But she agreed that the same rules I insisted on will apply.'

Vicè nodded. Imma had gone to see Cesare the day after they had got back together. Glancing down at her beautiful face, he felt a rush of pride in his wife for facing up to the man who had once dominated her whole life.

She'd given her father an ultimatum: change, or she and Claudia would cut him out of their lives forever.

And Cesare had capitulated. In fact, he had blubbed like a child, apologised, and then made promises which, so far, he was keeping.

'Why are you smiling like that?' she asked slowly.

'I was just thinking what a great aunt you'll be, Zia Imma. Of course I'll be the most fantastic uncle too.'

She laughed. 'That won't be hard as you'll be the only uncle.' Her face softened. 'Vicè, if you're half as good at being an uncle as you are at being a husband and a boss, you'll be better than fantastic.'

'Let's see if you still think that after the harvest,' he said lightly.

'I will.' Her eyes met his. 'I spoke to Manfredi this morning. He said that you have the same feel for the olives as your father.'

He felt his heart contract.

Stepping into his father's shoes had been nerve-racking. He still had doubts about his ability to pull it off. But with Imma by his side...

He felt a fierce, unpremeditated quiver of anticipation. She was his partner, his equal. Together they had already faced their fears. And together they would meet whatever happened in the future.

* * *

Watching the mix of sadness and pride in Vicè's eyes, Imma felt her heart swell.

She knew how much this estate meant to him. It was his father's legacy and one day it would be his.

Her breath caught in her throat.

'So, are you going to be Zio Vicenzu or Zio Vicè?'

'Not Vicenzu.' He shuddered. 'Too serious. Vicè is what a cool uncle would be called, and I am definitely going to be a cool uncle.' His eyes gleamed. 'I cannot wait until this baby is born. Hopefully he's going to be just like me. That'll keep Ciro on his toes.'

'It might not be a boy.'

'It is.'

She raised an eyebrow. 'And you know this how, exactly?'

'Man's intuition.' He grinned. 'It's very rare—only the most impressive males of the species have it.'

'Right... And I'm guessing it's infallible?'

He nodded, and keeping her expression innocent, she took his hand and rested it gently on her stomach. 'So what are *we* having, then?'

He stilled, his eyes widening with shock. 'You're pregnant?'

She nodded. 'I did a test after Claudia rang. Actually, I did two. Just to be sure.'

'And it's definite?'

She drew a deep breath and nodded again. 'I was going to wait for the perfect moment to tell you, but then I realised that every moment is perfect with you.'

There was a shake in her voice that matched the tremble in his hands as they tightened around hers.

Looking up, she bit her lip. 'Are you pleased?'

'Pleased?' His eyes filled with tears. 'I'm ecstatic.'

He pulled her against him, burying his face in her hair, pressing her close to his heart, which was hammering as wildly as hers.

'You're having my baby.'

He kissed her gently on the lips and she felt his mouth curve into a grin.

'Of course, with my man's intuition I already knew that—'

She punched him lightly on the arm. 'You are such a bad liar, Vicenzu Trapani.'

'Thanks to you,' he said softly.

His smile sent a shiver of heat down her spine. 'I love you, Vicè.'

Tipping her mouth up to his, he kissed her again. 'I love you too, Imma. That's the truth and it's going to stay true forever.'

She felt her pulse twitch as he gazed down at her, his dark eyes gleaming.

'That dress, though—that's coming off right now.'

And, scooping her up into arms, he carried her into the villa and upstairs to their bedroom.

* * * * *

COMING SOON!

We really hope you enjoyed reading this book.
If you're looking for more romance, be sure to
head to the shops when new books are
available on

Thursday 6th August

To see which titles are coming soon, please visit

millsandboon.co.uk/nextmonth

MILLS & BOON

Coming next month

CONFESSIONS OF AN ITALIAN MARRIAGE
Dani Collins

"Get in," Giovanni said.

The sight of him struck like a gong, leaving her quivering. He had a shaggy black beard and dark glasses, and his black hoodie was pulled up to hide all but his familiar cheekbones, but his legs stopped above the knees and she recognized the tense line of his mouth.

Alive. Her heart soared so high, it should have shattered the sky.

At the same time, a thousand furies invaded her like a swarm of killer bees. There was no triumph in learning she was right. There was only a crippling heartbreak that he had abandoned her. If he'd been truly dead, she would have been angry, but she wouldn't have blamed him.

This, though? He had put her through horrifying hours of actually believing he was gone. She had endured his gut-wrenching funeral, convinced it was a sham. Then, two short weeks later, she'd suffered another unbearable loss that would never heal.

He'd forced her to go through all of that alone.

For every minute that had passed since that awful day, she had longed for him to reveal himself, but now her feet only carried her forward so she could bitterly hiss, "Go to hell."

"Where do you think I've been?" he growled.

"I'm calling the police!" Teresina yelled from deep in the alley. Two of Teresina's employees were recording everything on their phones.

A man in a suit was running toward her. She instinctively moved closer to Giovanni, heart jamming with fear.

Giovanni's hard arm looped around her and he dragged her into the back of the car. He clutched the door for leverage, but his strength was as annoyingly effortless as always.

She didn't fight him. In fact, once he grabbed her out of her stasis, she helped, kicking against the edge of the door to thrust herself inside, desperate for whatever sanctuary he offered.

They wound up in a heap on the back seat while the man who was chasing her came up to the open door and reached for her leg.

She screamed and kicked at him with her sharp heels. He dodged her shoes and threw the yards of silk in after her, then slammed the door before he leaped into the passenger seat in front of Giovanni.

"Go," Giovanni said to the driver, and he pushed himself upright.

As the SUV sped into traffic, Freja rocked deeper into the seat, stunned to her toes.

Continue reading
CONFESSIONS OF AN ITALIAN MARRIAGE
Dani Collins

Available next month
www.millsandboon.co.uk

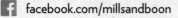

MILLS & BOON

THE HEART OF ROMANCE

A ROMANCE FOR EVERY KIND OF READER

MODERN

Prepare to be swept off your feet by sophisticated, sexy and seductive heroes, in some of the world's most glamourous and romantic locations, where power and passion collide.
8 stories per month.

HISTORICAL

Escape with historical heroes from time gone by. Whether your passion is for wicked Regency Rakes, muscled Vikings or rugged Highlanders, awaken the romance of the past.
6 stories per month.

MEDICAL

Set your pulse racing with dedicated, delectable doctors in the high-pressure world of medicine, where emotions run high and passion, comfort and love are the best medicine.
6 stories per month.

True Love

Celebrate true love with tender stories of heartfelt romance, from the rush of falling in love to the joy a new baby can bring, and a focus on the emotional heart of a relationship.
8 stories per month.

Desire

Indulge in secrets and scandal, intense drama and plenty of sizzling hot action with powerful and passionate heroes who have it all: wealth, status, good looks…everything but the right woman.
6 stories per month.

HEROES

Experience all the excitement of a gripping thriller, with an intense romance at its heart. Resourceful, true-to-life women and strong, fearless men face danger and desire - a killer combination!
8 stories per month.

DARE

Sensual love stories featuring smart, sassy heroines you'd want as a best friend, and compelling intense heroes who are worthy of them.
4 stories per month.

To see which titles are coming soon, please visit

millsandboon.co.uk/nextmonth